I0601620

Anonymous

Some Municipal Records of Carlisle

Vol. 4

Anonymous

Some Municipal Records of Carlisle
Vol. 4

ISBN/EAN: 9783337406981

Printed in Europe, USA, Canada, Australia, Japan

Cover: Foto ©Andreas Hilbeck / pixelio.de

More available books at **www.hansebooks.com**

SOME

MUNICIPAL RECORDS

OF

CARLISLE.

SOME

MUNICIPAL RECORDS

OF THE

CITY OF CARLISLE,

VIZ.,

THE ELIZABETHAN CONSTITUTIONS,
ORDERS, PROVISIONS, ARTICLES, AND RULES
FROM THE DORMONT BOOK,

AND

THE RULES AND ORDERS OF THE EIGHT
TRADING GUILDS,

PREFACED BY
CHAPTERS ON THE CORPORATION CHARTERS AND GUILDS, ILLUSTRATED
BY EXTRACTS FROM THE COURT LEET ROLLS AND FROM THE
MINUTES OF THE CORPORATION AND GUILDS.

EDITED BY

R. S. FERGUSON, M.A., F.S.A. (LON. & SCOT.),
MAYOR OF CARLISLE 1881-2 & 1882-3,

AND

W. NANSON, B.A., F.S.A.,
LATE DEPUTY TOWN CLERK OF CARLISLE.

CARLISLE: C. THURNAM & SONS.
LONDON: GEORGE BELL & SONS.
—
1887.

THE SOUTH WEST PROSPECT OF THE CITY OF CARLISLE IN 1739.

SOME

MUNICIPAL RECORDS

OF THE

CITY OF CARLISLE,

VIZ.,

THE ELIZABETHAN CONSTITUTIONS,
ORDERS, PROVISIONS, ARTICLES, AND RULES
FROM THE DORMONT BOOK,

AND

THE RULES AND ORDERS OF THE EIGHT
TRADING GUILDS,

PREFACED BY
CHAPTERS ON THE CORPORATION CHARTERS AND GUILDS, ILLUSTRATED
BY EXTRACTS FROM THE COURT LEET ROLLS AND FROM THE
MINUTES OF THE CORPORATION AND GUILDS.

EDITED BY

R. S. FERGUSON, M.A., F.S.A. (LON. & SCOT.),
MAYOR OF CARLISLE 1881-2 & 1882-3,

AND

W. NANSON, B.A., F.S.A.,
LATE DEPUTY TOWN CLERK OF CARLISLE.

CARLISLE: C. THURNAM & SONS.
LONDON: GEORGE BELL & SONS.

1887.

Cumberland and Westmorland Antiquarian and Archæological Society.

FOUNDED 1866.

Patrons :

THE RIGHT HON. THE LORD MUNCASTER, M.P., Lord Lieutenant of Cumberland.
THE RIGHT HON. THE LORD HOTHFIELD, Lord Lieutenant of Westmorland.
THE RIGHT REV. THE LORD BISHOP OF CARLISLE.

President :

R. S. FERGUSON, ESQ., M.A., LL.M., F.S.A., Carlisle.

Vice-Presidents :

JAMES ATKINSON, ESQ.
E. B. W. BALME, ESQ.
THE EARL OF BECTIVE, M.P.
W. BROWNE, ESQ.
JAMES CROPPER, ESQ.
THE DEAN OF CARLISLE.
H. F. CURWEN, ESQ.
ROBT. FERGUSON, ESQ., F.S.A.

GEORGE HOWARD, ESQ.
W. JACKSON, ESQ., F.S.A.
G. J. JOHNSON, ESQ.
HON. W. LOWTHER, M.P.
H. FLETCHER RIGGE, ESQ.
H. P. SENHOUSE, ESQ.
M. W. TAYLOR, ESQ., M.D., F.S.A.
HON. PERCY S. WYNDHAM.

Elected Members of Council :

W. B. ARNISON, ESQ., Penrith.
G. F. BRAITHWAITE, ESQ., Kendal.
REV. R. BOWER, Carlisle.
REV. W. S. CALVERLEY, F.S.A., Aspatria.
ISAAC CARTMELL, ESQ., Carlisle.
J. A. CORY, ESQ., Carlisle.
J. F. CROSTHWAITE, ESQ., F.S.A., Keswick.

C. J. FERGUSON, ESQ., F.S.A., Carlisle.
T. F. I'ANSON, ESQ., M.D., Whitehaven.
REV. THOMAS LEES, F.S.A., Wreay.
REV. CANON WESTON, Crosby Ravensworth.
ROBERT J. WHITWELL, ESQ., Kendal.

Editor :

R. S. FERGUSON, ESQ., M.A., LL.M., F.S.A., Carlisle.

Auditors :

RICHARD NELSON, ESQ., Kendal. | FRANK WILSON, ESQ, Kendal.

Treasurer :

W. H. WAKEFIELD, ESQ., Sedgwick.

Secretary :

MR. T. WILSON, Aynam Lodge, Kendal.

1887.

1304271

TO

B. SCOTT. Esq..

MAYOR OF CARLISLE, 1884–5,

IN ACKNOWLEDGEMENT OF THE INTEREST
HE HAS MANIFESTED IN
THIS WORK.

Publications of the Cumberland & Westmorland Antiquarian & Archæological Society.

EIGHT VOLUMES OF TRANSACTIONS.
T. Wilson, Highgate, Kendal.

EXTRA SERIES.

VOL. I.—BISHOP NICOLSON'S VISITATION AND SURVEY OF THE DIOCESE OF CARLISLE IN 1703-4. Edited by R. S. FERGUSON, F.S.A. Messrs. C. Thurnam & Sons, English Street, Carlisle. *Price* 12/6.

VOL. II.—MEMOIRS OF THE GILPIN FAMILY OF SCALEBY CASTLE, by the late Rev. William Gilpin, Vicar of Boldre, with the Autobiography of the Author. Edited with Notes and Pedigree by W. JACKSON, F.S.A. Messrs. C. Thurnam & Sons, English Street, Carlisle. *Price* 10/6.

VOL. III.—THE OLD CHURCH PLATE IN THE DIOCESE OF CARLISLE. Edited by R. S. FERGUSON, M.A. and F.S.A. Messrs. C. Thurnam & Sons, English Street, Carlisle. *Price* 15/6.

VOL. IV.—SOME MUNICIPAL RECORDS OF CARLISLE. Edited by R. S. FERGUSON, M.A. and F.S.A., and W. NANSON, B.A. and F.S.A. Messrs. C. Thurnam & Sons, English Street, Carlisle. *Price* 15/-.

VOL. V.—THE PRE-REFORMATION EPISCOPAL REGISTERS OF CARLISLE, now in preparation, to be edited by R. S. FERGUSON, F.S.A., and the Rev. T. LEES, F.S.A.

TRACT SERIES.

I. FLEMING'S DESCRIPTION OF WESTMORLAND. Edited By Sir GEORGE DUCKETT, F.S.A. T. Wilson, Highgate, Kendal. *Price* 1/-.

II. DENTON'S ACCOUNT OF CUMBERLAND. Edited by R. S. FERGUSON, M.A. and F.S.A. T. Wilson, Highgate, Kendal.

PREFACE.

One of us once conceived the ambitious idea of writing a History of Cumberland on the old-fashioned lines and scale: nor has he yet wholly abandoned the idea. But it seemed a more practicable and useful task to first print some of the materials from which such a history would have to be compiled. The Cumberland and Westmorland Antiquarian and Archæological Society took up the notion, and on the opposite page is a list of what they have accomplished : little enough ! But they hope to do yet better, and to deal with the local monastic chartularies, while the municipal records of Carlisle will easily furnish another volume.

With regard to the present volume, the editors have endeavoured to reproduce the original grammar and spelling : the caprices of the writers in the use of capital letters they have had to ignore, chiefly from the difficulty of deciding what was or was not a capital letter. They have refrained from overloading the pages with footnotes, but no better notes to, or illustrations of, the transcripts from the Dormont Book and the orders, &c., of the guilds could be given than Chapters XIII and XIV and the extracts given in previous chapters from the minute books of the guilds.

We have to express to Mr. B. Scott, late mayor of
Carlisle, our warm thanks for presenting the frontispiece
and the pictures opposite pages 14, 41, 42, and 59.

The question may be asked,—why we have not first
published the charters of Carlisle, and then followed up
with the laws, &c., of the guilds ? The answer to that is,
the charters are in safe custody, and can be published at
any time ; the records of the guilds are not.

CONTENTS.

ILLUSTRATIONS.

ERRATA.

page 89, John Christian Curwen was not M.P. for Carlisle in 1784 when he presented silver cups to the guilds : he was the candidate.

page 122, Fitchfield should be Titchfield.

Chapter I.*

THE CORPORATION AND CHARTERS.

The Saxon Chronicle, under the date of A.D. 1092, says :—

The King (*i.e.*, William Rufus) went northward with a large army to Carlisle, and repaired the city, built the castle, and drove out Dolfin, who had before governed that country ; and having placed a garrison in the castle, returned south, and sent a great number of churlish folk thither with wives and cattle, that they might settle there and till the land.

Thus the present boundaries between England and Scotland were established, and Carlisle became for *the first time part of the English kingdom.*

William Rufus retained the district round Carlisle in his own hands, but in the time of his successor Henry I, we find it as the earldom of Carlisle, or of Carleolium, in the possession of a person generally called Ranulph de Meschines, but whose proper name is Ranulph le Meschin, or cadet, a son of Ranulph de Brichsart, viscount or sheriff of the Bressin in Normandy. Ranulph divided the lands on the exposed frontier of his earldom into three baronies, which he bestowed on his followers, Gilsland and Lyddale, to guard the passes into Scotland by land, and Burgh to guard the sea coast.

In 1118, Richard, earl of Chester, perished in the White Ship with the unlucky Prince William, the only

---

* This Chapter was originally given as a Lecture to the Carlisle Scientific Society, March 7th, 1882.

son of Henry I, and his possessions and earldom fell to the crown. Ranulph de Meschines became earl of Chester, and surrendered to the crown the earldom of Carlisle. Now the crown had discovered that the policy of entrusting the defence of its borders and marches to great earls who enjoyed *jura regalia* was a very bad policy for the crown, because these great earls were hard to control. Thus it came to pass that no new earl of Carlisle or Carleolium was appointed ; and so no county palatine of Carleolium, an *imperium in imperio* with its own barons and courts, like those of Durham and Cheshire, which lasted until modern times, has come down to us.

The earldom of Carleolium, the barony of Kendal, and the strip that intervened between them were handed over to sheriffs and divided into the two counties of Carliol and Westmarieland, and these counties were accounted for by their sheriffs in the Pipe Roll of the 31 Henry I under these names. But Henry I followed the policy of Meschines and parcelled out five additional baronies, Coupland, Allerdale, Wigton, Greystock, and Levington, reserving to the crown *the city of Carlisle and the forest of Cumberland.* This reservation of the city of Carlisle to the crown is that which entitles Carlisle to be called a royal city, a title it may well claim, for all its charters were granted direct from the crown. Thus Madox, in his " Firma Burgi," gives Carlisle as one of eleven towns, of which he says the crown was seized in the reign of Henry I, and he cites as proof the following entry from a roll, which he states to be of uncertain date, but which is the Pipe Roll of the 31st Henry I :—

Chaerleolium. Hildredus reddit compotum de XIIII li. & XVI s. & VI d. de veteri firma de Chaerleolio & de Maneriis Regis. Et in operibus Civitatis de Chaerleolio, videlicet in Muro circa Civitatem faciendo liberavit XIIII li. & XVI s. et VI d. et quietus est.

From these towns in royal demesne, the King raised a revenue by rents, and by other means, just as from any

other property he had : there was no difference originally
in the mode of managing the crown's town property and
the crown's country property. The revenues of both were
collected by the sheriff, and both alike were subject to
the sheriff and to the county courts. The only difference
between the town property and the country property was
that the inhabitants were thicker on the ground in the
former than in the latter. It was the duty of the sheriff of
each county to collect all the crown rents and revenues, and
regularly pay them into the exchequer, first deducting his
disbursements, for very much of the royal expenditure
went through his hands, and was paid by him. Thus, in the
above extract, Hildred, the sheriff, accounts for £14 16s. 6d.
as the profits of Carleol and the manors, but as he has paid
just that sum for building a wall round Carlisle, he has
nothing to pay into the Treasury ; and the account says,
"*Et Quietus est*," and he is quit. In addition to crown
rents, the sheriff collected all sort of miscellaneous items,
such as the profits of the forest of Cumberland, timber and
hay sold, pannage or the charge for people feeding swine in
the forest, poundage fees on stray cattle, fines of all
sorts, the *geldum animalium* or noutgeld (a cornage
rent or crown rent paid in cattle), and a variety of
other items of revenue. Against his receipts the sheriff set
down all sorts of payments which he was authorised to
make, such as an annual allowance of 27s. 4d. to the
canons of Carlisle ; expenses connected with the repair of
Carlisle castle, and its chapel, mill, bridge, and gaol ; the
maintenance of its garrisons ; similar expenses for Appleby,
Prudhoe, Pontefract, and Bamburgh ; money laid out in
buying large quantities of military arms and stores, sometimes for Carlisle, sometimes for Ireland ; in discharging
the expenses of royal writs ; in buying hawks, and hounds,
and in sending them to the King ; &c., &c. With so much
money passing through his hands, it is not to be wondered
that the office of sheriff came to be a very lucrative one.
The crown let it out to farm, and the nobility began to bid

against one another for the post; thus the bishop of Ely tendered for the fee farm for the counties of York, Lincoln, and Northampton, 1,500 marks, cash down, and a hundred increase upon the usual farm of each county, but this was capped by Geoffrey Plantagenet, who bid another 1,500 marks. The sheriffs began to regard their offices as means by which to make money. General dissatisfaction arose in consequence of the severity with which these officers performed their functions, so that in towns and populous places people clubbed together and negotiated to pay fixed sums and so be rid of the sheriff.

Now Carlisle had, at a very early period, some sort of organised government; thus, in 1156, the sheriff appears on the Pipe Rolls, as accounting for *xx li de dono civitatis Carleolii*. In the next year the same entry appears as *de dono Burgi de Carleolio*; and the inhabitants appear as *Cives* and *Burgenses*, but we hear nothing of any mayor or corporation. In the 6 Ric. I, 1195, we find an entry which shows they wanted to manage their own affairs.

In Soltis, per breve Regis Ipsius Vicecomiti LII li. pro LII li. quas Burgenses de Carleolio commodaverant domino Regi ad facienda negocia sua de firma ejusdem Civitatis, quam ipsi Burgenses tenent in Capite ad firmam de ipso vicecomite.

In payments by the writ of the King himself to the Sheriff of £52 on account of £52 which the burgesses of Carlisle had advanced to the lord the King in order to do their own business relating to the farm of the same city, which the burgesses themselves hold as tenants in chief at farm of the sheriff.

It is not clear what they did in the years immediately following, but we find a tallage levied on the royal property in Cumberland, which is made up thus:—

Homines de Scottebi	... ...	30s.
Homines de Dalston	... ...	40s.
Homines de Penred	... ...	4 marks.
Homines de Salkeld	... ...	2 marks.
Homines de Langwadebi	... ...	20s.

| Homines de Steinweges | ... | ... | 10s. |
| Cives Carleolii | ... | ... | £50 |

The distinction between the *cives* of Carlisle and the *homines* of other places, shows that some regular government, beyond a mere constable and a township jury, existed.

In the 3rd of King John, 1201, the citizens of Carlisle made a proposal to farm the city themselves: they agreed to pay 60 marks down, and £3 advance of rent over what the sheriff paid. The sheriff, however, offered the same increase, and £20 a year more on the royal manors. The King then threw over the citizens and accepted the sheriff's offer, and apparently made a bad speculation, for the sheriff died within three years without paying the 60 marks, and leaving the rent in arrear. The rent was then reduced to the old amount.

We now come to a very important document. This is a writ of Henry III to the sheriff of Cumberland, dated 29th September, in the fifth year of his reign [1221], and preserved in the Chancery Fine Rolls. It contains most valuable information as to the early municipal history of Carlisle. It begins by reciting that an inquisition had been made by the King's command, whereby it was found that the citizens of Carlisle had formerly held their city of the sheriff of Cumberland at a yearly rent of £52, and that, together with the city, the citizens were accustomed to have his mills, which were under the city, and a certain fishery in Eden (the King-garth fishery) and the *toll of the shire* (*theolonium comitatus*) to make up their rent. It then states that the King has granted to the citizens their city with the appurtenances to farm during his pleasure at a yearly rent of £60, to be paid by the citizens at the Exchequer half-yearly, at Easter and Midsummer, and commands the sheriff to cause the citizens to have full seisin of the city, together with the mills, and fishery, and tolls, to enable them to pay the yearly rent of £60.

This writ thus records a most important era in the history of Carlisle.

From it, and from what has been stated before, it is clear the *cives Carleolii*, the citizens of Carlisle, had, prior to 1221, prevailed upon the sheriff to let them rent from him the profits of the city at a fixed sum. The sheriff was saved the trouble of collecting, and the citizens levied the amount of the rents proportionately among themselves, thus getting rid of foreign interference. The sum of £52, which they paid yearly to the sheriff, includes the rent of the city or *firma burgi*, made up of the rents the citizens paid for their burgage tenements; it also includes the rents of two mills, the King-garth fishery in Eden, and the shire toll. The King, as lord of the city, was entitled to require that all citizens should grind their corn at his mills. The citizens now rented the mills from the sheriff, and compelled all the people living in the town to grind their corn at them. They also took the fishery, which they probably found means to make more profitable than the sheriff could, and they were allowed to collect the shire toll. They sublet the mills for forty marks a year, and the fishery for fifteen. What the toll brought in does not appear. For the balance they would have to assess themselves in some way to make up the £52.

By this arrangement the citizens freed themselves from much interference, but the city was still only a part of the county under the jurisdiction of the sheriff, who was yet able to exercise his power to the annoyance of the citizens if he was so disposed.

The next step was to get rid of the sheriff altogether, and pay direct to the crown. This is what was effected in 1221. The sheriff is directed by the writ of Henry III of that date to hand the city over with the mills, fishery, and toll to the citizens, and they held it of the King at £60 a year during his pleasure. This arrangement was not binding on the King, and it is probable that the sheriff in a year or two offered a higher rent, and got back the city for

a time at least; the citizens, however, were in possession
in 1292, when Edward I issued a *quo warranto* against the
Maiorem et Communitatem Karleoli, and a *quo warranto*
was a writ of which Edward I, who was a great lawyer,
was very fond. He sent out justices itinerant to enquire
under what warrant the great barons, the clergy, and the
boroughs held their franchises and properties. The earl of
Warenne replied by flinging his sword on the table. The
citizens of Carlisle were not so bold; they appeared at the
assizes at Carlisle, before Sir Hugh de Cressingham, and in
reply to the King's attorney, William Inge, pleaded their
charters, but a jury of county gentlemen, Robert de la
Ferte, John de Hoddleston, Thomas de Oulewenne, Robert
de Haverington, Thomas de Derwentwater, Thomas de
Newton, John de Terreby, Hugh de Multon de Hoff, Hugh
de . . . ton de Lazingby, Robert de Croglin, John de
Hoton de Alanby, . . de Johnby, decided that the mills
and fishery were without the jurisdiction of Carlisle, and
in the county; further, that they were not the city's, but
the King's, and that the mills were worth 40 marks a year,
and the fishery at King-garth 15 marks. The fact was the
only two charters the city had ever had, namely those of
Henry II and Henry III, were burnt, and the city had no
title deeds to show.

It is probable that the citizens found it expedient to
make the King a present, or that he considered theirs a hard
case, for the *quo warranto* resulted the following year in a
charter, that of 21 Edward I, 1293, which contained an inspeximus of the tenor of the charter of Henry III, and, after
reciting that it was burnt, granted an exemplification of it.

However, in the ninth year of Edward II (1316) the
city, tolls, fishery, and the vacant places in the city were
granted by charter to the citizens of Carlisle at a fee farm
rent of £80, and they were also made free of "toll, pontage,
lastage, passage, wharfage, carriage, murage, pavage, and
stallage for all their wares and merchandise throughout the
kingdom." The change which was effected by this charter

of Edward II is remarkably evidenced by the Pipe Roll of the Exchequer for the last half of the 11th year, and for the first half of the 12th year of Edward II. From this it appears that in the 8th year of Edward II the city was in the hands of the sheriff. For that year the sheriff renders account of the issues of the city of Carlisle from the Feast of St. Michael in the 8th year to the 14th day of May following, on which day he delivered the city to the citizens; and the citizens of Carlisle accounted for the issues of the city, from the 14th day of May in the 8th year, on which day the King committed the city to the citizens, so that for the *issues of the same they might answer* at the Exchequer, until the 12th day of May in the 9th year, on which day the King committed the city to the *citizens at fee farm.* The 12th May is the date of the charter of the 9th Edward II, and the date corresponds exactly with the statement in the Pipe Roll. The rent of £80 continued to be paid until the first year of Edward IV, who reduced the fee farm rent to £40, on account of the impoverished and ruined state in which the city was left after the Wars of the Roses, and that sum of £40 is, at the present date, 1885, still paid out of the city fund every year to Lord Lonsdale as the grantee of the crown.

We have thus traced out the steps by which Carlisle became a city apart from the county, and got out of the jurisdiction of the sheriff, for clear of him the city is, as a later charter of Edward III more fully proves, and Carlisle is, in all but name, a county of itself, and perfectly independent of the county of Cumberland and all county jurisdiction, having its own bailiffs to execute the office of sheriff and its own coroner. But at this point it will be convenient to go back in point of time, and to endeavour to trace the constitution of the governing body of Carlisle, which, in the manner related, secured for the city its liberties and independence.

It has been already pointed out that in the Pipe Rolls for the reigns of Henry II, Richard I, and John (1154-1216) the inhabitants of Carlisle are called *cives* and *burgenses*, in distinction to the term *homines*, used of the inhabitants of Penrith and Scotby. This shews clearly that at Carlisle there existed at that day some sort of municipal authority beyond a mere township jury, but it does not necessarily imply that there was a mayor or corporation.

Let us now look at the earliest charter granted to Carlisle, namely, that of Henry II, after he had recovered the city from the Scots, who had held it during the reign of Stephen. This charter was burnt, but it is recited in a later—that of 35 Henry III, of which the exemplification granted by Edward I is still amongst the corporation muniments. It contains a confirmation of the liberties and customs which the citizens of Carlisle had theretofore freely enjoyed. It grants them exemption from toll, passage, pontage, and all customs belonging to the crown, and gives estovers of wood in the forest of Carlisle for burning and building, and a free merchant guild ; *gildam mercatoriam liberam ita quod nihil inde respondeant aliquibus.* This free merchant guild would be an association or brotherhood of the leading merchants and citizens of Carlisle. It no doubt existed long before it got the royal licence. Its object would be partly trade purposes, partly good fellowship and works of piety. The royal licence would confer on it power to settle disputes among its members, and exemption from the jurisdictions to which their county neighbours were amenable. These merchant guilds possessed a number of peculiar customs, which kept the burgesses or townsmen of the kingdom as a class by themselves, although they never, as in Scotland or Germany, adopted a confederate band of union, or organised themselves in leagues, like the Hanseatic League.

The grant to a town of a free merchant guild is the earliest stage in the development of a municipal constitution, and it was granted to such as were too humble or too poor to ask for more, for the King took payment for his favours. The next important steps were to oust the sheriff and his

exactions (how that was done has been already detailed), to
have the free election of magistrates, and the maintenance
of ancient customs.

The first mention of a mayor of Carlisle is the *Quo
Warranto* of 20 Ed. I, 1292, which is directed against the
mayor and commonalty of Carlisle. But the subsequent
charter of Edward II, in 1316, is directed to the citizens
without any mention of the mayor at all, so that he may
have been a mere spontaneous or voluntary creation of
the citizens which the crown did not recognise. This
charter of 9 Edward II, as already said, granted to the
citizens of Carlisle the King's mills in the city and the
King-garth fishery of Eden at a fee farm rent of £80;
also the King's vacant places in the city and suburbs, and
freedom from tollage, pontage, &c. The next charter,
9 Edward III, contains an inspeximus and confirmation of
the charter of 21 Edward I. The next charter which
mentions a mayor is that of 26 Edward III, 1353, which
recites among other things (we quote from a translation
made for the purpose of a trial about the fisheries in Eden)
that

The citizens of our city of Carlisle have been accustomed to have
among the liberties and customs belonging to the said city the
full return of all writs as well of summons of the Exchequer as of
all other writs whatsoever, and one market twice in every week, that
is to say, on Wednesday and Saturday, and a fair on the Feast of the
Assumption of the Blessed Mary in every year, for fifteen days next
following the said Feast. And *a free gild* and *a free election of
their* mayor and bailiffs within the said city, and two coroners
amending the assize of bread, wine, and ale broken gallows infan-
genthcof; and also to hold pleas of our Crown, and to do and
exercise all things which *belong to the office of sheriff and coroner*
in the city aforesaid; also the chattels of felons and fugitives condemned in the aforesaid city, and *to be quit of all fines and amerciaments of the county and suits of the county and wapentake.*

The charter mentions several other things—the city mills,
the King's fishery in Eden, the right to dig and carry away

turf on Kingmoor, to have the Battailholme to hold markets and fairs on, and to devise their tenements in Carlisle *by will;* and it goes on to say that "the aforesaid liberties and quittances belonging to the said city they have had from time whereof memory is not," *i.e.,* by prescription. Now, legal memory begins from the first year of King Richard I, or 1189, and we may therefore suppose Carlisle had a mayor, bailiffs, and coroners at that time. Probably they had, or pretended to have; but they certainly had not got the full liberties claimed in this charter of Edward III, (1353), for in 1195 they are negotiating for liberty, *ad faciendu sua negotia,* to do their own business, as told before. But by 1353 they had clearly got, and had had for some time, full liberty to "do their own business," and that liberty of local self-government Carlisle has retained from that time down to the days of the Local Government Board.

This charter further states that in the 23rd year of Edward III, the sheriff of Cumberland, Thomas de Lucy, had hindered the citizens in the enjoyment of their liberties, and it therefore confirms and grants to them all their liberties as of old. The charter puts the rights of the citizens very high. The learned town clerk of Carlisle, in a report to the corporation, says :—

It appears evident that under the above charter the city was, in all but name, a county of itself, being perfectly independent of the county and all county jurisdiction, having its own bailiffs to execute the office of sheriff, and its own coroners, and being free from the payment of any purvey or rate to the county.

So that the high sheriff of Cumberland is a mere nobody inside the city, and the mayor and his bailiffs are high sheriff there.

These rights have been confirmed by several subsequent charters, and finally by the charter of Charles I, known as the governing charter, for under it (modified by sundry acts of Parliament) the city is now governed. The inter-

mediate charters are those of 5 Richard II, 2 Henry IV,
13 Henry VI, 1 Edward IV, 1 Richard III, 3 Henry VII,
1 Henry VIII, 1 Edward VI, 5 Elizabeth, 9 Elizabeth,
2 James I.

The charter of Edward IV, as mentioned before, reduced
the fee farm rent from £80 to £40. It also gave for nothing
at all another fishery, in addition to the King's fishery in
Eden (the King-garth one), viz., the sheriff's net or frithnet,
or free net, now known as the free boat right. The charter
of 9 Elizabeth is important. It recites an inspeximus of a
writing, with schedule annexed, made by the commonalty
of the city of Carlisle, under their common seal. This
instrument states it was agreed that the government of the
city should be by the mayor with eleven worshipful persons of the city, and that the mayor should not do any act
without the assent of the majority of the eleven. Also
that the mayor and eleven should choose to them twenty-
four able persons, and that the thirty-six should choose the
mayor. That on the death of any of the thirty-six they
should fill up the number. This is signed by several of the
citizens. The charter contains also an inspeximus of several
resolutions of the corporation in the nature of bye-laws.
They are contained in the Dormont Book, and are printed
in this volume.

The charter of Charles I, the governing charter, is
a magnificent production of the conveyancer's art. It
begins :—

Carolus Dei Gratia Angliæ Scociæ Franciæ & Hiberniæ Rex
fidei Defensor, etc., Omnibus ad quos præsentes literæ pervenerint
salutem. Inspeximus literas patentes præclarissimi nuper patris
nostri Domini Jacobi nuper Regis Angliæ, etc.,

and continues with a most intricate piece of conveyancing,
reciting the previous charters, each charter reciting within
itself its predecessor, like a nest of Chinese ivory balls.
Each King who granted a charter is said to have inspected
the preceding charter, or, if it was burnt (as was the case

with those of Henry II and Henry III), then he is said to
have inspected the tenor of it, and caused it to be testified to.
The operative part of the charter commences by confirming
all liberties, customs, &c., and by granting a pardon for all
past sins of omission and commission.   It then gives a new
constitution, and incorporates the governing body by the
name of the "mayor, aldermen, bailiffs, and citizens of
the city of Carlisle."   One of the aldermen is to be appointed mayor, and eleven honest men *(undecim probi viri)*
besides the mayor are to be aldermen ; two other men
are to be bailiffs, two discreet men *(viri discreti)* to be
coroners, and twenty-four others to be capital citizens.
It is curious that whereas the eleven aldermen are
required to be honest, and the two coroners discreet, the
mayor is not required to be either one or the other.
Powers are given to this body to meet in the Guild
Hall from time to time, and to make bye-laws and
enforce them.   Richard Barwise, *armiger*, is appointed the
first mayor under the charter, and eleven honest men for
aldermen are found in Henry Baynes, William Barwick,
senior, Edward Aglionby, Thomas Blennerhasset, Thomas
Gent, Matthew Cape, Peter Baynes, Sir George Dalston, Sir
Thomas Dacre, William Barwicke, and Ambrose Nicholson.
Thomas Bushby and Thomas Kydd are the bailiffs, and
William Atkinson and Leonard Milburn are the discreet
men who are made coroners.   The twenty-four capital
citizens are Edward Barwise, Henry Monke, Edward
Dalton, Thomas Tallentire, Thomas Wilson, Robert Collyer,
Simon Brathwaite, Robert Shepherd, Robert Jackson,
Richard Dobson, Thomas Threlkeld, John Barker, Thomas
Bushby; Simon Jackson, James Knagg, Robert Watson,
Andrew Forster, Nicholas Hudson, Thomas Syde, Thomas
Barnfather, Clement Barnfather, John Bell the elder,
Thomas Dalton, and Hugh Gibson.   A recorder is also
appointed, and he, the mayor, and the two senior aldermen
are to be justices of the peace, and a long list of matters is
enumerated into which they may inquire, including all

manner of felonies, witchcrafts, enchantments, sorceries, necromancy, trespasses, forestalling, regrating, engrossing, and extortions; also, of all such as presume to go or ride armed, or to lay in ambush to maim and slay people. Next the mayor is appointed clerk of the market, and there is to be a common clerk, or town clerk, who is to be "honest and discreet."

Next in order follow powers for the appointment of a *Portator Gladii nostri coram Maiore Civitatis*, a bearer of our sword before the mayor; and also of three *servientes-ad-clavas*, or sergeants-at-mace, and the charter goes on to say—(we quote from the translation)

And further we will and ordain and by these presents for us, our heirs and successors, do grant to the said mayor, aldermen, bailiffs, and citizens, and their successors, that as well the aforesaid bearer of *the sword of us our heirs and successors*, as the aforesaid sergeants-at-mace in the same city to be appointed, shall carry and bear maces of gold or silver, and engraved and adorned with the *sign of the arms of this our kingdom* of England everywhere *within the said city of Carlisle and liberties of the same* before the mayor therefor for the time being.[*]

---

[*] Municipal pageantry has a meaning. The citizen of olden times looked upon the municipal insignia with a political significance. When he saw the mace and sword (says Mr. Thompson in his Municipal History), when he saw the banner of his community unfurled, his heart exulted in the thought that his fellow-citizens and he constituted a body enjoying entire independence, their own civil and criminal jurisdiction, and a name in the land which kings and lords respected.

The language of this extract should be noticed. In the first place, the official who is to carry the sword is

Portator gladii nostri coram Maiore.
(The Bearer of our Sword before the mayor.)

"The sword of us our heirs and successors," that is, the bearer of the King's sword, not the mayor's or the corporation's. The sword is the emblem of civic independence, of the right of the citizens to govern themselves; and also of the criminal jurisdiction wielded by the mayor. At Amiens, in France, the insignia of supreme justice consist of two swords of antique shape carried in the hands of officials, and a similar custom prevailed among all the great corporations of France, which, undoubtedly, had a continuity from Roman times. The sword is always carried sheathed, denoting the reserve of force behind the civil power: it is always to be carried point upright, even in church. The dean and chapter of Chester litigated the question with the corporation of that place, and it was decided that "as often as the mayor repaired to the church to hear divine service or sermon, or upon any great

GREAT MACE, AND SERGEANTS' MACES, CARLISLE.

T. .... Carlisle.

To face p. 14.

The governing charter next grants to the mayor authority to take recognizances. It also grants a court leet, and view of frankpledge. It contains a reservation of the accustomed fee-farm rents. It grants faculty for the corporation to hold land, &c., not exceeding the annual value of £40. It confirms the grant of the Battailholme for holding the markets and fairs.

Up to this point each successive charter, granted to Carlisle, broadens its municipal liberties; we now come to two charters which were intended to curtail them, but, except for a short time, they have always been regarded as waste parchment.

The 17th century witnessed many political changes. Many political questions still under debate cannot be understood without at least referring back to the middle of that century. No one should venture to speak on the political questions of the 19th century who does not understand those of the 17th. The power of Parliament was immensely augmented, and it was the interest of the Court to pack that body, or to bribe its members. Bribery was resorted to with the Parliament that succeeded the Convention of 1660. It sat from 1661 to 1678-9, and was called the Pensionary Parliament. In this Parliament commenced that system of bribery which Walpole afterwards perfected. The well-known Andrew Marvel printed at Amsterdam a list of the members who received pensions. On the dissolution of this Parliament the court tried to pack the next. They invented, for the first time, faggot voters; they instituted, also for the first time, the system of conveying voters to the poll free; they further did all they could to gain over the corporations in boroughs, and to pack them, with a view to influence the borough elections,

---

occasion, he was to be at liberty to have the sword of the city borne before him with the point upright." In fact it is lowered to neither prince nor prelate, but to the crown alone.

The maces are to have upon them the arms, not of Carlisle, but of England, and they denote that part of the royal authority which is entrusted to the mayor during his year of office.

for the corporations had gradually, by usurpation, become comptrollers of their local elections in derogation of the rights of the original voters. At Carlisle the crown had, during the time of the Pensionary Parliament, tried this system. In 1664 it imposed on Carlisle the charter of 16, Charles II, which re-enacted the governing charter of Charles I, but required that the officers should take the oath of obedience and supremacy, and that the recorder and town clerk should be approved of by the crown. This was acted upon, for in the Dormont Book is this proclamation—

CHARLES R.

Charles the Second by the Grace of God, King of England, Scotland, France, and Ireland, defender of the faith, &c. To all persons to whom these presents shall come greeting. Whereas our Trusty and well-beloved Maior, Aldermen, and Common Council of our good Citty of Carlile, have by an instrument under the Publicke Seal of that our Citty, bearing date the third day of this instant January, humbly signifyed unto us that upon the death of John Pattinson, gent., late Toune clarke of that our citty, they by virtue of our Royal charter to them granted, had on the nineteenth day of December last past elected and chosen James Nicholson, gent., to succeed in that place and office, humbly beseeching us that according to the power to us reserved in our said Royall charter wee would be pleased graciously to approve of such their choice. Know ye that wee taking the same into our Princely consideration, and having now received good testimonie of the loyalty and good affection of the said James Nicholson to us and our Government, and of his ability to performe and execute the said place and office have accepted, ratifyed, approved, and confirmed, and for us, our heirs and successors, by these presents sufficiently accept, ratify, approve, and confirme him the said James Nicholson, so chosen as aforesaid, to be Toune Clerk of our said Citty of Carlisle, to have, hold, exercise, and enjoy the said place and offices with all and singular the rights, priviledges, advantages, and emoluments thereto belonging and appertaining. Given under Signet and Sign Manuell at our Court at Whitehall, the fourteenth day of January, in the eighteenth yeare of our raigne, 1666.

By his Majestic's comand,

ARLINGTON.

As both the members for Carlisle were on Andrew Marvel's list of pensioners, the crown did not think any further deprivation of the city's rights necessary, so long as Sir Philip Howard and Sir Christopher Musgrave were returned. Those gentlemen sat for three Parliaments, but in 1680–1 the city turned restive, and dismissed the tory Sir Philip Howard in favour of the whig Lord Morpeth. Vengeance was not long delayed; chief justice Jeffreys came the northern circuit. A courtly jury decided that the charter had been infringed and forfeited ; the corporation, partly bullied, partly subservient, surrendered it, and the chief justice carried it off. The date of the surrender is August 7, 1684.

On the 16th of September, Jeffreys wrote the following holograph letter, the original of which is among the corporation muniments :—

Mr. Mayor,—

I thinke my selfe obleiged to retorne you and the rest of your Loyall Brethren the aldermen and other members of your Corporation my hearty thanks for the greate favours and respects I mett with when I had the hapiness to bee among you, and particularly for your great expressions of Loyalty to the King which you soe plainely demonstrated by laying your selves at his Majestie's feete, which according to the best of my understanding I acquainted his Majestie with, with all advantages to you ; his Majestie was pleased to express with greate pleasure his gratiouse acceptance of the Testimonies you gave of your Loyalty and therefore commanded me to acquaint you therewith as alsoe to lett you know you shall find the effect of it in the Renewall of your Charter, and required my particular care therein.   And to the end you may not loose his designed Bountie I thinke myselfe obleiged to give you this advice. That you consider what priviledges or advantages belonging to your Towne which were either omitted or not sufficiently granted to you by your Old Charters may be supplied by this New one, and I shall take care that it may be done. I came to towne but last night from Winchester and therefore lay hold upon this first opportunity to acquaint you therewith, and withall to let you know his Majestie's

C

designe to be here in London on Thursday sevenight and to continue
here eight or ten days at most and then to goe to Newmarket and
there continue three weeks soe that he will not make any stay here
in London till the Terme.   Now I apprehend that the persons you
designe to come up with your Charter and solicite the affaire may with
more ease and less charge attend his Majestie's retorne from Newmarket then any time before, for it is his pleasure that this your
Loyalty may meete with as little trouble and charges in ye renewall
of your Charter as possibly may be, And be assured his Majesty's
Gracious intention towards you shall meete with all the assistance I
can possibly give it.   I begg you will tender my hearty service to
the rest of your Corporation, and be assured I will with all zeale
and industry imaginable embrace all opportunities wherein I may
manifest myselfe to be a hearty friend to your Corporation and
particularly,

Sir,

Your faithful friend and servant,

GEO. JEFFREYS.

London, Sept. 16th, 1684.
For the Worshipful the Mayor of the City of Carlisle,
att Carlisle.

The smooth words of the chief justice were honeyed
poison.

A new charter, the 36 Charles II (1684), came down.
It re-enacted most of the provisions of the governing
charter, and it conferred some further privileges.   The six
senior aldermen were to be justices of the peace; the
recorder might have a deputy ; a fair in June, and a court
of *pie poudre* were granted.   But the sting was that it contained a *provision enabling the Crown at pleasure to
remove any of the chartered officers.*

The rod was made for the citizens' backs, but it was
left for James II to lay it on.

Carlisle returned two tories to the only Parliament of
James II, but this Parliament, strongly tory as it was,
declined to repeal the penal laws and test act.   The King
set to work to pack a Parliament that would.   Sir George
Duckett has published a most interesting book, which tells

how the King tried to manipulate the counties. The lord-lieutenants of the counties of Cumberland and Westmorland —the earls of Carlisle and Thanet—had been dismissed because they were not sufficiently subservient to his Majesty's wishes. Lord Preston was appointed to both offices, and held at Penrith, on January 25th, 1688, a meeting of the justices and deputy-lieutenants of the two counties, but whigs and tories alike declined to accept the King's policy, or to promise to return such candidates as he wished. Even catholic Lancashire resisted.

But we have to do with Carlisle. Secret agents were sent round the boroughs to canvass and spy on the King's behalf. The reports of many of these agents exist, but the one for Carlisle has not been found. Perhaps none was made. The corporation of Carlisle was a mere board of court nominees. In March, 1687, it had made the papist Sir Francis Salkeld a freeman and an alderman, and it had also admitted nine commissioned officers of the garrison, all Irish papists, to the freedom of the city. It sent up the following address :—

To the King's most excellent Majesty.

The humble address of the Mayor, Alderman, Bailiffs, and Citizens of Carlisle.

Dread Sovereign,

Being now at liberty, by the late regulations made here, to address ourselves unto your Majesty, we beg leave to return our late but unfeigned thanks for your Majesty's most gracious Declaration of Indulgence, which we will endeavour to maintain and support against all opposers. We likewise thank your Majesty for the royal army, which really is both the honour and safety of the nation, let the Tikelites think and say what they will. And, when your Majesty in your great wisdom shall think fit to call a Parliament, we shall choose such members as shall certainly concur with your Majesty in repealing and taking off the Penal Laws and Tests, and not hazard the election of any person who hath any ways declared in favour of those cannibal laws. Surely they do not consider what a Sovereign Prince by his royal power may do that oppose your Majesty in so gracious and glorious a work—a work which heaven

smiles upon and with no less blessing, we hope, than a Prince of
Wales.   That there may never want of your issue to sway the
sceptre, so long as the sun and moon endure ; that your Majesty's
reign may be long and prosperous, and blessed with victory over all
your enemies, are the daily prayers of

Gracious Sir,
Your Majesty's most obedient and
dutiful subjects, &c.

In Rapin's History of England, it is stated that this address was drawn up by a jesuit priest, and sent down to
Carlisle by the popish party to be signed there.   It was
then published in the *London Gazette* as a spontaneous
effusion from an important city.

. But the committal to the Tower of the seven bishops,
for refusing to allow the King's "Declaration of a Liberty
of Conscience" to be read from the pulpit, aroused a more
genuine outburst of public feeling.

On June 10th, 1688, occurred the birth of an heir to
James II, which was celebrated in Carlisle market place
in strange fashion.   The Irish officers of the garrison made
a great bonfire there, "where they drank wine till, with
that and the transport of the news, they were exceedingly
distracted, throwing their hats into the fire at one health,
their coats the next, their waistcoats at a third, and so on
to their shoes, and some of them threw in their shirts, and
then ran about naked like madmen."*

Yet the corporation were not servile enough to please
the King, as the following proclamation shows :—

At the Court, at Whitehall, the 23 June, 1688.

Whereas by the charter lately granted to the City of Carlisle,
in the County of Cumberland, a power is reserved to his Majesty,
by his order in Council, to remove from their employments any
officers in ye said city, his Majesty in Councill is this day pleased to
order, and it is hereby ordered that Edward Earl of Carlisle, Bazil
Fielding, Esq., Aldermen Henry Riddell, Chief Bayliff; William

---

* Memoirs of Thomas Story of Justice Town.

Barwick, Thompson Sympson, William Bushby, Robert Jackson, junior, Nicholson Robinson, Thomas Jackson, John Sowerby, Michael Collin, Richard Wilson, George Lankake, Francis Atkinson, and John Carnaby, capital or common Councilmen be, and they are hereby removed and displaced from their said offices in the said City of Carlisle.

Sir John Lowther, of Lowther (first Viscount Lonsdale), in his "Memoirs of the Reign of James II," a most valuable, but fragmentary work, privately printed, says :—

It is to be observed that most part of the offices in the nation, as justices of the peace, deputie-lieutenants, maiors, aldermen, and freemen of towns are filled with Roman Catholics and Dissenters, after having suffered as manie regulations as were necessary for that purpose. And thus stands the state of the nation in the month of September, 1688.

Events moved fast after this. On the 12th and 13th of October, 1688, Claverhouse, with three thousand horse, foot, and dragoons, and a train of guns, marched through Carlisle to swell the royal forces in Yorkshire and Lancashire. But the King had taken alarm : he tried to undo the work he had been doing. On the 17th of October an order was issued restoring all the corporations in England to their ancient privileges, displacing all corporate officers who claimed their places by any grant made by the crown since 1679, and reinstating all those turned out. The order bore date the 17th of the month, and no sooner reached Cumberland than Sir Christopher Musgrave and Sir George Fletcher, who had been mayors of Carlisle under the old charters, took possession of the corporations of Carlisle and Appleby, "entering into the ffirst in a kind of cavalcade and ostentation of merit, (writes Sir John Lowther, of Lowther) when in reality they had so far complied with those times as to deliver up the charters of Carlisle, Kendal, &c., which was the illegal action now redeemed."

There was a great drink in Carlisle that night, as

appears from entries in the books of the guilds. Luckily
the surrender of Aug. 7, 1684, had never been enrolled, and
so was void.

Then, still in that month of October, occurred the first
local overt act in favour of the Prince of Orange. William
Huddleston of Hutton John, an ardent protestant, the first
protestant of his family, received information that a ship
was expected to arrive at Workington laden with arms and
ammunition for the popish garrison at Carlisle. He put
himself in communication with the Lowthers; he and Sir
John Lowther of Whitehaven armed their tenants, marched
them by night to the sea coast, and forced the vessel, then
probably in Workington harbour, to surrender. The
Lowthers, who were in communication with the Prince of
Orange, timed this dashing move to coincide with his expected arrival in England. Their calculations failed. A
" popish wind " scattered the Dutch fleet, and news came to
the north that the expedition was put off for a year. This
must have been an anxious time for the Lowthers; had
that report been true, the Lowthers would probably have
gone to the scaffold. They and Huddleston must have
wished as ardently for a favouring gale as did the crowds
which blocked up Bow churchyard watching for the vane
to veer and indicate a protestant wind.

The protestant wind came soon; the Prince landed, not
at Hull, where the Lowthers expected him, but at Torquay.
Sir John Lowther of Lowther seized Carlisle (the Irish
garrison stealing away in the night) and thus blocked the
north road, and cut off Claverhouse's retreat.

Edward Stanley of Dalegarth, known as the "oak-
hearted," then high sheriff of Cumberland, proclaimed
King William III at Carlisle Cross, and there ends the
history of the charters of Carlisle. Never since then has
the crown meddled with the governing charter, and under
it, modified by the municipal corporation acts, Carlisle is
now ruled.

CHAPTER II.*

THE CORPORATION AND GUILDS.

In the previous chapter we have traced the various steps and noticed the different charters by which the citizens of Carlisle gradually won from the crown their municipal rights and franchises, such as the free election of their magistrates, exemption from the exactions of the sheriffs, and liberty *ad facienda sua negotia*, and we summed up the result in the words of the learned town clerk of Carlisle :

It appears evident that under the above charter (26 Edward III, 1353), the city was in all but name a county of itself, being perfectly independent of the county and all county jurisdiction, having its own bailiffs to execute the office of sheriff, and its own coroners, and being free from the payment of any purvey or rate to the county.†

It is our intention in this chapter to endeavour to deal with the municipal history of Carlisle from a more domestic point of view ; to discuss the strife between citizen and citizen, rather than between the citizens and the crown.

We have seen that the earliest charter granted to Carlisle was that of Henry II, after he had recovered the city from the Scots, who had held it during the reign of Stephen. This charter was burnt, but it is recited in a

---

* This Chapter was originally given as a lecture to the Carlisle Scientific Society, January 9th, 1883.

† Ante p. 11.

later—that of 35 Henry III. It contains a confirmation of
the liberties and customs which the citizens of Carlisle
had theretofore freely enjoyed, and it grants them a free
merchant guild, *gildam mercatoriam liberam ita quod
nihil inde respondeant aliquibus*. This guild mercatory,
or free merchant guild, is the germ from which the present
corporation has grown. No records remain to tell us anything
about it : we have only mention of it once in the recital
(in the charter of Henry III) of the burnt charter of
Henry II. But the name long survived, as the designation,
and the proper one too, of the building now commonly
called the Town Hall, but whose name in the corporation
records is always the Guild Hall or Moot Hall. That fact
it is important to preserve, as taking our history back to
the free merchant guild, or guild mercatory, and back
further than that to the moot of an early English *tun*.
The free merchant guild of Carlisle was very shortly ab-
sorbed into another organisation,—that of the mayor, bailiffs,
and citizens of a later charter, and did not, as at Preston,
drag on a curiously intermittent existence. But though
the name almost wholly disappeared, the struggle which
everywhere took place between the oligarchic guilds
mercatory and the democratic craft guilds was long
waged in Carlisle, until it culminated in the storms of
the famous Mushroom Elections of last century. It can
hardly be said to have died out until the old corporation
of Carlisle died itself in the clean sweep made in 1835,
by which time the craft guilds themselves had become
oligarchies as narrow as that against which they had so
long struggled.

Much learning has of late been expended in researches
into the history and origin of guilds. Mr. Coote, in his
able work, "The Romans of Britain," finds the origin of
the English guilds in the *collegia* of ancient Rome; while
Dr. Brentano, whose essay is prefixed to Toulmin Smith's
"English Guilds," refers them to the German tribes in
Scandinavia. But Bishop Stubbs well says :—

The simple idea of a confraternity united for the discharge of common or mutual good offices supported by contributions of money from each member, and celebrating its meetings by a periodical festival, may find parallel in any civilised nation at any age of the world. The ancient guild is simply the club of modern manners.

The ancient guilds were burial clubs, charitable clubs, dinner and drinking clubs, trade-unions, local boards, and the like. The craft guilds were trades unions, while the free merchant guilds, or guilds mercatory, were local boards. In all sorts of guilds the following characteristics are to be found—the members are *fratres* or *brothers*; great importance is attached to the due burial of the dead; and great importance is also attached to the dining or drinking together on certain occasions. Further, a religious character is always attached to a guild: of some guilds, like the famous guild of the Corpus Christi at York, the objects were purely religious. But even in the craft or trade guilds of Carlisle, which were mere trade unions, the religious character stands out well marked. The craft guilds of Carlisle took part in the celebration of Corpus Christi day. In the rules of the tailors' guild we find—

It is Ordained and appointed by ye said Occupacon that upon Corpus Christi day as old use or custome before time the whole Light and ye whole Occupacon and Banner be in Gt. Maries Churchyard at ye Ash tree at 10 of ye clock in ye forenoon and he yt comes not before ye banner be raised to come away pay VId. each offender toties quoties.

This picturesque order gives us an idea of what mediæval Carlisle looked like on a great church festival. Early in the morning the guilds, with banners and candles, would assemble in S. Mary's churchyard; probably they carried with them the images of their patron saints—the shoemakers still possess an image of S. Crispin—or men would be dressed up to play the characters. High mass would be celebrated within the cathedral, and then, to the strains of solemn music, a long-drawn procession of prior and canons and ecclesiastics of high degree would wend down the Norman aisles and emerge from the western door. As the pyx containing the consecrated bread was borne past under its magnificent baldachino or canopy, every head would be bared; then would succeed, radiant in jewellery and stiff in brocade, a life size image of the patroness of the city, the blessed Virgin Mary; the guilds, with their banners, would fall into the rear of the procession, and the pageant would wind in and out the narrow streets of the quaint old city, past a background of half-timbered and gayly-painted houses, to witness in the market place the performance of a miracle play. And to wind up the enjoyment of the day, the butchers' guild would find a wretched bull or two to be baited in the bull ring under the windows of the guild chambers in Redness Hall.*

The religious character of the local craft guilds is further marked by their days of meeting being usually fixed by festivals of the Church. Thus the quarter days of the shoemakers were fixed by reference to S. Sébastian's and S. Fabian's Day, S. Philip and James, S. Mary Magdalene, and SS. Crispin and Crispianus; the smiths regulated themselves by S. Helen's Day and Lammas Day, All Saints Day and S. Blazes' Day.

The craft guilds of Carlisle possess all the characteristics which have been mentioned as belonging to guilds; they called themselves fraternities, and their members brothers. Each guild kept a hearse cloth, or funeral pall, for the use of the members; and the whole fraternity were bound to attend the funeral of any brother who had "departed to God's mercy," or of any brother's wife, child, or apprentice.

Also it ordered (by the fraternity of Taylors) that when any brother or brother's wife of this occupation deceases that [they] have ye whole light with ye banner ye son or daughter to have half-light with ye banner and ye apprentice a third of ye light with ye banner.

---

* Redness Hall takes its name from Richard de Redness, merchant, to whom it belonged in the reign of Richard II.

As for dining and drinking together the rules of all the
Carlisle craft guilds are precise and full on the subject of
"quarterly drinkings" and periodical dinners.

These remarks, though a little anticipatory, serve
to illustrate the general characteristics of guilds. We
must recur to the germ from which the corporation of
Carlisle grew, the free merchant guild, or guild mercatory.
We cannot cite the rules of the free merchant guild as
we can those of the trade or craft guilds, because those
rules do not exist ; but the special objects of these merchant guilds are well known. They arose from the frith
guilds, or peace clubs, associations voluntarily formed by
neighbours for mutual protection and local government.
In them each member was responsible for the deeds of
his colleagues, as in earlier days he was held responsible
for those of his kin ; thus going back to the early
village communities, wherein each man was related, and
all were responsible one for the other. In towns, and
towns are only larger villages, the frith guilds became
town guilds, and, as commerce became more and more
the mark of a town, the town guilds came to be called
free merchant guilds or guilds mercatory, as being the
bodies that made laws for the regulation of trade. But as
in the village community, so in the town, the possession of
land was essential to the notion of a full townsman or free
burgher, and the merchant guild was a club of the landed
proprietors of the town, a ruling oligarchy, an autocratic
local board, which often, as at Carlisle, York, etc., developed
into the fully incorporated " mayor, aldermen, and citizens,
in council assembled."

Our first chapter shows how the free merchant guild
of Carlisle became a town council, and we need not recur
to its struggles and contests with the crown. This chapter
will call attention to another side thereof : its relations
with its fellow townsmen, the working craftsmen. The
governing body, constituted of landed proprietors, excluded
from all part in municipal affairs the craftsmen, the traders

without land, the new settlers in the town, and the poor
generally; so these combined and formed guilds for their
own protection and for the furtherance of their own
interests. These guilds are the trade or craft guilds, of
which Carlisle possessed eight, namely (1) the weavers;
(2) the smiths, who included blacksmiths, whitesmiths,
goldsmiths, and silversmiths, or all that live by the
hammery art; (3) the tailors, or merchant tailors, as they
called themselves in later days; (4) the tanners; (5) the
shoemakers or cordwainers; (6) the skinners and glovers;
(7) the butchers; (8) the merchants. These trade or craft
guilds are very old, but no record exists of any of them
older than the middle of the sixteenth century. It is
curious that there is no guild of carpenters, nor of any
trade connected with building; and it is noteworthy to
find three guilds which work in leather, while a fourth, the
butchers' guild, deals in hides.* Seven of the guilds are
guilds of manual craftsmen; the eighth, the merchants'
guild,—quite distinct from the free merchant guild or
guild mercatory, which became the town council—included
the shopkeepers, some grocers and seedsmen, others drapers,
haberdashers, apothecaries, &c. Nothing is at present
known about the early struggles between the town council
that had grown out of the free merchant guild and the
eight trade or craft guilds. We know that in other places
these struggles were severe, resulting, as at London, in
rioting and bloodshed. We may suppose something of
the sort occurred in Carlisle, for Carlisle had a turbulent
population, who are recorded, in the fourteenth century,
to have mobbed the bishop and his suite, and would have
little hesitated to stone the mayor in the event of their
having any serious difference of opinion with him as to
their rights.

In the year 1561, however, we emerge from the sea of

---

* The leather trade was regulated by several acts of parliament, under
which the manufacture of leather was divided into at least four distinct trades,
exercised respectively by tanners, curriers, skinners, and leather cutters.

conjecture, and set foot upon the firm ground of historical records, commencing with the Dormont Book. The title of this volume is as follows :—

This §

CALLED § THE § REGESTAR § GO

VERNOR § OR § DORMONT § BOOK §

OF § THE § COMONWELTH § OF § THI

NHABITANCES § WTH IN § THE § CITIE §

OF § CARLELL § RENEWED § IN § THE § YERE § OF §

OWR § LORD § GOD § 1561.

It contains a code of bye-laws for the government of the city of Carlisle, which must have been compiled with great care and much deliberation, for amongst the corporation papers, two original drafts of them remain. These bye-laws are preceded by a prologue, which states that

The Mayre and citisens of this citie with the advice of the citisens commonaltie wth lerned counsale of the same: : : : have taken parte labor, travell and Diligence of zeal and gudwyll to devise orders &ct.

and it concludes

In witness herof as well the mayre and counsale with foure of everie occupation of the foresaid citie for and in the naym of the hole citizens and th inhabitances thereof haith subscribed this book wth oure proper hands as also annexed hereto there comon seall.

Now, the point to be noticed is this, that the bye-laws are made by the mayor and citizens with the advice of the council and corporation, and that the testing clause is by the "mayre counsale with foure of everie occupation" or guild, as representing the citizens : thus shewing that the trade or craft guilds of Carlisle had asserted themselves, and become powerful checks on the town council or guild mercatory. This runs all through the bye-laws. Though the mayor and council are the administrative body, yet they are prohibited from laying out money without the consent of four of every occupation : two of the four keys of the common chest of the city are to be in the custody of the occupations : the recorder, auditors and other officers, not specified in the then existing charters, are removable by the "mayor and counsale and foure of everie occupation," who are to appoint successors to officers so removed. The two points of most importance, as having been most frequently the subject of local squabbles and litigation are the claim of the craft guilds to control the audit of the city accounts, and the following bye-law, which is No. 19 :—

Item, that the mayor of hymself shall not hereafter make any out-men freemen without the advice of the moste parte of the counsale and foure of euere occupacon, which is agreeable to the ancient custom and constitution of the citie.

The words "outmen" and "foure of euere occupacon" are interpolations. As the rule at first stood, the mayor, and the majority of the council acting together, could have admitted strangers or outmen to be freemen, but apparently the representatives of the guilds refused to sign the bye-laws, until they had a check put on a power which might be used in a way detrimental to their interests. There is on record an instance of this 19th bye-law being carried out. In the chamberlain's books, under date of 1569, is an entry that John Blennerhasset, who had been a freeman and councillor, and disfranchised for having withdrawn himself from the city, being again come to reside there, " by the mayor and council, with the full consent and agreement of the occupations is admitted freeman and councillor again." These two points, the supervision or audit of the city accounts, and the power of the mayor to make freemen, continued for long to be in dispute, and out of them arose the exciting episodes in the political history of Carlisle known as the Mushroom Elections.

The charter of Elizabeth, 1566-7, contains an inspeximus of these bye-laws and a confirmation of them. Under this charter the town council consisted of the mayor and eleven

others : how they got on with their 32 masters provided by
the occupations or guilds we have little to tell us until the
middle of the 17th century. That century witnessed many
important political changes. Among others the power of
parliament became immensely augmented. It became the
interest of the court to pack that body or to bribe it. Thus
the parliamentary franchise and the power of making freemen became of great value. It has been related in the
previous chapter how James II packed the corporation of
Carlisle with his nominees. In his reign also it appears to
have become worth while to manipulate the freemen of
Carlisle. Now, neither the governing charter of Charles I
nor the two charters of Charles II (which were afterwards
repudiated) prescribed how freemen were to be elected ;
the corporation in March, 1687–8, being well packed with
Irishmen and papists, seemed to have assumed that the
bye-laws of 1561, or at any rate the restrictions contained
therein, were either obsolete or superseded. Accordingly
they admitted and swore in a large number of freemen
without consulting the guilds at all. The corporation that
perpetrated this political job was purged by the order of privy
council of 17th October, 1688, which restored all corporations
in England to their ancient privileges : the Irish and Popish
swashbucklers that garrisoned the castle and sat on the
corporation benches got over the city walls and ran away
in the night. Their rightful successors soon took steps to
clear out the intruding or "Mushroom freemen."* An order
of council, dated November 14, 1689, runs thus :—

That whereas in March, 1687–8, and May and July, 1688, a great
many freemen had been unduly elected by the then new modelled
corporation, not having the least right to the freedom, being strangers
or foreigners, which tended to the ruin of the corporation, they are
thereby ordered to be disfranchised of their pretended right.

In this instance the corporation and the guilds do not appear
to have clashed ; but it is evident that, during the reign of

---

* So called because they sprang up in a day, without serving a seven years'
apprenticeship.

James II, the political virtue of the guilds had been tampered with, and that it continued ever afterwards somewhat easy. This alarmed the corporation, and the following lengthy order was passed by that body :—

At ye Common Councill holden the 14th day of March
Anno Domini 1697.
Present Mr Maior etc.

Whereas divers undermasters and Clarks of severall Guilds or Fraternitys of this Citty and Corporation of late years and more especially during the Raine of the late King James ye Second have at their own will and pleasure and as often as they thought fitt summoned called and procured the brothers of the said guilds or ffraternitys to meat together in their guilds within this Citty of Carlisle and at such meetings have taken ye Oppertunity by false insinuations and undue preparations of the said brothers to make and foment factions and divisions in ye said ffraternitys whereby ye freedom of Ellections wthin this Citty hath been greatly and frequently disturbed and divers other mischieves have ensued both to ye Cittizens of this Citty in their right of Ellections and in other their ffranchises and immanities. And whereas divers persons on purpose to carry on the said evill practices have procured themselves to be admitted to the fredome of the said fraternitys contrary to Law and ye Ancient Customs of this Citty And whereas it appeareth to us that the said Severall guilds within this Citty have made Severall Orders or by Laws to the hurt of ye Publique and to the trying and abuse of the freemen and inhabitants of this Citty in particularly that they have contrary to Law Imposed severall sums of money on the Brothers of the said ffraternity and others for the breach of ye said illegal Orders and by Laws. Therefore for the reformation of the above mentioned evills and abuses It is by the Mayor Aldermen and Capital Cittyzens of this Common Counsell assembled ordained and established that noe undermaster or Clarke undermasters or Clarkes of any the severall guilds or fraternities of this Citty and Corporation shall without ye allowance of the Comon Councill of this Corporation, &c., &c.

We need not cite any more of this long document; it forbids a repetition of the irregularities. The gist of it is

THE CORPORATION AND GUILDS.				33

this : The election agents of the 17th century were just
as sharp as those of the 19th century. There is no modern
election dodge, except the great card trick, that was not
first hatched in the reigns of Charles II and James II. At
Carlisle the practice was, by connivance of the clerk of a
guild, to call a meeting at some irregular time on short
notice. Many members would be unable to attend, and a
packed meeting would be easily secured, at which new
members would be admitted without much regard to any
qualification, but that they were of the right colour. The
persons thus irregularly admitted were presented at the next
court held by the mayor for the admission of freemen. As
the mayor was refused an inspection of the guild books, he
could not detect any irregularities, and was bound to admit
those presented, who thus obtained the parliamentary
franchise. The corporation do not appear to have been
able to enforce their order ; spite of it, and spite of similar
orders made by the guilds themselves, these irregular meetings continued to be held. In later days the mayor was
generally a political partizan, and fixed the date of the
court for the admission of freemen to suit the convenience of his own side, while the other side had no notice,
and his worship found it inconvenient to have another
court until the election was over. Of course, the candidates paid all the expenses, which were calculated on a very
liberal scale. They included the travelling expenses of the
new freeman, perhaps from London, or other distant place
of residence, his fees for brotherhood, and the arrears of his
father's quarterly dues, which sometimes had been unpaid
since the date of the father's admission.

About the end of the 17th century the corporation
made several *ex gratiâ* or honorary freemen, without the
concurrence or assistance of the guilds, namely, captain
Bubb, sir Christopher Musgrave, doctor Law, Leonard Gay,
and the earl of Carlisle, the last of whom was made
an alderman before he was made free of the city. At the
disputed election of 1711, the question of the right to vote

was avoided ; six honorary freemen voted, but as they were
not enough to turn the poll either way, no attempt was made
to question their right, beyond lodging an objection, which
was not pressed.   The guilds, however, appear to have been
alarmed at this, and, probably at their instance, the corporation passed the following order :—

Sept. 21st, 1713.   Order of Common Council.   That none be
made free who have not duly served their times to some who had
right to take apprentices, or have right to claim their freedom by
birth ; and this, be it observed, is not to be infringed on any pretence.

This produced no final settlement of the question.   In 1720
the opinion of the recorder was taken upon it, and in the
following year an order was made for its repeal,

as it had been found by experience to be doubtful and uncertain.

Henry viscount Lowther, his brother Anthony, colonel
Charles Howard, William Harrison, captain John de Roos
(who assumed the name of Stanwix and became well known
as major general Stanwix), Thomas Dobinson, Humphrey
Senhouse, Daniel Wilson, and Montagu Farrar were all made
ex gratiâ or honorary freemen between the rescinding of the
order of 1713 and 1750.   Many, but not all, of these gentlemen became brothers of some or one of the guilds after
they had been made freemen.   These creations, and also the
management of the corporation property, appear to have
stirred up the guilds to further action, and in the year 1750
the corporation, upon

the application of the freemen of this city, setting forth that several
ex gratiâ or honorary freemen have of late been made within this
city, which they apprehend is an encroachment upon their liberties
and very prejudicial to their just rights, as also that the city's
revenues have of late years been greatly misapplied and lessened,

entered into a bond to make no more ex gratiâ freemen,
and to have their accounts audited and submitted to
the guilds.   This order was made under the threat or
pressure of litigation, for in the books of the merchants'

guild is an order, under date of February, 1750-1, for the payment of the expenses of securing the right of freedom of the city, and to prevent making *ex gratiâ* freemen. The lessening of the city's revenue refers to the defalcations we shall mention presently, and to a trial at York about the corporation's right to demand mulcture, and to compel the inhabitants to have malt ground at the city mills. This trial the corporation lost, and with it much of their revenue, for, as they had neglected to keep a stallion horse, a boar, and a bull, they could not substantiate their right to the mulcture and the compulsory use of the city mills. Further litigation arose, between the freemen and the corporation, about the management of Kingmoor. Alderman Christopher Hodgson took the part of the freemen, and was disfranchised in order to give evidence against the corporation. This suit ended in March, 1757-8, in a compromise, under which the corporation paid the costs of the suit, restored Hodgson to his civic dignity, and gave a similar bond to the one they had given in 1750. In 1759, the order carrying out this compromise was repealed by an order reciting,

that it had been inconvenient by excluding from the corporation persons of worth, probity, and distinction, who might be useful to it.

The repealing order went on to direct that

from thence the common council should have authority to make freemen as they had immemorially enjoyed it, and of right ought.

Sir James Lowther (afterwards the first earl of Lonsdale) and P. Sowerby, a butcher, were immediately admitted *ex gratiâ* freemen, and five days later an order similar to those of 1750 and 1758 was enacted, and a new bond sealed to secure its observation in a penalty of £1,000.

The admission of sir James into the corporation was the commencement of a new order of things. He, at first, espoused the side of the freemen in the long quarrel between them and the corporation, and compelled an investigation into the corporation accounts from 1738 downwards : by means of a committee of investigation, of which sir James was a member, it was discovered that under the rule of the party dominant in the corporation during those years (the whigs), the corporation property, its revenues, and its landed estates (Kingmoor to wit), had been most grievously mismanaged and squandered. Sir James's entry into the corporation thus appears to have been a victory for the party who had been for some time struggling to compel an audit of the corporation accounts ; it brought about a return to the old lines of the constitution, by a deviation from which the corporation had assumed an uncontrolled authority over the city property and funds, and had recklessly and wickedly wasted them.[*]

Between 1759 and 1784 no new *ex gratiâ* freemen were made, but several of them, such as sir James Lowther, major Farrar, and Humphrey Senhouse, voted at contested elections. During this period the freemen appear to have had litigation with the corporation on various points. In 1784 the position of affairs was this : There had for upwards of two hundred years been disputes between the freemen, who were members of the eight city guilds, and the corporation, not alone as to the right to make *ex gratiâ* freemen, but on other points ; and the corporation was only restrained in its own view from making such freemen by an order of its own, and a bond dated five and twenty years back. On the 11th and 28th of October, 1784, the corporation unanimously—for the few dissentients stayed away—repealed the orders and bye-laws of 1759 ; they repealed also all orders and bye-laws requiring admisssion to a guild prior to admission to the freedom of the city, and all orders and bye-laws made to take away or limit the power of the common council to make freemen. On the 29th of

---

[*] The report of this committee was printed at Newcastle as a tract, and is known as "The Black Book of the Corporation of Carlisle." It was afterwards re-printed by the publishers of the *Carlisle Journal*. Both editions are rare.

October the corporation made Mr. Norton and several other persons freemen, and on the 30th they made no less than one thousand one hundred and ninety-five, the names being taken from lists supplied by the agents of the earl, for sir James now had that title, one agent handing in a list of five hundred of his lordship's colliers. Between 1688 and September 1784, one thousand five hundred and twenty persons had been admitted freemen of Carlisle : between September 1784 and February 1785, one thousand four hundred and forty-three were admitted to that dignity, of whom eight hundred and thirty-one were sworn in, coming up to take their oaths in droves, headed by the Lowther agents.* These new freemen soon became famous under the name of "mushrooms," a name apparently even then of some antiquity as applied to *ex gratiâ* freemen. The mushrooms not only had no qualifications on the ground of either birth or servitude, but they had none on any other ground. Had the earl raised his mushrooms from among the inhabitants of Carlisle, he might have defended his doings on the ground that he was only going back to the ancient lines of the constitution, and abolishing unfounded restrictions which had grown up. Probably this view never entered the earl's head. He found a quarrel existing that had existed for centuries, and he took advantage of it by espousing now one side, and now the other. Finally he took the corporation side against the guilds, and made that body his tools for his own end. To our ideas he seems to have done something dreadful, but in 1784, we fancy the defeated side alone held that opinion ; nay, they probably admired him for it, and wished they had been in a position to do the like. At the two bye elections for Carlisle in 1786, and at the general election of 1790, the mushroom voters of course swamped the genuine ones ; but their rights were hotly contested before committees of

---

* Many came from Russendale (now Ravenstonedale) in Westmorland, a place famous for the devotion of its inhabitants to tory principles and to the Lowthers.

the House of Commons, and in the law courts, and reports
of the proceedings will be found in "Luders on Election
Cases" and "Merewether's History of the Boroughs." The
two select committees appointed in 1786 and 1787 evaded
laying down the law on the matter, and were content to
strike out the mushroom votes, and seat the candidates
second on the poll, but a third, in 1791, settled the question
for ever by deciding that

> the right of election for the city of Carlisle in the county of Cumber-
> land, is in the freemen of the said city, duly admitted and sworn
> freemen of the said city, having been previously admitted brethren
> of one of the eight guilds or occupations of the said city, and deriving
> their title to such freedom by being sons of freemen, or by service
> of seven years' apprenticeship to a freeman resident during such
> apprenticeship within the said city, and in no others.

And this decision was confirmed in 1795 by another
committee.

Proceedings in the law courts had also been taken :
Robert Bennett, the son of a freeman, but not the member
of any guild, obtained at a trial before Lord Kenyon a
mandamus compelling the corporation to admit him to the
freedom. This decision clashes with that of the committee
of the House of Commons, and is better law. "Thus," says
serjeant Merewether, "was the connection of the guilds
with the municipal constitution of the place properly
annulled." There would be very few of the mushrooms
in the same category as Bennett, who was the son of a
freeman, for the mushrooms, almost to a man, were utter
strangers to Carlisle. Other legal proceedings were taken
against them. Two large cattle dealers to whom the freedom
from toll would have been of great pecuniary importance,
and a gentleman named Wheatley, also a mushroom, who had
become an alderman, were proceeded against by writs of *quo
warranto*. The pleadings raised the question of the right
of the council to make freemen, and the causes were set
down for trial at the summer assizes of 1790 ; but before

the hearings came on the defendants withdrew their pleas and submitted to judgments of *ouster*. Mr. Wheatley lost his alderman's gown, and all three lost any rights they fancied they had as freemen.

We agree with serjeant Merewether's law, and not with that laid down by the House of Commons. The different opinions as to what class of persons originally possessed the elective franchise in ancient boroughs are reduced by Mr. Hallam to the four following theses :—1st. The original right, as enjoyed by boroughs represented in the Parliaments of Edward I, and all of later creation [where one of a different nature has not been expressed in the charter from which they derive the privilege] was in the inhabitant householders resident in the borough, and paying scot and lot, under these words including local rates and probably general taxes. 2nd. The right sprang from the tenure of certain freehold lands or burgages within the borough, and did not belong to any but such tenants. 3rd. It was derived from charters of incorporation, and belonged to the community or freemen of the corporate body. 4th. It did not extend to the generality of freemen, but was limited to the governing part, or municipal magistracy. The first of these theses, known as the " common law right," was laid down by a committee of the House of Commons in 1624; the second was supported by lord Holt in the case of Ashby and White, and is called the " right of burgage tenure." The third thesis has been most generally supported by decisions of the House of Commons, but more rarely by lawyers, and is now exploded : while the fourth, which was invented by doctor Brady to serve the purposes of James II, has at this day no supporters. Take either of the first two : the resident householders of Carlisle in the reign of Edward I and the owners of lands at that time would be almost identical, for men did not then rent houses; they would form the oligarchic guild mercatory, with which the democratic craft guilds struggled so long—with the final and curious result of excluding from the franchise all householders unless they belonged to the craft guilds. And it is a fact that prior to the reform bill of 1832 the bankers and manufacturers of Carlisle, the Forsters, the Lambs, the Carricks, the Fergusons, the Stoddards, the Mounseys, and the Loshes, had no votes at the parliamentary or municipal elections: neither they nor their ancestors had practised any trade which would qualify them for admission to the craft guilds, and owing to the encroachments of the craft guilds nothing else would give them the franchise.*

---

* For a full history of the mushroom elections, as part of the political history of Carlisle, see Ferguson's *Cumberland and Westmorland M.P.'s from the Restoration to the Reform Bill.* Chas. Thurnam & Sons, Carlisle, 1871. The original right to the franchise is there discussed at length.

Sir John Lowther, Bt., M.P.

From " Boletarium," a political squib of 1786.

TITLE PAGE OF THE DORMONT BOOK.

See p. 42.

To face p. 41.

Chapter III.

THE DORMONT BOOK.

This book consists of about 300 pages of thick hand-laid paper, each exactly 15 inches high by 10¾ inches broad. The mark of a jug or pot tankard shows that the paper is Dutch, manufactured in the Low Countries. The sheets are sewn on three bands of stout leather, each nearly an inch broad. The binding is calf, solid leather without any stiffening of board, and has a flap to lap round the fore-edge. It has vellum end papers, pasted down on the leather; it also has loose ones, lined with leaves from a Roman catholic black letter service book* with illuminated initials and coloured capitals. These leaves contain the greater part of the psalm "Diligam te, Domine" (psalm 18th). The binding is a fine specimen of English calf binding of the 16th century, hand and blind tooled, though some of the corner ornaments may once have been gilt. The tooling has been done with a stamp or tool on a wheel, differently to the tool-work of earlier date, which was done by frequent repetition of a flat stamp or tool. The book has been at some remote period hinged and strapped, like a modern ledger, with three leather bands, sewn on one side of the book with flat silk cord, on the other with strips of vellum. The central band, recently renovated, goes round the book, and clasps with a brass hook in an oval loop. The initials W. T. occur thrice on the upper side of the book, once in an escutcheon, twice with a knot be-

---

* These books (and other objects of "superstitious use") were ordered at the reformation to be got rid of. They were largely purchased by bookbinders, who cut them up for end papers.

tween them. They are probably the initials of the original binder ; not of the mayor of Carlisle, as in that case they would have been followed by M. C. On the top edge of the book an ornament, now almost obliterated, has been painted in black and red, and the marks made by the artist's compass legs are still to be seen. Issuing out of the back of the book are the remains of a green and white cord, to which the city seal was once attached, for the authentication of the ancient ordinances or bye-laws for the government of Carlisle contained in the volume. The book is in good condition for its age, but has been injured by damp and mice. It has recently been carefully repaired.

On the first leaf of the book is a highly ornamented and floriated escutcheon of the city arms, a cross fleurie between four roses, all red, the same with the arms on the market cross and the town hall. The fifth, or central, rose, which appears on the reverse of the common seal of the city of Carlisle, is absent.*

The second leaf is the title page, the centre of which is taken up by a gigantic T, six inches high, and five broad on the cross piece, which forms a grassy plateau, on which a huge raven sits on the top of a flower, while grotesque figures manœuvre around the sable bird. The drops of the T end in red roses. The title has been already given (ante p. 29), but for convenience is repeated : it is as follows :—

T<small>HIS</small>

CALLED § THE § REGESTAR § GO

VERNOR § OR § DORMONT § BOOK

OF § THE § COMONWELTH § OF § THI

NHABITANCES § WTH IN § THE § CITIE

OF § CARLELL § RENEWED § IN § THE § YEAR § OF

OWR § LORD § GOD § 1561.

---

* On the subject of *The Armorial Bearings of the City of Carlisle*, see Transactions Cumberland and Westmorland Antiquarian and Archæological Society, Vol. VI, p. 1.

THE CITY ARMS, CARLISLE, FROM THE DORMONT BOOK.

To face p. 42.

As the vellum end paper preceding this title has the date MCCCCCXXXXIX written on it, the process of renovation possibly took some years. At the top of the page are some Latin mottoes :—

1. Domine saluum fac poplm̄ tuum.
2. Vbi nullus ordo, ibi sempiternus horror.
3. Nouo malo, nouū remedium est apponendū.

with others partly torn away.

It was formerly supposed that the name "Dormont Book" was a degraded form of *Liber Dominationis*, but when the book was exhibited before the Society of Antiquaries of London, the suggestion was made that the name was similar in character to the "coucher book" of a monastery or to the "ledger book" of a commercial firm—all three terms signifying large books that lie permanently in a certain place to which they relate,* in opposition to smaller ones which are intended to be carried about for ready reference. Skeat in his *Etymological Dictionary* defines *dormant* as sleeping, and instances "a table-dormant" from Chaucer, C. T. 355.

The first six pages of the book are occupied with the oaths of admittance to be taken by various officials, namely, the mayor, bailiffs, chamberlain, town clerk, sergeants, attorneys, and coroners, and also by a freeman. These are written in a cramped Elizabethan court hand of the date of the book, 1561. A number of blank pages follow, and then come the "Constitutions orders provisions articles and

---

* "Leiger-books are books that lie permanently in a certain place to which they relate."—*Westwood's Dictionary of English Etymology*. London, Trübner & Co., 1862, vol. II, p. 322. "It is not improbable that the word (*coucher*) is sometimes to be understood, as meaning some large volume intended to 'lie' upon a desk for the use of the choir."—*Monumenta Ritualia Ecclesiæ Anglicanæ Maskell*, 2nd Ed., vol. I, p. cl. See also *Mackenzie Walcott's Sacred Archæology*, p. 187. But "coucher" is said by Dr. F. G. Lee to be an abbreviation of *Collectarium*. See *Glossary of Liturgical and Ecclesiastical Terms*, p. 88.

reules to be observed in maintainance of the Comonwelth."
They occupy some 24 pages in the same cramped hand,
and an index in secretary hand has been prefixed to
them in 1667, probably by James Nicholson, then town
clerk.

The constitutions are written so as to leave wide mar-
gins, on which are explanatory notes, and additions to the
context written so as to be made part of the original.
The additions are in the same style of writing but in a
different hand and ink. The constitutions are signed by
Thomas Pattenson, mayor, and eleven others; also by four
of each occupation or guild. In 1594 and 1609 some
omissions in the bye-laws are supplied. With these ex-
ceptions no use seems to have been made of the book until
a much later date.

After an interval of a blank page or two we find the
whole corporation, on the 9th of October, 1662, from Henry
Barnes, mayor, and sir Philip Musgrave, alderman, down to
William Knagg, George Body, and William Slagg, the
sergeants, making the following declaration :—

I doe declare that there lies no Obligacon upon me or any other
person from the Oath comonly called the Solemne League and
Covenant and that the same was in it selfe an unlawfull Oath
and imposed upon the Subjects of this Realme against the Known
Lawes and Liberties of the Kingdome.

This declaration continues to be made by all taking civic
office until 1689, and to it are appended some valuable
autographs, *e.g.* Thos. Denton the recorder (appointed in
1663), John Aglionby the royalist, sir Philip and sir
Christopher Musgrave, the first earl of Carlisle, sir George
Fletcher, all fine bold signatures. In 1666, the appointment
of James Nicholson as town clerk is also recorded, being under
the charter of Charles II, which required the consent of the
crown to the appointment of recorder and clerk. These
complete the entries in this, or the fore, part of the book.

During the time of the commonwealth the book has been

reversed, and it is titled at its other, or latter end, " The
Citty Book " and

𝕿𝖍𝖊 𝕮𝖎𝖙𝖙𝖞 𝖔𝖋 }
𝕮𝖆𝖗𝖑𝖎𝖑𝖊 }

𝕬 𝕽𝖊𝖈𝖔𝖗𝖉 𝖔𝖋 𝖆𝖑𝖑 𝕯𝖊𝖊𝖉𝖘

of sale of certaine free Burgage houses within
the said Citty ordered to be entred in this Booke
by the Maior Aldermen and Comon Coun-
-sell of the Citty aforesaid in this pre-
-sent yeare 1654

Only about a dozen assurances are registered under this
order, all being conveyances of estates which had been
taken from the bishop and from the dean and chapter.
All but two of them are

inrolled in this Book of Record by me Jo: Pattinson Clk of
yᵉ court of yᵉ City of Carlile

between the 23rd and 26th of January, 1654. The other
two are enrolled in 1659. Alexander Dalton seems to have
been mayor in 1654.*

In 1672 a new use for the book seems to have occurred
to the then town clerk, James Nicholson, viz., as a register
of the indentures of apprenticeship of the future freemen ;
and about 800 have been registered between that date and
1844. Of late the practise has been discontinued, it having
now no object. These 800 indentures form a most important
mass of genealogical matter relating to the freemen of
Carlisle. They should be indexed and the register of them
paged.

The history of this fine book is clear. Purchased
prior to 1561, it was the Register Governor or Dormont

---

* An account of these assurances will be found in the Transactions
Cumberland and Westmorland Antiquarian and Archæological Society,
Vol. VI, 297, 301.

Book of the Commonwealth and of the Inhabitants of
Carlisle.   For nigh a century it was used for no other
purpose than to contain the form of the oaths to be taken
by the city officials, and the bye-laws of the city.   But
during the time of the protector it was reversed, and used
as a register of deeds of title to property which had been
taken from the bishop and from the dean and chapter.
The corporation, after the restoration, found two other uses
for it : a register of the declarations taken against the
solemn league and covenant, and a register of indentures of
apprenticeship. · The book is now over 300 years old, and
the various purposes for which it has been used are all
obsolete.   It has large store of blank pages yet : but its
work is done : its value as a record increases year by year.

Ancient armorial bearings of the Corporation of Carlisle.

Chapter IV.

TRANSCRIPTS FROM THE DORMONT BOOK.

THE MAIORS OTHE

1. Ye shall trewly serve the quenes ma^tie her heres and successores as maior of this her citie.

2. Ye shall trewly obey and serve all maner of processes writts and comandments sent from her highnes or others in authoritie onder her grace·and therof trew retorne make.

3. Ye shall to thuttermoste of your power mayntend and defend all this citie inheritances possessions rights dueties customes and services performe fulfill mayntend and kep all and all maner of constitutions and orders contened in this Dormont book and put the same fully in execution.

4. Ye shall reseive none of the townes money rents fermes nor other dueties but therof shall se a trew and a perfect accompt mayd of all the forsaid money rents fermes and dueties by the chambilanes at the next audit in lent.

5. Ye shall trewly minister justice as well to the pore as riche and suffer noe mayntenance ne imbrasery to be w^thin the same citie.

6. Ye shall see or cause to be sene nyghtly the watchmen of the walles of this citie trewly set serchet and kept for thonor of the quenes ma^tie the savetie of her subiects and discharge of you and other officers within thys citie.*

7. Ye shall make no reparations ne works of your owne self wth the citie guds above xx^s onles ye haue the advice of the most parte of the hole counsale.

---

* Marked in a copy of the date of 1626 as " not in use."

8. Ye shall folowe and tak thadvice of the counsale in all poynts touchinge the government of this citie and the comonewelth therof etc according to thauncient orders.

All thes poynts and articles and other thyngs contened in this book concernyng your office ye shall well and trewly kep accordinge to the lawes and customes of this citie to thutter moste of your pouer so help you god and the contents of thys booke.

THE BALIFS OTHE

1. Ye shalbe trew officers and balifs of this citie and at all tymes redye to serve the quenes ma^{tie} your mayr and thare lawfull comandments.

2. Ye shall impanell in your enquests betweene partie and partie honeste trew and indifferent men who wyll discharge thare conchiance of all such things as shalbe comitted to thare charge by thadvice of the mayr etc.

3. Ye shall suffer noc mayntenance ne embracerye in the court nor suffer noc officer member of the court to use any partiallite but that Justice be trewly and indifferently ministred as well to the pore as riche.

4. Ye shall se or cause nyghtly to be sene set and serchet the watchmen upon the walles. And if ye fynd ony default declare it to the maior.*

5. Ye shall se that all maner of vitelles cumyng to this market be gud and holesome and sold at a resonable price.

6. Ye shall suffer noc forestallors ne regrators to be wth the precinct of this citie ne the liberties therof.

7. Ye shall to thuttermost of your power mayntend and defend all the cities inheritances possessions rights customes and dueties.

8. All thes poyntes and articles &ct as in thend of the mair othe.

CHAMBILANES OTHE

1. Ye shalbe trew chambilanes and husbands of this citie And at all tymes redy to doe that thynge wch ye shalbe appointed by the maior and counsale.

---

* Not in use 1626.

2. Ye shall kep all such constitutions as ar contened in this booke all such somes of money rents fermes ducties and customes as ye shall resauve or otherwise cum to your hands pertenyng this citie ye shall make a trew hole and full accompt therof at the next audit.

3. Ye shall disburse noe money for noe works above xx^s onles ye be appointed by the mayr and counsale.

4. Ye shall deliver in at or afore your forsaid accompt all such implements as ye haue in charge or delivered ouer to you pertenyng the citie.

5. Ye shall deliver noe somes of money to the mayr hands ne others by the mayr sole comandment except before whersad without thadvice of the counsale or the more parte of them.

6. Ye shalnot suffer ne knaw of any waiste or spole of any thyng belongyng to this citie but ye shall make it previe to the mayr and counsale for the tym beyng.

All thes poynts and articles &ct ut supra.

THE CLERKES OTHE

1. Ye shall kep the mayr and balifs counsales attend the court euery court day from the begynnyng to the same be retorned and all other tymes when thofficers haith ony besinesse to be recordyt for the citie (onles special license of the court obtened).

2. Ye shall observe fulfill and kep all such orders and constitutions as is contened in this book concernyng your office.

3. Ye shallnot be a counsale wth any partie plantyf or defendant in this court ne take more for the entre of a playnt copies or answeres but as assigned by this book.

4. Ye shall quarterly seit forth the americements of this court and the same deliver to the mayr and balifs.

5. Ye shalnot carrye the court book out of the moithaull saving only iiii days afore thinquest passeth.

6. Ye shall deliuer ouer to thauditor of this citie for the tym beynge a trew and perfect note or transcript signed with your hand of all such dimissions as shalbe yerely maid by the mayr and counsale of thys citie soe that immediately the same auditor may know what is graunted for how long for what fyne or rent And who the taker that he may charge accordingly.

E

7. All thes poynts and articles and other thyngs contened in thys book concernyng your office ye shall well and trewly kepe according to the lawes and custuomes of this citie to thuttermoste of your power soe help you god &ct.

THE SERGEANTS OTHE

1. Ye shall trewly serve the mayr balifs and citizens and redy to serve att all tymes when ye shalbe comandit.

2. Ye shall mak your arrests lawfully of all persons and trewly present the same to the court.

3. Ye shall observe performe fulfill and kep all maner of constitutions and orders contened in this book concernyng your office.

4. Ye shall suffer noe persons comitted to your charge either for execution of det or otherwise comanded, to depart the haule wthout licence either of the mayr or balifs as ye wyll answer for the same.

All thes poyntts &ct.

ATTORNES OTHE

1. Ye shall trewly serve the court of this citie and trewly answere all parties hauing matter therin pertenyng to your office.

2. Ye shalnot be of counsale wth plantyfe and defendent ne tak furth any processe but in open court afore the mayr and balifs.

3. Ye shall trewly answer your clients of all such recoueries and somes of money as shalbe recouered in the court And trewly acquit and discharge the mayr and balifs therof wthout delay.

4. And finally to thuttermost of your knowledg ye shalbe upright and indifferent to all maner of persons in thexecution of your office.

All thes poynts and articles &ct ut supra.

THE CORONERS OTHE

1. Ye shall trewly serve the queues ma^{tie} her heres and successores and the maior of this citie in your office and all maner of writts and comandments direct to you in her name and trew retorno therof mak.

2. Ye shall impanell in your inquests honest trew and indifferent persons upon the view of such bodies as ye shall syt upon trewly and indifferentlie reseve there veredicts indented betweene you and them without any kynd of corruption accordyng to the law.

3. Ye shall tak noe other fees but such as is appointed by the law.

4. All thes poynts and articles &c't ut supra.

A FREMANS OTHE

1. Ye shalbe trew citizen to the quenes ma^tie her heres and successors trew and obedient to the maires and officers of this citie and to thuttermost of your power mayntend and defend all thinheritances and francheses rights possessions customes and dueties of the citie and the same kepe harmles in that that in you is.

2. Ye shall enter nor occupy any maner of occupation w^thin this citie or the liberties thereof onles ye agre wth that occupation afore.*

3. Ye shalnot implead nor seu ony freman out of thys citie whills ye may have right and law w^thin the same.

4. Ye shall tak noe apprentice to serve you for noe lesse terme than sevyn yeres and such one as ye may lawfully take And that w^thin two monthes his indenture to be enroulled afore the mayr and counsale therto remaine of record.

All thes poynts and articles etc ut supra.

DEO ET VIRTUTI OMNIA DEBENT.
PROLOG.

LYKE as the Universale noumber of subiects and people in all realmes and countres cannot haue continuall encreas nor good surties in unitie and peas but only by good providens godly orders and holesome Lawes provided mayd and orderyt after thare estate wth dew execution of the same by good governors and officers

---

* The Guilds were commonly in Carlisle called "Occupations."

which ledeth the people to one perfect submission unitie and trayd of concord wherupon resteth all the comonewelth for the encrease of the gude people in vertu and correction of the Evyll in vice.

AND FORASMUCH as it is necessarie for euere realme countre and comonaltie of people to haue gud lawes reules and seuerall orders to gouerne and rule the multitudes wthn thare charges thereby as a godly and a necessarie thynge so it is meyt that euere one of the people and noumber understand and haue knowledge thereof to kepe and obey the same lawes reules and orders as a decent thynge and reule to be used in a comonewelth to leve by. And forasmothe as the mayr and citesens of this citie wth the advise of the counsale and corporation of the same and considerynge the daly Iniuries Disorders Offences and Decays that grewe aswell to the corporation of the said citie the liberties jurisdictions and inheritances of the same as the mysuses and oppressions committyd by ignorant persons to ev^{rie} of the inhabitantes wthn the same which would be in tym the utter rewyne and decay of the comonewelth of the sayd citie and liberties of the same and great noisance to thinhabitants (yf remedy be not providyt) which thyngs consideryt and that there is nothyng more to be imbrased in a comonewelth than holsome lawes and ordinances to be dewly ministered and executed. And forasmoth as a comonaltie standith wth sundrie kynds of people gathered together which be of diverse mynde and contrarie appetites it cannot be avodit that besinesse shall aryse therin unless the same be well foresene wth wysdome in rewles and officers for yf wisedome reigne in Authorite comonewelthes cannot decay so longe as thei haue a brotherly affection amongst them mayntened justice prosecute vice and is void of couetusness havynge a fervent zeale to the comonewelth and the mayntenance therof that for lack of wysedome in thautoritie how soyne comonewelthes decreaseth and falleth into manifold calamities trobles and misaries for thembrasyng of vice and forsakyne of vertu Consider also how danngerous a thynge it is to begyne alterations in a comonewelth how invy and hatred rysyng of small causes haith the distruction of great kyngdomes and countries And that disobers of hyer powers and such as rebelled against maiestraites never escapyt unpunyshed nor com to goode end. THE MAYR AND CITISENS of the said citie havynge no small care over

the same for thencrease of vertu punishment of vice and discharge
of conshance wth full deliberation advice consent and agreement of
the citizens comonaltie with lerned counsale of the same haith
therin takyne parte labor travell and diligence of zeale and gudwyll
to devise orders make and setfurth certaine orders constitutions
provisions and Rewells contened in this book for the good gouernment and reule and order of the comonewelth of the same citie and
thinhabitantes therof all which orders constitutions provisions and
rowles in the same contened is agreed consented graunted and
appointed to be observed kept and used as a law positive consonant
and ground[t] as well upon the lawes of god as upon the comone lawes
and statutes of this realme and the laudable custom of the said citie
to be kept used obeyed and put in dew execution w[th]n the said citie
and liberties of the same. WHEREUNTO the said mayr and citisens
for them and theire successores consenteth graunteth and agreeth
that the sayd mayr citisens theire ministers and officers for the tym
beynge and thare successores hereafter shall put exercise and use the
same in dew execution as a comone rewle law provision and order
for euerye partie w[th]n the said citie and liberties upon the paynes
daunger penalties and punyshment contened in the same orders constitutions and rewles to euerie partie which thynge done and trewly
put in execution shalnot only pleas god but great quiete and
augmentation of the said citie the comonewelth of the same and
the inhabitances thereof shall daly grow wth great increase of vertu
which god graunt to his honor.

AMEN.

IN WITNESS hereof as well the mayr & counsale wth foure of euere
occupation of the forsaid citie for and in the naym of the hole citisens
and thinhabitances thereof haith subscribed this book wth thare
owne proper hands as also Annexed hereto thare comon Scall the
IX day of July An° Elisabethe dei gratia anglie francie et hibernie
Regine fidei defensoris etc tertio 1561.

CONSTITUTIONS ORDERS PROVISIONS ARTICLES AND REULES TO BE OBSERVED IN MAYNTENANCE OF THE COMONEWELTH.

(1.)

Auncieuts to be preferred.

When the mayr haith occasion to assemble his brethen not only the counsale of the citie But as well the men of occupations as shall seyme to him at —— that then thei and euere of them which haith borne noe office w^{th}in the citie shall give place to those auncients such as haith borne office and franckly and gentilly suffer to sit or stand over them accordinge to their vocation on payne of punishment or else to forfeit that and euere lyk offence euere tyme iii & iiij^{d.}

(2.)

Orderly advise by the counsale.

Itm when the mayr and counsale is assembled and the cause and matter wherefore thei come proponed and declared that then euere counsalor there present to answer the matter proponed in order and say his opinion and mynd fully therein and that noe person interrupe or troble any in the tyme of his declaration so that noe person there present shall alledg that he could not be hard to say his opinion upon payne of euere offender to be put furth of the counsale for that tym only.

(3.)

Obstinance in counsalors to be reformed.

Itm if any counsalor beyng present be obstinate or led by affection and stand in ple against all his fellows beyng counsalors and not reconsiled that then the mayr either to punishe hym extremely or else to exclude from that company for that cause or matter only And the determination of the residue of the counsale to be good and effectual

(4.)

Disclosers of counsale to be expulsed.

Itm when the mayr and counsale is together and a matter beyng proponed amongst them in counsale And the same matter after reveled and proponed abrod in the citie or else-where to the great slander and infamye of the said mayr and counsale which thynge cannot be but only by one of the counsale that then he beyng a counsalor reportynge the same shall not hereafter be takene as one of the counsale but clearly abied from the same as a man not worthe vocation.

(5.)

for not coming to counsale.

Itm when the mayr haith occasion to assemble his consale and send a sergeanne to warn them and appoint them ane houre and place certaine to cum to hym he that cumeth not at the houre and place resonably appoynted (unless he haue a sufficient and lawful excuse declared to the mayr) shall forfeit for euere tym vi^s viii^d and further to be used at the mayr and counsale pleasnr And the same to be payd afore the meattynge or entre of the counsale againe.

(6.)

Appearing of grudges in counsale.

Itm yf there be any grudge betweene any of the counsale that the mayr wth iiij of the counsale shall order the same And yf thei cannot then thei to abyde the orders of the residew of the counsale w^{tho}^{t} further delay and yf any hereafter refuse to abyd thare order then he or thei so refusyng to be expulsed out of that company and accept as none of them.

(7.)

Procurers of Elections.

Itm yf any freman hereafter procure or cause to be procured any election either for marialte balife chambilaines sergeants or coroners of any fremen that then upon dew proof wth ii witnesses afore the mayr provyd shall forfet for euere election procured vi^s viii and the consentor as moch according to the ancient order.

(8.)

Ralynge in counsale to be reformed.

If any counsalor in the presence of the mayr spek any ralynge or contemptuous wordes and wylnot be persuaded and orderyt by the mayr and counsale but obstinatelye continew in the same that then he or thei so offendynge be sharply punished by the mayr and counsale discretion or else expulsed from the counsale at the discretion of the mayr and most part of the residew of the counsale.

(9.)

Disorder in the mayr to be reformed.

Itm yf any inhabitant haue any cause of complaynt against the mayr for the tym beyng or balyfe that then he or thei shall put in thare bill to the counsale fyrste and not to make exclamation or sut againste the mayr or balife to the disworship of the citie and thei to se the same orderyt accordinge to justice upon payne thoffender to be punyshed in ward at the discretion of the mayr* & iiij of the counsale And if the mayr and counsale doe give noe order thereon then the partie to be at liberte to sew the comon law.

(10.)

Absens at election.

Itm when the day of election of the mayr and other officers of this citie shalbe that noe freman appoynted shall purposely absent themselfs that day (god and the service of the crowne excepted) wthout a reasonable cause or excuse made to the mayr for the tyme beyng and in especiall one of thos of the counsale of the citie as in case any tumult or soden disorder should arise amongst the commonaltie that then he being a counsalor or other freman and absent shuld be thought an inventor or giver of encouragement of any such sedition but rather put himself to acquaint and abolish the same to his uttermost power on payne of forfeit to the comon chyst xx^s

(11.)

Attendance upon the mayr.

Itm as often as any nobleman or strangers worthy shall cum to the citie that then upon warnynge from the mayr all the counsale wth the most parte of the honest men of the citie in thare decent apparell shall attend and accompany the mayr for the worshop of the citie upon payne of euere default iii^s iiij^d

(12.)

ray or sodene fyer.

Itm that all men shalbe in a redinesse immediately to cum to a fray or soden fyer and that all men attend and assiste the mayr wthout havynge respect or ayd either to frend

---

* The words "the mayr &" are scored out.

foe or adversarie And the offenders therein if any be hereafter shall haue condign punyshment or else be discharged of his frelidge (if thei be fremen) for not attendynge nor obeying the mayr etc.

(13.)

Settyng of the watch and lockyn of gates.   Itm that the watch nyghtly of the walls shall not be sett nor appointed tyll half an houre after the gaites be locked And that the mayr nor his deputie shal not give the watch word to hym that shal be the first watch to after nine of the clock in the nyght nyghtly And that all the gates of the citie shall nyghtly be locked immediately the comon bell rounge And yf the porters doe the contrarie to either to pay such fyne or else such order as the mayr and counsale agreeth unto or the most part of them.*

(14.)

Disbursement of the Townes Money.   Itm that neither the mayr and counsale that now is nor others hereafter shall lend lay furth or disburse any of the townes money or guds to any person or persons upon sute or other consideration without consent of the corporation and reserve not into the comon chyste a gage of that value for the trew repayment thereof that then the said mayr with all such of the counsale as was assembled and previe shall put in gage as made or obligation into the foresaith chyst And to answer the citie of the said money or guds at the next audit without further delay upon forfeit of their fredom and to answer the det And also that hereafter noe money shalbe layd furth lent or disbursed without consent of iiij of euerie occupation.

(15.)

Auditt.   Itm that the audit of the citie shall hereafter yearly begin and sitt the fyrste or seconde week in lent and so to continue unto the same be fynyshed and the fote thereof openly declared as heretofore haith bene accustomed and that the bok of

---

* The setting of the watch appears to have been abandoned after the accession of James I. to the Throne of England. See *ante* p. 47 n.

account to be subscribed with the mayrs hand in the presense
of the occupations and after to be recorded in the audit booke
And the said audyt to be yearlie finished and determined
before Easter.

(16.)

books of
accompt.

Itm that th' old books of accompts wth the new be brought
in afore the mayr and counsale there to be paste and examined
and after to be layd in the comon chyste upon payn of euerie
pson conscalynge or wthdrawyng of any such record and
deteynynge after requeste mayd to loase his frelidge And that
noe record pertenynge to the towne remaine in the custodie of
any private pson but only in the comon chyste or else wher
the mayr and counsale shall assign yt but a president of the
accoumpt to remaine styll in the custodie of thauditor.

(17.)

Accoumptes
of
chamberlaines

Itm that at the audits and accoumpts hereafter the
chamberlaine shall accoumpt and deliver as well of the
remaine of timber gavillocks hackes pikes ropes and other
necessaries in thar charge belonging the citie as of all such
yearly rentts and workes of thare year and the same to be
delivered over to the chamberlaines next ensewynge by bill
indented or other specialtie witnessynge the same upon payn
of the trew value of the losse.

(18.)

iiij keys of the
comon chyst

Itm where there is iiij keys of the comon chyste it is
orderyt that the mayr for his yere shall have one one of the
anncient and most discret of the counsale one and thother
two keys to be in the kepynge of two of thoccupations by
assignment of the mayr and counsale all which keys shalbe
and remaine in the dwelling houses of those to whom they
shalbe assigned in arediness at all such tymes as by the mayr
and counsale shalbe called for upon payn of the wthdrawer to
be imprisoned at the mayr and counsale.

THE COMMON CHEST OF THE CITY OF CARLISLE.

Now in the Museum.

To face p. 59

(19.)

Mayr alone shall make noe freemen *of out men*

Itm that the mayr of hym self shall not hereafter make any *outmen* fremen w^tbout thadvice of the moste parte of the counsale *and foure of euere occupac'on* wch is agreeable to thauncient custom and constitution of the citie.*

(20.)

rent payd to the mayr hands w^thout consent of counsale is noe payment

Itm yf any fermor of the citie pay deliver or disburse any part or parcell of his yerely rent to the hands of the mayr for hys tym beyng onles it be agreed by the consent of the counsale or the most parte of them that then the said fermor shall pay the same rent againe at the next audit or ells to remaine in ward to yt be payd.

(21.)

townes inheritances demysed etc to be of record in the chyste

Itm yf any person haue any of the townes inheritances or possessions by virtu of any lease graunted from the citie ouder thare seale for terme of yeres lyf or otherwise and noe counterpayne ne record thereof remaine in the comon chyste that all persons so havynge or claymynge to be called and com before the mayr and counsale and at a day gewen and appointed to brynge in and shew thare leases to the mayr and counsale that the matter therein contened (for that noe counterpayne ne record thereof remaneth in the comons chyst) be sufficient A copie thereof to be made and the said copie either to be put in the comon chyst or recordyt in this book†
And yf the persons refuse to brynge in any such leases to the mayr and counsale upon demand mayd that then the mayr and counsale shall enter to thare inheritance and possessions and the same to inioy and occupy unto such tym as the parties be willinge to brynge in thare leases and doe all maner of duties and services yerely for the same accordinge to the tenor of the same leases.

---

* The words in italics are additions in the margin, apparently made in 1573 ; see notes to rules 46 and 47. On this important clause hangs the history of the Mushroom Elections.

† No such copies are recorded in this book, *i.e.*, the Dormont Book.

(22.)

Town dykes. Itm the possessions and inheritances of the citie not beynge graunted by lease shalbe in disposition of the mayr and in especiall the towne ditches which is to be used w^{th}out pasturing of cattell for the preservation of the walles of the citie.*

(23.)

Reparations by the Mayr to xx^s ultra by advise. Itm that the mayr for the time beynge shall mak noe reparations nor workes wth the townes money or guds aboue xx^s onles he haue the advise of the moste parte of the counsale.

(24.)

The collection of the townes rent against thaudit. Itm that the mayr and chambilaines for thare yere shall provyde that all the townes rentts be fully gathered and levied against the tym of the audit and if any rentts or somes of money remayne in any mans handes or custodie unlevied in default of the mayr or chambilaines or other that then the same rent or somes of money to be allowed in the mayrs fee And if the default be in the chambilains then thei to be and remaine in ward unto such tym as the same det or some ought to the towne be fully ansuered and payd or yf the fermer beyng in ward or refuse to pay his rent and ferme and therein obstinatly stand that then the mayr and balife not only to enter to that ferme which he or thei that refuseth to pay haith and the same to use and occupy to the profit of the citie but also his guds to be distressed for the same to the value of the rent unto the same rent wth tharreragns be payd.

(25.)

Cause to discharge auditor recorder or others. Itm that the mayr and counsale wth iiij of the election of euere occupacon w^{th}in the citie upon gud and lawful matter hard and proved afore them shall hereafter haue auttoritie to

---

* The chamberlain's accounts contain many items of expenditure for cleaning the town dykes, removing dead animals, cutting down bushes, &c.

displace the auditor recorder or any other officer not expressed
in our charter and in thayre places to appoint others meater
for the same offices.

(26.)

Takyne of
plegt or gaget.

Itm yf any person or persons doe hereafter take any pledge
or gage or by any kynd of guds of any suspect person which is
not thayre owne that pledgeth or selleth yt yf any person
chalenge the thinge so pickgeth or selleth and make dew
proof before the mayr and other officers that the thinge so
pledged or selled is or was thare owne proper guds and haith
bene taken from them wrongfully That then all such guds so
pledged or selled shalbe restored to the owners againe and the
partie that tok or reselt the things to loase their money And
to be further punished at the mayr discretion.*

(27.)

leders to the
mylnes.

Itm that there shalbe noe comone leders† of noe freman
or woman's corn inhabitynge w^{thin} the cities or liberties of
the same to any mylne But only to thre‡ mylnes of the citie
whereunto all citisens are bound And that the moultergranes§
and fermers wth thare servants shall grind and use those
duties to all thinhabitantes of the same citie in such maner
and forme as thei ar bound by thare lease graunted by the
citie And yf any mylner hereafter offende any citisen in
grinding thare corne or takyne moulter that then the partie

---

* 1 James i, c. 21, enacted, that the sale of any goods wrongfully
taken to any pawnbroker in London, or within two miles thereof, should
not alter the property ; but prior to the 30 Geo. II. c. 24, there was no
general legislation on the subject of illegal pawning, and consequently
a local by-law was requisite.

† "To lead" means to cart corn. See Halliwell's *Archaic and
Provincial Dictionary* ; also the *Promptorium Parvulorum*, sub voce
"*Cartyn*." There was a trade of "water leders" at York. Originally,
probably, it meant to carry on horseback.

‡ There were three mills belonging to the City, viz., the Borough
Mill, the Castle Mill, and the Bridge End Mill : the City also leased a
fulling mill from the Dean and Chapter.

§ "Moultergraue." No official of this name occurs in Gomme's
"Index of Municipal Offices," but it may be parallelled with the
"Moor Grieves" (*gerefa*) or superintendents of the moors of Alnwick.
The moultergraue (*gerefa*) of Carlisle was evidently the superintendent
and the farmer of the mulcture taken at the mills.

grieved first to complean to the moultergraue who shall reforme the thinge to the person plaintif And yf the moultergraue will not reforme the thinge then the plaintif to complean
to the mayr who shall reforme the wrong according to justice.

(28.)

persons remainge at the mylnes.

Itm that there shalbe noe moe remaininge at any of the
townes mylnes but the mylner and the leder only upon payne
of forfitor of iii^s iiij^d for eure tym which som shalbe levied of
the guds of the moultergraues so often as thei suffer the same.

(29.)

Toulles.

Itm that the fermors of the toulles shall tak of all maner
of vitells and graine cumynge to the market in lyk manner
and form as heretofore haith been accustomed and that thei
shall tak no toulles of no kynd of vitalls cumynge to the
market beyng onder the value and price of v^d ob upon paine
of euere tym using the contrarie to forfet iiij^d.

(30.)

Kinggarth and frenet.

Itm that the fermers and there assignees of the King-
garth and frenet* after the years expired that the fermers now
haith shall yerely present the market wth the half part of all
such fyshe as thei shall gyt at the same for the better furnish-
ment and releef of all the inhabitances of the same citie upon
paine and forfitor for euere default vi^s viii^d which default
shalbe found and presented by inquest and the forfitor to be
levied and taken of the fermors.

(31.)

Sculding or mis raportyng.

Itm yf any person or persons hereafter do scold rayll or
misraport any man or woman inhabitynge wthin this citie or
the liberties of the same and the same complened upon to the
mayr and proved wth ii sufficient witnesses that then if he be
man to pay for euere severall offence vi^s viii and yf it be a
woman to pay iii^s iiij^d beside further punyshment of his or
her body at the mayr discretion.

---

* For the Kinggarth fishery see *ante* p. 5. The free net was
granted by the charter of 1 Edward IV *ante* p. 12.

(32.)

Undecent words.

Itm yf any man inhabitynge w^{th}in this citie or the liberties of the same doe speke or report any unhonest undecent or slanderous words or unreverently use them against the mayr or counsale contrarie to thare oath and profeshon If he be a counsaler that offendes shall for his first tym of offence forfet xx^s which shalbe levied of his guds immediately and punishment at the discretion of the mayr and counsale and for the second offence to be excluded the company of the counsale and loase his frelidge of the citie If he be a commoner that offends the first offence to loase his frelidge and further to be punyshed at the discretion of the mayr and vi of the counsale The prouf hereof to be had either by inquest confession of the partie or thre credible witnesses And the second offence to be excluded the citie and liberties thereof.

(33.)

Chamberlaines.

Itm that all chamberlaines hereafter upon the determination of thare severall accoumpts yerely w^{th}in twentye days after next ensewyng shall make full payment of all such somes of money or the arrearagies thereof as cum to thare hands And in default and lack thereof thei and euere of them to remaine in ward to such tym as thei bane fully discharged the same somes.

(34.)

Presentment of the turmes.

Itm that all presentments and orders hereafter found by the thre head inquests at the mayr turnes* meyt and convenient to be putt in execution for the comon welth shalbe recorded in this book and put in execution as other articles and constitutions is at the discretion of the mayr and counsale.

(35.)

Watching nightly of the walles.

Itm that the watchmen appointed to watch of the walles nightly shalbe such able honest and discreet persons both in bodie and guds as shalbe able to discharge thare duties and truste wherein thei ar put as well towards the dewties of theire

* The Mayor's Turn was another name for the Court Leet of the City.

sovergane as the suretie of thinhabitances both in body and guds w[th]in the same citie and the precinckts thereof And that noe watchman hereafter to be appointed but only w[th] thadvise of the mayr and counsale or the moste parte of them And that euere man so appointed shall watch his owne watch hymself and noe deputie except license obtened of the mayr upon payn of forfitor of euere default iii[s] iiij[d].*

(36.)

petie micherie.

Itm that all persons expulsed or presented for petie mycherie† forestallynge regratynge or any other lawful cause done shal not hereafter be received ne suffered to dwell againe w[th]in this citie or the liberties thereof at any tym hereafter on payne of vi[s] viii[d] to be levied of the guds and catells of the resetter‡ of them so expulsed.

(37.)

freman departynge the Citie and dwell in the countrie.

Yf any freman hereafter depte this citie and not returne againe w[th]in the space of a hole yere and a day that then all such persons from henceforth shalbe reputed and takyne to be noe freman and loase his frelidge onles sufficient cause or excuse as the mayr and counsale will alloue.

(38.)

Inheritances.

Itm that the mayr of hym self shalnot sell or let any of the citie possessions or inheritance without advise of his hole counsale *and four of euere occupation.*§

(39.)

Casting of corruption in wells.

Itm yf any person or persons hereafter caste any maner of corruption as deyd dogs catts nolt‖ hornes or any other thinge corrupte in any of the comon welles w[th]in this citie or

---

* See *ante*, rule 13 n.

† A "Micher" is a sly thief, a pilferer, an idle fellow. See *Mich* in Halliwell's *Archaic and Provincial Dictionary.*

‡ *To resett* is to receive an outlawed person. Cowell's *Law Dictionary.*

§ Marginal interpolation, see *ante* note to rule 19.

‖ *Nolt*, black cattle. *Neat*, horned oxen. "Noltsfoot oil" or "neatfoot oil" was formerly, and is probably now sold in Carlisle.

doe lye any myddinge, doonghill towards any of the said comon wells or w^{thin} xii feet thereof that euere offender therein to forfet for euere tym and severall offence vi^s viii^d immediately to be levied of thoffenders guds or else to be extremely punished by the mayr as of the pillorie or otherwise.

(40.)

Dighting or wyndoenge of corne.

Itm that no person hereafter shall dight* or wyndo any kynd of corn or grain in the comone or open streete or upon the townes walles shall forfeit for euere severall offence iii^s iiij^{d.}

(41.)

Swyne.

Itm that yf any manner of person or persons hereafter suffer willingly thare swine to goe abroad in the open or comone street shall for the firste offence forfet vi^d the second xii^d and the third time the swine to be forfet to the mayr and balif And that noe person sett any swine trough in the open or comone streete on payn of forfetor of euere default iii^s iiij^{d.}

(42.)

Reparyng of mylnes and dampes.

Itm that the mayr and balifs shall yerely view the mylnes dampes and houses and if thei fynd any default in reparynge thereof by the fermors then the mayr and bailif to give them warnynge to repare the same w^{thin} fortie dayes in payn and forfitor of x^{li} to be levied of the fermors guds w^{thin} one quarter of a year next after.†

(43.)

Clerk of the market.

Itm that the mayr and counsale shall yerely appoint two clerks for the market to take the oversight of all kynd of vitells cumyng and beyng w^{thin} the citie and market on the market days and that all unholesome vitells takyn either by the mayr balif or clerk of the market shall either be burnt or otherwise disposed to the pore people by the mayr and balyfs at thare discretion.

---

* *Dight*, to prepare or dress.

† The chamberlain's accounts contain constant items of expense for wood, rise (small brush wood), &c., for the repair of the dams.

(44.)

Vitells.   Itm that in all vitells cumynge or beynge in the market
the mayr shalbe fyrst served then the aldermen and counsale
next and after all honest men and women according to thare
vocation inhabitynge wthin the citie upon payne of euere severall
offence comitted to the contrare iii^s iiij^d which incontinent
shalbe levied by thofficer of thoffenders gnds.

(45.)

caters.   Itm that no man hereafter shall presume be cater or
viteller for any man either in the towne or countrie except he
be known to be a servant or comon cater appointed upon
payne of forfitor of thinge so bought and thoffender to be
punished accordinge to the statute of forestallers and regraters*
all which forfitors to be takyne to the mayr and balifs use
only for the tym beynge.

(46.)†

Out men   Itm yt is ordered that no artyfyer or man of occupation
prentice.   w'thin this citie hereafter shall take any man to be aprentyce
borne beneth Blackford on pain of x^{li} to be forfeited to the
Cytye by any on that shall doo the contrarye.

This order was revived and corroborated at a court leet
holden 23 April 1602. Whereunto William Barwise then
mayor wth his bretherne and the occupations subscribed and
that this order should also exclude all such as are borne beyond
Irdin   quare per presentment‡

---

* 5 & 6 Ed. 6, c, 14.

† The whole of rule 46 is an interpolation, and the first part of it is
in the same ink and handwriting as the marginal interpolations "four
of evere occupation" (see note to rule 47). The second part is in a
later hand. The numbering of the rules is not affected by the interpolation of No. 46, as the numbers throughout are obviously of a much
later date than the text.

‡ Blackford is about four miles north of Carlisle and Irthing about
the same. The conscript fathers of the city were determined not to
admit Scotchmen or even dwellers near to Scotland to learn a trade in
Carlisle.

(47.)*

Mayor's fee.

Itm that the maior fee from henceforth shallbe fourtye marks yerely in respect of all charges and to be payd yeraly before Martinmas viii^li vi^s viii^d at our ladyes day in lent vi^li xiii^s iiij^d And at pentecost vi^li xiii^s iiij^d

Itm that the mayr for his year beynge shall receive for his fee viii^li vi^s viij^d for wynne vi^li and for apprentices in his house one Saint John Evyn and Saint Peter Evyn iii^li †.

(48.)

Mayr and counsale.

Itm in all consultations hereafter had wth the mayr and counsale noe order ne weighty affares finally to be ordered or determined onles the moste of the hole counsale be there present.

(49.)

Arreragues.

Itm that the detts and all manner of arrearagues belonginge to the citie shallbe quickly called for by the mayr and balifs and in especiall all such dettes whereof remaineth noe record ne specialtie in writinge   And for not paying within one year then sute to be entered in the law for the same.

(50.)

Storehouse,

Itm it were convenient to have a comone storehouse for the towne wherein tymber would be layd and other necessaries provided all ways in aredinese to be kept for the mayntenance of all necessarie worke and reparations concerning the citie when neid requireth and also all implements for worke of the citie in lyk maner of the which house the mayr for his tym yerely to have the charge and custodie if the counsale thereunto agre.

(51.)

things remanying in the comon chyst.

Itm in this booke shalbe written all such plate jewells or somes of money as remaneth and is in the comone chyst for this consideration yf any parte thereof be taken furth for any

---

* The upper part of rule 47 is in the handwriting of the first part of rule 46, and a date over it shows the revision to have been made in 1573. The lower part of rule 47, the original rule, is scored out, and the new rule written over it at the top of the page.

† From the 2nd "Item" is scored out.

necessarie business to the townes use the same to be recordit
in this booke or other writtynge And in lyk maner yf any
remane of money hereafter be put in the said comone chyst
the same to be recordit herein so that neither there shalbe put
in or taken forth ont of the forsaid chyste anythinge but the
same shalbe knowne to the mayr counsale and comanaltie or
els a bill to be mayd and put in the purse wthin the comone
chyste declarynge the thinge therein etc.*

(52.)

**Sureties by
recognisance.**

Itm that the mayr and citisens hereafter shall only tak
surties of recognisance of all the fermars of the citie And for
nonpayment of the same or any parte thereof the fermors or
thare surties after the audit in lent to remaine in safe ward
wthout bayll to such tym as the hole somes of the yerely rent
be fully ansuered.

(53.)

**Cartes in the
street.**

Itm if any man or woman hereafter leave any cartes or
carres standyng in the srreet iii nyglites together the owners
thereof to forfet to the mayr and balifs for eueric severall
offence vi^d also that all carres or cartes specially be removed
euere holyday out of the street upon lyk payne and forfetor.

(54.)

**Scotts
unchartered.**

Itm that no unchartered Scott shall dwell wthin this citie
or the liberties hereof upon payne and forfetor of all his guds
and punyshment of his bodie at the mayr pleasure And he or
she that rescate or kepes them shall forfet for euere oflonce
vi^s vii^d.

(55.)

**Scottmen and
women.**

Itm that noe Scottsman nor woman shall walk wthn this
citie after the watch bell be rounge at thare perill onlesse thei
haue a freman his son or servant wth them upon payn of
imprisonment at the discretion of the mayr and counsale.†

---

* This book, the Dormont Book, contains no such entries, so it would
seem the alternative methods were adopted.

† See Rule 13 n.

(56.)

Brewinge or bakinge. Itm that noe persons inhabitinge wthin this citie or liberties thereof shall brew or bayk to sell but only fremen and thare wifes and that all comon brewsters and bakers shall kepe thassisse and measure of bread and ayll* and the same to be gud and holesome for mans body except the tym of open faires and such as shall be licensed by the mayre.

(67.)

Hot ashes. Itm yf any person or persons hereafter caste out any hot ashes in the comon street or layne or elsewhere wthin the citie or the libertes of the same shall forfet for euere offence vj^{d.}

(58.)

Making cleane of evere forefront. Itm that euere inhabitant wthin the citie shall cause their fore fronnt to be mayd cleane to the myddle of the pauement weykly or at least once in the moneth on payne of forfitor of euere default vij^d And in lyk manor all thos that hath any garthes wthin the boundes of the laite gray freers† euere one of them according to thare portion and bounder to mak the street cleane to the myddell on payn aforesaid.

(59.)

Unlawful games. Itm yf any person or persons suffer hereafter any unlawfull games to be played at or wthin his house gardynge or close shall forfit for euer tym   And the player at the same games vj^s viij^d according to the statute Henry viij xxxiij except such as be licensed by statute.

(60.)

Walkyn after x of the clock in the nyght. Itm that noe mans sones servants nor apprentices shall walk or goe abrod in the street wthin the citie aft^r tene of the clok in the nyght except it be upon thare fathers or masters

---

* 51 H. 3.

† Great part of the property once held by the Grey Friars remained garden ground until within the present century. It extended from the Citadels along the east side of English Street to about Bank Street.

business upon payn of punyshment two houres in the stok the
next day after and further to be orderyt by the mayr discretion.

(61.)

**Comon
backhouse**

Itm that thare shall not hereafter be kepd at any of the
comon backhouses any moe persons or servants then the wife
or maister of the backhouse and two women or servants the
names of whom to be written and delivered to the mayr And
that all thos that bryngeth or cometh wth thare leven or
dough to bak at the backhouse shall pay hereafter for euere
bushell baken two pence in money half a bushell a penny a
peck a half penny and no dough nor leven ne bread to be
geven for the same. the offenders herein to pay for euere
default iii^s iiij^d to the use of the mayr and officers. And if
any default be found hereafter in the kepors of the backhouse
in bakyn of any persons bread that then upon prouf of ii
witness before the mayr or balifs had the forsaid kepers to
mak double mende.

(62.)

**Mastive
doges.**

Itm that all mastive doges going abrod in the street
unmuscled thowner and maister thereof shall pay and forfet
for euere tym that hys doge is taken unmuscaled vi^d which
jmmediately shall be levied and taken by thofficers that shall
fynd the same.

(63.)

Cotagies.

Itm that there shalbe noe cotagers wthin this citie upon
payn of forfitor of iii^s iiij^d for euere moneth that thei remaine
which same shalbe levied of thowner or fermer of the cotage
except such as shall fynd surtie to the mayr and counsale for
thare gud demenor hereafter.[*]

(64.)

**Warnynge
of tenents.**

Itm when a tenend wthin the citie holding at wyll and
wil goe and surrender the same tenament that then he shall

---

[*] The penalty imposed by 31 Elizabeth, c. 7, on persons erecting
cottages, or maintaining same, not having 4 acres of ground laid to
them, did not extend to cottages in boroughs and market towns.

geve a warnynge to the landylord before he departe that is to
say of houses or tenements that be of fortie shillinge rent and
onder he shall geve warnynge by one quarter of a yere And
if the houses or tenements be above the yerley sume of
xl^s then warnyng to be geven by half a yere at the perell of
the tenend And lyk warnynge to be and continue to be geven
by all tenends inhabityng wthin this citie what ferme or rent
so euer they sit on.

(65.)

Apprasers. Itm that the mayr and balifs for the tym beynge shall
appoint iiij honest men to be apprasers who beyng sworne
shall appraise all such guds and catells as shalbe brought
afore them which guds and catells so being apprased shalbe
offered fyrst to the defendant putynge in sureties to answer
the debt wthin twentye days next after ensewynge Yf the
defendent refuse to take the guds so apprised then the guds to
be offered to the plaintif and yf the plaintive refuse the guds
and distresse then the same to remaine in the apprisers hands
and thei thereof to answer the plne wthin xx dayes prout
supra.*

(66.)

Dounghilles Itm that no inhabitant shall lye or suffer to be layd any
or myddyngs. dounghill or myddynge afore his front or dore But that the
same be carried away wthin eight days after it be layd there
And yf any hereafter doe or offend in the contrarie that then
thei and euere of them so offending to forfet for euere second
day that it lye uncartied away after the said eight days vi^{d.}

(67.)

Vacabunds Itm that noe vacaboundes ne valeant beggars shalbe
and beggers. sufferit to goe wthin this citie openly onles such pore and
impotent persons shalbe allowed by the mayr and counsale
according to the statute† mayd in that behalf which pore

---

* Appraisers valuing goods too high were bound to take them at
their own value.   11 Ed. I, Statute of Acton Burnell.

† 13 Ed. I, c. 4 (Statute of Winton) ; 5 Ed. III, c. 4 ; 25 Ed. III,
st. 1, c. 7 ; 34 Ed. III, cc. 10, 11 ; 7 R. II, c. 5 ; 12 R II, 7, 8, 9, 10 ;
11 H. VII, c. 2 ; 19 H. VII, c. 12 ; 22 H. VIII, c. 25 ; 28 H. VIII,
c. 6 ; 33 H. VIII, c. 10 ; 37 H. VIII, c. 7 ; 1 Ed. VI, c. 3.

persons to haue tokens and badges declaring that thei be
allowed by the mayr and counsell and others to be punyshed
by the mayr and balife according to the statute.

(68.)

Mayr turmes.

Itm that all presentments fonnd by the thre inquests at
the mayr turnes* hereafter shalbe delivered to the custodie of
the town clerk for the tym beyng which clerk shall record the
same in a register book there remaine of record and after to
be wrettyne in thys book.

(69.)

Writtings
taken by thold
mayr shalbe
delivered ower
to the new
mayr.

Itm that wthin twentye days next after thelection of the
mayr th old mayr shall deliver ower to the new mayr all
maner of writtings recognisances obligations and other muniments as he haith or tuk duryng the term of his marialte
wch writtings either to be put in the comone chyst or otherwise
used wth th advise of the counsale.

(70.)

Scales for
bushells pecks.

Itm that the comone scales wherwth bushells half bushells
pecks etc is sealed shall all ways remaine hereafter in the
kepynge of the mayr and in non other officer.†

(71.)

Clerk
to attend.

Itm that the clerk of the citie for the tym beynge shall
euery monday which is not holyday wayt and attend the court

---

* The meetings of the Court Leet of the City, see *ante* p. 63 n, which
were held three times in the year. The following is an extract from
the Court Leet Rolls :—

Civitas ⎰ Turnus maioris sive curia leta civitatis Carlioli tentā ibidem
Carlioli ⎱ die Veneris viz vicesimo secundo die Aprilis anno regni
domine nostre Elizabethe dei gratia Anglie Francie et Hibernie regine
fidei defensoris etc 39 annoque Domini 1597 coram Thoma Blenerhasset
armigero tunc Maiore civitatis predicte Eduardo Monke et Willelmo
Barwicke ballivis ejusdem civitatis per sacramenta.

Johannis Syde	Alexandri Knagge
Johannis Slater	Richardi Warwick
Henrici Syde	Thome Grame
Johannis Calvert	Willielmi Wilson
Thome Barnes	Willielmi Hetherynton
Thome Monke	Eduardi Barne

† See statutes 7 H. VII, c. 3, and 11 H. VII, c. 4, relating to
standard weights and measures.

of the mayr and balife in the moithaull at the house of ix of
the cloke afornoon and there styll to remaine to such tym as
the court be reiourneth And further that the said clerk shall
all other days be redy to attend the said mayr and balife or
any of them so longe as any ple of execution is to be raised
or any other business for the towne to be applied in payn of
forfitor of his office and revenu onles he haue speciall license
graunted by the mayr for the tym beynge.*

what pleas
shall be
holden.

Itm that no action be entred in the court but where the
cause of action is commenced wthin this citie or libertes of the
same And yf the plaintiff soe doe then he shall loase his
entree.†

(72.)

Clerk
not to be a
counsalor.

Itm that the town clerk shall enter in the court actions
only and not to be of counsal wth noe ptie And that he shall
graunt nor geve furth neither copies ne precepts but by
thappointment of the mayr and balifs in open court on payn
of forfitor his yere wages.

(73.)

The book of
entries to
remaine in the
moithall.

Itm that the book of plees and playnts wth other matters
shalbe and continually remaine hereafter wthin the moythall
and not to be carried nor removed from thence at noe tym on
payn of forfitor of the clerks office onles it be removed to the
clerks chamber or house for the space of iiii dayes beyng next
afore that th inquest shall pas and leye betuenne partie and
partie for an abstract to be takyn of the plaints thereof and
then to be brought in againe.

(74.)

Fees for the
clerk.

Itm that the clerk shall tak nothinge for the copies
or ansuers of any personall playnt but ii^{d.} and thattorney

---

* With rule 71 commences the rules of the "Court of the Mayor
and Bailiffs," called the "City Court," a civil court. The city also
possessed a Court of Quarter Sessions and a Court of Pie powder.
The Court of the Mayor and Bailiffs, at the time of the report of the
Municipal Corporation Commissioners, 1835, was doing an increasing
business, about 50 cases annually where the sum in dispute was under
40s., and 60 where it was over. Defended cases were rare, about four
of each class annually. · It held its sittings weekly.

† This rule has never been numbered, and is scored out.

nothinge And for recordyng of matters put to arbitrement or taken up by the parties nothing otherwise it is extortion.

(75.)

Sergeant to tak surtie.

Itm that the sergeant hereafter shall arrest noe outman or woman to answer the court and partie but he shall tak such sufficient surtie wthin the liberties as shalbe able to ansuer and discharge the court or ells the sayd sergeant to ansuer the partie of his det and further to be punyshed at the mayr discretion.

(76.)

No officer to be a suretie.

Itm that noe officer ne member of the court at noe tym hereafter shalbe taken surties in any action And yf that any officer chaunce hereafter to be cum surtie for any person or persons then he shall pay the debt and damages to the ptie and pay further fyne at the mayr and counsale pleasur.

(77.)

Attornies.

Itm that the two attorneys shal be appointed by the mayr and counsale such in wisdome and honestie as wyll discharge the matters and actions personalis comitted to them by thare clients as well for thadvoydinge of the slander of the court as the satisfience of the parties upon payne of forfitor thare office answeringe the parties of the dett and to mak fyne at the discretion of the mayr and counsale.*

(78.)

Attorneys.

Itm that the said attornies ne neither of them shalnot take and detain any money in thare handes beyng levied or recorded for any person or persons partie but the same wthin viii days to be delivered to the partie in panment upon payn of expulsyng thare office answering the partie of the dett and money and remanynge in ward durynge the mayr pleasur and that one attorney shal not be of counsale wth both the parties on payn aforesayd.

---

* In 1835, the court enjoyed the services of 20 attorneys.

(79.)

Metts and measures.
Itm that the mayr and balifs shall yerely take vew of all measures and metts wthin this citie ons in the yere And if they fynd any unlawfull measure either bushell half bushell peke half peck galone yard wands or other measures that then the mayr and balifs to brek them and euere of them and cause new to be providt Yf any man kepe in his house any double measure that is to say a great one to by wth and a lesse to sell wth that euere one offendinge therein shall pay for euere severall offence ,vi^s viii^{d.} *

(80.)

Courte.
Itm that the mayr balifs and other officers sittynge in court and actions comenced afore them either by the plaintyve in proper person or by his lawfull attorney and called that then the defendant to appeare and answer the matter either in proper person or by his lawful attorney And if he mak default he shalbe amerced the firste and second days and after appearance to haue a day given peremptorie to cum in and answer the matter And if he make default he shalbe condemned in his action The first day yf heanswer not he shallbe amerced ii^d The second day iiij^d and so longe as the partie runneth in amercement yt to double to such tym as the matter and plea be amerced unto.

(81.)

foroners.
Itm that euere foroner or outman that comenssed any actione in the court against another foroner or outman as well the plaintiff to put in surties wthin the liberties to folow his actions as the defender to answer either by themselfe or attorneys And yf the defendant make default to be amerced as is above sayd.†

---

* See rule 70 *ante.*

† A "foroner" means an utter stranger, but an "outman" seems to mean one who had some connection with the city, probably a member of one of the guilds, but who resided outside of the precincts.

(82.)

Court. Itm in actions of trespase the partie defendant may wage*
his law wth so many hands as the court shall award. Yf a
man infranchised be impledit by way of trespasse for gnds
taken or beating where no blood is shed as brosene stroke or
for other trespasses supposed to be done on contempt of the
peace such fremen so impledet may wage and mak his law by
custom of the citie that he is not culpable with vi hands as
afore is sayd and used.

(83.)

In lyk maner women shall wage their law wth women or
men in actions where wager of law lieth.

(84.)

Yf any defendant ansnere not the plaintyf in his ple the
first or second days and therebie is amerced And that the
plaintyf take a precept to bringe in the defendant that after
the precept taken noe copies shalbe graunted *by custom of the
citie.* And if he make default the thyrd day to loase his
issues and so to contenew to his apperance And if he mak
default after apperance then for his default he shalbe condempned. *Not wthstanding the custom of the cytye yeat the
law wyll the deffend appearing upon the precept or distringas
and demand a copie he shall have yt graunted And if he mak
default &ct ut supra.*†

(85.)

Jurors. Itm when the mayr thynketh oportunelie and will proclame
and owtraw thenquest betweene partie and partie and poynteth
a day certaine when the same shall holde and ane impanell of
the names of the jurors geven to the sergeantts to warne all
thos therein contened that all thei so warned and summoned

---

* Wager of law is where an action for debt is brought against a
man on simple contract, without deed or record, and the defendant
swears in court in presence of his compugators (hands) that he owes
the plaintiff nothing in manner and form as he hath declared.—See
postea, rule No. 94.

† The words in italics are interpolations in a later hand. The Town
Clerk seems to have discovered that the common law could not be over-
ridden by the custom of the city.

shall not absent themselfe from the said inqueste wthout a resonable cause which thei shall prove before the mayr or ells he or thei so willingly absenttyng them selfe shall forfet for the fyrst fault iii^s iiij^d which immediately shallbe levied by the mayr and balifs.

(86.)

Itm if any somes of money hereafter be recovered by veredict of xii men or jury or otherwise lawfully of any freman or others inhabitynge wthin the citie or the liberties of the same that then thei and euere of them upon warninge shall entre themselfe in the moythaul thare to answare the said recovery and yf thei doe not entre accordingly that then thei not only to pay the recovere but also to be punyshed by the mayr and officers in ward for thei contempt.

(87.)

Itm that all foroners condempned for det or other action judged either by inquest or confession of the partie or other ways lawfully that all such persons hereafter to be and remane in the law chamber in the moyt hall * in sauf custodie unto such tym as the debt be fully answered. fremen to have the libertie of the moythaull upon thare gentil demeanor.

(88.)

Itm that the mayr and balifs wth other ministers of the court for the tym beynge shall after twentie days next ensewing thenquest past betwene partie and partie levie and rase all such somes of money and recoveries as is judged found and presented by thenquest and see the parties answere thereof accordingly And if any officer let any maner of person at libertie out of ward which remaneth for execution or otherwise that then thei which gave the partie libertie immediately to ansuare thoder partie of the det or ells to remaine in ward to the debt be ansuered and fully discharged

---

* There was within the present century a lock-up entered from St. Alban's Row, in the basement under the Town Hall. It was a small dark chamber commonly called "the dog hole." The old Town Hall or Moot Hall would appear to have been provided with a similar convenience for the temporary accommodation of foreign debtors against whom judgment had been recovered in the City Court.

(the kynge or quen. wrytte of prohibition supersed replevin or such lyk etc. excepted) yf the partie that recovered be not ansuered of the dett after the recoverie had by inquest that then he of whom the det is reconered or his surtie shall remane in proper person in ward to the debt be payd.

(89.)

Itm that all mares and balifs for thar severall tymes here-after shall kepe one quarter day of the yere one inqueste that is so say iiij inquests yerely And that all thexecution and pre-sentment by the forsaid inquests shallbe raised levied and ansuered afore the next inquest be called or warned (except god and the service of the crowne or other lawful matter let the same) upon payn of forfitor of enere default xiii^s iiii^d to be rased of the mayr and balifs guds to thuse of the citie.

(90.)

Itm that all yssues and amerciments risinge of the courte be stated furth by the tonnes clerk and delivered to the mayr and balifs quarterly who shall levie the same wthin the next month foloning And the same to be ansuered thaccompt next ensninge and therewth to be charged except that thei can shew gud and sufficient matter to the contrarie upon payne of enere default in thofficers to forfet vi^s viii^d to tho use of the citie.*

(91.)

Itm the mayr and balifs hereafter shall impanell in thare inquests between partie and partie such wise substantial and indifferent men as will both discharge thare oath to god and advoid the slander of iniurye of the worlde and minister justice to enere partie.

(92.)

Itm when any surties be arrested and comit to ward for the dett of the partie for whom they were surties assone as thei can brynge in the principall for whom thei were bound he shalbe comit to ward (and the surties shalbe let to libertie) or so moche guds dischargable for the dett.

---

* From and including "th accompt," &c., scored out and the words
" to the mayr and balifs " substituted.

(93.)

Itm yf any playnt be brought against any freman or against any other man sufficient and resident within the citie or the liberties thereof the defendent shalbe sumoned by a sergeant to cum to the court and answere the plaintif Yf he make default he shalbe amerced according to the custom And then it shalbe awardyd that the distrese of the defendant shalbe closed to such tym as he cum and answere the partie in the court And if he cum not he shall losse issues which shall euere court day double And after apparance for default to be condempned.

(94.)

Actions of det and covenant be mayntenable against executors and administrators by custom of the citie when thei cum to answer thei may wage thare law as the court will award (where noe specialte or writtynge obligation is to prove the action) upon thes wordes that thei know nothing of the det condition nor covenant thei trust by thare conscience that the testator at his deth ought nothinge to the plaintif nor noe covenant to hym had broken and by this the defendant to be discharged.

(95.)

If a man be impledit by playnt of det for vitell specified in the house of the plantif or for house rent in thes cases the defendant shal not wage his law noe protection in this shalbe taken or allowed.

(96.)

Where a wife that haith a husband use any craft wᵗʰin this citie or the liberties of the same besides her husband crafte or occupation and that he mel not wᵗʰ her sayd crafte this wife shalbe charged as woman sole And if the husband and the wife be impledit in such case the wife shall plead as woman sole. and if she be condempned she shall goe to ward unto she haue mayd agrement And the husband nor his

guds shalnot in this case be charged And if the woman refuse
to appeare and answere the husband or servand to bryng her
in to answer.

(97.)

If ane action of trespase be brought aganst a man and
his wife of a trespase done by the wife only then the wyf shall
ansuer solie without her husband yf the husband cum not w^{th}
her she shall have plee as woman sole And if she be attaynt of
trespase she shalbe condempned and comit to ward unto she
hane mayd agreament.

(98.)

If a playnt of trespase be brought by the husband and his
wife for beatynge of his wyfe in this case her husband shall
persew recover and receive damages against the defendent or
the wife in the absens of her husband may sew and recover as
a woman sole.

(99.)

Where a playnt of det is brought against the husband and
the defendent saith that he mayd the covenant with the
plantyf by the hand of his wyf then the defendent shall haue
ayd of his wyf And shall haue day geven to the next court to
counsale with his wyf and the same day shalbe geven to the
plantif.

(100.)

Itm yf two or moe be bounde w^{th}in the citie and euere of
them in the hole then yf one of them so bounde pay the hole
to hym to whom thobligation was mayd and pursue w^{th}in this
same citie to recover the det againste one of them that was
bound   Then he that haith payde the det or so is condempned
may seu against the other that was bound by playnt of dett
iontly or severally for to make contribution so that euery of
they may pay his part accordinge to the custom of the citie.

(101.)

Attachment of guds in other hands in default of sufficient of the defendant in his own guds.

Money or coyn is not distreanable except thei be in bagges or otherwise sealed.

Itm when playnt of debt is brought before the mayr and balyfe and recordit by the clerke or other officer that the defendent haue not sufficient w^{th}in the towne of guds to discharge the thynge And by the plaintif is alledged and knowne that the defender haith guds catell or detts in other hands or in other keepinge w^{th}in the toune whereof he haith propertie And desire be mayd by the said plantyf that such guds cattels or detts in other hands may be arrested. And the sayd defendent then at the sute and suggestion of the plantyf shalbe wth such guds and catells where thei be found w^{th}in the towne arrested and the court ansuered.

(102.)

Obligations.

Itm yf any sew ane obligation which bearth date w^{th}in this citie and the defendent alledge ane acquittance of a parcell of the same mayd in a foren countrie that acquitance nea alledgment shalnot be allowed on plee of barr of action but the reste to be inquired upon by inquisition w^{th}in the citie.

(103.)

frais bloods and batteries.

If ane inquest of office be taken afore the mayr and balifs to enquire of frays blods and batteries against the peas it shall not be traversed by an new inquest by custom of the citie.

(104.)

Yf any custom or usage be pleaded in or alledged in the court afore the mayr and balifs the same shalbe dyscussed by the mayr and counsale.

(105.)

Of causes of actions within liberties.

Actions of dett be mayntenable by usage and symple grante and of assignment of pledges and of covenant symple w^{th}out specialte mayd or done w^{th}in the liberties of the citie.

(106.)

Itm the mayr and balife by custome may hold whatsoever persons before them condempned for det in ward and not to suffer them to go abrod.

G

(107.)

All contracts mayd between merchand and merchant in all places wthin this realme dwelling in this citie the same shall be tried in this court and orderit either by inquest or otherwise by consent of the parties and thinquest shalbe taken of merchands inhabityng wthin the tonne yf the parties there-unto submit them selves.

(108.)

Itm where the parties have appered in open court of the the mayr and balifs it is used that the plantifs may amend their ples and bills at all tymes before the same parties be at issue or plead in judgement.

(109.)

A debtor wthdraune and found wthin the citie.

If a person fynd his debtor sodenly wthin the citie which debtor haith wthdrawne himself before or is a fugitive which debtor would escape before that the creditor myght haue an officer to mak tharest It is accustomed in such a case that the freman himself bye ayde of neghbors wthout an officer may arreste his sayd debtor and brynge to an officer of the towne therto to putt in surties to answer.

(110.)

ii balyfs iiii chamberlayns on euere inquest.

Itm that in euere one of thinquests which hereafter shall trye betwene partie and partie therein shalbe ii balyfs iiii chamberlayns appoynted and the reste to be taken of other honeste inhabitants.

[Two pages left blank here.]

MARKET AND THOFFICERS OF THE MARKET CLERKES.

(111.)

Proclamations.

Itm that noe outman shall brynge any fleshe to the market to be sold onless thei bryng the skynes therewith and that all sheep skynes be faste to sum part of the carcase on payn of forfitor of the same.*

---

* This was to prevent the skins from being hoarded up until prices were high.

(112.)

That noe maner of person or persons shalby any maner of vitells before thei cum in to the market to be sold upon payne of forfitor of the same and to be punyshed as a forestaller.

(113.)

Itm that noe butcher shalby kyddes or lambes one the market dayes or make any bargaine for the same afore one of the clocke at afternone upon payne of forfitor of the same and further to be punyshed at the mayr discretion.

(114.)

Itm that noe outman one the market days shalby any kynd of corne to make malt or meyll to sell againe on payne of forfitor of the same. And that no outman shalby any corne in the market before xii of the clocke on payne of forfitor of the same And so to be used as a regrator.

(115.)

Itm that noe outman shall sell any corne to any forenor to such tym as the market beil be rounge on payn of forfitor.*

(116.)

If any butcher rube any sewet on any fleshe to mak it seym fate or otherwise gresed he shall forfet the moitie thereof and further to be punyshed at the discretion of the mayr and balifs for the dyssayt used to the subiects.

(117.)

That noe person nor persons shall by any fleshe or fyshe comynge to the market to sell againe at a derer price upon payne of forfitor of the same and to be punyshed as a fore-stallor.

(118.)

That noe person in the market shall cut any fyshe but thos that brynge the same from the watter to the market to be sold upon payn of forfitor of the same.

---

* See note to rule 81. In this case the outman was a neighbour selling his own produce, but he was not allowed to sell it to another stranger, a merchant from a distance.

(119.)

If any houkters pretend to sayt on the market days or ony other days in the market place or by any butter cheyse eggs pullen frute or any other kynd of vitells in or cumynge to the market (to retale againe) afore one of the clok of any market day that then the thinges so bought to be forfett and thoffender to be punyshed at the mayr discretion.

(120.)

Itm that noe man nor woman hereafter shall suffer any corne to be sold bought or metted wthin thare houses on payne of forfitor of vi^s viii^d but to suffer all cornes to be bargained bought and metted in opene market openly.

(121.)

Yf any freman of this citie by any manor of corne or grane to thuse of any outman by color or deceat that then the corne so bought not only to be forfet but also the byer to loase his frelidge the second tym or yf any freman suffer any outman to sett any corne in his house which is unlawfully bought to make malt or meyll that then he shall forfet for euery time he knowynge thereof vi^s viii$^{d.}$

(122.)

Itm that all maner of persons brynginge ony fyshe to the market shall present the same wth all such as he or thei bryngeth and suffer noe parte thereof to remaine in any house of intent to bryng it furth at several tymes by fyshe and fyshe to be sold the derer parte to thendeathnge of the market upon forfitor for euere tym vi^s viii^d

(123.)

Itm that noe butchers herhafter shall bawcon* ony sheyp skynes either of thare owne kyllyng or of others in payne of forfitor for euere tym therin offendyng xx$^{s.}$

---

* Dry or cure, so that they could save them until the market was dear, and thus make the tanners pay high prices.

(124.)

Itm that glovers shall bawcon noe shep skynes hereafter on payne aforesaid.

[Two pages left blank here.]

(125.)

Rentle of the inheritauce of the citie.

Itm a rentale of the possessions and inheritances pertenynge to the citie to be mayd by the collector and reservor thereof wherin is to be contened the names of euere fermer tenend or occupier and what estate or tearmes he occupied and what yerely rent ferme or service he or thei onght yerely to pay and atwhat termes or days the same is dew.

(126.)

Rentle.

Itm the same rentale so mayd to be entred in this register book or in parchment in a roule put in the comon chyst to remane as a record for the towns possessions.

(127.)

The mayr and counsale wth iiii of euere occupation may ade or mitigate.

Itm that the mayr and counsale for the tym beynge wth ouer of the moste discreat persons of euere occupation of the citie upon thair discreet consideration shall and may at any tymes hereafter for better intent or cause alter ad unto or mitigate any provision or order agrement payne or penaltie afore specified for any better provision or mayntenance of the comonwealth and justice to be ministred to th offenders.

(128.)

Pleas and matter not ordered to be used as afore.

Itm that the mayr and balifs for the tym beyng shall use all severall pleas and matters not aforesaid orderyt in lyk maner and forme as heretofore haith bene accustomed.

(129.)

Itm that at all times hereafter when as the mayr and counsale meyt together in the moyt haull At thare fyrst syttyngs doune the haull to be mayd emptie and cleane of all maner of persons the haul dors to be shott and locked and the

key thereof to be brought and layt besides the mayr duryng
the counsale aboed onles occasion be to let in or furth sum
persons and such as the mayr and counsale shall assigne.

Rewle.   At all tymes and in all plees between partie the service of
the crowne the visitation of sekness and flood watters is to be
allowed.

                        by me Thomas Pattinson, mare
                              John Aglionby
                              Richard Blennerhasset
                              Thomas Benson
                              Achilles James
                              Robert Dallton
                              Antony Rumige
                              Robert Scharpe
                              Symonde Brisco
                              W. Mulcaster

                                  Edward Sewell and } Bailyfes.
                                  William Bowman   }

                        Merchaunts
                              Cuthbert Pattyson
                              Robert Pattyson
                              John hewitt
                              John hodshon

                        Weavers
                              Robert James
                              thomas lowson
                              thomas Sawcall
                              thomas Sorby

                        Smythes
                              Eduarde nixon
                              xtofer Knagge
                              John barne
                              Wyllm yonge

                        Taylours
                              Robert Blanerhasset
                              Thomas Vyccars
                              thomas kyd
                              Robert Sympson

Tanners
> Henry Tallentire
> John Branch
> Edwarde Ralton
> Robart Sewell

Cordyners
> John Satrethwaite
> Willm Keyne
> Richard ffisher
> Richard Kitchinge

Glouers
> John Stodert
> Willm Saterthwaite
> Thomas Smythe
> Thomas Stanger

Butchers
> Willm bewley
> Nicholas moore
> Roburt Paton
> Richard Bowman

Obverse.   Reverse.

Common seal of the citizens of Carlisle.

Chapter V.

THE MERCHANTS' GUILD.

The books of the merchants' guild are three in number.

1. Is a paper book, which has lost its binding; it measures 12¾ inches high by about 8½ broad and 1½ thick. Twelve pages are gone at the beginning, and the first existing page is numbered 13, and starts with January, 1620. Among some loose papers I found the fragments of two or three of the missing leaves. From an entry made in 1623, it is possible that the earliest entry in this book was of the date of 1557. The earliest existing entry is one of the year 1586, appointment of William Barwise and Thomas Person as masters. The latest is about 1732.

2. Is a paper book bound in dark calf, 12 inches high, 8 inches broad, 2 thick without the cover. It is in very good condition and has been little used. It commences in 1656.

3. Is a paper book bound in vellum, 12 inches high, 7½ broad: it commences with a list of the guild in 1736, and contains entries up to the present time.

These are all in possession of the clerk of the guild. The quarter days of this guild were the Friday after the Feast of S. Peter, the Friday before Michaelmas, the Friday before Candlemas, and the Friday before Low Sunday.

The regalia of the merchants' guild consisted of, in 1526, banners, standard (yard wand of iron), and the keys of the box. To these articles another banner was afterwards added, and a table cloth, at one time a blue one, later, green. This guild has no plate, and has never had any. When the late J. Christian Curwen, then M.P. for Carlisle, sent to each of the guilds a present of a silver cup, the merchants sternly and virtuously returned the one sent to them. The merchants included mercers, drapers, grocers, apothecaries, &c., in fact all traders in Carlisle who were not actual manual workers. This guild was of all the eight the most independent politically, as shown by their refusal of presents of plate, and by their declining to admit strangers to brotherhood [see rule 7 in book 2]. They furnished Carlisle with more mayors and aldermen than any other guild. The younger sons of many brothers were successful in the learned and military professions. As these gentlemen took up their brotherhood by inheritance for the sake of the privileges it conferred, we find on the roll of merchants, General Studholme Hodgson, Colonel Lowry, Captain Dalton, Captain Hodgson, Captain Davison, Captain John Hutchinson, Captain W. Potts, Lieutenant Archer Pearson, Captain Isaac Davison, Rev. N. Robinson, Rev. R. Jackson, Rev. W. Dawson, Rev. John Lowry, Drs. Hutchinson, Brownrigg, and James, Mr. John Pearson (the town clerk) &c.

We give lists of the members at various periods.

A trew and perfitt record of all such names as are remayning of record within this booke and the yeare of theyre entrance newlie collected and found oute by me henry Monke clarke to the worshipfull the occuption and fraternitie of merchants this twentye daye of Februarie in the year of our Lord god 1623.

Peter Hewett	1557	William Chambers	1572
Robert Scott	1558	Edward daltonn	1580
Barnaby Toppinge	1558	John Skelton	1580
George Browne	1559	Thomas Browne	1580
John Calvert	1560	Anthony Nixon	1582
Adam Blakelock	1562	John Hodgson	1582
Thomas Monke	1564	Symon Wilson	1582
John Boake	1568	John Monke	1584
John Warwick	1570	Thomas James	1585

Name	Year	Name	Year
William Barwick	1587	Robert Chambers	1616
Thomas Pearson	1587	Thomas Chambers	1616
Edward Ivyson	1587	John Caipe	1616
William Symson	1588	James Pauton	1617
John Toppinge	1588	William Bownes	1619
Edward Barnes	1590	Robert Syde	1920
Robert Mulcaster	1592	Tho. Tallentyre	1620
Robert Dalton	1592	Anthony Coulter	1620
Thomas Atkinson	1594	Thomas Atkinson	1622
Thomas Pattinson	1594	Thomas Porter	1622
John Lyde	1595	John Glaister	1623
Thomas Barwicke	1595	Richard Barwick*	1624
Edward Barne	1596	Richard Wilson	1625
Mathew Caipe	1596	William Hewett	1625
Richard Pattinson	1596	William Barwicke	1627
Christo Slee	1597	John Caipe	1627
Thomas Dawson	1597	Richard Lowrey	1627
George Romeley	1599	Alex. Doulton	1627
Francis James	1598	Thomas Carliell yonge	1628
Thomas Barwis	1599	Andrew Nixon	1628
Henrye Monke	1599	William James	1629
Richard Lowrye	1601	Robert Chambers yonge	1630
John Jacksonne	1602	Carthew Pattinson	1632
Thomas Carlioll	1603	John Thomlinson	1632
Thomas Robinson	1605	William Atkinson	1633
Thomas Warde	1605	Matthew Wilkinson	1654
Edward Dalton	1607	Joseph Jefferson	1634
William Browne	1607	Thomas Warde	1634
Michaell Warde	1607	William Slee	1634
Edward durrance	1608	Thomas Monke	1634
John Hewett	1608	Robert Sewell	1635
John Ratlife	1609	William Atkinson	1635
Robert Lowther	1609	Edward James	1637
Thomas Warwick	1609	John Langborne	1638
Ambrose Nicholson	1612	Thomas Craister	1638
Isaac Browne	1612	Richard Laine	1639
Thomas Lowther	1613	Edward Hardon	1640
Robert James	1614	Thomas Dalton	1640
Edmund Craister	1614	Christopher Hardon	1640
Adam Warde	1614	John Taylor	1640
Dalston Dalton	1614	Thomas Skarrow	1640
Caires Orbell	1615	Henry Gill	1642
Thomas Blaymire	1614	Thomas Taylor	1642
Richard Orbell	1615	Peter Norman	1642
John Armer	1616	Robert Atkinson	1643

* All the names after 1623 are additions.

Name	Year	Name	Year
Cuthbert Studholme	1644	Christopher Parker ..	1663
Edward Sturdye ..	1644	Rich Richardson ..	1664
John Glaister ..	1647	Wilfred Brisco ..	1665
Richard Monke ..	1647	Stephen Whinfeild ..	1665
Richard Glaister ..	1647	John Sewell ..	1665
Richard Sewell ..	1647	Luke Simpson ..	1666
William Milborne ..	1647	Hugh James ..	1666
Ambrose Atkinson ..	1649	Anthony Simpson ..	1666
Isaac Tullye ..	1650	Robert Jefferson ..	1666
John Wilson ..	1650	Christopher Lough	1667
Hugh Wilkinson ..	1651	Thomas Baxter ..	1667
Adam Ward ..	1651	Robt Potter ..	1667
John Hewson ..	1651	Wm Barker ..	1668
Willm Atkinson ..	1652	Anthony Stagg ..	1669
John Scott ..	1654	William Lowther ..	1670
James Harden ..	1654	Tho Stanger ..	1670
Edward Craister ..	1655	Edmond Norman ..	1670
Edward Lowry ..	1655	Wm Skelton ..	1671
Richard Norman ..	1655	William Milborne Jnr	1672
Thomas Pattinson ..	1656	R. Browne ..	1672
Mr George Barwick	1656	Jenkin Pow ..	1672
Thomas Ward ..	1656	Nicholas Robinson ..	1672
Robert James ..	1656	John Wilson ..	1672
Richard Scott ..	1656	Robt Glaister ..	1673
John Thomlinson ..	1657	Robt Atkinson fil. Ambrose	1673
Willm Pattinson ..	1657	Wm Johnson ..	1673
John Monk ..	1658	Jos Reed ..	1673
Thomas James ..	1658	ffranciss Cape ..	1673
Isaac Milner ..	1658	John Glaister ..	1673
Willm Brisco ..	1658	Row^l Hodgson ..	1674
Timothy Haddock ..	1659	Daniell Cape ..	1674
John Atkinson ..	1659	Wm Jackson ..	1674
Edward dalton ..	1659	John Cape	1675
Joseph Jefferson ..	1659	John Sturdy ..	1676
Thomas Holme ..	1659	Tho: Simpson ..	1676
Thomas Carlile ..	1659	Tho Milburne ..	1677
Matthew Pattinson	1660	Lancelot Jefferson ..	1677
James Halton ..	1660	Tho: Norman ..	1679
Thomas Mason ..	1661	Wm Barwicke ..	1680
Willm Nicholson ..	1663	Tho Dawes ..	1680

The form of oath is also given as follows :—

Oath of every brother that shall be admitted——

You shall well & truely use exercise and keepe true weights and measures both for buying & selling without any manner of fraud cossenage or deceit.

You shall well and truely maintaine the orders and priviledges of this trayd and conceale all things belonging to the secrets of the obligation.

You shall not know of anything whatever prejudicial or hurtefull to this occupation or to any brother of the same fraternity but you shall acquaint them theirwith and to y^r best endeavour defend the same all these you shall well and truely keepe to the best of y^r knowledge & power soe help your God &c.

Another list shows the state of the guild at the close of the 17th century.

A true list of the names of the fraternity of march.
29^h Aprill 1698.

Mr Robt Atkinson x	Mr Joseph Parker x
M^r Wm Atkinson	Mr James Haddock
Mr Robt James x	Mr James Dalton x
Mr Timo Haddock x	Mr James Raines
M^r Wm Nicholson x	Mr Matthew Pattinson
Mr Anthony Stagg	Mr Jonathan Barwick
Mr Tho Stanger	Mr Jacob Davyson
Mr Nichol Robyson	Mr Rich Browne
Mr Jos Reed x	Mr Tho Lightfoott x
M^r Wm Jackson x	Mr Geo Lamplough
Mr Francis Cape	Mr Rich Swinburn
Mr John Sturdy x	Mr Edward Lowry x
Mr Tho Simson x	Mr Isaac Huntingdon x
Mr Tho Milburn	M^r Wm Tate x
M^r Wm Barwick	Mr Joshua Haddock x
Mr Tho Dawes	Mr John Lidell x
Mr James Pow	Mr Barnard Skelton
Mr Ambrose Atkinson	John Jeferson ⎫
Mr Rich. Lowry	Wm Sturdy ⎪
Mr John Tomlyson x	Joseph Robyson ⎬ Addition
Mr Ambrose Nicholson	Tho Railton ⎪
Mr Matthew Cape	Wm Robyson ⎭

In the same book we find—

A new call roll entered the 5th July 1706 being S. Peter quarterday 1706.

It contains the names marked ✗ in the last list, and also the following :—

Mr John Hodgson
Mr Barnard Skelton
Mr John Jefferson
Mr Wm Sturdy
Mr Joseph Robyson
Mr Tho Railton
James Atkinson
John Atkinson
Robert Norman
John Emerson
Tho Pearson
Phillip Hetherington
John James
Joseph Jackson
Jeremiah Jackson
Walter Phillip

The following is a list of the clerks during the 17th and 18th centuries :—

Thomas James 1614	Henry Monke 1624
Thomas Monke 1645	John Thomlinson 1655
Peter Norman 1670	Edward Lawson 1685
Timothy Haddock 1685	Wm Nicholson 1698
Joseph Parker	William Tate 1736
John Dawson 1748	John James 1768
Rob James 1784	

The following are the rules, oaths, and most interesting memoranda taken from the books :—

BOOK No. 1.

1624.

A brief rule to finde oute every order conteyned in this booke that is to saye the ffirst leafe the figure i the second leafe the figure 2 and so constanentlic euery leafe the figure in order.*

---

* This is from book No. 1, and is an index, written in double column, to a set of orders ; these have been written on the first twelve pages, which have been torn out, and are, with one exception, lost ; the index, which we print, is very full and partly supplies the loss.

i. First that undermaisters give warneing to the company to appear in our chamber or guild hall on y^r quarter dayes and at other tymes upon occasion.

That our dinner daye be kept as hath been accustomed upon Sunday before Michaelmas.

No under maister is to haue his dinner ffree ffor his attendance. Euery one to paye for his brotherhood yearlie towardes the charges of the dinner for strangers invyted 4^d quarterlye.

Those that be absent at our quarter dayes to yeald their consent to anie good order made as though they were present.

2. None to open shopp windoes upon Sundayes or other festivall dayes.

Our quarters to be duelye kept ffriday after Saint Peter, fridaye before Michelmas ffriday before Candlemas and ffriday before Low Sunday.

Maisters to give warneing to the company upon occasion.

None to take an apprentice but to a merchant. ✓

3. Noe distresse to be taken but to be delivered again upon payment.

The occupation to goe to the church at the buriall of the departed.

3. The youngest to reverence their elders : no foriner or outman to be taken partner or admitted to use the trade.

4. Boundering of the kinges moor none to haue the dinner but by due course and for obteyning a fee. Apprentices to be enrolled quarter day next date of his indenture None to use his ancestors unreverentlie None to sell sickles or sythes or anie other merchantize suffred to be sould by strangers : But onelie at the two faires.*

5. None floryner or stranger suffred to sell anie merchandyse but in tyme of our faires None to × × × × cottons or frise under couller ffor Scottes men.

Every apprentice to pay for his enrolement VI^d to the clarke None to speake before his elder haue spoken.

---

* This paragraph has been crossed out at some period. Kingmoor, about two miles from Carlisle, is now nearly all enclosed, and lost to the citizens ; but it was once a large open area, over which, by their charters, they had extensive rights. See a note infra to rule 7 from Book No. 2. The two fairs were in August and September.

Every florryner absent at our quarter dayes without lawfull excuse amerced XII^d *

6. All those that doe trayde to pay euery quarter daye twelve pence.
   No Scotes man suffered to retaile eyther in market or houses.
   Every apprentice being admitted a brother VI^s 8^d

7. No apprentice to be taken under 14 yeares of age the master giving over trayding must offer his apprentice to the occupation.

8. None suffred to take an apprentice onles he use and exercise the trade.

9. An acte against George Rumley for refuseing the merchant dinner.
   Our demand of his ma^tie at hys being at Carlisle.†

The XVI daye of May 1617.

Memorandum that when the marchants did meat in ther chamber about the comone good of this cittye we ware agreed to demand iiii thinges of the kynge, the first thing we desyer is to haue a lycense for transposing of wool and woolfells the second is to haue a noble man to lye in Karliell castell the third thing is to haue one of the three sittyngs of York ouse in the yeare to be keapt in Carlyell and the iiij^th thinge is if it please his majestie for the honor of his name and his posterytye to creat one unyversitie in this poore cittye of Carliell.

1624.

All such as desire to be admitted to this brotherhood ought to take this oath.
You shall well and truely use exercise and kepe true weights and measures both for buying and selling using no manner of fraud cosinage or deceyt.

---

* See *ante* p. 75 n. In the last clause of this rule, "fforryner" must mean a trader from a distance, who, on payment of some composition to the guild, had been permitted to trade in the city.

† The "demand" is on a loose leaf, and is given above. The removal of the garrison and its officers from Carlisle, after the two kingdoms were united under James I., was a serious money loss to the citizens; the having to resort to York for their more important law cases was also a grievance.

You shall well and truely maintaine and conceale all thinges belonging to the secrettes of this occupation.

You shall not know of anie thinge whatsoever prejudiciall or hurtfull to this occupation or to anie brother of the same ffraternitie but you shall acquaint them therewith and to your best endeavour defend the same.

This and all other orders articles and agreaments conteyned specyfied and declared in this our booke of orders you and all of you on your partes and behalfes shall well trewlie and ffaithfullie observe performe ffulfill and kepe to the best and uttermost of your power so help you god and by the contents of this book.

1644.

All such as shall be appointed under maisters ffor the occupation must tak oathe to be ministred as ffolloweth at theyre entrance You shall well and faithfully performe the office of wardens and under masters and be alwaies duetifull and readye to doe and exercise all things ffor the profitt and benefit of the trayde You shall make a true and perfect account of all such moneyes ffines and amercyments as shall come to your hands.

Thes and all other thinges belonging to your charge and conteyned in our book of orders and which are and ought on your part to be duly exercised you shall well and truly perform to the uttermost of your power Soe help you God.

The oath of every brother that is to be admitted.

You shall swear that you well & truely use exercise & keep true weights & measures both for buying & selling without any manner of fraud cozenage or deceit. You shall well and truly maintain the orders and privileges of the trade and conceal all things belonging to the secrets of this occupation.

You shall not know of anything whatsoever prejudiciall or hurtful to this occupation or to any brother of the same fraternity but you shall acquaint them therewith and to your best endeavours defend the same : all these you shall faithfully keep to the utmost of your power and knowledge. So help you God.

THE CLERKES OATH.

You shall swear that you will faithfully & diligently perform the place and office of clark to the fraternity you shall not

shew your orders nor give copies thereof to any person or
persons or act any other thing whatsoever that relates to this
occupation without the licence or consent of the majority of
this company So help you God.

THE UNDER MASTERS OR WARDEN OATH.

You shall swear that you will faithfully perform & execute the
office of warden or under master to this fraternity & true
accounts give of all such amercyments or other moneys that
shall come to your hands for the use of this occupation &
deliver up all manner of things that is in your possession
before you part with your place.

So help you God.

BOOK No. 2.

Orders belonging to the company of marchants reuised
corrected read and consented to by the whole socyete of
marchants upon Friday the fourth day of Julie 1656 being
S. Peter quarter.*

An order for them that are absent upon warneing to submitt to such
orders as shalbe made by them that are present.

1. Imprimis It is ordered by the company of marchants aforesaid
that if any brother of this society be warned lawfully at any
tyme to appeare in the marchants guild chamber by the wardens
or maisters for the tyme being and doe not appear accordingly
then every one that are soe absent shall performe and keepe
all such acts and orders as shalbe made for the good of the
trade by them that are absent as though they themselves
were there in their persons at the same tyme under the
penalty of five pounds.

An order for fower quarter dayes yearly

2. It is ordered and agreed upon by the consent of the whole
company that there shalbe kept and observed fower quarter
days yearely that is to say the first on Friday after the feast

---

* These orders, &c., are from book No. 2.

H

of S⟨t⟩ Peter the second on Friday before Michaelmas day the third on Friday before Candlemas day and the fourth on Friday before Low Sunday and as often more as the company shall think fitt upon warneing given by the wardens or maisters the day before And noe excuse to be admitted of except sickness upon paine of sixpence for every such default which the wardens or maisters are to levy and account for before they be discharged of their places.

It is ordered and agreed upon by the consent of the whole company that in regard our market day is changed from Satterday to ffriday that euery of our quarter dayes aboue mentioned shalbe likewise altered and changed from the seuerall fridays aforesaid to be held and kept upon the Tharsday immediately preceding euery such quarter day Peter quarter being   *This latter order is 3 July 1662 crossed out by common consent and our quarters to be kept the seuerall ffridays aboue mentioned.**

An order that the wardens or maisters shall forfeit three shillings four pence if they forgett to warne the company

3.   It is ordered and agreed upon by the consent of the whole company that if the maisters or wardens of the said trade doe not give lawfull warneinge to euery one of y⟨e⟩ company according to the former order That then the said maisters or wardens to forfeit three shillings fourpence soe often as they doe offend therein *And the under maisters to be present to attend to doe what is by the trade required.*†

Noe stresses taken by y⟨e⟩ wardens or maisters to be deliuered againe but by the consent of y⟨e⟩ trade

4.   It is ordered and agreed upon by the consent of the whole company that noe warden or maister that shall take any distresse from any person whatsoever of this occupation shall deliuer or cause the same to be deliuered againe except it be by the consent of the said company under the forfeiture of

---

* From the words "It is ordered" to "such quarter day" is a subsequent addition, as shown by the handwriting, and from "Peter quarter day" to the end is a still later addition. The change of market day in Carlisle from Saturday to Friday took place during the Commonwealth, but the Saturday was reverted to after the Restoration.

† The words in italics are a subsequent addition.

three shillings four pence to be taken without favour unless the same be paid that the goods are distrained for.

An order that upon notice geuen to the wardens or maisters upon the death of any brother they to warne the trade to attend the burial.

5. It is ordered and agreed upon by the consent of y⁰ whole company that whensoever any brother or sister of this trade doth depart this life that upon warneing thereof geuen to the maisters the maisters for the tyme being shall give warneing thereof to y⁰ whole company that at least one of euery house may resort to the church and euery one so offending to forfeit vi^d. And if the maisters doe not giue warneing upon warneing giuen to them then the said maisters to forfeit for euery default xii^d

An order that the juniors or youngest of y⁰ trade doe carry themselves respectively towards the seniors or ancients thereof.

6. It is ordered that at all publique meetings in our chamber the juniors or youngest of y⁰ trade doe upon all occasions carry themselves modestly and respectively toward the seniors and ancients thereof both in their words and actions And if it shall happen that any difference or trouble doe arise betwixt any brothers of that society relateing to the trade then it is agreed that six or foure of the most ancient of that company do order the same And those that refuse to submitt to any such order soe made to forfeit for the benefitt of the trade vi^s viii^d. to be taken without favour.

An order that noe stranger or outman be admited a brother of our trade.

7. It is ordered by the consent of y⁰ whole company aforesaid that there shalbe noe stranger or outman of what rank or degree soever he be admitted as a brother of this trade for any sum or sums of money whassoever And whatsoever he be that moued the contrary to forfeit vi^s viij And whosoever shall give his consent to admitt of any such shall forfeit for euerry default xl^s *

---

* This guild was a very independent one in political matters and declined to admit candidates or M.P.s to membership, merely as such, but troublesome "fforyners or strangers," who persisted in trading, were sometimes admitted to certain privileges on payment of a composition.

An order that the trade upon warneing attend Mr Maior to the kings moor.

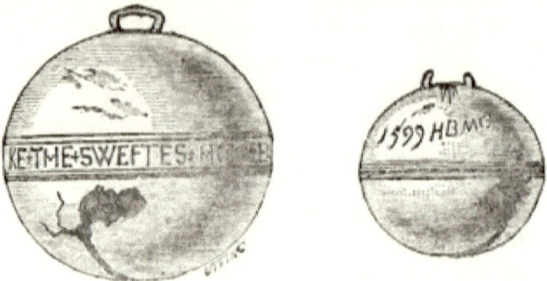

Racing bells of 17th century belonging to corporation of Carlisle.

8. It is ordered that upon notice geuen to y^e whole company euery one thereof doe attend upon Mr Maior for the tyme being to the kings moor And who euer is absent to pay six-pence for euery default unless he haue a lawfull excuse.*

An order that euery apprentice is to be inrolled ye next quarter day after his indentures be sealed.

9. It is ordered by the consent of ye whole company of marchants that euery brother that shall at anytime hereafter take an apprentice hee shall the next quarter day after the sealing of his indentures bring in the same indeenture before the whole company and inroll his said apprentice upon paine to be taken of the maister if he offend therein the sume of ten pounds.

An order for ye clarkes fees

10. It is ordered by the consent of the whole company of marchants that the clarke of that company for the time

---

* The mayor went on Ascension Day (Hallow Thursday) to beat the bounds of the estate at Kingmoor given to the citizens by the charter of Edward III. The occasion was one of high festivity, and prizes were given for horse racing. The chamberlains' accounts contain items for money laid out for saddles and bridles as prizes for these races. Later, the prizes were given by the local members of parliament, and the candidates for such honours. The corporation even now have silver bells which were run for on Kingmoor; of these an engraving is given in the text.

being shall haue the benefitt of all indentures makeing and to haue for euery paire makeing the sume of iii^s and for euery inrolment xii^d and recording euery brothers son or apprentice vi^d. The clark is likewise to haue of the trade for his ffee yearly xvi^d.

*It is likewise ordered that euery brother's son shall pay for the benefitt of the trade the same of iii^s iiii^d for his admittance. And euery apprentice for his admittance for ye benefitt of ye trade ri^s viii^d. ***

An order that while any matter is under debate noe younger brother to speake out of course without leave obtained.

11. It is ordered by ye consent of ye whole company whilst any matters shalbe propounded or debated in our chamber that noe brother thereof shall unreverently use his ancients either by ansuereing without license obtained of the seniors of ye trade or by any other frivolous talke or crablinge words untill such time as his ancients in their seuerall places and callings haue first geuen their judgements upon paine that euery such troubler of ye chamber or gild shall forfeit for euery offence vi^s viii^d to be presently levied without favour.

An order that noe brother of this trade shall suffer any Scotsman or others to retaile any goods preindeciall to the rest of ye marchants.

12. It is ordered by the consent of the whole company that noe brother of this company shall at any time suffer either Scots-men or others to retayl in his house any flax† onionseed or any other comoditie which may be preindeciall to the company of merchants upon paine of euery brother soe offending to forfeite for the use of the trade the summe of forty shillings euery default.

An order that noe apprentice be taken under the age of 14 yeares.

13. It is ordered by the consent of ye whole company that noe brother of the trade shall take an apprentice unless this company be sufficiently satisfied at the time of his enrollment that euery such apprentice soe taken is at least fourteen yeares

---

* The words in italics are subsequently crossed out.

† A good deal of coarse flax was at one time sold in Carlisle by country people. See *Hutchinson's Cumberland, Appendix, Carlisle.*

of age And if any be found to be under that age not to be inrolled at all.

An order that euery apprentice after the death of his maister shall the next quarter day offer himself to the trade.

14.   It is ordered by the consent of the whole company that euery apprentice after the death of his maister shall (if his mistresse haue no further imployment for him) offer his service to the trade the next quarter day after his maister's death And if none of the company imploy him he is at libertie to goe and live where hee pleases and after the expiracon of his indenture to be admitted a brother of this company and if he refuse to offer himselfe as aforesaid he shall not be admitted a brother of this trade untill he haue compounded with the trade for his neglect therein.

An order that noe brother shall joyne partner with a stranger or foranner.

15.   It is ordered by the consent of the company of marchants aforesaid that noe brother of this trade shall joyne as partner with any stranger or forraigner in the trade and occupacon of a marchant either within the cittie or libertyes thereof. Neither shall any brother of this company give any account of proffitt or gaine to any stranger or non-freeman concerninge their trade upon penaltie That euery brother that offends herein to forefeit for the benefitt of the trade the sume of ten pounds.

An order that noe brethren shall take an apprentice but such as trades.

16.   It is ordered and agreed upon by the consent of the whole company of marchants that noe brethren of this trade shall take an apprentice to the trade or faculty of a marchant but onely such brother as doth trade or hath traded at least for the space of six months before the takeing of euery such apprentice : and it is further ordered yᵗ all apprentices otherwise taken then as aforesaid shall not be admitted of nor inrolled and euery brother that offends against this order to be fined ten pounds for the benefitt of the trade.*

---

* See also Rule 24.

An order that euery brother that liues in the country shall appeare upon St Peter quarter day.

17. It is ordered by the consent of ye whole company that euery brother that lives in the country shall appeare in our marchants chamber euery St Peter quarter day or els to pay yearely for their defaults to the wardens of this trade for the time being the sume of twelve pence and neither themselues nor their children to haue any benefitt of this trade till all arrears be paid and discharged if any such happen to be due.

An order that noe brother depart out of our chamber without license.

18. It is ordered by the consent of the company aforesaid that noe brother of this trade shall upon any of our quarter daies or at any other tyme when he shalbe warned to appear in our guild chamber shall depart thence without leave and license first obtained of the company then present upon ye penaltie to pay for the benefitt of the trade the summe of thirteene shillings fourpence to be levyed without favour.

An order that euery brother shall take his place in our chamber according to his seniority.

19. It is ordered by the consent of the company aforesaid that euery brother of this trade upon our quarter daies or at any other meeting in our guild chamber take his place there according to his inrollment or seniority whether he be alderman or other unless it be in the year of his maioralty upon paine for every time soe offending to pay three shillings foure pence.

An order that noe brother chosen clarke shall refuse the place.

20. It is ordered by the generall consent of this company that if any brother shalbe elected clarke and doe refuse to take the said office upon him he shall forfeit to the company fortye shillings to be fourthwith levied by the wardens for the tyme being for the use of the company.

An order that noe warden shall refuse to take that office upon him being elected thereto.

21. It is ordered by the generall consent of this company that if any brother of this trade shall hereafter refuse to be warden

or under maister of this company except such as lines in the
country and trade not in the citty* when he or they shalbe
elected thereto in their due course he or they soe refuseing
shall forfeit to the benefitt of the trade the sum of fortie
shillings

July 4 1690.

This order confirmed saue the rasure of this order.

An order to read the orders euery Peter quarter day.

22.   It is ordered by the generall consent of the company aforesaid that all our orders shalbe publiquely read in our guild
chamber euery Peter quarter day that thereby none may
pretend to be ignorant thereof.

An order that noe brethren is to take a second apprentice untill his
first have served five yeares.

23.   It is ordered by the generall consent of the company of
of marchants that noe brother that hath taken an apprentice
for seuen yeares shall haue liberty to take another apprentice
untill such tyme as his first apprentice hath served completely
five years or unless before that time his first apprentice be dead.

An order that no brother of that trade shall take an apprentice but
such as trades and liues within ye cittie and to employ him in noe
other trade.

24.   It is ordered by the generall consent of the company that
noe brother of this trade either married or unmarried is to
take any apprentice unless it be such a brother as doth dwell
reside and keepe shopp within the libertys of this cittye And
further ordered that noe brother that trades or keeps shopp
shall take an apprentice to imploy him in any other employment but in his own vocation and calling either at home or
abroad under the penalty to forfeit for the benefitt of the
trade the sume of tenn pounds.†

---

* The words "except such," to "in the citty," are erased.

† See also rule 16, of which this seems to be an amended and later
edition.

25.* It is ordered by the consent of the company upon the 15 day of April 1658 that if any apprentice shall misdeameane or carry himselfe scornfully or uncivilly towards any brother of this trade and the same sufficiently proved by one witness in our chamber that euery such apprentice soe offending shall acknowledge his fault and make submission to the trade and the partie offended before he shalbe admitted a brother thereof.

26. It is ordered that the clarke of the company for the tym being shall not at any tyme give a coppy of any order to any brother without the consent of the company upon paine of 6ˢ 8ᵈ.

26.† It is ordered that if any brother of this trade doe not appear in our guild hall euery quarter day before his name be recorded in the bookes he shall forfeit sixpence though he doe appear afterwards in our chamber.

27. Ordered that euery apprentice shall pay to the trade at his first enroleing as an apprentice 2ˢ 6ᵈ and when he is brothered into the trade 3ˢ 4ᵈ and alsoe that every brother's sonne shall pay for his brotherhood when he is admitted a brother into trade iiiˢ iiijᵈ

28. July the first 1681 It is ordered by this occupation that the under maister of this trade shall make deligent inquiry of all such persons as exercise the trade of a marchant being not qualified according to law that they may be presented according to law And that the undermaisters shalbe keept harmless for their soe doing by the whole company of marchants.

29. June 30
1682.
An order that noe brother of this trade tak an apprentice till yᵉ first haue serued fiue yeares compleat.

30. Sᵗ Peter quarter day July 5 1689. Ordered by the consent of this company that all the yearly men leaning in the country shall pay six shillings eight pence if they does not appeare every Sᵗ Peter quarter day for the future.‡

---

* From this point the rules are later additions, as the writing shows, and have no headings.

† Two consecutive rules are both numbered 26.

‡ See *ante* rule 17.

31. St Peter quarter day July ye 1st 1692. It is ordered by the consent of this company whereas there was the sume of sixty pounds was giuen to this company by Mr Rob^{bt} Rodham deceased its ordered y^t the interest of ye money ariseing yearly shalbe paid in at this chamber upon this quarter day euery year and to be disposed as the company there present shall think fitt.

32. An order for the re-imbursing of undermasters for what they shall lay out for ye use of the trade upon ascension day.

Low Sunday quarter
feb 13 1694

It is ordered by and with ye consent of the company of merchants that all undermasters shall be obliged to provide oil and other necessarys fitt for ascension day And what soever they shall justly lay out for the use of the trade shall be reimbursed by the s^d company of merchants upon St Peter quarter day next following.

24th Fber 1703 being St. Michall quarter it is ordered and agreed by this company of marchants here present that noe brother of this fraternity shall take to an apprentice the son of any person whoe is a quaker or ownes himselfe to be such to forfit to the benyfit of this occupation the sum of forty pounds currant English money.

MISCELLANEOUS ENTRIES.

1586. That Wyllm Barwick and Thomas Person is chosen and appointed to be maisters of the company of the marchants this xxiii day of September A^{o.} dni 1586 A^{o.} Regni Regine Elizabethe xxvii and hes taken delnerains of the boourke and yard wand from John Hodgson and Symond Iveson who hes × × × these accounts and charge the same day for the year aforegong 1586.

1617. The Mayor Mr Thomas Pattinson was fined 6^d for absence on a quarter day.

1624. The insignia handed from one set of undermasters to another were the banner and a "yeare wand" and in 1626 a pewter pot & candlestick, which were held in pawn by the undermasters to secure arrears due from Edward Dalton & Edward Durrance.

The account of Mathew Caipe and Thomas Atkinson taken & received the 30 of June 1626 for the precedent year they being wardaines for the company.

The said accomptants doe charge themselves to haue received at theyre entrye ..	03 : 5 : 0
More of Mr Richard Barnes	02 : 10 : 0
By William Hewett for his brotherhood ..	0 : 6 : 3
At our dinner of 20 that doe not trad ..	01 : 06 : 8
Of 9 other that doe use trading 22^d	0 : 06 : 06
Of 5 weadars at 10	0 : 4 : 02
For amerciaments this yeare	0 : 3 : 0
Of the chamberlane	0 : 2 : 06

8 : 14 : 06.

Whereof disbursed.

Imprims 45 persons that were at our dinner ..	02 : 02 : 06
For wine at our dinner	0 : 13 : 0
To the cooks and undercooks	0 : 03 : 0
For musick	0 : 01 : 0
For beare	0 : 06 : 06
For charges on hallow Thursday	0 : 09 : 0
For chamber rent	0 : 02 : 0
To the clerk for his fees	0 : 01 : 04

Some of disbursements xlii^s & iiij^{d.}

So as now there remains good to the occupation all accomptes and disbursements payed vi^{li} ii^s iv^{d.} delivered (upon bond) to the succedent wardanes being Henry Monkouse John Jackson And the sade John hath engaged his lease of his manshon house for his securitye and lendes his bond (delivered to Mr Cape his custody).*

---

* This entry is given as a representative one, and it will be noticed the addition is not correct. The "5 weadars at 10" would be small traders in groceries and other small articles, relicts of departed brothers. The chamberlain's 2 .. 6 was the annual contribution from the corporation, of which that body received back 2s. for the rent of the merchants' chamber in the guild hall. The charges on Hallow Thursday (Ascension Day) would be in connection with beating the bounds of Kingmoor.

A coppy of the order betweine the tradesmen informers and the country usurpers dfds.

Whereas there hath beene informations heretofore made in the quarter sessions at Carleel in the countye of Cumberland by Andrew Nixon and Anthony Coulter informers against Christopher Astrigg Thomas Hodgson, Henry Robinson John Carliell Robert Carliell John Peat Robert Peat and Thomas Robinson for setting upp using and exercising sevr¹ craftes mysteries and trades contrary to the statute in that caise provided And whereas upon hearing of the matters in the said courte of quarter sessions houlden in the weeks after the feast of Saint Michaell the Archangle last past. The said informations and all the matters therein contained were by all the said ptyes with the license and allowance of the said court referred to the arbytrament and order of Sr Patricious Curwen baronnett Sir Henry Blencowe knight Richard Barwise esquire and Willm Barwick gentleman citizen of Carliel Now the saide arbitrators having this present daye heard the allegations of both the saide ptyes and takinge due consideration of the matters in the said information conteynd doe now order and   ×   ×   ×   that all the suits between the said parties shall cease and be no more presented And that the said defendants nor any of them shall not at any time hereafter sett up use or exercise any craft mystery or trayde contrary to the statute in that case provided In witness whereof the said arbitrators have hereunto sett theyr handes the xxiᵗʰ daye of March in the sixt yeare of the reyne of or soverayne lord Charles by the grace of god of England Scotland France and Ireland kinge defender of the faithe 1630.

> Patricius Curwen
> Henry Blencowe knight
> Richard Barwis esqr.
> William Barwick gente.

Candlemas quarter being the 29 of January 1635 Friday before Candlemas. Received the day aboue written of William Atkinson for admitting him a brother & haith payed for his enroylement vi. 8.

William Atkinson notary publiqe admitted a brother of this trade upon a letter from the Bishop of Carliell Lord William Howard &ct at the entreaty of Sir Richard Græme and Mr Anthony Holton & has payed composition for marryng before this yeare were fourth ye some of 3^li 10^s.*

1641. John Watt hath submitted himselfe to the censor of this occupation to undergoe and pay what they shall set done the next quarter day for his default in keeping unlawfull weights and measures wch he hath confessed.

1647 Whereas Willom Milborne haith traded beiore he was brothered into the occupation of merchants and did sell goods contrary to our order therefore ye occupation hath fined to pay at or before St Peters quarter the some of fortye shillings haith payed xxx to ye undermasters & x^s forgiuen.

1647. Leonard Lowther son of John Lowther of Roose† was admitted. Whereas Leonard Lowther did marry before ye expiracon of seauen yeares contrary to an order yet in regard of the discretion of having his m^r consent the tyme the occupation haue thoght fitt to fine ye s^d Leo Lowther to pay viii^li in manner folowing St Peter quar to pay 2^li and soe quarterly till ye some of viii^li be fully payed.

Candlemas quarter the 30 day of January 1651. It is ordered this day y^t whereas Leonard Lowther mentioned in severall orders haue utterly disobeyed the payment of viii^li for marrying for seauen year was expired And therefore further order y^t Leonard Lowther shall pay the sum of viii^li according to a former order or els y^t he shall haue no benefitt of this trade but from henceforth he & his be cleare excluded out of this occupation at or before the next quarterday.‡

Low Sunday quarter the 19th day of April 1650. Amerced this quarter day by generall consent M^r Jo Caipe Richard

---

* The Bishop of Carlisle was Barnaby Potter. Lord William Howard is well known : Sir R. Græme was afterwards Lord Preston. For the restrictions on marriage see an entry below as to Leonard Lowther.

† For the Lowthers of Rose Castle see an article on the Dalston registers in the Transactions C. & W. A. & A. Society, vol. vi.

‡ Printed out of order that it may follow the last.

Monke Is Tomplinson Mr Tho Craister.* Whereas dinerse
of this trade haue been psent this quarter day and now is
gone away obstinatelie without leaue of this occupation therefore this occupation haue thought fitt to fine these persons
according to our orders follouing Edu Dalton Peter Norman
Willom Atkinson Tho Scarrow

2nd July 1652. Willom Atkinson this quarter day haue
submitted himselfe to his trade ffor obstinately going out of
our gild and hath payed according to o^r order iii^s iiii^d abated
by generall consent ij^s iiij^d †

19 April 1651. Isaack Tullye‡ ye sonne of George Tully of
ye Citty of Carlisle gentleman, late apprentice to Mr John
Langhorne is admitted a brother of this trade by ye generall
consent of this occupation and has payd for his entrie vi^s viii^d

1651. It is ordered this quarter day at our next quarter
Isaack Tully shall submit himself to pay a fine to this trade
if they shall think it fitting for taking his sister to keep & sell
waires for him contrary to our order & soe referre him to this
occupation.

It is ordered this Michaelmas quarter 1651 y^t Isaack Tully
shall pay ye next quarter day following xi^s for his offence to
the trade.§

Candlemas quarter being the first of February 1655 It is
ordered by the Company of marchants then present that
Mr Isaac Tullys business concerning the payment of forty
shillings for keeping his sister in his shop contrary to order be

---

* For not appearing.

† Printed out of order to follow the last.   Atkinson's offence probably
consisted in shirking his liquor.

‡ Isaac Tullie, in his eighteenth year, was author of a tract entitled
A Narrative of the Siege of Carlisle, 1644 and 1645 printed by Jefferson,
Carlisle, in 1840.   He was descended from one of the German miners, who
settled in Keswick tempore Elizabeth.   He was Mayor of Carlisle at the
Restoration.   From him descended Thomas Tullie, Dean of Ripon, 1675-1676.
George Tullie, Prebendary of Ripon, Rector of Gateshead, and Sub-Dean of
York, 1625 ; and Thomas Tullie, Chancellor of Carlisle and Dean of Carlisle,
1716-1726.

§ Tully was obstinate and would not pay, as various entries show.

deferred to be fully determined and ended upon St John quarter next following.*

Michaelmas quarter this 26 day of September 1651
Whereas it is ordered this quarter day y^t severall psons sell waires in ye street to ye great pudice of this trade. Therefore we raquire ye undermrs Edu Monke and Richard Glaister to take notice of such persons as doe sell waires in ye streete y^t they may be able to informe the leete court juraye next to be houlden and see to psent the same.

2nd July 1652 Complaint being made this quarter daye y^t Richard Monke was ptner with Willm Oliuant a forriner in buyng & selling a can of vinegar th ye sd Richard being questioned for the same doth acknowledge the truth of ye information and submitts himselfe the sentence of ye coort is this y^t upon confession he is acquitted for ye same promising neuer to doe ye like it being ye first fault & he indyed ignorant of our orders.+

St Peter quarter day ye 3 of July 1663 Ordered by the joynt consent of the whole company this day (*nemine contradicente*) that Thomas Holme and Thomas Carlile shall continue undermasters untill St Peter quarter day next for regard that they did not the last quarter day bring in such an account as the trade could allow of for which cause they are continued.

Low Sunday q^r 27 March 1668 Ordered this day by the consent of the whole company this quarter day that Willm Woods the sonn of John Woods of Ravenglas apprentice to Richard Scott late deceased is debarred for euer being a brother of this trade in regard that the said William Woods did refuse to be entertained as an apprentice to John Thomlinson the next quarter day after his masters death dureing the remainder of his years then unxexpired wch is contrary to the fourteenth order in our book of orders.

---

* The result does not appear. This order is interpolated in the book immediately after the last.

+ In 1656 Mr. Peter Norman is charged with a similar offence as to a bargain of herring, and in 1659 as to some wool ; in the first case fined 10s., and in the second he was acquitted.

Michaelmas quarter day 25 Sept 1668   Ordered this quarter day that whereas Mrs Studholme hath employed James Moorehead Scotsman to vend and sell goods in her shop contrary to an order of this company wee doe order that the wardens of our company shall fourthwith acquaint Mrs Studholme y^t she must not be admitted to entertain him any long^r in her employm^t but that before our next quarter day she take some other course for keeping her shop and y^t he be noe longer employed therein till y^t time.

1671. Candlemas quarter Jan 26/71
Ordered this q^rterday by gen^ll concent that Anthony Sympson doo forthwith putt all ye glass windows in sufficient repair and soe keep them dureing his naturall life and alsoe make a new floore of good boards in ye marchands guildhall or chamber all over and maintain them also in good & sufficient repair and that they be made at or before Ascenscion day next & soe keepe such floore & glass windows & euery part of them in good & sufficient repair dureing his naturall life. that then the undermasters of the merchants shall pay unto the sd Anthony Sympson during his life naturall the summe of ten shillings English money yearely the first paym^t to begin on St Peter quarter day next & soe to continue to be paid to him the sd Anthony Sympson dureing his life upon the sd day yearly.

Candlemas q^r day 1677.
Ordered this quarter day that the undermasters of this company doe psent one bill of indictment or more if need require aganst those fforeigners that trade in the country not hauing served their apprenticeship according to law.

> At ye common councill holden
> the 14th day of March anno
> domini 1697
> Present Mr Maior &ct.

Whereas divers undermasters and clarks of several guilds or fraternitys of this citty and corporation of late years and more especially dureing the raine of the late king James ye second haue at their owne will and pleasure and as often as they thought fitt summoned called and procured the brothers

of the said guilds or ffraternitys to meat togeather in theire
guilds within this citty of Carlisle and at such meetings have
taken ye opportunity by false insinuation and undue prep-
rations of the said brothers to make and foment factions and
divisions in ye ffraternitys whereby ye freedom of ellections
wthin this city hath been greatly and frequently disturbed
And divers other mischieves have ensued both to ye cittizens
of this citty in their rights of ellections and in other their
ffranchises and immunities And whereas divers persons on
purpose to carry on the said evill practises have procured
themselves to be admitted to the fredome of the said fraternitys contrary to law and ye ancient customs of this citty
And whereas it appeareth to us that the said severall guilds
within this citty have made severall orders or by laws to the
hurt of ye publique and to the trying and abuse of the fremen
and inhabitants of this citty and particularly that they have
contrary to law imposed severall sums of money on the
brothers of the said ffraternity and others for the breach of
ye said illegal orders and by laws.

Therefore for the reformation of the above mentioned evills
and abuses it is by the mayor aldermen and capital cittizens
of this comon Counsell assembled ordained and established
that noe undermaster or clarke undermasters or clarkes of any
the severall guilds or fraternitys of this citty and corporation
shall without ye allowance of the comon councill of this corporacon first had and obtained at any time after ye twenty
first day of this instant month of March (except on Ascension
Day and the usual quarter days yearly and days appointed
and notified or to be notified or appointed for elections
sumon or call or procure ye brothers of the said guilds to
meet togeather in their guilds And that noe brother or brothers
of any of the said guilds or fraternitys shall without such
allowance as aforesaid att any time after the said 25th day of
this instant moneth of March (except on the days & times
before excepted) meet togeather in theire guild upon paine to
forfitt to ye chamberlaine of this corporation for ye time
being to the use of the mayor aldermen baliffs and cittizens
of this citty the sume of 40^s of lawful moneys of England
for every time wherein such undermaster clarke or brother of

I

any such guild shall offend contrary to the true intent and
meaning hereof And further that noe person or persons who
have been admitted or shall be admitted to ye fredome of any
of ye said guilds or fraternitys w^thout being entitled to such
freedome by birth or service or by grant or allowance of this
corporation shall have take or claime any benifitt privilide or
immunity or any right to meet or vote as a brother in any
the said guilds by reason or conlour of any such admittance
upon paine likewise to forfitt to ye chamberlaine of this
corporation for ye time being to the use of this corporation
the sum of 40^s of lawful English money for every offende
contrary hereunto And likewise that all and every ye clarks
of the said severall guilds shall upon notice to them for that
purpose respectively to be given by the maior of this corporation for the time being and as often as they shall be
hereunto required lay before ye comon councill of this corporation the book or register of ye orders of their respective
guilds that they may be inspected and considered whither the
same orders are agreable to law and fitt to be put in execution
upon paine that every of the said clarks who shall refuse or
neglect to lay before ye common council of this corporacon
the booke and register of his or their respective guild or
guilds as aforesaid shall forfitt to the chamberlaine of this
citty for the time being to ye use of this corporacon the sume
of forty shillings for every such refusal or neglect All which
paines penalties forfeitures and sums of money to be forfitted
by vertue of this ordinance shall be recovered by action of
debt bill or plaint to be comenced and prosecuted in the name
of the chamberlaine of the said citty of Carlisle for the time
being in the king's mat^ie court to be houlden in the guild
hall of ye said citty of Carlisle before the maior and bailiffs
of the said citty wherein noe esoine or wager of law shall be
allowed for the debt And that the chamberlaine of the said
citty for the time being shall in all sutes to be prosecuted by
vertue of this ordinace of offender recover ye ordinary costs
of suite to be expended in and about ye prosecution thereof
And lastly it is hereby ordered that this ordinance for ye better
observation thereof shall be entred unto ye books or registers
of the acts of said respective guilds by the respective clarks

of the same guilds And that ye town clark of this citty doe give them coppys of this ordinance to be by them entred as aforesaid.*

1699. George Usher son of George Usher† of Arthuret clerk is bound apprentice for 7 yeare to Timothy Haddock.

1703. James Lowther esq gave the fraternity 2 guineas.

1704. Christopher Musgrave esq gave two guineas for the use of the trade also "at once payed for a Bowle of Bunch 14ˢ 1ᵈ for another Bowle of Bunch, 14ˢ"‡

The same year Brigadier Howe and Coll Stanwix gave 40ˢ.

1719. Sᵗ Peter qʳ day July 3 1719.

Mʳ Jnᵒ Simpson present warden or undermaister is appointed by this company to endeavour to get proof before the next qʳ day against the several persons under mentioned for keeping open shops or retalery of goods contrary to the statute in that behalf made.

Mʳˢ Sybil Hetherington.

Mʳˢ Mary Nixon.

Mʳˢ Jane Jackson widow in Richard gate without

Mʳ John Hicks   Mʳ Wᵐ Carlile

William Armstrong   Tho Forster

July 20 1732. At a private meeting in our gild chamber came Mʳ Edŵ Lowry jun the son of Mʳ Edŵ Lowry and the brothers present agreed to make him a brother of the fraternity viz

Mʳ Jos Parker senʳ	Mʳ Jas Aktinson
Mʳ Edŵ Lowry senr	Mʳ Jos Parker jun.
Mʳ Mungo Langcake	Mʳ Tho James
Mʳ Jacob Hodgson	Mʳ James Atkinson
Mʳ Wᵐ Coulthert	Mʳ Jas Graham

---

* This order seems to have been frequently broken, as in 1712 and 1754 further orders are made by the council against admission of brethren on other than quarter days. The object of these irregular meetings was to slip on freemen of the political colour favoured by the officials of each guild. It seems doubtful how far the mayor and corporation could enforce this order, but it marks an era in the history of parliamentary elections. See *ante* pp. 31, 32, 33.

† Rector of Arthuret 1673 to 1688.

‡ To judge from the writing of this entry the clerk made it while under the influence of the "bunch." These generous donors were candidates for Parliament.

The day aboue Mr Edn Lowry jun of London is this day
admitted a brother of this occupation and hes paid to the use
of the trade 18/4 to John Graham and takes the usual oaths.*

April 7. 1741.   It is ordered that Mr Jos. Potts, James
Jackson, H Pearson and the undermaster of this guild for
the time being carry on a prosecution against Richard Hodgson
for exercising the trade of a mercer not having served an
apprenticeship.†

Low Sunday quarter Aprill 8th 1743.   Mrs Parker having
this day paid into the hands of Mr Chris: Hodgson the sum
of fiftyfive pounds for the use of the ffraternity wch said snme
is to be applied to carry on any law suit y^t may be brought
against any that shall incroach the privileges of this company.‡

Ex gratia   Candlemas quarter Friday ffeb 1 1750/1.
freemen
                 .
The question being put whether the expenses of securing the
right of freedom of this citty and to prevent makeing *ex gratia*
freemen be paid by the undermaster for the time being or not
was carried on the affirmative by 15 to 4.§

[Two orders   Order that the roads from Reeds town to Caldue bridge
as to roads]   be inspected and where found to be insufficient the
(circa 1751-2) inhabitants to be prosecuted at the expense of this
               guild and that John Dauson and the undermasters for
               the time being direct the prosecution.

Ordered that five guineas be given out of the companys stock
towards the expences of a turn pike from Carlisle to Cockermouth and so to Workington and that the undermasters for

---

* This seems one of the meetings against which the Council Order of 14th
March, 1697, was directed.   Mr. Thomas Phillips, son of Mr. Walter Phillips,
of Whitehaven, was similarly admitted, December 8th, 1732, and Mr. Geo.
Lowry, son of Rich. Lowry, of Kendale, in 1733.

† Many similar instances could be cited : the usual infringement was by
exercising the trade of a grocer.

‡ It does not appear what this sum was paid for ; it seems too large to
have been paid as a fine or composition for trading in infringement of the
rights of the guild ; probably it was the repayment of money lent on bond out
of the joint stock of the guild.

§ This refers to legal proceedings as to *ex gratia* freemen.   See *ante* p. 33-35.

the time being pay the said five guineas towards the expenses
of obtaining an act of Parliament for that purpose to Mr Jere
Adderton.*

1756. John Crozier, late apprentice to Mr William James
deceased offered himself this day to this fraternity and none
of the trade having occasion he is at liberty to dispose of
of himself as he pleases the remaining of the seven years.

Michaelmas q^r Septr 23 1761.

Ordered that Mr Monkhouse Davison† have the thanks of the
ffraternity for the colour which he has sent for the use of this
guild that Mr John Pearson write the same.

Low Sunday q^r April 1 1785.

Whereas the mayor and corporation has admitted seven or
eight hundred persons mostly strangers to the freedom of this
city who were not entitled thereunto either by birth or
servitude which we consider as a gross violation of our rights
and privilidges we therefore having taken the above transaction into consideration at a special guild held this day for that
purpose do nominate and appoint William Halton our representative to meet a freeman appointed in like manner from
each guild as a committee to enquire particularly into the
above transaction and to do what in their judgment may seem
meet in procuring every necessary information to form a
proper case for the opinion of council and ascertain our
accustomed rights and privilidges.‡

May 5 1786.

At a meeting held this day May 5th 1786 it is ordered and
agreed that all or any of the books of this guild belonging

---

* These two orders show a patriotic spirit on part of the merchants, which
is not found in the other guilds. But the commodities that the merchants
dealt in mainly came by sea to Whitehaven and Workington, and hence the
roads mentioned were of importance to them.

† Mr. Monkhouse Davison, a member of the guild, made a fortune as a
grocer in London, and in 1761, he purchased the Dalston Estates, near Carlisle,
from Sir George Dalston, for £5,000. These estates were sold by Mr.
Davison's trustees to the Sowerbys in 1795. Mr. Pearson was town clerk.

‡ This and several following extracts refer to the celebrated "Mushroom
Elections," see the introduction, p. 33-40, and see also Ferguson's (R.S.)
Cumberland and Westmorland M.P.'s from the Restoration to the Reform
Bill. C. Thurnam and Sons, Carlisle.

the merchants company be delivered to the care of M\ Henry Dobinson in order to be taken for inspection on a warrant from the speaker of the House of Commons ordering the clerk of this trade to attend the tryal of the legality of fourteen hundred new freemen chiefly tenants of the earl of Lonsdale and by such freeman our mayor Richard Jackson returned Jn° Lowther esq duly elected Jn° Christian esq^e on such proceeding petitioned the hon^ble the House of Commons and after a full hearing the hon^ble house declared that John Christian esq ought to have been returned who took his seat accordingly.

At a public meeting held this day June 23 1786 a motion being made wheather any brothers shall be admitted being already legal freemen carried by 13 to 4   Whereas we have been alarmed by a violent and tyrannic attempt to create fourteen hundred new freemen possessing no title or servitude in direct and open violation of our antient custom and to the destruction of our liberties and most valuable franchises We the brethren of this guild at a special meeting assembled in order to these rights liberties and privileges in a state of the greatest possible security have agreed unanimously that the following gentlemen shall be admitted brothers of this trade being citizens and brothers of the guilds set opposite to their names.

At a meeting held this day Nov 20 1787 the majority eleven to six have ordered and agreed that 2 guineas be advanced from the stock belonging this trade in conjunction with the other guilds to take oppinion of counsel to know the propriety of restoring to the freemen their ancient rights respecting their lands &ct call'd king moor which the corporation granted titles to several people which is believed they having no such right so to do.*

---

* This and the next order refer to the disastrous litigation under which the freemen lost their rights over the greater part of Kingmoor, *ante* pp. 94, 100. During the early part of the 18th century, the corporation let large areas on Kingmoor to various people of the right political colour, on leases for lives. At the close of the century, these people claimed the right to enfranchise on easy terms, and after protracted litigation carried their point.

Pursuant to an advertisement in the public papers a special
meeting was held this day March 13 1790 in order to take
into consideration the propriety of voting twenty pounds from
the stock of this trade for the use and purpose of prosecuting
the claim of right upon king moor which upon motion was
carried nem. con. and the said 20lb put into the hand of
Mr Wm Halton he being appointed cashier for all the trades.

At a meeting held this day Feb 4 1791. It is unanimously
agreed that the books belonging this trade be given in
charge to Mr Dobinson to be taken to London in order
to be inspected by a committee of the House of Commons
Rd Jackson mayor having admitted to poll a majority of
illegal votes and by such made a return of two members to
serve in Parliament contrary to the ancient custom of this
city

Members returned { James Clark Satherwaite
                  { Edw Knubley

Petitioners { Jno Christian Curwen esq
            { Wilson Braddyll esqe

All books &ct given in charge to Mr Dobinson as above was
returned safe to the clerk of the trade.

The election of a member to serve in parliament in the year
1788 in the room of the earl of Surrey now call'd to the
upper house on acct of his late father the duke of Norfolk
the candidates were Edw Knubley and Rowland Stephenson
esqs the mayor Jerh Wherlings returned Edw Knubley by
admitting the votes of honorary freemen the ancient freemen
with Rowd Stephenson esq petitioned the honble the House of
Commons of the illegal proceedings and after full hearing
declared that Rowd Stephenson was duly elected and ought
to have been returned.

In consequence of a dissolution of Parliament Mr Jno
Christian Curwen and Wilson Braddyll offer'd to serve this
city in the ensuing Parliament as also did James Clark
Satterthwaite and Edw. Knubley and notwithstanding the
committee of the House of Commons decided twice that

120 THE MERCHANTS' GUILD.

honorary freemen of the city of Carlisle had no right whatever to vote for a member to serve in Parliament yet
R^d Jackson did admit such honorary freemen to vote and by
such returned James Clarke Satterthwaite and Edw. Knubley
duly elected the legal freemen with Messr Curwen and
Braddyll petitioned the hon^ble the House of Commons against
the said return which was ordered to be heard the 22nd March
1791 on which day the under mentioned members were
appointed a committee viz Edward Philips esq chairman
member for Somersetshire

John Nesball	Galton
Captain Henry Burrard	Limmington
John Randall Bird	Thetford
Fra^c Gregor	Cornwall
David Howell	St Michaels
Honble John Sommers Cox	Ryegate
Sr James St Clair Erskine	Morpeth
Honble Henry Hobbert	Norwich
Isaac Hawkins Brown	Bridgenorth
S. W. Coke	Norfolk
Christ^r Hawkins	St Michaels
Sr Wm Montgomery	Peebleshire

Nomminees { Honble Thomas Grenwell for the petitioners
Sr John St Clair for sitting members

House of Commons.
Jovis 3° die martii 1791.

Mr Phillips from the select committee who were appointed to
try and determine the merits of the petition of John Christian
Curwen and Wilson Bradyll esq^rs and also the petition of
severall persons whose names are thereunto subscribed being
freemen of & citizens of the city of Carlisle in the county of
Cumberland and having a right to vote in the election of
citizens to serve in Parliament for the said city severelly com-
plaining of an undue election and return for the said city;
inform'd the house that it appeared to the said select committee that the merits of the petitions did in part depend

upon the right of election and that thereupon the said committee required the council for the several parties to deliver to the clerk of the said committee statements in writing of the right of election for which they respectively contended. That in consequence thereof the said select committee having duly considered the statements and the evidence adduced before them touching the right of election for the said city of Carlisle have determined.

That the right of election of the city of Carlisle in the county of Cumberland is in the freemen of the said city duly admitted and sworn freemen of the said city having been previously admitted brethren of one of the eight guilds or occupations of the said city and deriving their title to said freedom by being sons of freemen or by service of seven years apprenticeship to a freeman resident during such apprenticeship within the said city and in no others

And the said determinations were ordered to be entred on the journals of the house.

That the deputy clerk of the crown do attend forthwith with the last return for the city of Carlisle in the county of Cumberland and amend the same by raising out the names of James Clarke Satterthwaite and Edwʳ Knubley esq. and inserting the names of John Christian Curwen and Wilson Braddyll esqᵉ instead thereof.*

Jovis 12 die martic 1795.

Mʳ Edwʳ James Elliott from the select committee also appointed to try and determine the merits of the petition of Thoˢ Wilson Morley James Paine Robᵗ Murray Edwᵈ Wastell John Richardson Robᵗ Yarker Thoˢ Wyley John White Rich Rowland Jos Yeuwert Ralph Elliott and Jos Brownrigg citizens of the city of Carlisle and also the petition of John Christian Curwen and Wilson Braddyll esqs and also of the petition of the several persons whose names are thereunto subscribed being freemen and citizens of the city of Carlisle in the county of Cumberland and having a

---

* See *ante* p. 38 n.

right to vote in the election of citizens to serve in Parliaments
for the said city respecting the right of election for the said
city inform'd the house that the said select committee have
determined that the right of election for the city of Carlisle
in the county of Cumberland is in the freemen of the said
city having been previously admitted brethren of one of the
eight guilds or occupations of the said city and deriving their
title to such freedom by being sons of freemen or by service
of seven years apprenticeship to a resident during such
apprenticeship within the said city and no other.

And the said determination was ordered to be entred in the
journals of the house

Jovis 12 die martie 1795.

Names of the committee.

Edw. James Elliott	Liskheard.
J. H. Addington	Winchelsea.
James Amyatt	Southampton.
Row^d Burdon	County of Durham.
Franc Greggon	Cornwall.
Charles Pierpoint	Nottingham.
John Osborn	Bedfordsh:
Lord Morpeth	Gloucester.
Morice Robinson	Bourghbridge.
Richd Glover	Penryn.
Marquis Fitchfield	Buckinghamsh:
William Holbeck.	Banbury.

Nominees.

Baldwin for J. C. Curwen & Mr Braddyll.
John Anstruther for W. Morley & others Cockermouth.*

————————

[Quarter   At a public meeting of this fraternity usual notice being
days]   given for the purpose it was unanimously determined to
          depute three persons to meet the same number from each
          guild in order to consult with them on the propriety of

————————

* See *ante* p. 38 n.

fixing the different quarter days on the same day and hour and to report the result of such association and conference at our next quarterly meeting this regulation appearing highly necessary to prevent innovations and attempts that may be made to injure or deprive us of our ancient rights and privileges as freemen when Mr John Patrickson Mr James Ebdell & Mr Robt James were appointed for the above purpose.

St Mich. quarter day Sept 23 1796.

Conformable to the determination of this guild on the 30th of June last we the undersigned with an equal number from each guild assembled at Mrs. Pringles the Grapes Inn Carlisle on Wednesday the 6th of July when it was resolved unanimously to recommend in our respective guilds the necessity of having all our quarterly meetings on the same day & hour and report this conference on our ensuing quarterly day.

Names of those deputed Mr Jno Patrickson
M^r Is Ebdell
M^r P James.

Whereas various attempts have lately been made on this and other guilds to obtain admission to their brotherhood by persons having no claim of title whatever we takeing into our most serious consideration the violence of such proceedings and for the better securing and preserving our rights and privileges as freemen of Carlisle do unanimously agree to the following resolutions

1. We repeal and declare null and void every rule order and institution only so far as respects the days on which we have been accustomed our quarterly meetings and that each meeting will no longer be holden on the said days in the guild.

2. We constitute and appoint our future quarterly meetings to be held on the following days viz the first Wednesday after All Saints Day the first Wednesday after Candlemas Day the first Wednesday after the third day of May the first Wednesday after Lammas Day.

3. We repeal and declare null and void every rule order and institution so far only as respects the notice given for meetings or assembling in the said guild and in future order and direct that twenty four hours notice shall be given to every brother or left at his place of abode within the liberties of the city of Carlisle or at usual distance before assembling in the said guild all which meetings meet during the day.

Moiety of the seal of the statute merchant of Carlisle, formerly kept by the town clerk.

Chapter VI.

THE WEAVERS' GUILD.

The books of the weavers' guild are five in number.

1. Is a paper book, bound in vellum, 11½ inches high and 8 broad. It begins in 1679 and ends in 1714. On the title is in old English lettering—

> The Register booke bel
> ing to the Weavers
> the Cittie of Carlisle
> Hic liber incipiebat octavo
> die mensis Nouemberi
> vicessimo tertio anno Car
> Regis anno d͠no 1647
> Gulælmus Atkinson Notarius Publicus
> clicus guilde Texatorum
> Sola salus servire Deo
> Mihi Christus omnia.

It begins with a list of the fraternity dated 8th Nov., 1647.

2. Is a paper book, same size as No. 1. It begins with 1716 and ends with 1784, and has a great many blank leaves.

3. Begins 1749.

4. Is 14½ inches high, paper, marked outside—

> Weavers guild
> 1825

It commences—

> " Mr William Dobinson in account with the weavers guild"
> 1824

5. A book of admissions.

1, 2, 3, and 5 were long missing, and were supposed to be buried in Mr. Dobinson's office, where a search was made, but ultimately they turned up in the house of some old freeman of the guild, and have been restored to the clerk.

The quarter days of the weavers' guild are Allhallows, Candlemas, Saint Elline (Helen), and Lammas. An account of their plate will be found in the appendix to *Old Church Plate in the Diocese of Carlisle*, R. S. Ferguson, (Chas. Thurnam & Sons, Carlisle). It consists of a silver beaker of Dutch work, and of a tall two-eared cup, given by John Christian Curwen. They also possess a huge punch bowl marked "Success to the Weavers' Guild," and a couple of wooden toddy ladles.

The list of members given in the oldest book, under date 8th Nov., 1647, is headed by Mr. John Aglionby, the man who was so conspicuous in local history on the loyalist side : he is the only one honoured as *Mr.* Among the names occur the local names of Bell, Gibson, Robinson, Blacklock, Pattinson, Wilson, Warwick, Studholme, &c. In 1659 the guild numbered twenty-five members, apart from eight more called country members. In 1678 it had forty, in addition to twelve styled governors, who constituted the ruling body. The names of Highead, Asmotherly, and Stubbs now appear on the roll. Colonel Gledhill, who contested Carlisle in 1710, was admitted a member in September of that year, and is recorded to have given "one large silver bowl, carved, and one silver chalice, carved"; but this does not correspond with the list of their plate in 1731, viz., "one cup and silver salver." Dr. Tho. Tullie, dean of Ripon, was a member of this guild. In 1764 the Hon. Raby Vane, Gov. Stanwix, Sir James Lowther, Mr. Dobinson, Captain Carlyle, Rev. E. Coulthard, and Alderman Hodgson appear on the roll.

The guild now [1886] is very small in numbers, consisting mainly of two names—Stubbs and another.

Orders provisions & constitutions concerning the good
government profit and advantages of the weavers trade
belonging to the city of Carlisle revised and confirmed
by the fraternity of weavers aforesaid the 5th day of
May anno dom 1679.

1. That every brother of the said trade shall be true and faithful
    one to another for upholding of their trade and craft that
    none doe disclose their counsells and consultations upon paine
    of 6^s 8^d for every persons offence proof being made thereof
    by one or more wittnesses before the company or occupation
    or the major part of them.

2. That noe brother of this company shall doe any work to any
    outman upon paine of 6^s 8^d.

3. That noe brother shall sue another in any court untill they
    haue first acquainted the masters or governors of this trade
    therewith or the major part of them.

4. That if any brother of this trade do trouble chide or slander
    another brother publickly or privately he shall forfeit
    3^s 4^d for every default if the same be made or appear to the
    said governors or the major part of them in the guild chamber
    before the said trade.

5. That noe brother shall take an apprentice for any tearm than
    seven years and the eight a hireman And that the said master
    shall not take another apprentice till five years after inrolment
    of his indenture upon pain of 20^s

6. That no brother shall take another's brothers servant to work
    unless the former master had fourteen days warning upon
    pain of 3^s 4^d.

7. That no brother of this occupation shall forestall work or
    ingross the same to himself as it is coming to the city upon
    pain of 13^s 4^d for every default proof being made thereof
    by one or more witnesses before the masters or the major part
    of them.

8. That all brothers of this occupation upon lawful warning and
    living within the city shall attend the corps of any brother
    or brother's wife or brother's child to the grave upon pain of
    6 pence.

9. That if any brother shall absent himself from the quarter
    day having lawful warning shall forfeit for every default six-
    pence.

10. That if any brother keep any worksmen not able and ex-
    perienced in work he shall forfeit 3^s 4^d if the insufficiency of
    such workmen be made appear to the masters of the said
    trade.

11. That all indentures be drawn by the clark of the trade in
    parchment & inrolled in the book before the trade in the
    guild chamber the next quarter day after the sealing of the
    indentures upon pain of 3^s 4^d for every default.

12. That no brother shall take an apprentice with intent to sell
    him again or make advantage thereof or put him away under
    any colour or pretence whereof the trade may be damnified
    upon pain of 20 shillings.

13. There shall be yearly two under masters of this trade who
    shall be accountable to the trade for all money by them
    received or disbursed for the use of the said trade which
    account shall be made at Lammas quarter yearly & new
    masters then to be chosen in their room upon pain of 6^s 8^d.

14. That no brother of this trade shall put his apprentice to any
    outman upon pain of twenty shillings.

15. That no brother of this trade shall lend any work gear to
    any outman upon pain of 5^s 4^d.

16. That if any brother shall take work in hand which he cannot
    get done in reasonable and convenient time : and therefore
    restore the work to the right owner they being clamorous and
    raileing for it if any other brother shall work the same after-
    wards without lycence of the former brother that had it he
    shall forfeit 3^s & 4^d for every such default.

17. It is ordered that no brother of this occupation shall under-
    value the trade by taking less rates for work than hath been
    used upon pain of 3^s 4^d.

18. That no out man come within the libertys of the city and
    take any work upon pain of £1 6^s 8^d.

19. That all matters and controversies concerning the trade and the benefit and good government thereof shall be ordered & determined by the trade and who refuses to submit to their orders or the major part of them shall forfeit twenty shillings.

May 4th 20. It is ordered that no brother of this trade who is a
1685 freemen and unmarried shall take an apprentice unless he pay a fine to the trade before the inrolement of the indentures (vizt' 5ˢ if the said brother live within the city and tenn shillings if he live without the liberties of the city. And those fines to be paid for every apprentice that they shall so take : And if the brother live within the liberties and be married he shall pay but five shillings for every apprentice he takes and these fines to be paid without any abatement.

21. It is also ordered that if any brother present at any meeting in the guild chamber shall depart before the business be dispatched not having leave from the fours of the trade or the major part of them he shall forfeit 3ˢ 4ᵈ for every default.

22. It is ordered that if any apprentice to any brother of this trade shall depart from his masters service before his term be expired no brother of this trade shall employ him or gett on work any such apprentice without leave from the trade upon pain of twenty shillings for every default.

THE UNDER MASTERS OATH.

You shall well and truely execute the office of undermaster you shall give notice within the libertys of this city twenty four hours before to every brother of the company every quarter day and upon all other necessary meetings you shall well and faithfully make a just and true account of all amerciaments and other money which shall come to your hands at Candlemas quarter day as usual all which you shall well and faithfully perform so help you God.

THE OATH OF A FOUR.*

You shall swear to be a true and faithfull four or warden of the company and brotherhood of weavers and uphold maintain

---

* *Ante* p. 126, and *infra* p. 132, n.

K

and keep all our antient orders and constitutions belonging to
the company all faults presentments and controversies which
shall come before you at anytime to be determined you shall
to the best of your judgement determine the same you shall
give your due attendance in our chamber every quarter day
and at all other times when lawful notice shall be given for
the said company to meet and consult for the good and benefit
of the company and brotherhood these and all other things
belonging to a four or warden you shall well and faithfully
observe to doe and perform to the best of your knowledge and
skill so help you God.

THE OATH OF A BROTHER.

You shall swear to be a true brother of the weavers company
true and obedient to the fours observe all orders and constitutions of this trade diligent and forward to the utmost of your
power defend and maintain all our antient rights and privileges
belonging to the same trade being lawfull you shall duely and
truely observe your quarterly meetings or pay a penalty of
6^d for each omission and pay all quarterly groats you shall
keep secret your private conferences & your meetings they
being honest and lawful all these whatsoever else belonging
to a true brother of this trade you shall faithfully perform to
the best of your power so help you God.

THE OATH OF A CLERK.

You shall well and truly execute the office of clerk to the
fraternity of weavers you shall be diligent and impartial in
keeping a perfect book of their proceedings and at all times
be ready to produce your book and appear yourself upon
proper notice you shall likewise be diligent in demanding all
fines and amerciaments that shall be due without favour or
affection these and all other things belonging to a clerk you
shall faithfully execute to the best of your skill so help you
God.

MISCELLANEOUS ORDERS.

1659 Thomas Barne of Tarraby ordered to pay 40^s and to
enter into a bond not to practice as a weaver within 7 miles of
Carlisle or be proceeded against by information according to law.

May 7 1677.

At this quarter day it is agreed that the Assention day called Allballows Thursday be from henceforth observed by this occupation and an entertaint or treatment provided at ye charge of ye occupation & that the Candlemas quarter day be from henceforth observed by all ye brothers of this trade and that it shall be first kept at ye house of ye senior of this trade & if any senior shall refuse it then the next to him in the call shall provide an entertainment for ye trade and so to goe by turnes.

Nov 8th 1697   At this quarter day it is ordered in the guild that Mr Jos Read write a petition or letter about the stopping of the sd weavers from bringing woollen and linen yarne to be wrought at Carlisle or places adjacent & soe to be returned after made into cloth. *

March y^e 20 173$\frac{1}{2}$ The day abovesd. the company having met together both brothers in city & some brothers in the county and have ordered and agreed that processes shall be sent out against George Cook and Jeremiah Chapman and that they shall be summoned against Easter sessions for keeping looms going within the city and have given them notice to defend themselves   It is therefore agreed that the sd 2 persons shall be prevented according to law and that there shall be a general collection made next quarter day to defend suit against them   And that John Matthews and John Mackwell be likewise prosecuted and all those who can be informed against who doe follow such illegal practice ag^t the rights and property of this fraternity of weavers.†

Aug 5 1731   The day & year abovesd Mr Randolph Losh one of our brothers being an antient man desired to be discharged from appearing any more in this guild for reason the sd Randolph Losh hath paid to the trade the sum of five shillings for which sum the trade unanimously agreed that he might have his liberty to appear no more in our sd guild.

---

* It does not appear who or what stopped the sd weavers.

† There is no further note of what was done in the matter of these prosecutions; the four persons threatened do not appear to have paid any composition to the guild or to have joined, so it is probable they shifted themselves and their looms out of the guild's jurisdiction.

May 6th 1745

It is ordered and agreed by and with the consent of the four and the whole fraternity that every brother's treat or the crown given for that purpose shall be drunk in the publick guild and not out of it and that the money so received shall be laid out for drink at brothers houses who keep alehouses equall in share as formerly.

February 26 1745/6 The day and year above written by the worshipful mayor or his deputy it was order⁴ and agree⁴ that all our company of weavers should meet in our guildhall to attend his highnes the duke of Cumberland so far as our freeledge goes without the Scotch gates and to heaue our colours flying before the company & to haue illuminations for the same at night.

Nov 1768 All saints quarter day at the guild A dispute arose amongst the fraternity whether their should be any more fours made amongst them or not and also whether the fraternity should be governed by the fours for the future or by a majority upon a pole was caled for and it stud as under

For the fours   Against the fours

13   16   *

The books of this guild contain a complete set of resolutions as to the mushroom elections, and the fixing of quarter days, similar to those passed by the merchants, &c., pp. 117–124. The later entries present little of interest.

---

* The ancient method of governing the society was by 12 governors: fours first occur about 1735.

Chapter VII.

THE SMITHS' GUILD.

The books of the smiths' guild are three in number, viz. :—

I.   A book which commences in 1819, and contains the minutes at one end and the accounts at the other.   It also contains the oaths of office, copied from No. III, and a table of fees.

II.   An index to the members, commencing in June, 1786.

III.   A small book containing the rules and oaths, evidently a copy from an older book.

No minute book prior to 1819 can at present be found.

These books are very dry and give but little information. From No. II we have made the following analysis of the principal names of members between 1786 and the present day :—6 Armstrongs, 3 Blamires, 15 Coulthards, 3 Cleggs, 3 Carnabys, 1 Donald, 10 Dixons, 1 Ebdell, 18 Gills, 2 Graysons, 1 Harrington (an M.D., a well known physician in Paternoster Row, Carlisle), 2 Holmeses, 1 Halton, 1 Hodgson, 7 Hinds, 6 Jacksons, 1 Longcake, 1 Lawson, 11 Lowrys, 1 Monkhouse, 1 Nevison, 2 Nicolsons, 1 Peel, 9 Parkins, 10 Robinsons, 1 Richardson, 1 Rowland, 1 Stephenson, 2 Sowerbys, 1 Simpson, 9 Senhouses, 1 Taylor, 1 Watson, 14 Waleses, 9 Wilsons.   Among the Senhouses we find Humphrey Senhouse, son of Humphrey, admitted Jan. 16, 1796 ; Samson Senhouse and Humphrey Fleming Senhouse, sons of late William Senhouse, admitted

Oct. 3, 1808 ; Edward Hooper Senhouse, of Watford, and James Lowther Senhouse, sons of late William, May 23, 1820 ; Jos. Ashby Senhouse, of Hensingham, and Michael le Fleming Senhouse, of London, son of Sir Joseph Senhouse, May 24, 1820.

The blacksmiths' plate consists of three silver cups, described in the appendix to *Old Church Plate in the Diocese of Carlisle* (Carlisle : C. Thurnam & Sons), namely, one presented by John Robinson to the company of smiths in 1742, another presented by Humphrey Senhouse of Netherhall, alderman of Carlisle, in 1760, and one by John Christian Curwen in 1874.

The quarter days are, Friday after St. Helen's Day, Lammas Day, All Saints, and St. Blase's Day (Feb. 3).

The occupation, as appears by the oath of a brother, includes the trade and mystery of a blacksmith, whitesmith, silversmith, or goldsmith, and by the old indentures of apprenticeship apprentices were bound to "the trade faculty mistery & occupation of a blacksmith whitesmith & goldsmith." By the 2nd article or rule, it will be seen the craft covered anything made "in the hammary way."

The accounts present nothing of interest: they paid a cullery rent of 1s. to the corporation for their chamber in the guildhall, and they received annually from the chamberlain £1 : 2s. 6d., the original 2s. 6d. paid to each guild, plus the additional pound subsequently added. They spent £6 or £8 over the feasting on Ascension Day, which dwindles to 10s. 6d. in 1872, and then the entries cease.

Since the Municipal Corporation Reform Act the admissions are few, and the last, of William Gill, was in 1867.

> Articles orders and constitutions plainly honest and brotherly agreed upon by the full consent and summon of the mayor of this antient city of carlisle to the blacksmiths dwelling and living within the liberties of the said city for good order and to the pleasure of Almighty God and for the maintaining

and upholding of the occupation in ye aforesaid city according to antient grants this 18th day of February 1562 in the 5th year of Queen Elizabeth.

> Jos. Hinde, clerk
> Jos. Clerk & John Barnes
> Undermasters.

Art 1. It is ordered and agreed upon that every one of the aforesaid occupation of smiths and hammerers shall at all times and time from henceforth be brotherly friendly loving helping aiding and assisting one to each in all things honestly godly and civil.

Artic. 2. Also it is ordered by the general consent of the aforesaid occupation that no Francis forringer* nor × . man shall at any time hereafter set up use or practise the aforesaid crafts and misteries or that makes locks or are smiths spurriers cutlers or any thing in the hammary way or any of them : in the aforesaid city liberties of the same untill such time as he has agreed with the said occupation and have paid his fine therefore upon pain of forfeiture of 6^s & 8^d to be taken of every person offending therein And as often as it appears or shall taking and proved to be guilty of the same.†

Article 3

Also it is ordered that no brother of any of the aforesaid occupation shall at anytime suffer any forener or stranger to take an heat in his furnace or fire upon pain of forfiture of sixpence to be taken of the master and ouner of the shopp where the offence is don and as often as he offends therein and the same to be employed to the use of the occupation.

Article 4.

Also it is agreed upon that none of the aforesaid occupation shall take any apprentice within the space of six years and for lesser term than seven years. And every apprentice which they or any of them shall take shall pay sixpence to the occupation. And if he be not able to pay the same then his master shall pay it for him at the next quarter day of their occupation after he hath taken him at

---

* Francis, or Frenchy. Frenchman included all who spoke an unknown tongue. The blank, no doubt, is Scotsman.

† The wording of this rule is most confused, though the drift of it is pretty clear.

which time also he shall shew unto the trade the indenture of his said apprentice and shall cause his name to be enroll'd in the books of this occupation.

5.

Also that tis condescended and agreed upon that no person or persons of the aforesaid occupation shall at any time hereafter set on to work or suffer to work with him any other mans apprentice or servant without license of his own master upon pain of forfiture of 10/ˢ for every offence known and proved to be employ'd to the use of the occupation.

6.

Also that tis ordered that no person or persons belonging to any of the aforesaid misterys crafts or occupation shall at any time hereafter exercise or use any of the other crafts or occupations of this city but only that which he hath and doth profess and was an apprentice unto or shall n t use meddle with or sell any wares or stuff belonging to any other of the trades of the city but such as belongs to his own occupation only : upon pain of forfiture of 6^d for every default known and prov'd.

7.

Also that tis agreed upon that no person or persons of any of the aforesaid crafts or occupations shall at any time from henceforth entice or draw away by any sinister means any customer or customers of any of his brethreren of this occupation whose work his said brother hath had a long time before upon paine of forfeiture of 6/8 to be taken without favour of them which shall be proved to offend therein for every default.

8 order.

Also that tis agreed that if that it shall by chance at any time here-after that any man being expert or skillfull in any of the aforesaid occupations do come to this city and require work of any brother of that occupation which he his of then it shall be lawful for him so required to set him on work for the space of twelve or fourteen days the clerk of the trade and most eminent of the occupation made privy thereunto before.

9 order.

Also that tis agreed upon by consent of all the whole occupation aforesaid that if by fortune that any dissention disturbance controversy or debate do fall between any person bretheren and free of the same trade wherby any suit or tryall in law might come then the party which shall find themselves agrived or to have wrong done them shall immediately make their complaint to the occupation and require reformation and not take suit therefore untill the fraternity had first had the assuring thereof for the avoiding of slander & further inconvenience which thereof might ensue.

The 10th order.

Also that tis agreed upon that no person nor persons being free of any of the aforesaid occupation their servants or apprentices shall at any time fight brawl quarrell scold chide or rale one with another and especially at their meetings upon their quarter days or other times nor undecently behave themselves in words deeds nor countenance quarrelling amongst any of their bretheren but the peace shall keep and use an honest and civil order and behaviour towards one another upon forfeiting and paying three shillings & fourpence to be taken of every person offending therein as often as they shall be known and proved to offend.

The 11th order.

Also that tis ordered that whenever any of the aforesaid occupation shall know understand or learn that any servant or apprentice of this occupation hath done any notorious mischief or that shall unskillfully or wrongfully waste or spoil any of his said master's goods he shall forfeit 6^s & 6^d as often as it shall be proved and made known to the occupation And if the apprentice refuses payment then to loose the advantage of taking up his brotherhood.

The 12th order.

that tis agreed upon that all and every person & persons belonging to any of the aforesaid occupation and being ffree of the same shall at all times hereafter have quarter days which are appointed for meeting of the occupation as follows that is to day Friday after St Hellens Day Lamas Day All Saints Day & St Blase Day and whosoever shall neglet appearing on these days aforesaid or any other time being lawfully summoned by the undermaster or servant shall forfeit 6^d unless they be sick or have some other lawfull excuse.

the 13 order.

Also that tis ordered that all and every person or persons belonging to the guild of the s^d occupation of smiths shall at any time here-

after disclose make known and discover any of the secrets of the said occupation or such things as shall be said or done amongst them at their quarter days or other meetings shall forfeit 3ˢ/4ᵈ to be taken of every person or brother of yᵉ trade for every default that they do.

the 14 order.

Also that it is freely agreed upon that no person or persons of any of the aforesaid occupation shall at any time hereafter buy any wares goods or tools of any unknown person or of those of evil fame upon pain of forfiture.

the 15 order.

Also that it is order'd that whensoever that it shall please Almighty God to call unto his mercy out of this transitory life any brother of yᵉ aforesaid occupation their wife child or apprentice then every brother of the occupation having his health shall give his attendance and accompany the corps to the church in a decent manner for conscience sake and whosoever shall be absent being lawfully warn'd by the under masters or servant of the occupation unless he can give a good reasonable and sufficient cause of excuse he shall pay 6ᵈ for every time that he doth offend therein.

the 16ᵗʰ order.

Also tis agreed upon that whensoever any brother of the occupation shall dye and depart out of this life shall not leave goods sufficient wherewith to bring him forth and discharge his funeral expenses then he shall be brought decently forth upon the costs and charges of the occupation.

The company of smiths hath had time beyond memory a power of making by laws for the good government of their occupation provided they are agreable to the laws of the land It was therefore order'd and agreed upon in the year 1620 that no brother should work upon any of the grandfeasts or holydays on forfeit of

3/4.

July 29ᵗʰ 1691.

It is ordered by us the mayor aldermen bailiffs and citizens of the said city that for the future no fraternity guild or company of this city do receive or admitt any person or persons to be a brother of their respective guilds or companys without the consent of the majority of such brothers of the said trade or company as do actually exercise the said trade except such as have been apprentices and only served their time according to law or are the sons of brothers of the same company upon pain that every person that shall at any time hereafter be made a brother of any trade or company of this city in other manner as aforesaid shall be dis-franchised and disabled from using the said trade or having the benefitt of any such trade as he or they shall so be made brother or brothers of.*

September 21 1696.

The order aforesaid was then taken into further consideration and confirm'd by yᵉ corporation And it is further order'd that no free-man of this corporation who inhabits without the liberties of this city shall be allowed to take any apprentice while such freeman continues to inhabit and dwell without the liberties of the said city aforesaid upon paine that such apprentice shall pay all tolls dues and duties to the corporation as persons not free of the city aforesaid and that every trade or company have a copy of this order.

Sept 21 1696.

Also that tis orderd that whensoever any of the aforesaid occupation that knowe understand or lern that any servant apprentice or under-master of this occupation hath done any mischief or that unskilfully or wrongfully waste or spoil or neglect is business in the place he fills he shall forfeit 6ˢ & 6ᵈ as often as it shall be proved and made known to the occupation and if any of the aforesaid offenders refuse payment then to loose the advantage of their brotherhood and the privilidge of the guild unto their debts and arrears are paid.†

---

* This order and the next order are orders of the town council, not of the guild, but they have been copied into the minute book of the guild ; they point to some difficulty between the guilds and the council, about making freemen, who were not properly qualified, to the lessening of the city's revenue from tolls. See the *ex gratia* oath *infra* p. 140.

† This is in a different handwriting to the foregoing.

A BROTHER'S OATH.

You shall sware that you will × × and truely use and occupy
the trade and mistery of a blacksmith whitesmith silversmith or
goldsmith without any manner of fraudelent or deceitfull dealings
and perform all that which you are bound to by your indentures.

You shall keep all things secret such as ought to be kept which are
spoken or done among your brethren of the same trade.

You shall also observe and keep all such articles and orders as are
already made or that hereafter honestly shall be made for the benefitt
and profitt of the same occupation or trade you shall not bring in
your name any other person by your means or procurement to use
the same otherwise then for your own use you shall also use true
weights both in buying and selling you shall maintain and defend
the said occupation and all things profitable for the same you shall
not know of any thing that is hurtfull to the same trade but to the
utmost of your power shall endeavour to lett and hinder the same or
make knowing whereby it may be prevented All these things and
what else belonging to a brother of this trade you shall well and
truly keep observe and fullfill to the utmost of your power So help
you God.

AN EXGRATIA OR EXONERARY OATH.*

Whereas the antient fraternity of blacksmiths whitesmiths silversmiths or goldsmiths of this city hath thought fitt to make you a
brother for and during your natural life you behaving according to
the rules and customs of their occupations.

You shall therefor sware truly to observe and keep all such articles
and orders as are already made for ye benefitt and profit of this
occupacon or trade.

You shall also sware truly to keep all things secret such as ought to
be kept which may be spoke or done among bretheren of this trade
when assembled in their chamber.

---

* The existence of this special oath shows that the "ancient and ingenious
society" had a habit of making ex gratia brothers : these they bound by oath,
not to prejudice the society, and left them to arrange other matters with the
town council. The "ancient and ingenious" probably found this pay, and this
oath should be read as a gloss on the orders of the town council of July 1691
and September 1696, ante p. 139.

You shall sware that you will not bring or set up (by yours means or procurement) any persons in your name to use practise or follow the said trade so as to damage any brother of this ancient and ingenious society and you shall truly maintain and defend the said occupation in all things profitable for the same.

You shall not know of anything that is hurtful to this trade but to the utmost of your power shall hinder the same and also make it known to this company that they may cause their endeavour to prevent it.

All thes things and what else belonging to a brother of this trade you shall well and truly keep fullfil and observe to the utmost of your power so help you God.

CLERK'S OATH.

You shall sware that you will well and truly execute the office of clerk of this company or fraternity of smiths you shall or cause to be drawn all indentures between masters and apprentices according to the form of the statute in that behalf made you shall keep secret all councils and matters relating to the good and benefitt of the said trade and to the utmost of your ability and power shall keep and observe all lawfull and wholesome constitutions and orders already made or hereafter to be made for the good rule and government of this occupation.

All these things & what other matters appertains to the clerk or a brother of this fraternity you shall observe and keep to the best of your power and knowledge So help you God.

UNDERMASTERS OATH.

You shall sware that to the best of your knowledge you will wel and truly execute the office of undermasters of this trade and occupation of smiths and give a true account to the trade of all monies by you received or disbursed for the trade use when thereunto lawfully required and make true payments of what shall happen to rest due to the occupation all these things and what else relaits to the office aforesaid you and either of you shall well and truly perform and execute to the best of your skill and knowledge so help you God.

A table of fees belonging to the smith company.

For the admission of a brother £1 „ 1.

The new brother has also to pay as below before taking the oath.

Whatever his father may be in debt to the company.   For the company's entertainment if upon a quarter day 5/ˢ at any other time 10,ˢ

To the clerk if admitted on a quarter day 1ˢ on any other day 2ˢ

To the undermaster for warning the brothers if it is not upon a quarter day 1 . 0*

1820.   Lammas qʳ·   The clerk reports that at Aug 2 the close of the late election he lodged in the banks of Messr Forster & Co on an interest check the sum of £50 being the principal part of the money then in his hand : it is ordered by the company that they approve of what he has done and the check remain in his hand.†

1821.   St Helen qʳ·   It having been reported May 9 to this guild that the corporation have let to Mʳ Studholme the race course at Kingmoor it is ordered that the clerk in conjunction with the clerks of the other companies waite upon the corporation to have it explained.‡

---

* This table is from the book dated 1820 : as the vote for Carlisle was a valuable possession, the guilds easily screwed out of a new brother all his father's arrears and debts, as well as his own fees. As a matter of fact, one or other of the candidates for the representation of Carlisle generally paid them, as also the new brother's travelling expenses, if he came from a distance. The new brother, if a non-trader, generally declined, after admission, to pay any annual fees to the guild, who patiently awaited their time until his sons came up for brotherhood.

† See the last note : a large number of brothers were always admitted immediately before and during an election.

‡ The people who got possession in the manner described, *ante* p. 118 n, ultimately enclosed the race course on Kingmoor ; some ardent freemen went and broke the fences and held the annual race, and out of this arose the assize trial of *Ismay v. Barnes*, tried at Carlisle in 1865, when the freemen lost their case, and the time honoured holiday of Kingmoor races came to an end.

CHAPTER VIII.

THE TAILORS' GUILD.

The records of this guild consist of a manuscript volume whose leaves are 11¾ inches high. It has been formed by binding into one volume, at no very remote period, the leaves of two or three older volumes, with a large addition of modern paper, so as to swell the thickness to 1¼ inch, the modern paper forming about one half of the bulk. A great many modern leaves have been cut out at the end of the book. The first page is headed

"The ffoure wardens of this occupacon theire names with the rest of the occupacon names

	Wlm Moresby	John Hodgson
	Alexander Stagg	Robert James
	Thomas Pearson	Edward Blacklock
	George Martine	Thomas Hudson
		Marmaduke Mandyn
		mort Lancellot Vartie
	Robert Sanderson	Robert Thomlinson 1659
	John Blacklock	
	Roger James	
	William Carlile	
	Richard Hudson mort	I John Bell doe prmis
	Robert Willson	to pay yearly to ye
	John Brathwht	fraternity of tailors ye
mort	William Johnston	sum of 2ᵈ and my
	Christopher Raskell	proportion for the ex-
	Thomas Hewatson	pense upon ascension
	Robert Scott	day for the wardⁿˢ
	Henery Clemetson	kindnes in takeing off
	Thomas Tomson	all my fines due since
	Thomas × × ×	my goeing to London
	Thomas Kidd	to this day
	William Stagg	ye 14 1697
	Anthony Craister	John Bell
	Thomas Craggell	Witness
	John Guy	ffrancis Backhouse
	George Rigg	Geo Brathway
		clerk

The above list is not all of one date, the names after Anthony Craister being subsequent additions, as also the word "mort" where it occurs. This guild appears to have been comparatively poor and unimportant; few of the local great men appear to have joined; many of the members are marksmen, and even the clerks, to judge from their handwriting and spelling, were very ill educated men; thus Stephen Watson, sworn as clerk in 1783, writes "cam in to gill, and produced one in Dentur," for "came into guild and produced one indenture."

Another call roll will be found among the miscellaneous entries relating to this guild. Their plate consists of three silver cups of various sizes and a small tumbler, all described in the appendix to *Old Church Plate in the Diocese of Carlisle.* The tumbler was given by Edward Tate in 1711, in which year also Leonard Proctor gave one of the cups. Another cup has on it

In gratitude to ye fraternity of merch^t taylors in Carlisle by
    Mrs Katherine Eglisfield 4 July 1701.

Legend says, for the book is silent, and she cannot be found in the local parochial registers, that Mrs. Eglisfield was a stay maker, with whose trade the guild were too generous to interfere. The other cup is one of the John Christian Curwen cups.[*] All this plate has been frequently pawned, and has been much misused; a pair of candlesticks are said to have been pawned and never to have been redeemed; they can hardly have been silver, or the book would have recorded them, as the silver articles are frequently specified in detail when passing from one official's custody to that of another. In 1670, prior to the acquisition of any silver plate, the articles handed by the under masters to their successors are described as "i Taffity colour ribons staffe and staffehead."

Their quarter days were Tuesday after S. Thomas day, Christmas Tuesday after Lady day, Tuesday after Midsummer day, and Tuesday after Michaelmas day.

---

[*] *Ante* p. 89.

ORDERS.

Orders of the trade entered out of the old booke the 5th January 1659. ffirste it is ordered and appointed that every man of the whole occupation shall be true and faithful to one another on the 12th day of September 1558.

Also it is ordered and appointed by the said occupacon that the tow ould maisters shall make there accounts between St Thomas day in Christenmass and the quarter day ffollowinge which is upon the 3 of January if it doe not fall on the Sabbath day and to be delivered in there chamber before the whole occupacon which occupacon is to appoint two other vnder maisters Euery mᵉ soe chosen shall accept thereof upon paine of viˢ viijᵈ

Alsoe It is ordered and appointed by the said occupacon that every man of the whole occupacon shall be true and faithful and all secrets and cousels shall keep to himselfe for if he doe not the same and it be proved one him he shall pay to the occupacon 3ˢ 4ᵈ for a forfeit without favour.

THE OATH OF A BROTHER WHEN HE IS ADMITTED.

ffirst you shall sweare that you shalbe true and faithful to the occupacon all secrets and counsells you shall keep. you shall know nothinge prejudicicill to this occupacon but you shall make or give warninge to the maisters or one of the 4 wardens. 2nd you shall obey all comandmants of the guild maisters or wardens for the time beinge that be lawful you shalbe deligent to all meetings for the behoofe or wealth of the said occupacon soe help you god and the contents of this book.

The 31 October 1608 Michallmas quarter day.

It is ordered and agreed upon by the consent of the whole occupacon that noe man shall sett any man to worke butt if they doe then the persons who shall doe the same shall hire the said person for one whole yeare and likewise they that shall hire any of the said persons shall make the foure wardens privid to the same before they sett them on worke upon pain of euery weeke to pay to the occupacon 3ˢ 4ᵈ and the maisters to answer quarterly for their persons soe hired 8ᵈ to the occupacõn

Also it is ordered and appointed by yᵉ said occupacõn that euery man and woeman that is widdowes of yᵉ abouesaid light* shall pay quarterly to yᵉ said occupacon iᵈ·

Also it is ordained and appointed by yᵉ said occupacon that noe ffreeman of this occupacon nor freeman's son set up shopp without license of yᵉ 4 wardens vpon paine of viᵈ for each offence.

Also it is ordered by yᵉ consent of yᵉ whole occupacon that when any wife child or apprentice of the occupacon shall deccase yᵗ each brother of yᵉ said fraternity shall either goe with yᵉ corps to church or send one of his house vpon paine of viᵈ

Also it is ordered by yᵉ whole fraternity that none shall be made free of this society without yᵉ consent of yᵉ whole occupacõn each person yᵗ is brothered in shall pay for his birgah† xiiᵈ and each person yᵗ served his apprentice to pay a year viˢ viiiᵈ

Also it is ordered yᵗ noe brother of this trade set any fforreiners on work without license of iiii warders and two vndermaisters vpon paine of viᵈ each offence.

Also its ordained and appointed that none of yᵉ occupacon shall take any apprentice vnder vii years and yᵉ viii year hireman by indenture vpon paine of xxˢ

Also it is ordered by yᵉ whole occupacon that none shall make their indentures between him and his apprentice but the clerk of yᵉ trade onely : and that yᵉ said indentures shall be

---

* The term "light," as a name for the guild, evidently comes from the religious side of the guild. See the two rules on p. 147, and several other instances. The two words " man and " in this rule must be inserted in the original by mistake.

† This word occurs in various places in this guild's book, as " birage," " burradge," &c. Does it mean " burgage," a fee for admission as a burgess, or has it something to do with beer ? The words " a year " mean " within a year," see a subsequent rule, and the admission of Matthew Wilkinson : payment was made by 20s. a quarter, pp. 149 & 155.

publiquely read to the whole occupacon ye first quarter day they are made and every maister that offends herein shall pay to ye trade ———.*

Also it is ordered by ye occupacon that noe brother of this society shall take law agst another brother untill first acquaint ye 4 wardens or some of them upon paine of xii^d each offence and if ye 4 wardens cannot agree them then to tak as many as they think fitt of ye said occupacon and to order it between them which said plaintif and defendant are to stand to and abide there arbitration (if ye debt or trespass be under xx^s) upon paine of vi^s viii^d each person y^t is refractory to their order.

Also it is ordered that none shall giue euill language to ye undermaisters when they are distreineing for any amercem^{ts} or forfitures upon paine of vi^d each offence.

Also it is ordered that noe brother of this occupacon his servant or apprentice shall work openly in his shopp door or window upon any holiday upon paine of vi^d each offence.

Also it is ordered that when any brother or brothers wife of this occupacon deceases that haue ye whole light with ye banner ye son or daughter to haue half light with ye banner and ye apprentice a third of ye light with ye banner and to carry them where ye maister appoints to ye church upon warneing by ye undermaister upon paine of vi^d each offender toties quoties.†

Also it is ordained and appointed by ye said occupacon that upon Corpus Christi days as old use or custome before time the whole light with ye whole occupacon and banner be in g^t Maries church yard at ye ash tree at 10 of ye clock in ye forenoon and he y^t comes not before ye banner be raised to come away pay vi^d each offender toties quoties.‡

---

* Left blank.

† This is crossed out, as if obsolete, as it would become after the Reformation.

‡ This is a most interesting entry, and carries us back to the pre-Reformation Corpus Christi procession in Carlisle. Great Mary's church would be the parish church in the cathedral nave, and its churchyard is now known as S. Mary's burial ground.

Also it is ordered that no Scottes taylor shall work within this cittie nor carry out any work without license of ye occupacon upon paine of iii^s iiii^d each offence.

Also it is ordered by ye said occupacon that none shall make any debate nor strife one with another nor gine any euill language in words nor scoff or brawl one with another nor thump upon ye table but that each shall carry himself decently toward his senior and superiors upon paine of xiii^s & viij^d for each offence to be taken without favour.

Also it is ordered by each occupacon that there shall be foure quarter days in each year to meet at our guildhall or chamber which daies are as follows Tuesday after St Thomas day in Christs Tuesday after Ladyday Tuesday after Mid summer day and Tuesday after Michaelmas day and that ye under-masters or their deputy give warneing to ye severall members of this society the eve before every quarter day or leave word at their dwelling each under maister neglecting his duty to pay iii^s & iiij^d and each brother that does not meet at one of ye clock each quarter day except hindered by sickness to pay vi^d for each offence.

Also it is ordered by the sd occupacon that no brother shall take an apprentice before his last apprentice haue served fiue years without license of ye iiii wardens upon paine of xx^s.

Also it is ordered by said occupacon yt noe brother shall imploy or lett any scotch man work as jorneyman but shall for euery offence pay to this occupacon ye sum of iii^s & iiij^d with-out favour.

Also it is ordered by ye whole occupacon that there shalbe chosen iiij of ye occupacon to be iiij wardens dureing their naturall life for ye welth of ye said occupacon and further it is agreed ye book what ye iiij wardens does and makes an end of whatsoever it be yt so be ended and done by all ye occupacons and further if there be any man yt findeth any fault with the aforesaid wardens without juste cause he shall pay for his aforesaid fault and slander iii^s & iiij^d as oft as he offends.

Also it is ordered that when any dinner is to be made for this occupacon that ye iiij wardens have power to appoint it; and

to place all persons according to their discretion and that none
depart without their license euery offender herein to pay iijˢ &
iiij⁴ toties quoties.

Also it is ordered by consent of yᵉ whole occupacon yᵗ if any
brother of yᵉ same doe take any work to make or finish upon
a sett time if yᵉ same be not done in yᵉ time but yᵉ owner be
driven to complaine to yᵉ whole company for want of his
clothes yᵉ party soe offending shalbe amerced iijˢ iiij⁴ for
bringing such a slander to yᵉ trade this to be taken without
favor.

Also it is ordered that yᵉ undermaisters shall at Midsummer
quarter each yeare gather of euery brother their quarter's
groat.

Also it is ordered that if any brother of this society haue
taken of any to make up and cutt it out no other of this trade
shall tak it on his head or mak it up without license of yᵉ iiij
wardens of this trade upon paine of iijˢ iiij⁴ for each offence.

Also there shall be a clerk chosen by yᵉ whole occupacon who
shall be clerk for his life and when he deceases yᵉ whole company to elect another all elections to go by votes and most to
carry it but if it happen either in this or any other vote to
be even or equal then yᵉ ancientest of yᵉ wardens to haue
yᵉ casting vote.

Also ordered by and with yᵉ whole assent & consent of this
occupacon that noe brother of this society shall take any
apprentice nor his son be admitted a brother of this fraternity
till he himself haue paid all yᵉ amercements and forfeitures
by him due to yᵉ trade   And that euery brother's son before
he be admitted a brother of this society shall pay to the trade
at one payment viˢ viij⁴ and xii birage* money and euery
apprentice before he be admitted a brother likewise pay at one
entire payment viˢ viij⁴ & xii birage* money and no brother
of this society shal! take an apprentice before his marriage
but shall pay to this trade forty shillings before yᵉ enrolment
of his apprentice without favour.

---

* Birage, see note p. 116 *ante*.

77 June 26*

Ordered this quarter day that the clerke of this company shall haue for the enroleing of every apprentice sixpence and for the enroleing of euery brother six pence and noe other sallary from y⁰ trade but only y⁰ benefit of making y⁰ indenture.†

Ordered this day by the consent of the whole occupacon that those men belonging to this guild who liue in y⁰ country for their convenience shall be acquitted from theire amercements euery yeare paying 1ˢ yearly to the trade upon every mid-summer quarter except those who live within one mile of the towne.

Ordered by y⁰ consent of y⁰ whole occupacõn that no freeman of this light‡ shall take any apprentice but according to act of parliament And y⁰ y⁰ said freeman shall haue y⁰ said apprentice according to y⁰ date of his indentures for seauen yeares and eight x x x hireman and not under And y⁰ y⁰ said freeman shall not x x x apprentice ouer to any brother of this fraternity or any other x x x shall forfeit to y⁰ fraternity without x x x x §

Ordered by the occupacon that hereafter shall no freeman of this occupacon belonging to this trade after the date of this order ofer any man to be a brother of this occupacon unlesse he the said apprentice haue serued seauen years apprentices to a freeman of this occupacon according to y⁰ ancient orders and privileges of this trade and if any brother of this light shall propose any brother to come in upon any composition in y⁰ guildhall butt according to y⁰ said orders he shall pay to this fraternity without favour y⁰ sum of five groats without favour toties quoties.

THE OATH OF A WARDEN.

You shall sweare y⁰ you shall be a true and just warden to y⁰ occupacon of taylors and to maintaine y⁰ same to y⁰ utmost

---

* But must be 1677.

† This rule and the next are in a different handwriting and ink.

‡ See note *ante* p. 146.

§ These two next rules are again in a different handwriting and ink, and are written across the paper at the bottom of a call list of the guild of 1701. One of them has been much thumbed and is illegible.

of your power   All controversies which shall come before you
of any of the occupaçon you shall not for any favour you
beare to yᵉ one nor hatred to the other so deale otherwise but
truely and justly in all causes as shall come before you you
shall giue your attendance at oʳ quarter days in our chamber
and at all other times betwixt our quarter days whensoever
you shalbe warned by yᵉ undermaisters you shall likewise be
reddy to giue your attendance to yᵉ mayor of this city whensoever you shall be warned either to yᵉ motehall or elsewhere.
These and all other things which doth appertaine to a warden
you shall truely observe and doe to yᵉ best of your knowledge
soe help you God & by yᵉ contents of this book.

THE UNDERMAISTERS OATH.

You shall sweare that you shall give warneing or cause to be
warned the whole occupaçon at yᵉ quarter daies appointed
Alsoe you shall giue warneings or cause to be warned at
yᵉ death of a brother or wif child apprentice or servᵗ the said
occupaçon to goe to yᵉ church and tarry to yᵉ corps be buried
Also you shall know noe outman work within yᵉ cittie or
liberties of yᵉ same but you shall present them to the
occupaçon you shall obey all comandments of yᵉ iiii wardens
yt be lawful you shall diligently mak searth and tak a notice
of all hiremen strangers which doth work of the occupaçon
within yᵉ liberties of this city you shall up or nominate two
undermaisters at your yeares end according to yᵉ statutes of
our occupaçon you shall make a true accomp of all such
amerciments forfeits or other things as you shall be charged
with in your yeare soe help you &ct.

THE CLERKE'S OATH.

You sweare to be true and faithful to this occupaçon and shall
well and truely execute the office of clerke of this company
you shall not for any favour or malice doe any otherwise but
justly these and whatsoever else belongs to yᵉ office of clerk
you shall faithfully doe to yᵉ best of your knowledge soe help
you god.

THE OATH OF A WARDEN BELONGING TO THIS ———

You shall sweare to be a true warden of this occupation and to maintaine y^e [same] to the utmost of your power all faults and controversies which shall come before you of any of this occupacon you shall neither for any feare you beare to the one or any hatred to the other deale any otherwise but truely and justly you shall give your atendance at our chamber euery quarterday and at all other times whensoever you shall be lawfully warned these and all other things belonging to your duty of a warden you shall well and truely observe and doe to ye best of your knowledge and skill soe helpe you god *

THE OATH OF A BROTHER WHEN HE IS ADMITTED INTO THE OCCUPATION.

You shall sweare that you shall be a true and faithful brother to this occupation all their secrets and counsels keepe you shall know nothing prejudicial to the same occupation but the same shall make known to the trade you shall obey all comandments of the masters for the tyme being that be lawfull you shall duely attend and appeare in this guild every quarter day unlesse you be hindered by god's visitation or the king's business and at all other meetings shall giue your assistance and attendance for the good and advancement of the occupacon upon warneing to you giuen by the undermaisters or either of them   So helpe you God.

THE OATH OF THE MASTERS OF THE OCCUPATION.†

You shall give warning or cause to be warned all the brothers of this occupation to attend in their guild or chamber every quarterday and at the deaths of any brother brothers wife or child to warne the whole trade to attend the corpse to the church and to stay till the same be interred.   You shall knowe noe outman worke within this citty or liberties of the same but you shall present them to this occupacon alsoe you shall obey all commandments of the wardens and brotherhood that

---

* This oath and the two next are from a different part of the book, and appear to be later in date.

† The terms "masters" and "undermasters" are used indifferently for the same officials.

be lawful and comoding for the occupacon you shall diligently
at Easter Whitsuntide ffaires and assizes and Christmas soe
longe as you continue in your office make search and take
note of all hiremen strangers which doth work with any other
occupacon presenting their names and finally you shall make
account of all such money and ffines and x x and dis-
tresses y^t you shall receive or be charged with all in your
yeare soe helpe you God.

MISCELLANEOUS ENTRIES.

June 29th 1652. It is ordered by this occupacon that hereafter there shall noe fforraner be a brother of this trade after
the daite hereof unless he doe serve seaven yeares and the
eight yeare hire man according to the ancient orders and
priviledges of this occupacon unless he be a gentleman and
hath desire to be a brother and if any break this order shall
forfeit ten pounds to this occupacon.

1657. We amercy Robert James vi^s viii^d for working with
John Parker without the lycence of the occupacon contrary to
afformer order anciently made by the s^d occupacon. We
amercy John Guy ffor the like offence.

Christmas quarter 1658

disbursed by the s^d George Martin ffour shillings by consent
of the whole occupation.*

1659. Matthew Wilkinson clerk of this occupation of tailor
x of December 1659 by the consent of the foure wardens
and of the trade and they did give him his oath the same day.
Disbursed by George Martin for chamber rent xii^d.†

The foure wardens of this occupacon their names with the rest
of the occupacons names the 3 January 1659.‡

---

* Drinks all round.

† Cullery rent to the corporation for the room in the guildhall.

‡ A new call list was made in October, 1666, when the following new
surnames appear—Twentiman, Boane, Dickinson, Bamber, Barnes, Robinson,
Norman, Monkhouse, Smith, and Bewley.

Imp. Alexander Stagg mort.
Thos Pearson mort.
George Martine
Robert Sanderson
John Blailocke
Roger James mort.
Wiiliam Carlile mort.
Robert Wilson
John Brathaite
Christopher Raskell
Henry Clemitson
Tho Thomson
Tho Kidd mort.
William Stagge mort.
Anthony Craister
Tho Cragall
George Rigg
John Hodshon
Robert James
Ednard Blalock
Tho Hindson
Marmaduke Maugre mort.
Robert Thomlinson 1659
Mathew Wilkinson 1659 mort
Joseph Sinton 1660
John Pattinson mort.
John Simpson
Joseph Lowson
John James
ffargus Vertee mort
James Twentiman
Thomas Pattinson
Peter Norman
Rob Johnson.*

* The new clerk, Mathew Wilkinson, immediately commenced a new call list in the book, ending with his own name; subsequent new members have been added from time to time, and "mort" added to several and to the new clerk himself. As John Pattinson became clerk in 1660, Wilkinson did not long survive his appointment.

Jan. 3, 1659.

Matthew Wilkinson is admitted a brother of this occupacōn and haith payed 12^d burrage money and 20^d at his entry & is to pay 20^d every quarter day following till 6/8 be payd.

January 7 1660.

Rec^d of John Blakelocke Roger James and Anthoney Craister for and towards the paym^t of the colours 0 : 1 : 6 *

April 1662. P^d by George Martin w^{ht} was got off Rob Littlejohn 0 : 10 : 0 †

Whereas an information was presented before his majesties justices of peace at a generall quarter sessions ag^t Robert Littlejohn a scotsman for exercising the craft & mystery of a taylor contrary to the lanes established in this kingdom of England after wch the s^d Robert Littlejohn came and addressed himselfe to this occupacōn & pleading poverty was willing to submit himself to the trade and paid the ffine thereon set upon him promising to depart this citty and never afterwards to worke within the liberties of the same to the prejudise of any brother of this occupacōn. And whereas the s^d Robert Littlejohn contrary to his promise hath come to this citty & taken the boldness to exercise the s^d trade and that Thomas Kidd hath of his own accord sett him on work contrary to sevral ancient orders of this occupacōn & to the prejudice of the same occupacōn It is this day ordered by this occupacōn that whosoever after this day shall take the s^d Robert Littlejohn to worke or sufier him to sitt working or any way employ him in the art or mistery of a taylor or any worke thereto belonging within the liberties of this citty That every pson soe offending shall forfeit for every quarter of a yeare the s^d Littlejohn shall soe be suffered by him to worke the sume of forty shillings to be sued for or otherwise levyed for the use of this occupacōn.

Chrismas quarter day January the 5th 1663.

This box this day vieued and the acc^t of moneys stated there remains is found to be 1 – 6 – 8 there being 19^s that was

* Other donations are entered.
† This will be the fine set on Littlejohn, as explained in the next entry.

taken out of the box wch at present cant be remembered by those y^t kept the keyes of the box & soe they stand charged with it & this day there is putt into the box two pounds foure shillings & eight pence.*

Lady day 1675   Whereby John Braithwait one of the 4 wardens of this trade was summoned by the undermasters to appear in the guildhall this quarter day & persistently refused to come contrary to his oath it was this day ordered by the s^d trade (*nemine contradicente*) that ye s^d John Braithwait be from henceforth discharged from being one of ye foure wardens.†

June 29 1675   Wm Stagg fined 20^s for taking an apprentice while unmarried.‡

1676   John Lawson junior was fined for taking an apprenticee before he kept a house or was married.‡

July 1679   John Linton fined 3 „ 4 for contumelious words agst ye wardens.

1679   Will Pattinson is amerced by the consent of the whole occupacon for raising debate and giving evil language to his superior contrary to an order in that case provided 3 „ 4§

April 1 1864   This day Timothy Lawson the son of John Lawson was admitted a brother of this occupacon and sworn and haith paid for his admittance 6^s 8^d and paid 12^d borrage

---

* The mode of doing business was on each quarter day to put into the box the balance of receipts over disbursements. In March, 1664, it is stated that there is £2..6 in the box. ".All accounts due to any psn of the guild is fully paid & discharged."

† "Thomas Thompson aliis Parker" was elected in his stead. This is the first recorded instance of the election of a warden. It is possible that, up to this period, the four senior members were wardens by virtue of their seniority, and that so no election was necessary. The executive officers were the under-masters, or masters, as they were sometimes called for brevity. Their posts were as onerous as honourable; they had to warn the trade for quarterly and other meetings—they were fined if they neglected to do so; they kept the accounts, and were detained in office for another year, if the accounts did not come right.

‡ Similar instances could be multiplied.

§ Similar instances could be multiplied—in some cases the *ipsissima verba* of the bad language are recorded.

money which was delivered to Mr Wilson to buy a cloath* for the trade.

Ascension day May^t 1684

Re^d in the guild from Sir Christopher Musgrave 10/^{s} which was delivered to Jo Lowson jun. & paid to Jo Braithwait the next day.†

Sept 1684 Ed Monkhouse was merced for giving uprobrious words to the four wardens 20^s This day Tho Kidd was amerced for giving euill word in questioning the four wardens in their authority 6^s 8^d

March 31 1685 this day was amerced Ed Monkhouse for laughing to scorne the clarke when he was in his office and saying God damm ye all.

Oct 6 1685 This day was amerced Joe Thomson for going out of the guild abruptly & in anger contrary to an order in that case provided 3^s 4^d

1686 Edward Monkhouse & Timothy Lawson were made undermasters & they charged the fraternity with the following bill for repareing the guild as foloweth "‡

Glass 23 foot new	0 : 13 : 3	Imp Ale	00 : 04 : 0
Two Stanches	0 : 0 : 4	Bisket 6^{lb}	00 : 04 : 0
nails 3 hundred	0 : 0 : 6	Bread	00 : 02 : 0
5 fir deales at 1 . 2	0 : 5 : 10	Wine 6 bottles	00 : 5 : 06
for prop	0 : 1 : 0	Tobacco 3 lb	00 : 01 : 9
for rails	0 : 0 : 7	pipes 6 doz	00 : 1 : 06
for making the table	0 : 4 : 6	candles	00 : 00 : 2
& setting it up		Music	00 : 01 : 00
		prentice	00 : 00 : 06

* Must have been a pall, as a bearing cloth or mort cloth afterwards is included in lists of the property of the guild : 12s. more was paid afterwards towards this cloth.

† Sir Christopher Musgrave, son of Sir Philip, and M.P. for Carlisle 1661 to 1690, and one of the leaders of the tory party in parliament—a well known and distinguished man (see *Cumberland and Westmorland M.P.s, from the Restoration to the Reform Bill*, R. S. Ferguson, p. 420).

‡ The account includes Ascension day expenses. Towards it Sir Christopher Musgrave gave 10s., the Mayor 2s. 6d., and those present 6d. apiece. Sir Christopher's 10s. becomes annual, and in 1688, Captain Babb, who was M.P. for Carlisle from 1689 to 1691 or 1692, when he died, also gives 10s., as does Mr. Aglionby.

1690   Ascension day.

for 3 bottles of Claret & one bottle of sack & bread & bisket	00 : 13 : 09
tobacco & pipes & candels	00 : 03 : 00
p'd to Anthony Collson p'd to y'e drummers musick & Apprentices	00 : 05 : 06
for 54 Flagons of Ale and 3d & 2d with John Hodgson*	01 : 01 : 02
	02 : 02 : 05

1690

Will Patterson is amerced 3s/4d for telling the wardens to kiss his a——

Ed. Monkhouse is also amerced for abusing the wardens to the maior and saying they were foresworn fellows & that he had more knowledge than they all.†

Lady day 1701. This day the whole fraternity ordered to have q'ter days and if any man shall absent himselfe he shall pay to y'e trade y'e sume of one shilling for euery default and the brothers are not to exceed sixpence upon those days in their expences and to haue their q'terdays at no hou e but a brothers or brother's wife.

1705   turn to y'e other book. All absenses, journeymen defaults and other business belonging to y'e talors guild are to be written in y'e new book. George Braithwaite clerk 1705.‡

May 10h 1711.

This day Mr Rouland Stagg of the citty of London son of Mr W. Stagg one of the foure wardens of y'e fraternity of

* That is at John Hodgson's public. "3d & 2d" are various kinds of beer. The Ascension day bill for 1698 includes an item of "expended by the fours when they ordered what we should haue upon Ascension day 00 : 2 : 4."

† This terrible tailor, he was always being fined for similar offences, was in a big way of business, for it appears he had four journeymen and took on another at the assizes, which were held once a year, at midsummer. Later on he pays for six journeymen at the assizes, a great apiece, while other members of the trade only pay for one or two. At Christmas he keeps only three. Ultimately he becomes Mr. Monkhouse. He was evidently the local Poole of the period, and made for the country squires, who attended the assizes. The levy of 4d., or a groat, on each journeyman, was made twice a year, at the assizes (midsummer) and at Christmas. In case of the journeyman being a Scotchman, the levy was 10 groats, or 3s. 4d.

‡ We do not recognise the leaves belonging to this new book of 1705, ante p. 143.

merch^t tailors in ye citty of Carlile did freely gine to
ye s^d fraternity one large red silk couller wth a large new
cross at ye head corner and his name siphered in gould at
ye middle wth ye yeare of our lord 1711 at ye bottom of
ye said siph^{er} as a free gift being made brother of ye said
light ye yeare before. And it is ordered by ye said wardens
and trade that his father Mr Wm Stagg shall keep ye said red
silke couller cleane and safe for ye use of ye afore said guild
and fraternity for his naturall life : and then his exrs or
assigns to delinr ye said large silk couller to ye 4 wardens
clarke or undermasters to be kept and preserved cleane & safe
from damage for euer for ye use of ye said light and for
ye sake of ye said Ronland Stagg our generous benefacter.

This day Leonard Proctor presented ye said fraternity wth a
silver cupp w^t two ears for ye favour done him by ye said light
in admitting him a brother of this fraternity of merch^t tailors
& ye said cupp was delivered to Geo Braithwait clerk to be
kept for ye trades use.*

The same day Edward Taite presente to ye said fraternity one
silver tumbler plaine for ye fauoure done him by ye aforesd
light in admitting him brother of this fraternity and ye said
cupp was del:vered to Geo: Braithwaite clerke aforesd

March 30 1731.*

It is ordered and agreed by the generall consent of the
fraternity of taylors whose names are hereunder written that
the undermasters or deputy wardens of this fraternity shall
give summons or warneing to the severall and respective
members of the same personally or by leaving notice at their
respective dwelling houses the eve before every quarter day or
quarterly meeting of the society that they appear at the
s^d meeting

And it is also ordered that if any undermaster or deputy
warden neglect to give notice or warneing as aforesaid the
s^d undermaster or deputy warden so neglecting shall forfeit
and pay to this fraternity or to the wardens thereof for the
time being the sum of three shillings and fourpence for said
neglect or offence.

* Both these cups are still in existence, *ante* p. 144.

Ordered that if any brother or member of this fraternity after haveing had warning or notice as afore^d shall neglect to appear at the hall of this fraternity exactly at one a clock in the afternoon of each quarter day or quarterly meeting (except hindred by sickness) shall forfeit and pay to this fraternity or the masters or wardens thereof for the use of the s^d fraternity the sum of sixpence.

June 25 midsummer q^r 1734.

At a generall meeting this quarter day by the general consent of this company it is agreed that whereas upon the Ascension day it is usuall in every guild in this city to entertain the mayor aldermen conncell and gentlemen in the city with punch brandy ale bisket tobacco pipes & severall other necessarys according to the old antient custome of this city which is very chargeable and cannot be ansuered to pay of charges without a general collection made in our s^d company in our guildhall And whereas the brothers in this city are obliged by our antient order to attend the corps of any brother his wife or children to the church and from thence goe back againe to their s^d house where mortality doth so fall out and spend each man 6 pence per man through the love and respect of their deaceased brother or friend upon which order the country brothers belonging to this company doe not appear, which is thought to be great hardship upon our citty brothers it is therefore unanimously agreed by the generall consent of the company that every country brother belonging to this company shall pay the sum of twelvepence and every city brother pay the sum of sixpence yearly and every year And the same to be collected by the undermasters every lady day q^r and be accounted for the same And if any city brother or country brother shall refuse to pay the said sum or sums so agreed upon shall forfeit to the use of this guild upon such offence the sum of ten groats without any abatem^t as witness &ct.

January 2 1738/9. Then was Jeremiah Dalston admitted an *ex gratia* brother by the gen^ll consent of the trade and gave to the trade one guinea and p^d to the trade 7^s 8^d & 6^d to the clerk.*

October q^r ye 2^d 1739.

This day was Mr George Rigg by the consent of all the company and brothers swore an assistant four to the company in the roome of Mr George Brathwait who refusing comeing to the guild when sent for.

January the 8th 1739.

It is ordered and agreed by the generall consent of this company that hereafter this guild or chamber belonging to our trade shall be lent out to no body whatsoever by any means And that if the undermasters shall lend the key of the chamber to any person whatsoever shall forfeit to the use of this company three shillings & fourpence to be p^d upon the first demand.†

January 27 1770. Be it remembered that this day Mr John Pearson a brother of this gill has been pleased to make this fraternity of our company of taylors a present of a most valuable new colour which is most gratefully acknowledged by all the brotherhood and we do all in general return him our most humble thanks for his valuable present and ever revere his memory for the same   Entered by order of the company   Thos Wallis clerk.

Taylors guild Thursday Feb 17 1785.

Whereas the mayor & corporation have admitted seven or eight [same order as the merchants *ante* p. 117].

[An order for guild books to be produced before the House of Commons *ante* p. 117].

---

* This is the first record of the admission of an *ex gratia* freeman to the guild. In most cases, when persons are admitted to brotherhood, it is stated whether they acquired the right by servitude or by birth. Occasionally this is not done, and in 1761, Henry Farrar and Thos. Yeats, Esq., Mayor, and in 1767 Thomas Nanson of London, merchant, and Will Betts of London, taylor, were admitted, but their qualifications are not stated ; the last two were probably entitled by birth, while Farrar and Yeats might be *ex gratia*. In 1765, Henry Aglionby, son of Henry, and in 1774, Christopher Aglionby, son of Henry, were admitted ; they probably had a right by birth, but the fact that the brotherhood was taken up by persons in their position, sons of a late M.P. for Carlisle, shows that the political reasons for doing so were important.

† Some of the guild chambers were let as schoolrooms ; at present, 1886, they are let for all sorts of purposes, from the breeding of pigeons upwards.

M

23 June 1786.

Whereas we have been alarmed by a late violent and tyrannic attempt to create fourteen hundred new freemen possessing no title or pretence of title either by birth or servitude in direct & open violation of our antient custom and to the destruction of our liberties and most valuable franchises, We the brethren of this guild at a special meeting assembled this day in order to put these rights liberties and privileges in a state of the greatest possible security have agreed unanimously that the following gentlemen shall be admitted brothers of this trade being citizens and brothers of the guilds set opposite to their names.

Mr John Jackson, blacksmith, shoemaker Carlisle
& Mr Edward Nevinson Carlisle gent weaver
& Mr Thomas Coulthard. Carlisle tanner
& Mr Willn Jackson Carlisle mercht
& Mr Henry Dobinson attorney-at-law, Carlisle weaver
& Mr George Blamire Carlisle storekeeper tanner
& Mr George Blamire junior　　　do　　　do
& Mr Thos Blamire surgeon　　　　　　do
& Mr John Hodgson Scotch Street shoemaker
& Mr Rob Harrington M.D Carlisle tanner
& Mr Rob James Carlisle mercht
& Mr John Carnaby Carlisle smith
& Mr Isaac Ebdale Carlisle mercht
& Mr James Craggle Grayson merch
& George Harrington esq alderman Carlisle tanner
& Mr Saml Coleman Carlisle shoemaker
& Mr Ben Holmes　　　do　　　do
& Mr Edward Rowland Carlisle tanner
& Mr John Blamire Carlisle merch:
& Mr John Simpson Carlisle shoemaker
& Mr Anthony Longcake Carlisle smith
& Mr John Jackson gentleman Catgill near
　　　　　　　　　　Whitehaven merch

　　　　All of which is entred upon
　　　stamps according to antient custom
　　of this fraternity of mercht taylors*
　　　　　　by John Brown
　　　　　　　　clerk

---

* The brethren were once content to be called tailors. This order was passed by all the guilds, and the same gentlemen thus became members of the whole of the guilds.

Midsummer quarter day 1788   At a general quarter meeting
it is unanimously agreed by each member that a general contribution be contributed from this time forward untill such
times as the whole fraternity think proper to disannull the
same each member to pay or cause to be paid into the treasury
or stock, one sixpence each quarter for the better accommodation of the trade and one sixpence more for the soal use of
defrayeing any necessary expences which may hereafter come
upon the guild occasion'd by any means that may be used in
order to obtain a right of common on Kingmoor, which
appears to have been ilegaly taken from the antient freemen
of Carlisle.

June 30 1796   [Same order as merchants (*ante* p. 122),
delegates to meet & appoint same quarter days]

Nov 6 1805   Whereas by the fraudulent practises of some
brothers belonging to this guild in takeing apprentices for a
less term than the charter of this city admits of and contrary
to the rules of this guild whereby the guild is deprived of
resources for its support and if allowd to go on will in time
be the cause of knocking up the guild entirely.   How can it
be presumed to stand as a member of the eight guilds if its
supporters are allowed to continue such fraudulent ways
Resolved that as the oath which a brother takes admitted into
the guild and more so the oath when made free is not a
sufficient barrier against such practices we do order that whoever his guilty of the like offence from and after above date
shall pay a fine to the guild of two pounds.

Aug 1812   Fees were fixed as follows ·

Every brotherhood	£2 ,, 2 ,, 0
Clark & undermasters for a brother to be made off a quarterday	0 : 5 : 0
On a quarter day	0 : 4 : 0
Clerk for enroling a brother	0 : 4 : 0
Brother's treat off a qu. day	1 : 1 : 0
do do on	10 : 0
Enroling an apprentice	2 : 2 : 0
Clerk for enroling do	4 : 0
Undermasters fees	3 : 0

Resolved that the culler is to go with the apprentice on Ascension day provided that the apprentice provides a man that the brothers judge able to bear it.*

Resolved that the plate &ct belonging the gild be lodged with the clerk.

1818.   A cashier is appointed.

1822.   That no money is to be taken out of the stock unless it is regular mentioned in the guild and voted for by a majority or otherwise the cashier will be charged with it.

---

* To Kingmoor ; no easy task.

Seal of priory of Carlisle : from the corporation muniments.

Chapter IX.

THE TANNERS' GUILD.

The only records of the tanners' guild, that can be found, are a bundle of admittances, some on parchment, from about 1700 downwards, and a large modern book, 16 inches high, which begins with a list of the quarter days, a list of fees, and the forms of the oaths. It contains no copy of the rules, which is probably due to the fact that the tanners' guild comprised, latterly, few brothers that tanned, consisting almost wholly of county magnates and residents at a distance. Thus the call-roll of Feb. 7th, 1821, shews 163 members, of whom only 14 resided in the city. No less than 36 were named Sewell. There were, upon the list, 5 Broughams, 6 Briscos, the earl of Lonsdale, Sir Philip Musgrave, and John Christian Curwen.

The plate consists of a silver drum tankard, on which is—

> The Gift of the Right Rever[nd] Thomas
> Lord Bishop of Carlile to the Guild or
> Fraternity of Tanners in the said City 1701

The quarter days were—

Candlemas quarter first Wednesday after 2[n] of January
Saint Helens   -   -   -   -   3 of May
Lammas   -   -   -   -   -   1st of August
Alhallows   -   -   -   -   1st of November

Fees, if made on a quarter day; if otherwise		
Brotherhood	1 : 0 : 0	1 : 0 : 0
Colours	0 : 1 : 0	0 : 1 : 0
Clerk	0 : 1 : 0	0 : 2 : 0
Treat	0 : 5 : 0	0 : 10 : 0
Stamp	1 : 0 : 0	1 : 0 : 1
Warning trade		0 : 2 : 0
	2 : 7 : 0	2 : 15 : 0

Tanners ⎫ The oath of a brother admitted
fraternity ⎭ into this company

You shall swear to be a true brother of the company ready and obedient to the lawful commands of this table as heads of the tanners' corporation You shall keep secret all such matters as are expounded in this place for the mystery trade and credit of the same You shall observe fulfill and keep orders and constitutions that have been made for the good of this trade so far as they are agreeable to law and to the uttermost of your power defend and maintain the same.

These and all other things appertaining to a true brother of the trade and company you shall well and truely observe and keep to the best of your power So help you O God.

THE SOLEMN AFFIRMATION.

I   do solemnly sincerely and truly declare and affirm that I will be a true brother &ct.*

THE OATH OF THE UNDERMASTERS.

You and either of you shall swear that you will duly and truly execute your place of undermasters and wardens of this company or society of tanners in giveing warning quarterly every brothers meeting that lives or follows the trade within the liberty of this city in this guild hall the night before the quarter day.

You shall also make a true and faithful account of all such sums of money now delivered to you as shall come to your hands by those profits amerciaments fines brotherhoods or slanders which you shall make a full account thereof observing due frugality in expences All other things appertaining you as undermasters of this company shall use all diligence therein as faithful men So help you O God.

1834 May 7th   At the quarterly meeting held this day it was agreed that if any member of this guild shall introduce or bring into the said guild any person not a brother therein (except any of the brothers in other guilds) that the person or brother belonging

---

* The merchants' guild had a positive rule against admitting quakers (see *ante* p 106. This guild was more liberal ; and at the present date the tanning trade near Carlisle is largely in the hands of members of the Society of Friends.

the same shall pay one shilling on entering or the person to leave
the guild immediately and on his refusal to comply the undermasters
shall call upon any brother or brothers of this guild to assist them
in compelling the person immediately to leave the same by force.

May 1 1845. It was resolved that no money belonging the funds
of this guild should be expended until the guild was totally clear of
debt except what should be ordered to be spent on each yearly day
of meeting during the year.

The following are taken from the bundles of admissions :—

1695 Robert Law dr of phisick
1704 Joseph Musgrave esqr elected
1709 Thomas Brougham esqr elected &ct
1709 Peter Brougham elected admitted & sworne*
1711 Wm Rooke elected &ct
1711 John Briscoe of Crofton esq elected &ct
1711 The Rev Geo Fleming clerk archdeacon of Carlisle elected &ct
1712 Sir Christopher Musgrave bt admitted
——— Christopher Musgrave esq elected
1714 Thomas Howard esqe
1720 The Reve Stephen Green a bro's son
1721 Richard Briscoe gent son of John Brisco of Crofton a brother
1721 Jos Pattinson clerke son of John Pattinson a brother
1725 Wm Salkeld Nicolson son of Joseph Nicolson clerke dead
1726 Mr Thomas Tullie son of Dr Thomas Tullie deed
——— Mr Jerom Tullie
1727 Jos Nicolson clerke son of John Nicolson esqr deced
1732 Mr John Briscoe son of John Briscoe esq
——— Mr Willm Brisco son of John Briscoe esq
——— Mr Musgrave Brisco son of John Briscoe esq
1733 Mr Wennersley Law son of dr Law
1733 Rev Mr William Fleming son of doctor Fleming dean of
     Carlisle
1733/4 Wastel Brisco son of John Brisco esq
     James Brisco   „   „

* He is "elected, admitted, and sworn." Those whose fathers were
brothers are "admitted and sworn."

1734/5 Philip Musgrave esqr son of Sir Christopher

1736 Ralph Brisco gent son of John Brisco

1739 Mr Hans Musgrave son of Sir Christopher

1739 Mr Christopher Musgrave son of Sir Christopher

1740 Mr Henry Richmond Brougham son of Peter Brougham esq a brother of the fraternity

1740 William Tullie gent son of Dr Th Tullie late dean of Carlisle and a brother

1752 John Stanwix colonel & governor of the city of Carlisle

1758 Rev Mr Chardin Musgrave D.D

1758 Peter Brougham son of John Brougham of Cockermouth

1758 Henry Brougham of Brougham Hall esq son of Samuel Brougham

1767 Henry Brougham of Brougham Hall

1768 James Law son of Winnersley Law

1768 Richard Horton Brisco son of Mr Musgrave Brisco of Wakefield

1773 John Brougham son of Henry of Brongham Hall

1776 Edward Dyne Brisco son of Musgrave Brisco of Wakefield

1780 William Lowther esqr a member of parliament for this city

1820 Christopher John Musgrave

1820 Musgrave Brisco of London son of Wastell

—— Wastell Brisco of London son of Wastell

1820 Henry Brougham* esq son of Henry Brougham esq of Brougham Hall

1833 Robert Brisco of the Oaks son of Sir Wastel

---

* Lord Brougham.

Carlisle siege piece.

Chapter X.

THE SHOEMAKERS' GUILD.

The records of this guild consist of two books. The earlier is bound in vellum, over which a leather case has been put. It measures about 11¾ inches by 7¾, and is rather over an inch thick; it is in a most dilapidated and tattered condition. The entries are in great confusion, running from both ends of the book. It commences at one end with the rules, of which the first pages are gone. After them the writer left a blank page or two and then headed a page,

"Brethren admitted."

He then left more blanks and headed a page,

Irolments of and for Apprentices.

The first entry, the enrolment of John Mulcaster, is in the same handwriting as the rules; it is dated 1595, and so gives a date to the rules. The more modern book is 12½ inches by 8, and is just under ¾ inch thick. It is bound in leather, and has a few leaves in parchment at the commencement, headed,

An Index to find every rule in this Book
Carlisle
1735

The quarter days of this guild were—

1. The Friday next after S. Sebastian and S. Fabian, 20th January.

2. The Friday next after S. Phillip and S. James (or S. Jacob), May 1.

3. The Friday next after S. Mary Magdalene, or 22nd July.

4. The Friday next after S. Crispin and Crispianus, or 25th October.

In two instances in the seventeenth century mention is made of St Helen's q^r, August 18, and in two instances of Quentyne q^r, or S. Quintin, October 31. Another quarter day is entered as St Sebastian and Mary Magdalene q^r, and another as " Sebastian quarter being 26th of July 1661." This arises from a confusion between S. Sebastian, an early saint, and Don Sebastian of Portugal, who disappeared in 1578, and whose return is still expected in Portugal and Brazil.

A list of the guild, date torn off, but of the seventeenth century, gives the following names :—

Peter Bowne	Robert Sewell
Simon Braithwaite	William Nicholson
Thomas Knagg	Thomas Cumston
Robert Shippard	John Nixon
Michael Pattinson	Robert Nicholson
Robert Kitchin	Thomas Waystye
Anthony Sanderson	John Blacklocke
Roger James	Robert Blacklocke
Cuthbert Booes	Ralph Smith
Robert Jackson	Robert Dalton
Henry Clemetson	John James filius Phillippi
John Rumpuey	John James filius Rogeri

Twenty-four in number. Other lists will be found below. In 1686 the guild had about 40 members, and in 1699 about 50 : among the names that of John Francis Charnley has a foreign sound. The others are all local names.

The *ex gratia* freemen on the roll in 1715 were Captain Thomas Morris, for whom see *Transactions Cumberland*

and Westmorland Archæological Society, Vol. VII, p. 245;
the Rev. Richmond Fenton: he was admitted in 1711 and
gave a guinea and a cup; the Rev. George Story, dean of
Limerick: he was admitted in 1682 and was brother to
Thomas Story of Justice Town, the eminent member of the
Society of Friends; Leonard Dykes, Esq., admitted 1684;
Hon. Samuel Glidhell (Colonel Gledhill, for whom see
Cumberland and Westmorland M.P.s, p. 87); John Hylton
of Hylton Castle, M.P. for Carlisle 1727 to 1746 (see *Cum-
berland and Westmorland M.P.s*) was admitted in 1739.
Other instances will be found among the miscellaneous
entries.

This guild, like the others, pays cullery rent of one
shilling to the corporation for its guild chamber, and
received 2s. 6d. yearly from the chamberlain, augmented in
the eighteenth century to £1 : 2s. 6d. In 1785 a marginal
note to this payment of £1 : 2s. 6d. says "an annual sum
acknowledged & paid by them for upwards of 68 years."

The plate belonging to this guild is fully described in
the appendix to *Old Church Plate in the Diocese of Carlisle*.
It consists of two candlesticks, and of a beautiful salver
on a foot (called a standard in the guild's books), on all of
which are inscribed—

> The gift of Col Samuel Gledhill citizen of Carlisle
> to the company of shoemakers Sept 21 1710.

A small mug, on which is—

> The gift of the Rev Mr Richm^d Fenton 1713.

A plain silver tumbler, on which is—

> The gift of Joseph Sewell son of Jo^n Sewell to ye fraternity of
> shoemakers at Carlisle 4 May 1722.

And a tall cup given by John Christian Curwen.

ORDERS &c.

All the ancient accustomed × × orders customs constitutions and
bye laws used and observed by the fraternity guild and × ×
incorporated company of shoemakers or cordwainers in the city of

Carlisle in the county of Cumberland And by all the time and by
many years whereof the memory of man is not to the contrary and
whereunto × × all sich time all and euery parson and parsons
× × × been are or shall be made admitted or taken a brother or
master of this same guild haue been and shall be strictly bound by
their oaths to keep and them or any other good and lawful order or
by lawes × × shall be hereafter made and agreed upon by the
said company × × × common benefit and good of the brotherhood.   For every and newly computed transcribed × × or
parchment for the continuance that the same constitutions and
by lawes might not be rent torn or decayed × × with ill usage
as heretofore the same hath been and to be red properly in this guild
or chamber

  it is by the general and mutual consent of the   body of
this guild and brotherhood and fellowship and company of shoemakers or cordwainers of the city aforesaid ordered acted concluded
agreed upon × × shall be four quarter dayes × × four × ×
dayes of meeting yearly at which × × consideration of all matters
  × × concerninge or belonging to the × × good order of the
said brotherhood excep × × parsons as shall be exempted the
same.   The first quarter to be observed and × × on Friday next
after Sebastian or Fabr or 20 ×   The 2nd quarterday to be kept
on Friday after Philip and × × on the first day of May.

The 3 quarter day to be kept on Friday next after Magdalene on 22
day of July.   The 4 quarter day to be observed and × × next
after the feast of Crispin and Crispianus or 25 × ×

Item That it is by the general and mutual assent of the whole body
of this guild now present it is × × × that if any brother shall
wilfully or willing × × att any of the above said quarter days
and hath had warning given to apear by the undermaisters or
  × × them att one of the clock on the sece × × his or their
name be caled twice each parson so neglecting or offending or
absenting shall pay unto the common box of this guild or × ×
for every quarter day unless agree as outer brother liveing out of the
ffreelidge or occasions shall require.*

---

  * The above is from a loose sheet of paper ; a strip has been torn from one
side, thus occasioning many blanks.

Enrolinge of an apprentice. 12. Item it is ordered and sett down   x   x   x
aforesaid that every brother of this   x   x   x
which shall take an apprentice shall   x   x   x
after the date of his indentures   x   x   x
apprentice in the register booke of this   x   x   x
x   x   upon paine and forfeit to   x   x   x
the said common b   x   x   x   *

The fee for his enrolesment iij. 13. Item it is agreed upon and by the con   x   x   x   said sett
down that such apprentice so bound   x   x   x   shall pay
for his enrolument to the bene   x   x   x   the common box
sixpence and to the clark   x   enrolwling him a penny.

None to take a apprentice till the other haue served five years. Item it is by the consent and assent of the brotherhood of this
gyld and fellowship condisioned concluded and agreed that no
brother of this brotherhood haveinge an apprentice shall take
to him another apprentice before that his first or   x   x   x
apprentice have served full five years upon paine that he who
x   contrary to this order shall forfeit and pay   x   x
common box vi⁵ viiiᵈ· †

A brothers sonne may be taken. 15. Item it is conditioned and agreed upon by the   x   x   x
brethren and the whole body of gyld that (not withstanding
the last and former order above sett downe) it shall and
may be lawful to any brother of this gyld haveing only one
apprentice to sett downe his owne sonne or a brother sonne
at any time when it please him and take him as an apprentice
for seaven years.

None to give work to anothers journeyman or apprentice. 16. Item by the general consent and assent aforesaid it is ordered
and sett down that no brother of this gyld or fraternity shall
give work or sett on worke any journeyman servant or
apprentice of another brother of this gyld without yᵉ consent

---

* The following rules, down to and inclusive of the one ordering
every brother to pay viijᵈ quarterly are from the earlier book : the
first leaves are lost, and with them the first eleven rules. These rules
are probably of the date 1595, that being the earliest date in the
book. Many of them are crossed out, and others altered, as if with
a view to an amended set being drafted from them. The leaves are
much tattered and worn.

† Altered in a more modern hand to—upon paine of xx⁵ to the
common box.

good will and license of his said brother to whome he is bound or with whom he is hyred upon paine of forfeit to the said common box vi^s viii^{d.}

Item by the assent and consent beforesaid it is ✕ ✕ ✕ ✕ sett downe and agreed upon that no young man of this occupation being unmarried and keeping or haning no shop of his own wherein dalye he keepes workmen shall take any apprentice before that he sett up shop and worke for his owne advantage upon paine of forfeite to the said common box.*

Item that no brother shall sett downe any which he intends to take to be his apprentice with an apprentice before he is bound apprentice upon paine of forfeit to the common box vi^{d.}†

Item that it is by the assent and consent aforesaid ordered and sett down that no brother of this gyld or fraternity shall secretelye or openly sell or convey to any Scotts man any tanned leather upon forfeit to the common box xx^{s.}†

Item it is agreed ordered and sett down by ye assent and consent aforesaid that no brother of this gyld or brotherhood shall bargain or buy any leather of any tanner which any other his brother of this gyld haith bargained or bought before upon paine of forfeit to the common box six shillings & viii pence or elles doe returne the leather so bought to the partie who first bargained and bought the same.†

Bespeaking of leather.

Item for avoydinge of encrease of price of leather it is by consent abovesaid ordered and sett downe that no person or persons being a brother of this gyld or fraternity shall bespeake bargaine or buy before hand any leather of any tanner before the said tanner haue dramnt dryed and maide his said leather ready for sight and sealinge upon paine of forfitor to the said comon box for every such offence xx^s ‡

---

* This is crossed out.

† These three are all crossed out.

‡ Searchers and sealers of leather were, under various statutes, appointed by the mayor of a borough to examine all leather and ascertain if it was sufficient and good. "Dramnt" probably means "drained."

Horseleather.
22.

Item by the assent and consent aforesaid ordered agreed upon and sett doune that no brother of this gyld or brotherhood shall secretly or publicly × × × any horse leather of any tanner or shall use cut × × any tanned horse leather in wayres upon paine of forfeitor as well of the said waires as also the paiement to the said common box xx^s. *

Selling of oyle.
23.

Item by the said consent it is ordered and agreed and sett doune that no person or persons of this brotherhood and gyld shall privately or openly sell any oyle to any other shoemakers or bootmakers dwelling in any common country towne hamlett or village upon paine of forfeit to the said common box vi^s viii^d.†

Measuring of oyle.

Item it is ordered and sett doune by the consent aforesaid that one gallon shalbe kept for mesuring traine or oyle : whosoever shall borrow the same to measure his owne oyle shall pay therefore 1^d.†

Any person or persons committing felline or petty × × to be deprived of his fraternity.

Item it is by the assent and consent aforesaid ordered and sett downe that if any person or persons beinge a brother of this gyld or brotherhood or beinge a servant jorneyman or an apprentice shalbe detected knowne or proved to haue committed or done any petye crime or other criminall offence whereby by verdict of jurye or by the officers of this cittie he shall be voided and putt forth or owte said this said cittie That such person or persons shall likewise be exempted and losse the benefit of a brother of this gyld and shall not be suffered to work within the liberties of the said cittie thereafter.

Item it is by the assent and consent of the × × brotherhood ordered and agreed upon that if a brother of this gyld or brotherhood shall worke or suffer any his servants journeymen or apprentices to worke openlye in his shopp the windowes lett downe or privately at his house any manner of worke belonging to this occupation upon the Satterday at night or upon any saint even bydden by the church to be kepte holyday after once the day be gone unlesse it be only

---

* Horse leather is too soft for making shoes.
† Crossed out.

for dispatching of sole or such like thing no which must needes be dispatches and the same to be wrought with the light of a candle and the shopp windoues not to be letten doun upon paine of forfertor to the box sixpence provided always and the premises notwithstanding it shall be lawful to every brother of this gyld at his and their pleasure upon Saint Thomas eve before Christmass (being not Satarday) to worke any worke either at his shop openly or at his house privately withyout paine or trespast.*

Item it is ordered agreed upon and sett downe by the consent aforesaid that no brother of this gyld or fraternitye shall his shopp windowes to be full opened on the Sabothday or other saint day or holyday bidden in the church except such saint day or holyday fall on the Satterday or Wednesday upon paine of vi^d for every falt committed against this order.†

Item it is by the consent aforesaid ordered sett downe and agreed upon that if any brother of this gyld shall misraport slander or defame any other of the brethren of this brotherhood to the hurt of the persons good name and credit so slandered mis-raported or defamed and cannot by due proufe prove the same trew the said misraporter slanderer or defamer shall forfett therefore to the benefitt of the aforesaid box twentye shillinge.

Consaling of matters

Item it is by the consent aforesaid ordered and sett down that if any brother of this gyld do ✗ ✗ any matter which may be hurtful to the estate or goods or which is or shall be done contrary to this ✗ ✗ ✗ agreement of the same and declare or reveale ✗ ✗ openly at the next quarter day or immediately upon knowledge thereof to the supervisors or undermaisters of the said ✗ ✗ or to the whole companie assembled in the chamber shall forfeit and pay to the benefit of the said box twenty shillings.

Declosinge of matters done in this gyld.

Item it is ordered agreed and sett downe by the consent aforesaid that what person or persons of this gyld or fellowshipp

---

* Crossed out. This very oddly worded rule applied to the eve of a saint day, tho following one to the saint day itself.

† Crossed out. Wednesday and Saturday are Carlisle market days, and the saints could not be allowed to interfere with country customers.

shall open disclose or make any council or thing which is in counsell dealt in within this gyld and brotherhood or amongst us in this our hall or chamber to any person or persons (except to one or more of ourselves which shall chance to be absent when that article or counsell was had and talked upon) shall forfeit to the comon box vi^s viii^d *

To be present at burial vj^d. Item it is ordered sett downe and agreed upon by the assent and consent aforesaid that the brethren of this brotherhood (when it shall please god to call away any of the brethren his wife sonne servant or apprentice to his mercy) shall attend and waite upon the corpse to the church and who so there himselfe his wife or one of his house to accompany the said corpse shall forfeit to ye foresaid box . . . *Provided always that the brethren be warned by the undermaisters which undermaisters shall give due warning upon paine for every default of 6^d.†*

A poor brother demise Item if that any brother brother's wife or brothers sonne shall depart to God's mercy and dye haueing not wherewithall to bring him forth or to pay his funerall then the said charges in bringing him forth and funeral expences to be taken on the comon box *as the trade or wardens shall think proper*.‡

Item if any brother of this gyld by himselfe his apprentice or journeyman shall goe into any place oute to worke any worke with any gentlemen or other private man in the nature as common bootmakers or unskillfull shoemakers in the country do that is by the consent aforesaid ordered and sett down that that brother which shall so do or direct his apprentice or journeyman so to do shall forfeit and pay to the said common box twenty shillings.

Younger brother to give place to the elder upon pain of xij^d Item it is by the assent and consent aforesaid agreed upon ordered and sett downe that in all markett townes whatsoever (Brampton excepted) wherennto any person or persons of this gyld or brotherhood shall repair for selling of his wayres that every younger brother shall giue place to the elder brother for

---

* This last line is a substitution for an erased one.
† An addition in a modern hand.
‡ Addition in a modern hand.

N

settinge and placinge his waires before the other upon paine
of forfeit to ye comon box twelvepence.*

To observe their oath. Item that all and every person and persons × ×   and
admitted to be a brother or a maister of this gyld and × ×
shalbe strictly bound by his oath upon a booke to observe
 × × whole industrie to keepe as well all the order aforesaid × × and many years heretofore sett downe as well
other hereafter × × for the benefit of this gyld and
brotherhood to be × × sett downe and agreed upon.†

Searchers vi^s viii^d Item it is by the consent aforesaid agreed upon and sett downe
that every quarterday two new searchers‡ shalbe app × to
search all maide wares maide by the brethren of this guild
which searchers shall haue authoritye hereby to enter into
any brother's shopp and search his wares And if they shall
find any not able or unsufficient or unsufficiently wrought
they hereby alsoe haue power to seize upon take and bring the
said waires away to the gyld haull or chamber there to remaine
and continue the good pleasure of the bodye of this occupation
And who shall withstand or will not suffer the said searchers
to do their duty herein shall forfeit to the benefitt of the said
box six shillings eight pence.

Refusing fines or amerciants Item it is ordered and sett down by the consent aforesaid if
that any of this brotherhood shall refuse to pay his fine or
amerciaments immediately upon the setting downe thereof or
upon demand thereof maid by the supervisors or governors
or one of them That then it shall be lawful unto the undermaisters to goe enter unto and distreant of the goods or things
whatsoever pertaining to th' offender and shall bring the
goods into the gyld chamber of this brotherhood there to be
forfeites prises for the amerciaments for discharge thereof And
who shall withstand and not suffer the said undermaisters to
do their dutyes herein shall pay and forfeit to ye benefitt of
this box twenty shillings.§

---

* The exception of Brampton is very curious, and is explained by a
rule below as to that market, pp. 180 and 181.

† A note says, "This to be placed nearer the beginning."

‡ These must not be confounded with the searchers of leather
appointed by the mayor under various statutes.

§ A note says, "To be amended."

Making of accounts by jorneymen.

Item it is by the assent aforesaid agreed upon and sett down that as well the undermaisters of this gyld and brotherhood as also the jorneymen shall at the quarter day called Sebastian quarter make a just accompt of all things come to their hands and the jorneymen how it standeth with them and how the condition of their stock and box is used and imployed.*

Item it is ordained and sett downe by the general consent of this whole body of this occupation that no brother of this gyld or maister of an apprentice shall at any time hearafter either suffer his owne apprentice or the apprentice of any other maister of this occupation to play at cards within their owne house upon paine for every time that he or they shall do the contrary to pay to the aforesaid comon box during his apprenticeship three shillings & fourpence.†

Playing as foresaid.

Item that no jorneyman of this occupation shall play with any apprentice at cards for either drinke or money at any time hereafter upon paine of twelve pence for every time to be livred to yͤ benefitt of the box of the jorneymen.†

Item it is ordered and concluded and by general consent it is sett downe that if any of this brotherhood do departe to gods mercy and haue one or more apprentices to be preferred to others the ancients of this occupation which have apprentices according to the orders of this book That no person or persons beinge of this brotherhood or to whom the said apprentices dewly shall fall shall not privately or openly compound agree or give any money or other consideration for any such apprentices upon paine of twenty shillings to this box.‡

Item it is ordered and sett downe by generall consent of this occupation that at what time soever that any apprentice shall happen to be lowst of his apprenticeship and intends nowe to be jorneyman and worke he shall first have foure paire of shoes given him to worke which shoes so by him wrought

---

* This is crossed out. In no other guild do we find the journeymen with a separate stock and common box.

† Both these rules are crossed out.

‡ A marginal note to this rule says "quære."

shalbe shewed to six of the aucient of this gyld to be veiwed and tryed which if the same be good worke and workmanlike then shall he be admitted a jorneyman otherwise he shall not haue any work but a hireman and haue wage according to his worke.[*]

Keeping of Brampton markett vi^s viii^d — Item it is concluded and agreed upon × × body of this occupation that the brethren × × shalbe divided into tow partes or parties after which th one partie or so many of them as will shall goe to × × markett with shewes on Tuesday and the other partie or × × many of them as please annother markett day so as th one partie go on thither but once in every fourteene dayes and any brother shall do contrary to this order shall pay for every so offending vi^s viii^d [†]

Making of foot balle. — Item it is fully condiscended and agreed upon by the fellowship of this gyld that no jorneyman or apprentice shall make any foot balle to sell or play withal without consent and knowledge of his or their maisters and that they shall not play at football within the liberties of this cittie upon paine everytime they shall do the contrary to forfeit to the comon box[‡] × ×

To makeng of boots & shoes vi^s viij^d. — Item it is ordered sett donne and agreed upon by the whole of this occupation at St Sebastian Twentyne § quarter 1600 that whosoever giveth more than thre pence for making of either single or double soled boots to any jorneyman shall forfeit to the benefitt of ye box six shillings and eight pence for every

---

[*] The difference between a journeyman and hireman is that the first had constant employ and pay ; the hireman was merely paid for each job, and might often want one. Journeymen, though originally meaning one hired for the day, came to mean one hired for a long period, — a year.

[†] Brampton is nine miles from Carlisle : probably the market was too small to make it worth while for the whole fraternity to attend at once. A later rule enforces this one. Brampton market is now held on a Wednesday.

[‡] Crossed out. Football playing led to rows and fights, but it was allowed on Carlisle Sands.

§ St. Sebastian Twentyne is a mixture of S. Sebastian and S. Quentin and is intended for the July quarter or Friday after Mary Magdalene : This St. Sebastian is not the early saint of that name, but Don Sebastian of Portugal. See *ante* p. 170.

time that he shall offend or for making any doble soled shewes alone eighteen pence the dossen and for pomps alone eight pence the dossen 12ᵈ *

None to sell his apprentice to make h'm a jorneyman.
xxˢ.

Item it is by general consent ordered and sett doune at Crispin and Crispiany quarter 1601+ that no brother shall over his apprentice to himselfe to any other but that he shall work as an apprentice and not as a jorneyman untill the apprentice haue served his yeare of apprenticeship upon forfeit to the aforesaid box twenty shillings.*

Item at Sebastian quarter‡ it is ordered and agreed upon by the general consent of this company that no man shall henceforth beinge unmarried shalbe admitted a brother of this occupation or companie but before his admittance he shall pay to the comon box xxˢ

Item it is ordered agreed upon and sett doun by the generall consent of this gyld that no person or persons professing the handycraft of a shoemaker and comminge to worke as a jorneyman of that trade not to be hyred or sett on worke by any of this gyld except he prove himselfe to be a skilful man of the occupation and shew his indentures or shew testimoney where he served his apprenticeship and for his tryell he so cumminge to worke shall haue first foure pares of dobble soled shewes cutt by mᵉ which he shall worke according to his skill and without help of any other which shewes shalbe brought and vewyed by this gyld. And whoso do the contrary to this order shall forfeit the said gyld twenty shillings.§

For goinge to Brampton fair.

Item Sᵗ Cryspiane quarter 1607 it is by yᵉ general consent of this gyld agreed upon and sett doune that every brother shall keepe the order for going to Brampton yea if the fare day fall on Tuesday, but if the fare of Brampton fall on any other day than Tuesday then it shall be laufull to every brother of

---

* Crossed out.

+ Crispin and Crispiany quarter was the October quarter. *Ante* p. 170.

‡ This will be the January quarter, St. Sebastian (the early saint) and St. Fabian. See *ante* p. 170.

§ Crossed out. A note says, "This to be considered."

this occupation at his will and pleasure to goe to the faire there with their goods shewes or other things.*

Item it is ordered and sett donne that no man shall keepe any stall in the streete upon paine and forfiture of ten shillings unless it be in the faire tyme.*

The clerkes fee for making indentures
Item at S Phillip and Jacob's quarter 1610 beinge ✗ of May it is concluded and agreed upon by the general consent of this occupation that our clerke shall haue ✗ ✗ makinge of every paire of indentures eighteen pence that is to say sixpence of yᵉ maister and twelve pence of yᵉ apprentice.

No brother shall buy boots or shoes in any other markett
Item it is concluded agreed upon by the whole consent of this occupation that from henceforth none of this occupation or brotherhood shall either in this cittie or any other place or markett buy either boots or shewes upon paine of twenty shillings.†

Byninge of horseleather
Item by the consent of this occupation it is ordered agreed upon and sett downe that no gyld of this gyld or brotherhood shall secretly or publicly buy any horseleather of any tanner or use cutt or worke any tanned horseleather in any waires upon paine of forfeiture as well of the said wares as alsoe to pay to the foresaid comon box for every default viˢ viiiᵈ ‡

If an apprentice die before 5 yeares be expired
Item it is agreed as aforesaid that when any apprentice is deade before he haith served five years his said maister may take another apprentice for asking leave of yᵉ head maisters.

Every brother to pay at
Item it is agreed upon and sett downe that every one of this gyld or brotherhood shall pay every quarterday at the house of meatinge viiiᵈ whether he comes or no.

— —— // — ——— .

✗ ✗ ✗ time of assembly in their gyld that there shalbe supervisors ✗ ✗ over the rest to keep them ✗ ✗ It is therefore by the general consent ✗ ✗ aforesaid ordained condiscended and ✗ ✗ the two ancientest and

---

* Crossed out.
† A note in margin says, "This to be considered."
‡ See a previous note as to horseleather, *ante* p. 175.

eldeste brethren   x   x   brotherhood shall duringe their
lives   x   x   taken and accompted supervisors or   x   x
of the rest of this ffraternity by whose and under whose
government the rest of this   x   x   shall submit themselves And he who shall not   x   x   at any meatinge or
assemblyes be esteemated to be obedient to thers commandment either   x   x   or th'one of them commanded to be
still   x   x   and otherwise shall loose forfeit and pay to th'
x   x   for every offence vi^{d.} *

Item it is by the said assent and consent agreed and sett
downe That yearly at the quarterday of Saint Sebastian there
shalbe two undermaisters appointed to execute the commandments of the supervisors or governors and bretherin of this
gyld   x   x   for warninge of the whole body of this
brotherhood   x   x   All or particular meatinges or for
other actions doings and belonginge to this brotherhood as
they shalbe commanded or directed.

Item it is by the assent and consent aforesaid ordered sett
downe and agreed upon that no person or persons shalbe taken
or accepted   x   x   admitted to be brothers of this gyld
or brotherhood but that haith served his apprenticeship in this
cittie fully And that no person or persons shalbe accepted or
admitted to be a brother of this gyld or brotherhood but only
on the quarter day next after Saint Sebastian day.†

     x   x   x   x   x   x   x

that every person or persons so to be taken or accepted and a
brother of this fellowship or brotherhood shall   x   x   sent
and pay to the benefitt of the common box of   x   x   gyld
thirteene shillings and fourpence sterlinge whereof six shillings
and eight pence at his firste cominge in and every quarter day
thereafter twelve pence untile the sum   x   x   of his
brotherhood be payed And he or they shall find one or two
oatmen pledged to pay the   x   x   his brotherhood within
one year.‡

---

    * This rule and the six following are on a loose and much-tattered
leaf ; they are in the same handwriting as the previous rules, and may
be part of the eleven missing at the beginning.

    † The clause beginning "And that no person" is crossed out.

    ‡ Crossed out.

Item that it is by the assent and consent aforesaid ordained sett downe and agreed upon that what person or persons soever as shalbe taken in and admitted to be a brother of this gyld shall either furthwith and presently thereupon sett up shopp and worke as a maister for hymself or otherwise shall chuse himself a maister of other of the brethren of this gyld with whom he shall worke in the nature of a jorneyman for one year thereafter and so from yeare to yeare untill he shalbe ready or able to set up for himself And whosoever shall attempt or do contrary to the intent of this order shall loss forfeit and pay to the common box ✕ ✕ ✕   *

Item the assent and consent aforesaid it is ordered agreed and sett down that no brother of this occupation shall take any person or persons to be his apprentice but only such as are naturall Englishmen and on this side Blackffourde upon paine and forfeit to the common box of this brotherhood xx⁵ †

Item that it is by the assent and consent abovesaid ordered agreed upon and sett downe that no brother of this gyld or occupation shall take an apprentice but by indenture written in parchment and for the tearme of seaven yeares at the least besides his hireman year And that both parties shall stand bound to other by obligation in the sume of five pounds for the performance of it upon ✕ ✕ ✕ forfitor to the comon box viᵈ viijᵈ *

Chrispin and Crispiane quarter day being the
· 30ᵗʰ of October 1663.

Memorandum yt it is this quarter day agreed upon with consent of the whole assent and consent of this ffraternity and brotherhood that from henceforth no quarter day shall be observed or kept saving only to meet together as formerly in the guild chamber each quarter and then ciuilly and orderly to treat and confer of things conducing to the good and benefit of this guild and hauing so done for each brother to depart to his owne imploy And that in lewe of the

---

* Crossed out.

† The line against Scotchmen was drawn not at the Scotch border, but four miles north of Carlisle, at Blackford. See *ante* p. 66 n.

quarterly drinkings at houses there shall be each year once one diner day upon the ffriday next after Chrispin and Crispiane quarter where every brother of this fraternity is to resort unto and to pay 12^d for his ordinary and to be vi^d in extraordinary the extraordinary not to begin till the diner be done And every brother absenting himselfe and not coming to the said diner nor one sent in his roome shall pay xii^d to him that shall provide the said diner The first diner day is to begin with Edmund Craister and so descend to each brother in order and course as their names stands in the call booke untill it be quite gone through the guild and then to begin with the senior and so in like manner goe round in order still descending to the next brother until it be gone through And if any brother haue not the × × himselfe to provide a dinner as aforesaid then he shall haue the liberty to appoint one who hath a × × house and make a good and sufficient dinner.

A note of the expences which was at the dinner day being at Edmond Craistores the 27^t of 8th 1663

Imprimis for M^r maior his 2 bayliffes & 3 sergeants	0 : 6 : 0	
Itm in wine - . . . . . -	0 : 4 : 0	
Itm to the musitians . . . . -	0 : 2 : 0	
Itm to the servants . . . . -	0 : 2 : 0	
	0 : 14 : 0	

This was paid by Edward Twentyman.

THE OATH OF A BROTHER OF THIS COMPANY OF SHOEMAKERS AS FOLLOWES VIZ

You shall swear to be a true brother of this company of shoemakers and shalbe obedient to observe all such orders and constitutions as are agreed upon or shalbe devised and set downe (being just and lawful) which may be for ye good and benfitt of this guild or brotherhood you shall duly and truely observe your quarterly meetings in the ye guild hall (without a lauful excuse) you shall keepe secret all private conferrances at our meetings and likewise if any thing shall come to your knowledge that may tend to ye preju- dice or harm of any member of this ffraternity you shall truely acquaint them therewith and to ye best of your knowledge maintaine and defend ye same all these and whatsoever else belongs to a brother of this company you shall faithfully observe perform and keepe to ye utmost of your power soe helpe you god and by ye contents of that book.

THE OATH OF UNDER MASTER

You shall sweare that as under master or warden for this company you will truely and carefully execute the same dureing the time you shall remaine in it that you will not wast nor negligently lay out the money belonging to this company that you will attend give notice and carefully execute all such duties as belong to one in your office to the best of your skill knouledge and obey the directions of the supervisors or elders of this fraternity soe help you &et.

In 1683 the trade did vote to the contrary that noe brother shall take an apprentice but such as haue formerly keept shopp or such as shall keepe open shoppe twelve months at the least before he take an apprentice.

It was afterwards ordered that no brother of this guild should take an apprentice befor that he had keept open shop six months and wrought as a master in this city and that he be a freeman of this city befor he takes aprentice to make him a freeman.*

Sebastian quarter day January the 23.
Anno dni 1684.

Memorandum that on the thirteeth day of December one thousand six hundred eighty and four his majestys gracious charter came into this city and the mayor aldermen and common counsell was pleased to giue to this fraternity the summe of a guinny to drinke his majestys good health and all the rest of that royall familly which was done accordingly.†

---

* " Robt. Stagg refused leave to take an apprentice."
In a later hand on the margin.

† This was the charter of Charles II, which deprived the city of many of its liberties. See *ante* p. 18. It is treated as a nullity.

S Sebastian quarter day January 23 1684.

Item it is agreed and ordered upon by the whole company that noe brother shalbe admitted into this company that hath married before his tearme of yeares of apprenticeship be expired but in such case

   ✕   ✕   ✕   fraternity   ✕   ✕   ✕   *

Item it is concluded and agreed upon by the whole consent of this occupation therefrom henceforth none of this company or brotherhood shall either in this city or in any other place or markett buy either boots or shoes of any foreigner or any other person exceptain always that any brother may buy the goods of any deceyed brother from his executor or administrator.

Whereas Ann Barrow the wife of Richard Barrow formerly one that by virtue of the Coldstream act brought shoes and exposed them to sell in Carlisle market he being long abroad and his said wife poor the trade is willing to permit the said Ann to bring and sell shoes provided always they be of the work of one former servant and noe more and for this permission she owns the trades favour and is thankful for it   Afterwards to witt the 5th of May 1704 agreed and ordered that every yeare she shall pay upon the 1st friday after Mayday 2 shillings.

May 5 1699.

Phillip and Jacob   } Then ordered and agreed upon by all the quarter day May 7 1702 } brethren of this trade (nemine contradicente) that whereas the decision of any difference is very much confused where all the numerous members of this society is consulted it is agreed upon that henceforth all differences matters and things whatsoever shall be ended and determined by these eight vizt Robert Jackson sen^r Edward Twentyman Michael Colling William Harrison Thomas Jackson John Sewell Joseph Nixon and John Scalby or the major part of them and if upon any poll these supervisors shall be equal then and onely in such case it shall pass to the vote of every member present   And further when any of the supervisors above mentioned shall die or be otherwise removed that then the said supervisors shall chuse another to be of their number out of the

---

* From this point we proceed with entries taken from the earlier book. These do not always follow in chronological order, as the clerks seem frequently to have inserted entries in any blank spaces available, regardless of any other aptness.

said ffraternity and alsoe that upon Whitsun Monday Tuesday and Whitsun Weduesday next these supervisors or as many of them as cann conveniently meet shall view the orders raze out continue or amend the same and whatever they doe shall be the sentiment of the whole society.

January 25 1705.

S Fab and Sebas.
Ordered the day and yeare abovesaid that whereas there is a prosecution begun against seaverall country offenders for exercising our trade not sufficiently qualified we order and agree that all shoe-makers belonging to our ffraternity that exercise the trade shall contribute proportionally to the charges of the suits begun or to be begun viz¹ not only those that doe exercise and worke in the trade but such as soe use the said trade or take apprentices to be made brothers thereof or having such other advantages as working brothes pretend so.

S Phillip and Jacob.
Quarter day May 31.1706 It is then ordered for deciding controversy relating to this trade proper to be decided by the trade in generall it is agreed that two considerable brothers elected for that purpose by the trade shall receive all complaints or applications relating to the breach of any of our orders those two haue power to dettermine calling in to their assistance the two undermaisters for the time being and if those think themselves notfitt to end the matter or controversy then they shall transmit the same to all the superiors appointed and chosen by the trade.

Stabin and S¹ Sebastian quarter day, being 24ʰ of January anno domini 1723 then ordered by the fraternity guild and occupation of the cordwainers and shoemakers of the citie of Carlisle in the county of Cumberland that they did agree to prosecute all persons that is not a brother of this guild and fraternity who shall make or presume to make any new shoes or boots or to translate old ones that shall take any shop or chamber within the frelidge liberties of the same in order to work or make new shoes or boots for fremen or others and mend or translate old shoes for themselves or himselfe by cutting new leather or by other equivocating wayes and means doth endeavour to lessen or hinder the priuiledges and immuuityes of this free guild and brotherhood who are a company incorporated by prescription who hath had and may have power to make bye laws for preserving the priuileges of traders in the art and mystery of cordwainers or shoemakers of this corporation and for excluding or hindring all persons not rightly qualified for working in this cittie.

I think this order was made when Will hall did pretend to set up shop to mend and make shoes but he presently left of upon the first discharging him.*

Copy of the shoemakers case about suppressing of the clog or wooden soles put in to new uper leathers.

It is enacted (amongst other things) that no person that shall occupy the mistery or occupation of cordwainer or shoemaker shall make or caus to be made any shoe or any part of them of English leather wet curried (other then deer skins calve skins or goat skins made and dressed or to be made and dressed like unto Spanish leather) but of leather well and truely tanned and curried in manner and form aforesaid or of leather well and truely tanned onely and well and substantially sewed with good thread well twisted and made and sufficiently waxed with wax sewed with good thread × × × stitches hard drawn with hand leathers or shall put in the utter sole any other leather then the best ox or steer hide and if the searchers find any shoes or otherthing wrought converted or used contrary to the said statute or insufficiently wrought they may seiz and retaine ye same till they be tried by the triers and all that shall be seized and tried to be forfeted shall be brought to the comon hall and thereto to be prized and of the value to be disposed to the poor and in other deeds of charity at the discretion of the mayor and another part to the mayor to the use of the comonalty of such city and the third part to the seizer thereof for his paines and by said statute judges of assize justices of peace and stawards of franchises leets and lawdays mayors and other head officers of cities have power in their sessions leets and lawdays to enquire of the premises and to determine the same.†

---

* This remark is in another handwriting.

† This recital is taken from the 1 Jac. 1, c. 22, section 23, &ct.

Notwithstanding which act vast numbers of people in the county of Cumberland and without serving any apprenticeshipe follone a method of nailing uper leathers to wooden soles which they call wooden shoes or clogs and expose great quantities thereof to sale in the market so that it is (computed) their is more leather curried in that county for upper leather for these wooden soles then for leather soles to the great discouragement of the shoemakers trade and exeding great prejudice to his majestys revenue of sole leathers for one pair of strong uper leathers will wear out two pair of wooden soles: though they be plated with iron on the heels and soles to make them as durable as two paire of shoes.

A copy of a petition sent from the shoemakers guildhall January 25 day 1738 to the members for Parliament.

To the Hon. Coll. Chas. Howard and Baron Hilton members of Parliament for the city of Carlisle.

The humble petition cordwainers of the city of Carlisle shew We having been fully aprised that a petition is presented to the honourable House of Commons by the curriers &ct praying leave to impower them freely to cut and sell all sorts of leather in any city town or corporation in England contrary to the laws now in being by which it is now apprehended that not only the shoemakers trade here but all over the kingdom will be destroyed : or at least irreparably damaged and the whole leather trade monopolised and ingrossed by the curriers to themselves wee your honours petitioners in order to prevent the framing of so pernicious a bill so destructive to our trade and which we are confident cannot tend to the public good notwithstanding the specious pretence wherewith it is introduced but must necessarily prove the ruin of many poor families in this kingdome do most humbly intreat your honours vot and interest in parliament against the same whereby you will not onely highly obleidge your petitioners but also saue them their children and posterity from ruine.*

      And greatly oblidge

          Your honours most obedient

Cordwainers hall   Humble servants.

 Carlisle Jan 25 1738.

---

* By the 1 Jac. I, c. 22, section 20, a currier could not be a "tanner cordwainer shoemaker butcher or other artificer usinge cutting of leather."

Robert Ford
Thomas Brown
Thomas Wallis
William Carruthers
Thomas Hodgson
Robert Hodgson
Thomas Hardin
Georg Scellon
James Collins
John Smith
Lenard Twentiman
Robert Sutton
Thomas Hewitt
Robert Bennet
Joseph Sewell
John Dixon
Will Routledge

Launcelot Beck
Richard Peall
Samuel Coleman
John Banks
John Graham
John Dobinson
Rob James
James Nicholson
Robert Nixon
Robert Norman
Georg. Dobinson
Joseph Sewell

John Sewell
Mich. Collin
Timothy Graham
John Hodgson
Will Addinson
Samuel halton
Robert Jackson
George Read
Will Carrick

To the Honᵉ Coll Charles
Howard at his lodgings
in Maddock Street
                London
                        these

//

A book of all the ancient laws customs constitutions and orders
accustomed holden and observed by the fraternity guild and brotherhood of the trade mystery and occupation of the cordwainers or
shoe-makers of the city of Carlisle and county of Cumberland
whereby every person or persons that are or shall be admitted a
brother or master of the said guild and company shall be bound by
oath to conform to and observe the following rules and orders agreed
upon by the mutual consent of the said brotherhood as also other
orders that shall be hereafter assented to or agreed upon for the
maintenance and common benefit of the said guild and brotherhood
And it is agreed and settled as a standing rule that these orders be
read all over publickly in the guild hall once a year at least viz on
Philip and Jacobs quarter day.*

---

* These rules are on the parchment sheet at the commencement of the
2nd book. On a loose sheet in the older book, we find, " Oct the 31 day 1735
then paid John Sewell the sume of five shillings for what he had done to
respect the new book. Oct 31 day 1735 then paid George Read junior ten
shillings for assisting John Sewell in writing the orders in."

First It is by the general assent and mutual consent of this guild
       brotherhood and company of the shoemakers of this city
       ordered concluded and agreed upon that there shall be four
       quarter days or four special days of meeting yearly at which
       the whole body of this brotherhood shall convene and meet
       together to confer and consider of all matters and causes
       touching concerning or belonging to the common benefit or
       good order of the said brotherhood The first quarter day to
       be kept the Friday after the 20th January The second
       quarter day the Friday after S Philip and Jacob 1st May
       The third the Friday after the feast of Mary Magdalene 22
       July and the fourth to be kept the Friday after Crispin and
       Crispianus being the twenty fifth of October.

Item 2. It is by the general assent and consent of the whole
       body of this guild agreed upon that if any brother of this
       company shall absent himself from the said quarter days when
       duly warned by the under masters or one of them without a
       lauful reason for so doing shall forfeit and pay to the common
       box of this guild for every such neglect six pence.

Item 3. By the mutual consent aforesaid it is enjoyn'd that
       every member of this company be present at the hall or
       chamber every quarter day at or before one of the clock in
       the afternoon and who shall be absent or come after one a
       clock be strucken and after the names of the brethren in the
       catalogue be called the second time shall pay to the said box
       sixpence.

Item 4. To the end that all and every of the brethren of
       this guild behave himself or themselves in their hall at their
       meeting soberly and with good manners as is fitting when the
       company or trade is convened it is agreed upon by general
       consent aforesaid that two wardens be chosen yearly by the
       votes of all the brethren in general provided that the wardens
       are chosen out of the twelve table-men* to avoid confusion in
       the election or such persons as the table-men shall appoint the

---

* No definition of the table-men is to be found, but it probably means the
twelve seniors, who found seats at the table in the guild chamber, while the
others sat round the room.

candidates so approv'd of by the tablemen not to exceed three the office of the wardens shall be to cause good order be kept in the hall and to reprove all cursing swearing or opprobious language and any disorder that doth disturb the guild and brotherhood and he or they that do not at the first reproof or commandment keep silence and behave as becomes a brother or depart the hall if desired or required by them shall forfeit and pay to the publick box 3ˢ 4ᵈ and further if it so happen that there be an equal poll at any time when any affair is put to the vote that then the senior warden have the casting vote.

Item 5. It is by the general assent and consent of the brethren of this guild agreed upon that there shall be chosen yearly at the quarter day next after the feast of Sᵗ Sebastian two under masters to execute the orders of the table-men and wardens of the guild and to warn and give timely notice to the whole body of the brotherhood within the liberties of this city at their aforesaid quarter days or other times as they shall have occasion to meet for the dispatching of business *and those persons that refuse the said office as by rotation shall pay to the box 2ˢ 6ᵈ.* *

Item 6. By the assent and consent aforesaid it is agreed upon and ordered that none shall be admitted a brother of this company but he that has served his apprenticeship seven years compleat in this city or has a claim thereto by birthright that is his father being a brother and freeman before him or a gentleman that may be of service to the trade and is voted in by a majority of all the brotherhood.†

Item 7. It is by the mutual consent aforesaid agreed upon that no brother shall take an apprentice but by indenture and for no less term than seven years and that they be such as may be taken by the statute viz fourteen years of age.

Item 8. By a general consent of this guild and brotherhood it is agreed upon that no person having a right to this guild shall take an apprentice before he hath been made a brother

---

* An addition in another hand.

† The last clause is important : points to a "patronus." No doubt the guild often found gentlemen useful, if only to pay for liquor on occasions.

and hath kept open shop for six months and any brother
taking an apprentice in this city shall enroll him in the
register of the trades-books on or before the first quarter day
after the date of his indenture and pay for the enrollment to
the benefit of the common box 6^d and to the clerk for
enrolling him a penny.

Item 9. By the assent and consent aforesaid it is agreed That
no brother having an apprentice shall take another apprentice
upon any account whatever before the other hath served five
years fully upon penalty of paying to the box 20^s and giving
up his apprentice so taken immediately except he be a brother's
son and in that case a master having only one apprentice may
set down his own son or a brother's son any time he please.

Opposite to rule the first of these rules is this

S Sebastian quarter ⎱ It is agreed by the general assent and
Jan 21 1780   ⎰ consent of this guild and brotherhood
that no master (having an apprentice) shall take another
apprentice before the other hath served three years fully and
then to pay unto the trade box at the execution of the said
indenture one pound one shilling beside the usual fees of
enrolment except he be a brother's son and that a former order
in this book N° 9 which restrains masters from takeing a
second apprentice before the first has served five years is
hereby made null and void and of no force.

Item 10. It is concluded and agreed upon that if any brother
depart to God's mercy or leave of the trade having one or
more apprentices to be disposed of to a new master inhabiting
within the liberties of this city that then the apprentice or
apprentices shall present themselves to the trade the first
quarter day after the decease of their former masters in order
to be assigned over to a new master.

Item 11. It is agreed upon by the mutual assent and consent
aforesaid That a master that taketh an apprentice by assignment of the executors of a deceased brother or of any brother
that shall leave off keeping open shop shall enroll his ac-
ceptances of him the first quarter day and his assignment the
quarter day following and shall pay to the common box every

quarter day during the time the apprentice has to serve one shilling.

Item 12. By the assent and consent aforesaid it is concluded and agreed upon that no master shall sell over to work as a journeyman during his apprenticeship his apprentice upon the penalty of paying to the box twenty shillings.

Item 13. By the general and mutual agreement and consent of all the brethren of this guild agreed upon that no brother of this company and fraternity shall employ or set to work a journeyman servant or apprentice of any other brother of this guild without the consent license and good will of his said brother to whom he his bound or with whom he is hired unless his former master doth not keep him employed as he ought to do and this to be made appear to the wardens by complaint in order for redress) upon the penalty of 20ˢ to the common box of this hall.

Item 14. It is agreed upon by the assent and consent aforesaid that no person that hath been bound by indenture and enrolled and registered in the book of this guild and marries before his seven years of apprenticeship be expired and ended shall be taken in or admitted a brother of this guild.

Item 15. By the assent and consent aforesaid it is agreed and concluded that if any person or persons shall contend with strokes or draw weapon or knife against any brother within the guild hall shall forfeit to the common box twenty shillings.

Item 16. It is ordered by the consent aforesaid. That if any brother of this guild shall refuse to pay his fine for the breach or neglect of any of the orders he hath sworn to perform or such a sum as the wardens and tablemen shall moderate it to that then the offender may be arrested and the under masters shall take out entry or summons and sue him to the mayors court of this city in order to recover the said fine and the under masters shall be empowered to employ such council and attorneys as are necessary for prosecuting the offenders out of the publick box.

N.B. That all these that have been table-men is to be esteemed as table-men and act and give their voice as such if present in the guild.

Item 17. By the assent and consent aforesaid it is agreed. Then when it shall please God to call any of this brotherhood to his mercy or his wife children or apprentice and shall request of the wardens clark and undermasters to have the trade warned That then the whole fraternity shall attend the corpse to church he his wife or one of his family and return after the interment to the house of the deceased and pay sixpence if requested and they that do not attend the corpse as aforesaid shall forfeit to the common box sixpence and further if a brother that is necessitus his wife or child die and application be made to the trade the first quarter day after the funeral the wardens and table-men may make them such allowance as they shall think reasonable for them out of the common box of this guild and brotherhood.

Item 18. By the general and mutual assent aforesaid it is agreed that if any person or persons being a brother of this guild or servant journeyman or apprentice shall be detected or proved to have committed any crime or felony and by verdict of a jury hath been convicted such person or persons so convicted shall be deprived of and lose the benefit of being a brother of this guild and shall not be suffered to work within the liberties of this city hereafter.

Item 19. By the assent and consent abovesaid it is agreed upon that no brother living and residing without the liberties of this city shall take an apprentice in order to make him free nor shall such an one be admitted to inroll an apprentice before he haith kept open shop within the liberties of the city six months and continue to keep his apprentice (if designed to be a brother and freemen) at work during all the time of his apprenticeship in the city or else assign him over to a master following the business aforesaid within the liberties of this city and further none shall be admitted to take or enroll an apprentice but masters that carry on the trade within the liberties of this city.

Item 20. Ordered and agreed by consent aforesaid that all brethren of this company living without the liberties if they request it shall be exempted from appearing save once a year on Philip and Jacobs quarter day on which they shall appear and pay for the year one shilling.

Item 21. [gone.]

Item 22. It is ordered and agreed upon by the general consent of the guild and brotherhood that no person whatever be admitted and sworn a brother of this society but upon one of the four quarter day unless such person or persons chuseing to be made on any other day than a quarter day then such person or persons shall pay (besides the usuall money to the box) double fees a ten-shillings treet to the trade and one shilling to the undermasters.

1750. Madg.* It is this day ordered by the consent and assent of this guild and brotherhood att their quarter day assembled to nominate Michael Collins to represent their incorporated trade in order to see the execution of a bond to be granted from the worshipful corporation of this city to the eight guilds and to be a trustee for the said guild to make ye bond binding.

Signed the day and year above by the wardens of ye guild. John Hodgson. Tho Hewett.

COPY FROM THE ORIGINAL.†

Know all men by these presents that we the mayor aldermen bailifs and citizens of the city of Carlisle are held and firmly bound unto the Rev Wm Nicholson Jackson of the said city clerk and a brother of the merchants guild within the said city George Blamire of the city aforesaid gentleman a brother of the tanners guild there Jeremiah Adderton of the same place gentleman a brother of the taylors guild there Thos Lowry of Blackhall in the county of Cumberland gentleman a

---

* Magdalen quarter day.

† This is the heading in the book. The bond that follows is not the one given in 1750, which is not set out, but a similar one given in 1759. For the intervening transactions see pp. 34, 35, 36 ante.

brother of the smiths guild within the said city Michael
Collins of the city aforesaid shoemaker a brother of the
butchers guild there Wilfred Reay of Caldewgate without the
said city a brother of the weavers guild in the said city and
Rob Railton of the city aforesaid innkeeper a brother of the
skinner and glover guild within the said city trustees appointed
by the said several guilds for this purpose and to enforce the
due execution and performance of the bye law or order of
common council of the said city in the condition hereunder mentioned in the sum of one thousand pounds of good and lawfull
money of Great Britain to be paid unto the said Wm Nicholson
Jackson Geo Blamire Jeremiah Adderton Thos Lowry Michael
Collins James Grayson Wilfred Reay and Rob Railton or to
their certain attorneys or to the survivors or survivor of them
or the certain attorney of the survivors or survivor of them
or to th. exors admors or assignees of the survivors of them to
which payment well and truly to be made we bind ourselves
and our successors firmly by these presents seald with our
common seal dated the eleventh day of September in the
thirty third year of the reign of our sovereign lord king George
the Second and in the year of our Lord one thousand seven
hundred and fifty nine.

THE CONDITION OF THIS OBLIGATION

that whereas at a meeting of the above bounden mayor
aldermen bailiffs and citizens of the said city of Carlisle in
council assembled in the guildhall in the said city in order
to put an end to all debates and disputes touching the making
of freemen for the future and also for the regular passing and
auditing the annual accounts of the said city it was amongst
other things then ordered as follows   Whereas the admitting
of persons to the freedom of this corporation who are not
intitled thereunto either by birth or servitude is adjudged to
be very detrimental thereunto   And whereas the auditing
annually of the accounts of the said corporation may tend to
the advancement of the revenue thereof   Therefore it is this
day ordered that for the future no person or persons whatsoever
shall be admitted a freeman of this city or corporation but
such as are clearly intituled to their freedom either by birth
or by having first served a legal apprenticeship to some

member of the said corporation inhabiting within the said
city notwithstanding any former order by law or usage of or
within this corporation to the contrary thereof And it is hereby
further ordered that the annual accounts of this corporation
shall for the future be made up and finished yearly at least
ten days before twenty fifth day of March in every year by
the accountant and accountants of the said corporation and
that such accounts after the same are so made up by the
proper accountant or accountants shall or may annually be
inspected and examined in full council by eight of the freemen
of the said corporation that is to say one proper person to be
elected and nominated yearly by and out of each of the eight
guilds of the said city or corporation for that purpose who may
attend yearly if they think proper and have the inspection and
examination of all and every the accounts relative to the said
corporation for the preceeding year and of all receipts and
vouchers vouching such accounts And for that purpose persons
may be appointed by the said eight guilds and that such
persons so appointed may be made acquainted with the time
or times of meeting yearly to examine and inspect such
accounts   It is likewise ordered that the mayor or this corporation for the time being do yearly give at least six days
notice in writing under his hand of such time or times to the
master or wardens of each of the said eight guilds for the time
being and that no account or accounts of the said corporation
or relative thereto shall hereafter be passed or the accountant
or accountants discharged thereof or therefrom untill such
account or accounts are inspected and examined and also
attested and subscribed yearly by a majority of the freemen
so nominated by the said eight guilds who shall and do
actually attend the inspection thereof and for the better and
more punctual observance of this order it is recorded and
ordered that the now mayor of the said corporation shall and
may execute under the common seal of the said corporation
one bond or obligation in the penal sum of one thousand
pounds with condition for the due performance of all and every
part of such orders according to the sense and meaning thereof
and which said bond shall be so executed and delivered to such
and so many persons as the majority of the now wardens of

the said guilds shall appoint for that purpose in trust for the said guilds and the rest of the freemen of the said corporation If therefore the said mayor aldermen bailiffs and citizens of the said city of Carlisle for the time being and their successors do and shall from time to time and at all times for ever hereafter in all things well and truly observe perform fulfill accomplish and keep the above recited bylaw and order of council which on their parts are or ought to be observed performed fullfilled accomplished and kept in such manner and form as is mentioned and set forth in the said order of council made this day according to the true intent and meaning of the same without any fraud or cozin or any act or other thing to be done hereafter by the said mayor aldermen bailiffs and citizens or their successors to obstruct or revoke the same then the present obligation to be void and of no effect or else to be and remain in full force and vertue with effect in law.

Signed
   Rich Coulthard Mayor

GREAT
SEAL

July 27 1785. We whose names are hereby signed being freemen of the city of Carlisle and intitled thereunto by birth or servitude according to the antient usage of the said city do hereunto promise to pay to the treasurer hereafter to be appointed to receive the same the sums set opposite to our names towards carrying on such process at law or otherwise as shall be thought proper for contesting the legality of the late made honnorary freemen and also the steps by which they were made. [*Ante* p. 117.]

[Signed by about fifty for various sums from 1s. to 2s. 6d.]

Magd· quar⎫ It was then ordered and agreed by the general
the 29th day ⎬ consent of this guild and brotherhood that
of July 1785⎭ every brother belonging this fraternity that
attends the quarterly call shall pay unto the common box three pence every quarter day. And also that all yearly brethren shall pay unto the aforesaid box the sum of two shillings yearly in order to support all necessary emergencys

that may happen for the good and benefit of the said guild and brotherhood.

The same day by a general consent of this guild it was put to vote and passed not one voice being to the contrary that all the stock should go first to support our rights and privileges against all opposers.

Magd. quarter }
July 28 1786 } It is ordered and agreed this quarter day that for the future no honorary or ex gratia brother be on any account what soever admitted in this guild but on a quarter day and that every brother legally entitled shall give twenty four hours notice to the clerk before he be admitted.

June 23 1786.

Whereas we have been alarmed &ct.*

Mr Edward Nevison weaver
Mr Thos Coulthard tanner
Mr Willm Jackson merchant
Mr Heny Dobinson weaver
Mr Geo Blamire jun tanner
Mr Thos Blamire   do
Mr Rob. Harrington do
Mr Geo Harrington do
Mr John Carnaby smith
Mr Robt James merchant
Mr Isaac Ebdell   do
Mr James Grayson butcher
Mr James Grayson butcher
Mr John Brown butcher

Mr Edwd Rowland tanner
Mr Antho Laucake smith
Mr Willm Halton merchant
Mr John Young butcher
Mr John Blamire merchant
Mr James Monkhouse smith
Mr Robt Lamonby weaver
Mr Joseph Beck skinner
Mr Willm Little butcher
Mr John Watson taylor
Mr Joseph Twentyman weaver
Mr John Atkinson merchant
Mr Tho Sowerby butcher

Carlisle 30 1796.

Series of restrictions as to quarter days, *ante* p. 122.

MISCELLANEOUS ENTRIES.

INROULEMENTS OF AND FOR APPRENTICES.

Phillip and Jacob qr 1595 John Mulcaster sonne to Richard Mulcaster bound apprentice unto Robert Blacklocke for eight years seaven as apprentice and the eight as an hired servant by indenture bearinge date the feast day

* A copy *ante* p. 162. The list of names added to the guild is not quite the same as that adopted by the tailors, *ante* p. 162. The shoemakers omit the three shoemakers (they were already members), but they add only one tailor, though they add several craftsmen, not added by the tailors: this is hardly reciprocal.

of ye Purification of the Virgin Mary 1594 and in the 38 year of her ma{tie} reigne.*

The names of the fraternity and brotherhood of the shoemakers living at Philip & Jacob 1647.

Ralph Smith	Edw James
Robert Dalton	Thomas Cholmely
Thomas James	William Christian
William Vaux	Edmond Craister
Robert Shepherd	——— Braithwaite
John Nickholson	Robert Jackson
William Stagg senr	William Robinson
Thomas Calvert	John Pingneys
Thomas Jackson	John Dethick
William Knagg	Edward Twentyman
John Nixon	Symond Nixon
William Stagg jun	John Pattinson
Henry Baines	Thomas Dixon

26

* This is the earliest entry in the earliest book, and is in the same handwriting as the rules and orders at beginning of that book. The enrolments continue from 1594 to 1725. They present no very special features of interest. In 1597 one John Pattinson, whose son is bound apprentice unto Christopher Walker, is described as called "reed John Tanner." The odd name of Achilles Stagg is found about 1600. In 1657, John Paxton of Stapleton is bound apprentice for ten years. From marginal notes made by some commentator, it appears to have been the custom to bind all those that were not brothers' sons for ten years. In 1662, the commentator notes of Jacob Reeve, "This is the first apprentice that was bound but 7 years that not a b's son." After this date the eighth year as hireman is generally omitted. One or two instances occur of indentures being cancelled after six months' trial. The entries get irregular and the handwriting very bad about 1678, but afterwards improve. In 1682, Edw. Hind alias Gibson son of John Darrance of the citty of Carlile is bound apprentice, but a note is added, "The above inrolled Edw . . . . hath so extravagantly and indecently behaved himselfe that he shal never be admitted brother or haue any advantage of the sd inrolmt." A similar note is made to John Sewell enrolled in 1683 : he was admitted in 1689 and was clerk 1725 to 1742. In 1720, Robert (name illegible) is enrolled apprentice, but the entry is erased and noted—

This could not be admitted
becos Michael Collins did not
follow the shoemakers trade nor
keep open shop an was refused
to inroll him in the city book.

In 1719, enrolment of Joseph Pattinson is cancelled because "he never served with his master in town." Some enrolments are erased, and no explanation given. In 1725, William Kirkbride's enrolment is noted. "Memorandum that the above sd Will Kirkbride ordred by a great majority to be crossed out of the book becaas he had marryed but some opposed it as that being a right which the master might despence with."

List of the guild 24 January 1661.

Ralph Smith, Robert Dalton, Robert Shepherd, John Nicholson, Thomas Jackson, William Knagg, John Nixon, William Stagg, Edw James cler. of the company, Mr Henry Baynes, Wm Grame, Edmund Craister, Hugh Braithwait, Robert Jackson, William Robinson, John Dethick, Edward Twentyman, Symon Nixon, John Pattinson, Thomas Dixon, ffrancis Wood, John Atkinson, Anthony Heniside, John Nicholson, John Dobinson, Edward Gibson, Rob Sealby, John Dixon, Thomas Hutton—29.

1661. Itm in expense at the king's coronacon   0 : 13 : 0*

Item in expense by the trade at severall times when they rode to Kendall to buy shoos 9s. *

8 p of children shoos at 12d a p is	00 : 08 : 00
Bought of John Brabbond	
12 p of shoos at 3s a p is - -	01 : 16 : 00
24 p of shoos all for women	
at 2s 1d a pr is - -	2 : 10 : 00
Bought of Jn Ronson	
9 p of shooes at 2s 4d a p is -	1 : 01 : 00
Bought of Rob Wharton	
21 p of wom: shooes at 2s 3d a p -	2 : 14 : 00
12 p of men shoos at 3s 3d - -	1 : 19 : 00
12 p of childrns shoos at 10d a pair or	0 : 10 : 00
&c. &ct.	
—— in all great & small	
331 paire summd - - -	35 : 16 : 07
For expence in going & coming	
from Kendall	00 : 16 : 08
For carrying of the sd shooes -	00 : 10 : 04
Jackson took nothing for horse	
Twentyman paid for his horse -	00 : 05 : 00
	37 : 08 : 07*

October 28 1664 being Crispon quarter.

Mr Thomas Lowther was admitted a brother of this guild.

---

* This is on a loose piece of paper. An entry elsewhere shows that Robert Jackson and Edward Twentyman were in 1661 appointed by general consent to buy boots and shoes, and that seven members of the guild advanced £5. The shoes were sold over again in batches to the trade.

The Ascension day bill 1664.

For drink - - - -	00 : 08 : 00
For bread - - - -	00 : 03 : 00
A creem chees - - -	00 : 04 : 04
Item ¼ ᵗᵇ best cut tobacco - -	00 : 01 : 00
Item ½ ᵗᵇ best cut tobacco - -	00 : 01 : 06
Item a quart of sack - - -	00 : 2 : 00
Item a quart of claret - -	00 : 1 : 00
Item in pipes - - - -	00 : 00 : 10
Item in candles - - - -	00 : 00 : 02
Item 1 ᵗᵇ of Biscuit - - -	00 : 01 : 02

1 : 03 : 00*

1676. William Taylor admitted a brother on condition that he do not trade or sett up within a mile of yᵉ citty.

1679. Vincent Coats of Penrith is admitted a brother of this guild upon condition that he shall not trade or sett up within a mile of the citty and he has payed for his brotherhood three pounds this quarter day and he is not to buy any shoes of any man to sell again in this market neither shall he worke any horse leather or any other leather prohibited by the laws of this kingdom In witness whereof I Vincent Coats have set my hand the second day of May 1679.†

1682. Henry Pearson is admitted a brother, but only to sell shoes in the market and not to worke or sett up shop in the city or libertie thereof.

Decemb 11ᵗʰ 1682.

Impr to Mʳ Joseph Read for taffety silk and other trappings for the culler	02 : 12 : 02
Paid to Mʳ Robert Smedley for paintyng it	04 : 00 : 00
Pᵈ John Addison for makeing the fringe & setting it on	00 : 08 : 00
For mending the culler staffe two staples & one loupe	00 : 01 : 00
For goulding & cullouring Crispiannus	00 : 15 : 00
More for other repairs to the culler -	01 : 1 : 2
	08 : 17 : 4
1683. For the box lock & bands - -	00 : 08 : 9

* From another bill it appears that the 8s. in drinks paid for 32 flagons or quarts. The sack and claret would be for the mayor and the swells who would call in with him.

† The guild, on the same day, lent Coats £3 on his bond : this was often done with new brothers who probably were not flush of cash.

1683. Memorandum that whereas Edward Twentyman was due to this fraternity six pounds by bond it is this day ordered that the sd bond shalbe cancelled & given him & his bond discharged.

It is ordered this day that Eliz. Nixon have given her towards her releife 2ˢ & never to trouble the trade more.*

Philip & Jacob quarter day being the second day of May 1864. Ordered this quarter day that the apprentices belonging to this occupation shall have two & sixpence to be mirry on Alhallow Thursday and neither they nor the journeymen shal truble the guild that day.

Rec. on Ascension day 1686 from Mʳ feilding by Sir Christopher Musgrave's order - · · · · · · 0 : 10 : 0†

Sept the first 1710. Reᵈ· from Mʳ James Maxwell two guineys by the Lord Carlisle's order upon Sir James Montague's acct.‡

Sept 1 1710. To Cornl Glidhills§ servant for bring the plate 51ˢ·

Sept 21 1710. Wee admit the Hᵇˡᵉ Capt Thomas Morris‖ to be a brother of this society by the generall consent of this fraternity Sept the 22 1710. The Honᵇˡᵉ Coroll Samuel Glidhill is admitted a brother of this society by the generall consent of this fraternity.

Received from Cornall Glidhill a silver standard and two silver candlesticks.

---

* She had relief before : instances of this kind might be multiplied ; sometimes the relief was a coffin, at 9s.

† This item frequently occurs. Sir Christopher Musgrave was M.P. for Carlisle 1661 to 1690. See *ante* p. 157. Captain Bubb, M.P. for Carlisle 1689 to 1691 or 1692, gives 10s. in 1690. See *Cumb. and West. M.P.s*

‡ Attorney General, afterwards Chief Baron ; represented Carlisle in the Howard interest 1705 to 1714. See *Cumb. and West. M.P.s*

§ Colonel Gledhill contested Carlisle in 1710. He was defeated and petitioned the House of Commons against Montague's return on the grounds of bribery, treating, and undue influence. Similar charges were made against Gledhill in retaliation, the silver standard (a salver) and the candlesticks, and also seven hundred pair of shoes, which Gledhill ordered for his regiment from this guild, being prominently advanced. See *Cumb. and West. M.P.s*, p. 87 *et. seq.*

‖ For Captain Thomas Morris see *Transactions of Cumb. and West. Archæological Society*, Vol. VII, p. 215.

Mem that Philip Sewell hath preferred his servitude to the trade & not being imployed he hath his liberty to procure a master where he can & to have his brotherhood at the expiration of his indenture. But he never served or came to mak any clame but dyed in dumfries.

May the 30th day 1712

  Payed for a blew table cloth - 0 : 10 : 5

May the 8 1713

  Lade out for the inscription of 0 : 4 : 0
    t^he plate

  Rec. from Mr Brisco for the use of
  Sr Christopher Musgrave & from
  Mr Parker for the use of
  Brigadeare Stanwix two guineys* 4 : 6 : 0

 9 Mr Maire as usual - - - 2 : 6

ffeb 17 1713. Then out of the box
  & paid for a funeral black cloth - £1 : 5 : 0

 2/^s to be paid for use of the cloth in
the country & 1^s : 6^d in the citties

1714 List of silver two silver kandlesticks & a silver stander in John Shaws hand & a silver kann M^r fenton gift. Paid for the inscription of the silver kann 1/^s †

Septr the 9th 1714 4 guineys given by Brig
  Adear Staix & Mr Strickland‡ - - 4 : 6 : 0

May the 4 1722 Joseph Sewell the son of John Sewell admitted & gave a silver cup. *He died at Westchester Sep 8 day 1730 & had been collector of the customs & left 3 sons John Thomas & Cuthbert.*§

---

* This means four guineas, and a guinea was £1 1s. 6d. For Brigadier Stanwix see *Cumb. and West. M.P.s* He was M.P. for Carlisle, 1702 to 1721.

† *Ante* p. 171.

‡ Sir William Strickland, M.P. for Carlisle, 1715 to 1722. See *Cumb. and West. M.P.s*

§ Words in italics are a marginal note.

October 1729. Memo that the four guineys that was given on the election day by colonell Howard & esq^r Hilton was all drunk out by order of the trade this day.*

May 7 1731. The day abovesaid it was ordered that Tho Scot a man that makes womans pattown clogs in this city and he not being a brother of this guild or freman of this city be prosecuted if he doth not remoue out of the libertys according to a discharge giuen him in this guildhall.

October the } Thomas Scot the sone of the late deceased
31 day 1735 } Richard Scot of Carlisle city singing man
being Crispin } bound an apprentice for seven years unto
& Crispian } Timothy Grahame a working master &
ye quarter day } keeping open shop in this city & as may
more fully appear by his indenture bearing date the ninth day of October 1735.†

John Hilton of Hilton castle esq^e admitted a member Sept 30 1739 and promised a present.

John Hilton esq of Hilton castle near ——— a honorary brother of this guild -——— member of parliament for this city gave as a present to the guild and brotherhood a colour valued ———

May the 8th day } This day remaining in the box the
1741 being Phillip } sume of thirty five pounds sixteen
& Jacob quarter } shillings & tenpence halfpenny.
day

1768 May Philip & Jacob the comp of cordwainers here remitt^d five guineas out of their common stock to assist the cordwainers comp: of London to procure an act for the drawback on leath^r export^d to be taken off but it did not succeed.

1770 Aug 10 then paid Jos Stephenson a bro of this guild for a new colour which he paint £12 : 12

---

* General the Honble. Charles Howard, M.P. for Carlisle, 1727 to 1761. John Hylton, Baron Hylton, M.P. for Carlisle, 1727 to 1746. See *ibid*.

† This is given to shew the usual form of entry at this date. Richard Scot, the father, would be a chorister at the cathedral.

May 14 1779. Laid out for Ascension day

expences	6 : 4 : 8½*
for a new funeral cloth - -	8 : 5 : 6†
for makeing do . - - -	0 : 5 : 0
for a box for the cloth - -	0 : 13 : 3
for blind Robin - - -	0 : 0 : 6
	15 : 8 : 11½

1753. Oct 26. The Hon^bl Colonel John Stanwix‡ of the city of Carlisle was this day admitted & sworn a brother of this society & inroled on a two shiling stamp.

1765. N B Genl Stanwix paid his arrears up to this day being Nov 1.

Sept. 21 1780. The R^t Honble Charles earl of Surry‡ was this day admitted & sworn a brother of this society & inrol upon a two shill stamp.

July 27 1781. Robt Collins late governor of Cape Coast castle in Africa & son of the late Michael Collins‡ was this admitted a brother of this guild & inroled upon a two shill. stamp.

April 21 1784. The Wor John Cristian‡ esq was this day admitted a brother of this society & enrol'd upon a four shiling stamp.

---

* In 1740 the Ascension day expenses were £7 10s. 10d., " being the moste extravagant bill & not to be brought as a presedent to futurety by other under-masters or wardens." In 1741, they were £5 12s. 3d., "it being a very extravagant charge."

† A list of the funerals to which the cloth was lent was kept. Some of the entries are odd : "Lord Surry's serv^t 1781. Mungo Dow g^r gunner 1782. Pattin the barber's funeral 1784. A recruit that was drownded. W. Benson's Grace's funeral. Christ: the chandler's wife 1791. A hatter in Botchergate 1792. Coulton's mother 1793. William Bell's mother 1794." The last date of the loan of the cloth is 1800, Aug. 5, to a funeral in Botchergate.

‡ General John Stanwix, M.P. for Carlisle, 1746 to 1760. The Earl of Surrey was M.P. for Carlisle, 1780 to 1786, when he became Duke of Norfolk. John Christian, afterwards John Christian Curwen, was M.P. for Carlisle, 1786 to 1812, and 1816 to 1820, and for Cumberland 1820 to 1828. For these three see *Cumb. and West. M.P.'s*. Michael Collins was clerk to the guild, and son of Tobit Collins, also a member.

CHAPTER XI.

THE GLOVERS' GUILD.

The name of this guild was originally "glovers" alone ;
but the title "skinners and glovers" first appears in 1730,
as will be proved below by the second set of orders : even
after that date "glovers" alone is generally used, but when
both terms are used, "skinners" always precedes "glovers."
From the books it appears that the guild controlled the
trade in skins long before the name of "skinners" was added
to that of "glovers." The difference between a "tanner"
and a "skinner" is that the former deals with skins of
cattle, &c., which he treats with bark, and makes into
hides : the latter with skins of sheep, goats, lambs, kids,
&c., which he treats with alum and makes into white
leather : that is they used to do so ; now chemicals are
used for both. The members of the guild of glovers made
other articles besides gloves,—breeches for instance ; and
they also dealt in white leather : at first, we fancy, they
only made white leather as a means to making gloves, but
gradually they came to deal in it, and to manufacture other
articles out of it.

The books of this guild consist of (i) a book $11\frac{1}{2}$ inches
high by $7\frac{1}{4}$ broad and $1\frac{1}{2}$ thick, bound in calf, with flap
over, two strings, and a clasp, now partly lost. In the
inside, on a fly leaf pasted down, is—

Our present Roll of all the glovers that belong to this company was
taken from the old book in the 13th year of the reign of king
Henry the 8th from thence extracted & copyed forth in the forty &

P

one year of the reign of queen Elizabeth & in the year of our Lord 1599 and the first brother on our roll is

> Sir Christopher Dacre knight
> William Skelton esq^r
> Robert Sewell esq^r e t c

Sir Christopher Dacre was of Lanercost, son of Sir Thomas the Bastard, and several of his descendants appear as members of the guild. This book contains entries from about 1674 to 1764.

The next book (ii) is titled a

> Day book belonging to the company of skinners & glovers,

and continues the entries until 1802. The subsequent one we have not been able to see. There are also two books of admissions, the first from 1761 to 1805; the second from 1806 to 1829. The first contains 227 admissions; the second 339, or 566 in all. In 1787 the society had 180 members, of whom only 42 were resident in the city. Among the names we have the earl of Lonsdale, John Christian, esq., William Dacre, esq., 3 Greenups, 3 Saiers, 11 Bells, 5 Feddons, 10 Hendersons, 5 Slacks, 6 Sewells, 8 Blamires, 10 Hodgsons, 3 Railtons, 3 Whelbys, 3 Wherlings, 2 Dobinsons, John Jackson, M.D., Robert Harrington, M.D., &c.

Between 1826 and 1837 this guild had about thirty brethren: after that the number came down to ten, and now it would be hard to find three.

The quarter days were—

> Thursday after St Helens, May 3
> Thursday after St Peter Advincula or Lamas, Aug 1st
> Thursday after Alhallowday, Nov. 1 and
> Thursday after Candlemas, Feb 2nd

The plate is specified in one of the entries below, and is fully described in *Old Church Plate in the Diocese of Carlisle.*

ORDERS, &c., FIRST SET.

The book of orders lawes constitutions and customes belonging to the occupation of glovers newly made and revised by Richard Monk clark to the said company by general consent of the said trade 1665.*

Whereas noe traid ffacoulty or occupation cann fflourish prosper or continue in any good order without men of ciuill gouernment knowledge and understanding to rule and direct them noe more than a kingdome or comonwealth without a ruler or a citty without a magistrate or some men of authority to gouerne the same.

4 quarter dayes yearly.

It is therefore ordered and agreed upon by generall consent of the company of glovers that for the better establishment of good order there shalbe kept yearly fower quarter dayes of meatinge of the said company and brotherhood in their guild hall to confer about the well orderinge and upholding thereof The first to be ever on the Thursday next after the invention of the cross and comonly called St Hellin mass quarter The second to be kept the Thursday next day after the ffeast called St Peter the Aduincle called Lamas quarter The third to be kept the Thursday next day after Alhallowday And the fourth to be kept the Thursday next after the ffeast of the purification of our blessed lady comonly called Candlemas day In the aforesaid guild hall.

2 Vndermaisters apointed yearly.

An order for chusing undermasters.

It is ordered and agreed upon by general consent of the company that there shalbe chosen 2 discreet persons of this guild to be vndermaisters as well to warne all the brethren of this guild to conuene and meat together at the foresaid quarter dayes as alsoe at all other times when the said traid shall have occasion to meat together and that they shall giue notice to euery brother of this guild the night before the quarter day or leaue warneing at his house upon paine of 6^d

---

* These orders are at the end of book No. 1.

None to be absent at our quarter or other meatinges in
our guild upon paine of 6ᵈ

None to be absent on quarter dayes. It is ordered and agreed upon by generall consent of the
company that euery brother of this guild shalbe present at
our quarter dayes or other meatings except sicknes by one of
clock in the guild hall that whosoeuer shalbe absent of the
said company their name beinge cald after the said houre
shall fforfeit and pay to the benefitt of this fraternity 6ᵈ to be
seized by distress (by the vndermaisters for the time beinge)
of the goods and chattels soe offendinge and the overplus (if
any be) to be returnd.

None to take an apprentice vnder 7 yeures. It is ordered and agreed by consent of the said company of
glovers that noe brother of this ffraternity shall take an
apprentice vnder the full end and tearme of seaven years ffully
to be compleat and ended to be bound by indentures with
obligation excepting brothers son or daughter and likewise
that noe brother shall take an apprentice till his former hane
served ffull fine of his seauen yeares and that noe brother of
this guild being vnmarried shalbe allowed to take an apprentice upon paine of twenty shillings to be leued by distress as
aforesaid.

Thre shillings to be paid for makes indenture 6ᵈ for inrolement and one shilling for yᵉ clarkes allowance.   6   It is ordered and agreed upon by generall consent of this
company of glovers that the clarke of this guild for the
time beinge shall haue for euery pair of indentures
drawinge three shillings for the inrolement of euery
apprentice sixpence and for his allowance euery quarter
one shillinge.

The prentice indentures to inrolled yᵉ first quarter day yᵉ apprentice is taken.   7   It is ordered and agreed upon by generall consent of the
said company of glovers that euery brother of this guild
after he hath taken an apprentice shall cause him to be
inrowled at the next quarter day after the daite of the
said apprentice indentures upon paine of euery brother
soe offendinge to forfeit and pay to the use of this occupation the sume of twenty shillings to be leuied by
distress as aforesaid.

April 25 65.

That none shall be a brother of this guild except he pay to ye benefitt of this guild 6^s 6^d and a penny for enrolleing his name.	8 It is ordered and agreed upon by the consent of the whole occupation of glovers that if any apprentice of this company haue serued the compleat tenrme of seauen yeares he shall if he desyre be admitted a brother of this company prouided he pay in ready money for the use of this guild six shillings sixpence and to the clarke for enroleing his name a penny.

Noe brother to sell any skinnes to any baconer or other person till the property be altered.

9   It is ordered and agreed upon as aforesaid that noe brother of this guild shall sell any sheep skinnes lamb skinnes kid skinnes or goat skinnes to any baconer* or any other person whatsoeuer untill they be converted into white leather or gloues upon paine of euery person soe offendinge to forfeit for euery skinne soe sould three shillings and fouerpence to be leued by distress as aforesaid.

None to by any skinnes till first present the open markett

10   It is ordered by general consent of this company of glouers that noe brother of this guild shall buy any sheep skinnes lamb skinnes veale skinnes kid or goat skinnes in any butcher's house or cominge to the markett till the said skinnes doe first present to the open markett neither shall buy any such skinnes as aforesaid till they be severed from the flesh upon paine of euery brother so offendinge to the benefitt of this company twenty shillings to be sewed by the undermaisters (by distrese) for the time beinge as aforesaid. *This ordinance to stand good though they was an ordinance to ye contrary only concerning calf skinnes & they be bought as others menconed in the ordinance aboue Aug 6 91.†*

And that noe person that buyeth any skines but shall presently remove ye skins from ye place they were bought to an other place of the market upon paine of every default 6^d

---

* See *ante* p. 84 n. The "baconers" seem to have been irregular practitioners, who infringed the privileges of this guild, and of the guild of tanners, by salting hides and skins to preserve them temporarily, treating them in fact as bacon is done.

† The words in italics are a subsequent addition.

None to
entertaine any
man's
apprentice.

11 It is ordered by the consent of this whole company of
glouers that noe brother of this fraternity shall entertaine any man's apprentice at vnlawfull or other times
either at cards dice or any other vnlawfull games and
we doe amercy euery brother soe offending for euery
default twenty shillings to be leuied by distress as aforesaid.

None to utter
any vndecent
behaviour
or raileing
language in
our guild.

12 It is ordered by general consent of this company that noe
brother of this company shall utter any railinge language
or utter any vndecent words that may defame and take
away the good name of any brother of this company
either at our quarter dayes or other meatings in our guild
that euery parson soe offendinge shall pay such penalty
and forfeiture as fouer of the seniors of the said company
shall inflict vpon him to be levied by the undermaister
by distress as aforesaid.

The under-
masters to
giue notice
euery quarter
day of all
abuses.

13 It is ordered by generall consent of this company of
glouers that the vndermaisters for the time beinge shall
presente shall euery quarter day present all offences
whereof they shall haue knouledge done by any member
of this fraternity contrary the orders of this guild or any
brother thereof upon paine of twelve pence euery such
offence.

Noe brother
shall be
partner with
any foriner.

14 It is ordered by and with the general consent and
ffraternity of this company of glouers that noe brother
of this company shalbe partner in the buying of any
skinnes either of sheep lamb kid or veale skinnes with
any Scottsman or other forrenor with intent to transport or
bacon* the same or that shall teach or instruct to any such
forrenor the art or mistery thereof shall forfeit and pay to
the use of this said occupation twenty shillings to be
levied by distress of the person soe offending (of their
goods and chattels by the undermasters for the time
beinge and the ouerplus if any be to be returned.

---

* Ante p. 84 n. and p. 213 n.

Noe apprentice to be taken without the consent of four of the seniors.	15	It is ordered by and with the consent and assent of the company of glovers that noe brother of this traid shall take an apprentice without the consent of fouer of the seniors of the said guild and that noe brother shall take an apprentice under the ffull age of fourteen yeares upon every such default shall pay to the use of the fraternity twenty shillings.
Noe unmarried man living in the country to take an apprentice under ye penalty above written.	16	It is ordered by and with the consent of this ffraternity that noe brother of this company livinge in the country beinge unmarried shalbe allowed to take an apprentice under the paine and penalty of ffortye shillings. *And that noe married man liveing in ye country shall take an apprentice under ye paine and penalty of 01£ . 00^s 0^d. and that noe unmarryed man liveing in ye citty shall take an apprentice under ye paine and penalty of £01 . 00^s 00^d* *
Noe brother to buy any skins over any brother's head.	17	It is ordered by and with the consent of this ffraternity y^t noe brother of this companie shall buy any skins over anothers head under ye paine and penalty of 00[£] : 06^s : 8^d.
Noe apprentice to marry in ye time of his years.	18	It is by and with ye consent of this occupacon of glovers y^t noe apprentice to any brother of this guild dureing the time of his apprenticeship shall neither marry or contract himselfe in marriage or consume his master's goods and other things which is in his indenture more fully expressed shall pay before he be admitted a brother of this guild the sum of tenn pounds to ye traid 10[£] 00 00^d provided y^t if his master or any brother of this traid shall make it appeare.
None to commit any fellonye.	20	It is ordered by ye consent of this occupacon of glovers that if any of this guild or brotherhood shall commit any fellony or petty larcynye or that any servant jurneyman or apprentice belonging to any brother of this guild doe commit or doe any fellony or petty larcynye and be throf convicted or flye for ye same fault he and they soe offending shall be clearely exempted from this brotherhood and be hindered of ye benefit thcarebye.

---

* The words in italics are a subsequent addition.

None to discover secrets.

21   It is ordered by the consent of this occupacon of glovers y^t if any shall discuse shew tell or discover to any other person then to his brother of this occupacon any cause matter or counsel done talked upon or spoken in y^e guild-hall of this occupation whensoever we shall convene or meet together there for any matter touching y^e state or good of this brotherhood y^t said person or persons soe offending contrary to this order shall forfeit and pay to the brotherhood for his default therein committed 01$^£$: 00^s : 00^d.

It is ordered by y^e occupacon of this guild of glovers y^t neither y^e wife y^e servant nor apprentice of any brother of this guild shall buy any skins whatsoever belonging to the occupacon in y^e open markett upon every default iii^s 6^d.＊

Noe brother no apprentice shall pull any skins for any other persons but for themselves.

It is ordered by generall consent y^t noe brother of this guild his servant or apprentice shall at ye request or for any gaine or paiment pull any skins haueing or bearing wool or haire for to ye use of any butcher or forranor or their servants upon paine for every default doeing contrary to this order 3^s 4^d. †

Undermasters to present almes every quarter day for their time being.

It is ordered y^t ye two undermaisters for their time being shall at every quarter day present all offences whereof they shall haue knowledge done by the brethren of this guild or any of them contrary to the orders shall forfitt 6^d

No brother of this trade to arrest another but by consent of 4 eldest of ye trade.

It is ordered noe brother of this guild shall areast or take suite in law against any other brother for any cause or matter before y^t ye same their greif be made known to ye elder masters of the guild or before y^t ye same be heard and license obtained upon paine of every default 12^d.

Noe brother to set any jurnaman in work without license.

It is ordered y^t noe brother of this guild shall sett any jurneymen in worke without license of two of ye head masters or of ye two under masters first obtained upon of every default vi^s viii^d

---

＊ This order is crossed out.

† This order is crossed out. To pull a skin means to take the wool or hair off : skins thus treated become "pelts."

None to by noe sort of skins upon sheep lamb kid goat or calves back.

It is ordered y^t noe brother of this guild shall buy any sheepe lamb kidds or veale skins before ye said skins be taken off ye flesh upon paine of every default three shillings fourpence 3^s 4^d

None to be absent at the death of any brother his wife or children or apprentice.

It is ordered by generall consent y^t all ye brothers of this guild haueing notice giuen of ye death of any brother or his wife or childeren shall attend and waite upon ye corps of any brother servants jurneymen or apprentices which it shall please God to call to his mercy and which shall dwell in this citty or shall be brought to be buried in ye churches or church yards of ye one of ye parishes in this citty upon paine of every default 6^d

None to buy any pelts pulled from any stranger.

It is ordered by consent of this guild y^t if any brother of this traid or his apprentice doe buy any pelts* y^t is puled from any stranger shall upon ye proofe thereof pay six shilling eight pence 6^s 8^d

None to take apprentices without the consent of 4 of ye eldest.

It is ordered by consent of this guild y^t noe brother of this guild shall from henceforth take any apprentice but he shall make fower of ye elders of this traid first acquaint therewith and request theire fauours upon paine of twenty shillings 20^s

The names of the elders
Thos. Sewell
Anthony At-kinson
Jo Beck sen.
Wm Tompson
Robt Hodgson
Christo Slack
John ffoster
Andrew Wilson.

It is ordered by generall consent of this fraternity of glou that there shalbe eight of the gravest and eldest bretheren of this guild chosen appoynted and named which said eight shalbe called the cheife masters of this brotherhood and shall haue power to reforme disorders assesse fines and order all causes betweene brother and brother of this as occations shall fall forth unto which the rest of this brotherhood shall submitt themselves and be obedient at their comandments (they being lawfull) and further if it fall forth that these eight cannot

The names of the younger sort
Jo Beck jun
Ed : Blacklock
Henry fforster
Tho. Nixon
Tho Huntington
Hugh Boes
Adam Robertson.

agree of any action comeing before them in plea then it is ordered that other eight of ye younger brethren shalbe appointed to order or giue judgement in that cause and if either the elder eight or the younger eight doe order any matter or set downe any fines upon any brother or brothers of this guild and ye brother of whom the said amerciament or fines shalbe assessed doe refuse to pay the same furthwith upon their

* "Pelts," in the trade, are skins without the wool or hair, see *ante* p. 216 n.

setting downe y[n] y[t] brother or brotheren so refuseing to abyde their orders or to pay his fine shall over and above the amercyment sett downe forfeit and pay to the benefitt of this guild for euery offence 3[s] 4[d] presently to be levyed and payed.

None to lend knife or apren to Geo. Wilkinson.

It is ordered that if any brother of this corporation shall lend any knife apron lymeeroofe* or any other instrument belonging to the trade to any forriner but especially to George Wilkinson saddler shall forfeit for euery default xx[s]

5[s] to be allowed when the undermaisters give in their accounts at Lamas quarter.

It is ordered by consent of this guild that there shall be allowed out of the trade or stock 5[s] when the undermaisters gives up their accounpts at Lamas quarter yearly.

Nov. the 2d 1676.

It is ordered by eight of y[e] ancient or oldest of this brotherhood or company of glovers that from henceforth y[t] there shalbe four quarter dayes kept in y[e] year at euery brother houses in this city to beginn at y[e] eldest and soe on by course

Every brother refuseing shall pay 12[d] for every offence.

and if any brother refuseing to come to y[e] said quarter dayes shall have benefitt of y[e] said trade or 12[d] and likewise it is ordered (behaveing ourselves civilly) to spend every man his twelvepence y[t] is to say sixpence y[e] first shott and 3 pence a peace two shotts after and y[t] then euery brother to depart when he pleases only there shalbe ordered bread and chsese with pipes and tobacco.†

It is ordered the 2nd day of November 1676 by eight of y[e] antient or eldest of this brotherhood or company of glovers (which eight are to reforme abuses or any differences y[t] shall happen amongst us) that from henceforth at euery quarterly meeting in our guildhall there shalbe kept at euery brother house beginning at the eldest and soe on until it come to y[e] youngest a mieryment or recreation as formerly hath been orderly amongst us spending first sixpence y[e] first shott and

---

* What is this? We have made much enquiry among the "conscript" fathers of the local trade, but they are unable to help us, beyond the suggestion that it is a knife. We suggest it may mean a splitting knife ; *roofe* means split, see *Halliwell*. The skinner's knife is circular in shape.

† This is crossed out.

threpence a peace 2 shotts after and then euery brother to
depart when he pleaseth and he or they y^t doe not come or
send twelvepence to ye said brotherhood by his wife or any
other whom he will appoint that he the said brother or
bretheren soe offending to forfeit and pay to the use of the
occupacon 12^d to be levyed of their goods by distress by the
undermaisters.

———————— // ————————

January 6 1678
It is ordered and agreed by and with the full consent of the
fraternity of glovers that a due preparation of bread wine
bisket mault tobacco and such like necessaries be duely
prepared against the Ascension day comonly called Holy
Thursday in order to accomodate the mayor recorder aldermen bayliffs and other gentlemen who accompany him or
them into our said guild and that certain quantities of several
necessaries aforesaid shall be ordered and appointed by the
due consideration of the fours and seniors of our said fraternity
and it is likewise agreed that if at any time any of our brothers
doe follow the employment of baking bread biskett brewing
of ale that then they the said brothers shall have the advantage
or benefitt of such like necessaryes as shall or may at any time
hereafter be required upon and the same to be equally taken
of them according to the discretion of the fours and seniors
aforesaid and it is also further considered and agreed upon
that the under masters of our fraternity for the time being
and yet to come shall take such diligent care as to take fetch
and bring in such like due preparations as shall be allowed
and appointed by the fours or seniors as aforesaid the night or
eve the said Ascension day and if they shall at any further
charge the said fraternity with more than what is ordered and
agreed upon then and in such a case the said under masters
shall pay the said overcharge and as a penalty for their dis-
obedience shall forfeit and be amereyed in disregard of the
same the sume of twenty shillings to be levyed of their goods
and chattels &ct.

June 10th 1680.
It is ordered by generall consent of this guild or fraternity of
glovers that noe brother of this company shall by any lamb

skins shevlings* calfeskins in Carlisle mirkatt above the rate of
fourpence halfpenny every brother y^t shall goe above ye rate
aforesaid shall forfeit for every default 6^s viij^d to be immediately levyed upon their goods or chattels this order to stand
to lammas next comeing.

ffebruaire 8th 1681.

The day and yeare above written we whose names are
hereunder written doe order y^t from henceforth noe brother of
this fraternity of glovers liveing without the libertys of the city
of Carlisle shall take apprentice as witness our hands &ct.†

May 4th 1682.

It is ordered by general consent of this fraternity that there
shall be two sufficient men to be overseers to make enquiry
and presentment of all such persons of this fraternity as doe
bring any unlawfull leather of what sort soe ere it be or gloues
made of any unlawfull leather into the markatt or any other
place within this city to sell or bargaine and every markatt
day or week day when occasion serves shall make search of
such leather and gloues and the same soe unlawfull found shall
imediately make distress and the same take away and cause to
be valued by four of the trade within the space of 14 dayes
next after the distress to the use of the said fraternity and he
or they that brings such unlawfull wares besides to be presented for every default 6^s & 8^d

If any shall think themselves to be wronged by the overseers
they shall haue the benefitt of chosen other foure of their
owne appointment.

October 1st 1684.

It is ordered by consent from henceforth noe brother of this
brotherhood shall give aboue the rate of 10^d a piece for any
sheep skin in this markat and every brother so offending for

---

* This term is unknown in the local trade, but some members suggest
it means the skins of calves that have gone on grass, that is have left the
cow, what are now called "kips." We give this for what it is worth.

† This rule is repeated on 3rd of October in the same year, with
this addition—"and y^t noe brother y^t followes not the calling of skinner
or glover shall have any." This is the first introduction of the term
"skinner."

every default to pay 6ˢ viijᵈ to be levyed of the goods of the offender by the undermasters till next quarter day And if any brother disclose this order to any butt a brother he shall pay to the benefitt of this company 6ˢ viiiᵈ

ffebruary 6ᵗʰ 1690.

It is ordered this quarter day yᵗ all country brothers belonging to this fraternity of glovers shall appeare butt one quarter day in the yeare which said quarter day shall be at allhallows quarter and shall pay yearly at yᵉ said quarter day 2ˢ to the benefitt of this company and they shall be excused from brother houses and upon their appearing at the said quarter day shall forfeit for every default or offence 3ˢ 4ᵈ

May 7 1691.
It is ordᵉᵈ that Ed Blacklock senʳ Thomas Nixon Ri Wilson Hugh Boase be admitted the fours of the guild and are to reforme and desyde all matters in controversy as amercyments fines &t which may arise betweene brother and brother.

It is ordered this quarter day that drinking at our brother houses as formerly hath been shall be giuen over and this is agreed that every brother of this guild shall pay 6ᵈ yearly to the maintaining and clearing the expences spent on Allhallow Thursday and if in case yᵗ the said 6ᵈ of every brother does not defray the said expenses there shall be more collected by the undermasters at Candlemas quarter and upon non-payment by any brother he shall pay to the benefitt of this guild 3ˢ 4ᵈ to be distrained of their goods or otherwise All brothers that agreed for 2ˢ yearly shall be excepted from this order.

Carlisle, July 29, 1691.
It is ordered by us the maior [ante p. 139].

Sept 21 1696.
The order aforesaid was then [ante p. 139].

feb 12 1696.

Ordered that Ri Carlile Ri Railton and Ed: Dalton be appointed elders and joined with Ed. Blaylock senʳ Thos Nixon and Hugh Boase Ordered that noe moneys shall be spent for the future out of the publick except itt be about extraordinary occasions concerning the trade and by the majority in the open guild.

Whereas severall abuses and undecent behaviours has been shewn and given by the brothers of our fraternity to the mayor and his company* at the approaching of our guild upon the Ascension day as refuseing to leave the said guild to make room for y^m when ordered by the fours and seniors to the great shame and disgrace of our whole fraternity and contrary to the custom of all other guilds in this city It is therefore by general consent of this fraternity of glovers unanimously agreed that for the time to come every brother whatsoever concerned in our said guild in order to give place and sufficient room for the mayor and his company shall at the first command of any one of our said four who are now present or may be hereafter immediately depart the said guild till such time as the mayor and his company be all conveniently dispersed and gone out of our said guild and if any of our said brothers shall seem in any obstinate manner to refuse to depart the said guild for the said time haveing been sufficiently requested by the said fours or seniors those persons so offending shall forfeit and immediately pay for euery such offence to the publick guild the summ of twenty shillings and the same to be levied by the undermasters by distress as aforesaid.

And it is further ordered and agreed by generall consent as aforesaid that if any brother in our said guild shall upon the Ascension day or upon any other quarterly meeting make any unreasonable noise in their discourse being too loud upon any concern or be offensive one to another contrary to the true meaning of this said order that information be made to our said fours by our present undermasters or by a person so offended And every brother offending for euery default shall pay to our publick guild the sum of 6^s 8^d and the same to be levied as in the above orders.

---

* The mayor with his sergeants and friends went the round of the guilds on Ascension day, *ante* p. 160.

August 6th 1702
Ordered this quarter day that every brother that lives in the
country shall pay twelvepence and every brother that lives in
the city shall pay every of them 6^d towards the defraying of
hall hollow Thursday yearly and in considecon thereof our
publick drinking at our brotherhouses shall be hereafter voide
and of none effect and this to be at St Helens quarter yearly
upon paine of every one making defanlt of payment as aforesaid 3^s 4^{d.}

Feby 4th day 1724.
Then agreed by the generall consent of this fraternity that our
clerk shall receive for his sallery every quarter day for keeping
the books and accounts the sum of two shillings and sixpence
per quarter but this during their pleasure and no otherwise.

August 3 1727
Then order'd and agreed by the unanimass consent of this
fraternity that the fours of this fraternity and the clerk and
other brothers convenient in this city shall goe to the mayor
of this city and require a copy of the charter relateing to our
trade and y^t the same be done before the next quarter day.*

November 7. 1728
Then ordered by the publick consent of this guild that the
clerk of this trade shall draw out a list of such persons are are
above a year's arrear and deliver ye same to Mr Jacob Davison
a brother of this fraternity who is hereby empowered to call
upon them for the same and such as shall refuse to pay the
said arrears before the next quarter day he the said Mr Davison
is hereby impouered to sue for the same according to the custom
of this corporation.

———————————— // ————————————

ORDERS, &c., SECOND SET.

The book of the antient orders lawes and constitutions belonging to the company traid fraternity and occupation of
skinners and glovers neuly made and renoued by Anthouy

---

* The mayor would have no other charter but the city charters.

Nixon clerk to the said company by the general consent of the whole traid in the year of our Lord 1730.*

*   *   *   *   *   *   *   *

None to take any shop over another's head It is ordered by the consent of this occupation of glovers that no brother of this fraternity shall at any time hereafter take any shop from any other of the same occupation or shall offer or profer a greater rent or consideration for such a shop but he shall first acquaint the party in possession therewith and whoso doth offend herein shall pay to the benefit of this guild one pound.

It is ordered and agreed by consent of this guild that if any brother of this traid or his apprentice doe buy any pelts that are pulled from any strainger shall upon the proof thereof pay six shillings eight pence.

November 8th 1734

It is this day agreed by this fraternity that the brothers inhabiting within the verge of this city shall be exempted from spending as usuall at the funeral meetings at brothers houses and that all brothers living without the liberties who before paid one shilling towards defraying the expenses of Holy Thursday shall now pay onely sixpence as those in the city usually before did and that if such contribution fall short of the said expences that then a further contribution shall be made by this fraternity and every brother neglecting to pay his rated proportion within the limited time as aforesaid shall for his said refusall or neglect forfeit and pay to the fours of the trade the sum of three shillings and sixpence over above the said dividend and this order to be in force for one year and no longer.

May 10t 1733.

This day it is agreed by the whole fraternny of glovers that all such brothers that are now standing out in arrear to the said trade be forthwith sued by a common writ and Mr Richard

---

* It is unnecessary to print this set of rules *in extenso*, as the only differences between them and the earlier ones are verbal; the title of the guild now became "skinners and glovers," and not "glovers" alone.

Goodman George Railton and John Davison do sue the severall persons so standing out by a writt or writts at the expense of the sd fraternity and that the said deputed persons doe first advise with Mr Recorder Gilpin in what manner such sute shall be commenced and that they shall begin the same some time before the next quarter day.

The order for Holy Thursday collections on Ascension day. It is ordered this quarter day that drinking at our brothers houses at quarter days as formerly hath been used shall be given over and this is agreed of by generall consent And likewise it is further agreed that every brother that lives in the country shall pay twelve pence and every brother that lives in the citty shall pay sixpence towards the defraying of Allhallow Thursday yearly and every year and this to be paid at St Helens quarter upon paine of every one makeing default of paym^t shall forfeit and pay to the benefit of this company three shillings and fourpence.

May the fourth 1738.

This day it is agreed by the whole fraternity of glovers and skinners that the fours of the said have a power to sue in the city court of Carlisle all such persons as are in arrears to the said trade And they are hereby impowered accordingly to employ an attorney to sue all such persons at the expense of the said fraternity by such methods and ways as they shall be advised to try which several sums so recovered shall be paid unto the undermasters for the time being.

February the 8th 1738/9.

It is then ordered and agreed by the generall consent of this company that noe brother hereafter shall be made in this company at any time but upon a quarterday and with the consent of the publick guild.

February 5 1740

Whereas the above order made in the year 1696 being not fully explained with respect to the takeing of apprentices out of the liberty of the city it is therefore ordered by the consent of the publick guild that no apprentice that shall be taken without the said liberty shall be admitted or enrolled as a brother in or by this guild witness whereof wee the fours and seniors of this company have hereunto sett our hands the day and year first above written.*

> Rich Goodman
> John Railton
> George Porter

August the 7th, 1740.

Ordered the day and year abovesaid that the aforesaid order shall be continued for ever in full force.

Then ordered and agreed by the general consent of this company that all the brothers that are in arrear for not paying Holy Thursday collections absences or any other ameerciaments due to the trade shall be drawn out of the book by the clerk and demanded by them and if not answered upon the first demand shall be immediately sued for the same.

Feb 5 1740/1.

It is ordered and agreed by the general consent of this company that no brother shal be made in this occupation except he pay five shillings for a treat and the usual brotherhood fee 6s 6d and one penny to the clerk and that the said sums shall be paid upon the table at one entire payment before the said brother be sworne without any denyall of the same as witnes our hand the day and year first above written.

> Rich Goodman
> John Railton his mark
> George Porter

May 7 1741.

Whereas it appears before this company that Martha the daughter of Joseph Robinson in the city of Carlisle hath undertaken to cut and sew and follow our trade haveing no right or priviledge to doe the same to the great damage of this occupation it is therefore unanimously agreed that the said Martha Robinson shall be persecuted according to law and that information shall be taken against her by the fours of this company which are to be laid before this trade the next quarter day unless she submit herself to the trade before yt time and desist.

> Rid. Goodman
> John Railton his mark
> John Dawson
> George Porter

---

* The order of 1696 is an order of the town council, for which see *ante* p. 139.

Feb 8   1748/9.

It was then orderd and agreed upon by the general consent of this company that such brothers as live in the country be exempt from fines every quarter day provided they come and appear on All Saints quarter every year.

And if any default be made by any brother in ye countrey in not appearing upon the said day each brother so neglecting shall pay the sum of two shillings to the comp^y for every default so made and before they receive this privilege so agreed upon they shall pay all former arrears to th company.

Geo Railton
Geo Porter
Jno Davison
Tho Walby

fours

A coppy of the case of the freemen of the city of Carlisle with the order that was made by the corporation of the said city the 26th day of March 1750 as handed into this guild this 10th day of May 1750 viz.

By the antient custom of the city of Carlisle no person was to be made free by the corporation unless first made a brother of one of the eight guilds or companies of that city: and also entitled to the same either by birth or servitude.

It has been usual for the corporation by agreement amongst themselves to permit every mayor if he thought fit to compliment any one friend of his with the freedom of the city and such freemen were called ex gratia or honourary freemen.

That of late years the same corporation have frequently made several ex gratia or honourary freemen without any consideration whatsoever which the freemen of the city looking upon as a great encroachment on their rights and liberties who had obtained their freelidge either by birth or servitude agreeable to antient custom therefore they applied to the corporation to redress this grievance and prevent such abuses for the time to come upon which the corporation thought fit to make the following order.

"Application haveing been made unto this corporation by the freemen of this city setting forth that severall ex gratia or honourary

freemen have of late been made within this city which they apprehend is an encroachment upon their liberties and very prejudicial to
their just rights as also that the city revenues have of late years
been greatly misapplied and lessned and desires and hopes that this
corporation will take such method as may effectually prevent such
abuses for ye future."

" This corporation haueing taken these matters into consideration
and finding them agreeable to the antient constitution do hereby
order that for the future no person whatsoever shall be admitted a
freeman of this city unless he shall be entitled to the same either by
birth or servitude and that the audit of this city's accounts shall
annually be made and finished ten days before the 25th day of
March in every year and that the same account shall be examined
not onely by the then mayor aldermen and council but also by eight
freemen vizt one of every occupation who shall have due notice of
the time intended for the auditing every account which persons
respectively shall be appointed yearly for that purpose by each
guild and if such account be found past then to be signed by the
said eight freemen as auditors and that no account for the future
shall pass that shall not thus be examined and witnessed And as an
assurance to the freemen of this corporation truly preserving keeping
and performing these orders they have agreed and do hereby impower
the present mayor to sign under their corporate seal a bond to the
eight occupations in the penalty of such a sum as may to him and
the said occupations seem meet."

NB. This order was made the 26th March 1750.

Q. As every one of the eight guilds or occupations have wardens in
what manner must this bond be given wheather must a bond be
given to the warden of each occupation or one bond to one of the
eight occupations in trust for the others or how otherwise to make
the order binding upon the corporation.

A. The proper method would be for the 8 occupations to name certain persons to be the person in whose names the bond should be
taken as trustees for the purpose of the order.

Signed by D. Ryder
25th April 1750

The above being publickly read.

It is ordered and agreed by the general consent of the fraternity of
glovers that Robert Railton be appointed trustee and auditor to the

settling of the corporation accounts and to take security for the better preserving the rights of freedom of this city against making ex gratia or honorary freemen.

Feb 9th 1786 Candlemas quarter day.

This day it was agree by the consent of the brothers present that the sum which Mr Henry Dobinson has advanced to Thomas Wallis & George Railton being four pounds four shillings for attending each twenty eight days at the guild during the time Mr Thomas Whibbel & his attorney or agents were taking copies of the books records &ct of & belonging to this fraternity be paid out of the publick fund of the guild as soon as so much money shall be in the hands of the clerk or undermaisters of the said guild.*

Jno Heslop clerk

4th April 1786

It was this day agreed by the consent of this guild that Mr Dobinson be allowed to carry the books of the skinner and glovers guild to London for the purpose of laying a proper case before the House of Commons or otherwise relative to the honorary freemen which were lately made by the corporation.

The brothers having taken it into consideration that the brothers who are obliged to attend the different quarter dayes frequently have a great deal of business to do which is detrimental to their trade or profession unanimously agreed that ten shillings should be spent on All Saints quarter day and five shillings on each of the other quarter days as a small compensation for their attending on the business of the guild.

Thursday 3 August 1786.

It is ordered and agreed this our publick quarter day that no person whatsoever shall hereafter be admitted a brother of this guild or fraternity but who shall be legally entitled to the same by birth or servitude.†

Jovis 12 die Martii 1795.
" Mr Elliott" as ante p 121.

Lamas quarter day 1796.
Conformable as ante p. 123.

---

* We have not found what this refers to, unless it is explained by the next entry.
 † Thirty-two ex gratia freemen had been made on 23rd June, 1786.

10 March 1796.

At a general meeting of the guild it was ordered and agreed that this guild do subscribe the sum of twenty pounds towards an intended prosecution against the occupation of the Kingmoor.*

Candlemas Q^r day Feb 8 1797.

It was this day agreed by the consent of this guild that if it be necessary for the books to go to London on account of a scrutiny demanded by Mr Knubley on the part of sir James Graham and himself at the close of the election in 1796 that Thos Sutton the the clerk of the said guild of skinners and glovers is to be intrusted with them.

St Helens quarter day
May 5th 1802.

Whereas the order was made Sept 14 1795† relating to the admission of brothers which order has been found detrimental to this company it was this day agreed by full consent of the guild that it should be repealed and the following made in its stead

viz

That all persons who have a legal right to the brotherhood of this company of skinners and glovers shall be admitted on any day (Sundays excepted) with having the consent of the brothers then present and giving proper notice to the undermasters and paying the undermasters fees viz

All persons made on a quarter day shall pay for his brotherhood 6^s 6^d treat 5^s clerk 1^s Stamp 6^s 1^d

All persons admitted on any other day except quarterdays for his brotherhood   *   *   *   *   *   *

THE CLERK'S OATH.‡

I A. B. chosen clerk by the publick consent of this fraternity do hereby take oath to make it my only concern and study to serve the said company honastly and faithfully in all concerns whatsoever relating or may relate to the aforesaid office.

So help me God.

---

* *Ante* p. 118 n.

† Apparently an order against admission on any day but quarter days, but we have not found it.

‡ These oaths are interpolated in the book with entries of about the date of 1747.

THE UNDERMASTERS OATH
when appointed as follows.

You shall swear well and truly to execute and perform the office of undermasters for this occupation for the next year following : you shall diligently and truely give notice and warning of your quarter days within the liberties of the town and meetings in your chamber or guild and other meetings there upon lawfull and just occasions : you shall make a true account of all fines merciaments and such other moneys as shall be committed to your custody and charge in this year to the whole company at the end thereof. So help you God & by the contents of that book. November the 6 1755.

A BROTHERS OATH.

You shall sweare to be true brothers of this company of glovers and and shalbe obedient to observe all such orders and constitutions as are agreed upon or shalbe devised and set donne (being just and laufull) which may be for the good and benefitt of this guild or brotherhood. You shall duly and truely observe your quarterly meetings in ye guild and likewise at ye brothers houses (without a lawful excuse) You shall keepe secret all private conferrances at an meeting and likewise if anything shall come to your knowledge y^t may tend to ye prejudice or harm of any member of this fraternity you shall truely acquaint them therewith and to ye best of your knowledge maintaine and defend the same all these and whatsoever else belongs to a brother of this company shall faithfully perform and keepe to the utmost of your power soe helpe you God and by ye contents of ye booke.

THE FOURS OATH WHEN ADMITTED.

You shall swear to be a true and just warden or fours of the occupation of skinners and glovers and to maintain uphold and keep all the orders sett forth by the trade for the good and benefitt of this occupation to the best of your power and all controversies that may happen between any brother or brothers of this company which may at any time come before you you shall justly and honestly determine without any favour or respect to the one or the other but in a just and honest manner settle the same you shall likewise give your due attendance in this chamber upon every quarter day or at any other private meetings . . . . . quarter day as the trade at any time

may have a just occasion to require your company being before
warned by the undermaster or undermasters of this company these
and all other meetings which do appertain to the duty and place of
a warden or four you shall truly and faithfully observe keep and doe
to the best of your knowledge skill and judgement so help you God
and by the contents of this book.

Whereas the antient fraternity of skinners of this city hath thought
fit to make you a brother for and during your natural life you
behaving according to the rules of this occupation you shall therefore
swear truly to deserve and keep all such articles and orders as are
already made for the benefit and profit of this occupation and trade
you shall duly observe all quarterly and other meetings when you
are regularly warned so to do you shall keep secret all private
conferences at our meetings and if anything shall come to your
knowledge that may tend to the prejudice or harm of any member
of this fraternity you shall truly acquaint them therewith all these
and which soever else belongs to a brother of this guild you shall
faithfully observe and keep.*

MISCELLANEOUS ORDERS.

Aug 1676.   Alex Hodgson is presented for calling of a buyer from
Thomas Nixons stall contrary to order therefore he is amercyed
3ˢ 1ᵈ·   he hath satisfied yᵉ trade & paid his amercmnt.

Willm Porter is psented by Thomas Tiffin for buying of a sheep
skin over his head therefore the trade amercyed him according to
order 6ˢ 8ᵈ he haith paid yᵉ trade.

Jo Brown is presented by Adam Robinson & Jo Harrison for buying
pull'd pelts from Mʳˢ Broadwood being contrary to order therefore
doe amerc him 6ˢ 8ᵈ John Brown hath satisfyed the trade.   We
likewise order yᵉ said John Brown to putt away his jorneyman
which he hath kept contrary to order of this guild before the 10ᵗʰ of
August 1676 or else to be amercyed 20ˢ·

* *Ante* p. 140 n.

Lammas quar being the 8th of August 1678.
We amercy Willm Barker for buying a sheepe's pelt contrary to an order of the trade therefore we do amercy him 6s viiid. pd in full & agreed.

We amerce Robert Railton for scandaleous words speaking against the trade therefore we do amercy him xiiis iiiid. pd & agred.

January 1678. Willm Barber hath presented Robt Railton for buying of skins upon the sheepbacks of Tho James butchr as upon his oath he hath declared & therefore we amercy him 3s 4d pd.*

May 7th 1679. John Twentyman of Hawksdale is admitted a brother of this guild by general consent & paid for being admitted being a strangr ye sume of forty shillings.

1680 ffebruary 3. The undermastr hath received this quart day ffrom Mr Maxwell upon Lord Morpethst account   0 : 10 : 0

May 13 1681. The day and year above written. The Right Honble Edward Lord Viscount Morpeth was admitted a brother of this guild and brotherhood ano regni dni nri Caroli sdi nunc regis angl & et tricesimo tertio
                    Ibid die et anno.
Thomas Warwick ‡ of Warwick Hall, esq was admitted a brother of this guild and brotherhood S. Helens quartr May 4 1682.

Upon Ascension day from Sr Christoper Musgrave 10/s §

May 8 1693. The undr masters hath recd of our parlmt men
                    1li : 0s : 0d

Aug 1701 Lammas quarter William Gilpin of Scaleby Castle esqr admitted a brother of this guild & hath paid in full of his brotherhood vis vid memoranda that Wilim Gilpin esq gave to the trade when he was sworn 2 guineys which is in the hands of Andrew Jackson.‖

---

* Similar instances could be multiplied.
† 2nd Earl of Carlisle. M.P. for Carlisle 1680-1.
‡ Head of an eminent local Roman Catholic family.
§ M.P. for Carlisle 1661 to 1690, see ante p. 157.
‖ William Gilpin, Recorder of Carlisle. He also gave them a piece of plate.

April 20th 1705. Collonell Thomas Stanwix* esquir the day & yeare abovesd gave one silver plete with the glovers arms upon itt as a free guift to the ffraternity.

September the 28th 1766. At a private meeting then was Colonel Gledhill† admitted a brother of the glovers taken his oath paid his fees and admitted according Colonell Gledhilt given to the glover fraternity one silver chalice carved and one silver candlestick.

St Helens qrt^r May 9th 1712.
Same day Richard Goodman esq‡ by a gen'all consent of the trade is made a broth of the glovers & sworne accordingly the fees for his brotherhood being vi^s vi^d.

1714. The four pieces of plate are delivered to George Railton all being put into a blew leather satchell made for ye same use.

Sept 9 1714. The same day the Honble Brigadeer Stanwix and William Strickland esq gane unto our fraternity 4 guineas Three of the s^d guineas was deliv^d unto the hands of John Railton upon the account of his son George Railton being then undermaster & the other guinea is to be dispersed of amongst the publick to drink the aforesaid gentlemen's health as by publick consent.

St Helens quarter May the 5 1715. This day amereyed Tho Wallas for giveing abuse in our publick guild in bidding the fours and seniors of our trade goe & seek their money from the devil he would pay none.§

1721. Richard Gilpin esq^r admitted.‖

November the 7th 1723.
A memorandum that I Joseph Nixon glov^r and malster hane receiv^d the day abone written those particular peices of plate (to witt) the cup given by Brigad Stanwix with his coat of arms upon.

---

* Brigadier Stanwix. *Ante* p. 206 n.

† *Ante* p. 205 n.

‡ He was keeper of Carlisle Gaol, a man of archæological tastes and knowledge, and a correspondent of Stukeley : several of his letters are published by the Surtees Society, see *Stukeley's Letters and Diaries*. He died 1746, *Mounsey's Carlisle* in 1745, p. 234.

§ It would be easy to multiply instances of fines for abusive language.

‖ Eldest son of William Gilpin ; he succeeded his father as Recorder of Carlisle.

The cup given by Collonell Gledhille with his name engraven
and a silver candlestick* with his name engraven and also a little
tankard given by loyar Gilpin† with his name engraven with the
trade colour and the bobb at the end of it and the black cloth all
which sd things I haue receiv'd from the trade to be kept for their
use and restored to them againe when they shall at any time demand
them for the trade use.

Allhallows qr November the 7t 1723.   Then ordered and agreed
by the publick consent of this company that a new black cloth and
six new towells be bought for the use of this company and before
the next quarterday.

	Cloth	-	-	0 : 18 : 0
1726	Napkins	-	-	0 : 7 : 0
New colour 3ll 16s 00d	Ribbon &	-		6 : 9
	setting on			
	Marking	-	-	0 : 3
				01 : 12 : 0

St Hellens quarter May the 6 1731.
Whereas John Taylor hath scandaleously reflected upon the fours of
this fraternity saying that the sd fours had spent 5s at John Topping
house that year when Samuel Sewell was undermaster at the buying
of the malt which the fours doe deny now if the sd John Taylor
doe not make this appear upon prove or sweare the same against
them on the next Ascension day he is and by the consent of the
whole fraternity shall be amereyed 6s 8d ‡

June the 28 1732.   Then was Mr John Gilpin§ admitted a brother
of the glovers fraternity and paid the sum of one pound one shilling
to the trade in gratuity of his brotherhood and fees.   Enterd upon
stamps June the 28, 1732.   Then received of Mr William Gilpin
the sum of twelve shillings being in full for all absences to this day.

---

* This candlestick was not in possession of the guild in 1882, when *Old
Church Plate in the Diocese of Carlisle* was published : it has recently [1886]
been purchased by the Corporation of Carlisle.

† William Gilpin, the Recorder.

‡ There is no further record on this matter.

§ Son of Mr. Recorder William Gilpin, and the Captain Gilpin of 1745,
see *Gilpin Memoirs* and *Mounsey's Carlisle in 1745.*

Lamas quarter August ye 1732. Mr Willm Gilpin* merchant in Whitehaven entred yearly man from this day.

August 2 1733. We amercy Edward Wallas the sume of one pound for discovering secrets of our company in the open streets.

St Hellens quarter May 9th 1734. Received of Captain Roose† this day ½ guinea being in full of his arrears and the rest to drink his honours health.

1735. Wee amercy Joseph Nixon for selling several hundreds of Lammas lamb skins bacond to Kendall contrary to our orders and therefor doe amercy him according to order of our book given upon oath by Richard Reay.‡

Aug the 26 1737. The day & year abovesaid was the R^t Honble Colonell Charles Howard§ a member of parliament admitted a brother of this company by the general consent of this whole fraternity per me Anthony Nixon clerk & enterd upon stamp— The Honble Colonell Charles Howard gave to the company the summ of one pound one shilling for the brotherhood fee which is lodged in John Taylor's hands the present undermaster and he gave the clerk 2^s for his fee.

Candlemas quarter February ye 9. 1737/8.

Receiv. this day of Mr Richard Goodman the sum of four shillings being for the use of four pounds formerly lent to his spouce & Joseph Nixon her father.

St Helens quarter May 4 1738.

Richd Bell being above eighty years of age is from this day excused from appearing in the guild or paying any more yearly money.

---

* Son of Mr. Recorder William Gilpin, died young, see *Gilpin Memoirs.*

† This gentleman assumed the name of Stanwix, and became General John Stanwix, M.P. for Carlisle. He was nephew of the Brigadier. His name appears in the books of this guild as Captain Roose, Captain Roose Stanwix, Captain Stanwix Roose, Major Stanwix, &c. For an account of him, see Ferguson's *M.P.'s for Cumberland and Westmorland, ante* p. 208 n.

‡ No amount stated.

§ *Ante* p. 207.

Ordered for Ascension day 1738.

> Two bushell and ½ of mault
> 2 gallon of brandy
> ¼ dozen of oranges
> 2 bottles Renish wine and 2 bottles more of other sort
> 1^{lb} ½ of loaf sugar
> 2^{lb} of cutt and dry tobacco
> pipes 1ˢ 2ᵈ
> 9 pound of biskit
> bread 6 dozen
> 6 and ½ pound halfpenny candles

September yᵉ 13 1738.
Then was Major Montague Farrow* admitted a brother of yᵉ company by the consent of the brothers within the city Major Farrow gave to the trade the sum of one guinea and one half.

Candlemas quarter February the 4ᵗʰ 1741/2
This day was Jeremiah Wherlings the son of James Wherlings being a brothers son was admitted a brother of this company and paid to the trade his brother fee 6 „ 6 and one penny to the clerk and five shillings for a treat.†

May 7ᵗʰ 1741. Then ordered and agreed by the generall consent of this company that a new table cloth be bought by the present undermasters for the sᵈ company to be laid on the table upon every Ascension day or when may be required. As witness our hands the day & year first above written.

> Richd. Goodman
> John Railton
> John Dawson

Lammas quarter August the 2ⁿᵈ 1744. This day wee amercy Mʳ John Dawson 6ˢ 8ᵈ for selling skins before they be converted into white leather and we also further amerce him two pounds for baconing‡ of them by his own confession.

---

* Montagu Farrer of Carlisle, was on the Grand Jury at the Special Assizes at Carlisle, 1746, for the trial of the rebel prisoners, also see *ante* p. 36.

† There were two Jerry Wherlings in the guild, but this will be the Jerry, famous in local song and caricature, who as mayor of Carlisle admitted the "mushrooms."

‡ *Ante* p. 84 and 213 n.

St Hellens quarter May the 9th 1745.

> All absences excused this
> by reasons bellow written.

Wee amercy Joseph Threlkeld and Thos Story present undermasters for not attending the guild with the key to let the company come in and was after one a clock before they could come into the guild we amerce them each 2^{s.} for the s^d offence. All brothers of this company were call'd upon and who did not appear were excusd by reason of the undermasters not comeing with the key till after one a clock aforesd.

Alhallow q^r day Novem the 7th 1745. No business done or admittances.*

February 26th 1745/6. It is the day and year above written by the worshipful mayor his deputy orderd and agreed that all our company of glovers shall appear with the Scotch gates at the freelidge stone with their colours goeing before the company for to meet his highnes the duke of Cumberland and to have illuminations for the same when required.†

St Helen quarter May the 5th 1748. It is this day ord^d in the publick guild that a new black cloth be bought for the use of the publick guild.

March 25th 1761. Then Sir James Lowther‡ baronet gave to the trade this to be spent the sum of five pounds five shillings which Joseph Slack has received and also the Honble Generall Jno Stanwix paid the sum of 19^s being the full of all his arrears to this day which is paid full of all Thos Blamire the undermaster has received.

March 28th 1761. The above said day came the Honourable Captain Raby Vane§ and was admitted a brother and paid two

---

* On the 7th November, 1745, the Highlanders entered Cumberland.

† The Duke was expected at Carlisle at this time, see *Mounsey's Carlisle in 1745*, p. 201, but the rumour was untrue. A similar order *ante* p. 132.

‡ Afterwards the first earl of Lonsdale. For this prominent local politician and potentate, and what he was doing at Carlisle, see *Cumberland and Westmorland M.P.s from the Restoration to the Reform Bill.*

§ M.P. for Carlisle 1761 to 1768, captain in the navy, and son of first earl of Darlington, and brother of the second earl, who had married Margaret, sister of Sir James Lowther. See *Cumberland and Westmorland M.P.s*

guineas out of which sum there was two shillings and a penny for a stamp and the remainder is in John Robinson's hands.

March 28 1761. The Honourable Sr James Lowther came this day and was admitted a brother of this trade and paid two shillings and a penny for a stamp. Joseph Dacre* esq came this day and was admitted a brother and paid the usual fees & also two shillings & a penny for a stamp.

November the 5th 1761. It is then ordered and agreed by the general consent of this trade that some brother of this trade shall use their utmost endeavours to find a prosecution against Benjamin Smithson who has no right or property to work in the liberties of this city.

St Helens quarter day May ye 6th 1763. This day it is ordered that notice be given to Benjamin Smithson to shew reason why he follows the business of a skinner in the liberties of this city having no right and property.†

Nov 5 1761. It is ordered by general consent of this guild that the clerk write and send a letter of thanks to Mr Jacob Danson for the very acceptable present that he has lately made to us of a fine new colour with this company's arms richly painted thereon and by entering the said order in our book it is intended as a means to make it known and be gratefully remembered by our posterity.

1776. To cash from 36 brethren at 6^d but one bad 6^d .. 17 „ 6

1776. To cash rec. from John Sutton on acct of putting Wm Herceg for the first three years to work at makeing at briches which was contrary to the laws of the guild which he submitted and by consent of the brothers onely took of him being the first fault 0 : 5 : 0.

  1778 Ascension day

By cash to the aprentices 2 : 6 drums &
 music 2^d ..   ..   0 : 4 : 6
By do to Thos Wallace for 1 lb bixits & 4 dosin
 bread   ..   ..   0 : 12 : 2
By do to Jane Railton for 1 lb do ..   ..   0 . 8 : 2

---

  * Of Kirklinton hall.   † Result not recorded.

By do Tho Henderson for 8 dosin bread .. 0 : 8 : 0
By do for 2 lb more bread .. .. 0 : 2 : 4
By do to Rd Sewell for 1 dosin lemons 2ˢ for
    1 lb lofe sugar 1ˢ for 2 dosin best pipes 6ᵈ 0 : 3 : 6
By do to do for 2¼ tobacco 6ˢ 11ᵈ for 2 dosin
    cake 3ᵈ candles 2ᵈ .. .. .. 0 : 7 : 4
By do to Jos Slack for 24 gallons at 16 pʳ gallon 1 : 12 : 0
By do to do for ½ gallon rum & brandy at 12ˢ
    per gallon .. .. .. 0 : 18 : 0
By do for the use of a dosin glasses* & one broke 0 : 0 : 0

The 21 April 1784.

Then came John Christian of Unrigg esq (the present high sheriff for the county of Cumberland) and was admitted and sworn honorary brother of this fraternity & at the same time gave 3 guineas a part thereof to pay for stamp the two undermasters &ct the remainder to drink his health he also propos'd to give the company a piece of sʳ plate for their fees.† This done by consent and order of near all the quarterly broˢ· and two undermasters.

---

* Broken glasses and bottles occur suspiciously often in the Ascension day bills. The "drums & musick" sometimes get 5ˢ and "a piper by chance, 6ᵈ": on another occasion a trifle is given to "drums musick and a French horn".

† John Christian (John Christian Curwen, M.P.) gave a tall two-handled cup, same as he gave to all the other guilds, except to the merchants', ante p. 89, where we have in mistake stated Curwen to have been M.P. for Carlisle, when he gave these cups: he was then only the candidate.

Chapter XII.

THE BUTCHERS' GUILD.

The records of the butchers' guild consist of five books. (i) The oldest of these was in 1883 in the possession of Mr. C. B. Hodgson, the Courts, Carlisle, having been left with him at the time of the trial of Ismay *v.* Barnes, in 1865, as to the right of the freemen to hold races on King-moor. It is bound in vellum, with flap-over and a brass clasp ; it is $11\frac{1}{2}$ inches high by 8 inches broad, is nigh 2 inches thick, the leaves are all loose, and the entries are very promiscuously arranged as to date. The first entry is

> Quarter daies for y^e company of butchers
> within y^e citty of Carlisle Mar 11 1665
> > ffirst Tuesday after Lamas day
> > ffirst Tuesday after All Saints day
> > ffirst Tuesday after Candlemas day
> > ffirst Tuesday after Maie day

A subsequent note says that on Feb. 9, 1686, the quarter days were altered to Wednesdays following the same.

The remaining books are with the clerk of the guild, and are—(ii) book of stamped memoranda of admission of apprentices and brothers, bound up together, not always chronologically arranged, extending from 1724 to 1836, and numbered from 1 to 510. The book is about $8\frac{1}{2}$ inches by 6 inches, bound in calf ; (iii) a paper book, $15\frac{1}{2}$ inches long by $6\frac{3}{4}$ broad, which is an index to the last book, giving names, dates of admission, and numbers on the admission papers ; (iv) another paper book, $12\frac{3}{4}$ inches by 4 inches,

R

an index to the admissions of freemen in books (i) and (v); (v) a folio bound in rough calf, 15 inches high, 10 inches broad, and 2 inches thick. It commences thus—

The fraternity of butchers 1797
Rules and orders to be observed.

This guild, was a very numerous and wealthy one, and the fees for the enrolment of apprentices and for the admission of brethren were at one time very high, as much as £20. In 1836 they had a balance of £600, which they divided among the members. The following analysis of the names of the 510 persons admitted between 1724 and 1836 may interest :—

15 Allisons.	7 Armstrongs.	11 Blaylocks.
11 Browns.	20 Bousteads.	4 Bowmans.
2 Bendles.	15 Carliles.	4 Curwens.
1 Christian.*	4 Creightons.	13 Daltons.
3 Dobinsons.	3 Donalds.	6 Edgers.
1 Eaglesfield.	3 Fishs.	18 Grahams.
6 Graysons.	9 Gates.	2 Gills.
4 Gashs.	7 Gibbons.	12 Hodgsons.†
3 Heads.	1 Ismay.	2 Jameses.
3 Jacksons	4 Lambs.	2 Lamberts.
6 Murrays.	1 Mulcaster.	5 Matthewses.
23 Nansons.	6 Normans	3 Nixons.
15 Pearses.	6 Pattinsons.	6 Peascods.
3 Parkers.	3 Pealls.	20 Robinsons.
3 Ravens.	4 Riggs.	2 Randlesons
6 Snowdons.	8 Skeltons.	17 Sowerbys.
5 Simpsons.	7 Staggs.	4 Sewells.
3 Stanwixs.‡	12 Thomlinsons.	1 Tate.
12 Tinlings.	3 Taylors.	2 Underwoods.
1 Warwick.	29 Wilsons.	1 Wilkinson.
1 Wallace.	5 Youngs.	

* John Christian Curwen, M.P.

† These include W. N. Hodgson, M.P., admitted 1823, and J. S. Hodgson, Canon of Carlisle, admitted 1826.

‡ All called Thomas, one being the Brigadier.

In 1797 the guild numbered about 150 members; a list
of 174 members is given in the first book, under date of
1665, but this appears to include all the names the clerk
could find, dead or alive, in an older book, now lost.
Among the 174 the Barnfathers, Nansons, Sowerbys,
Bewleys, Jameses, Bowmans, Blacklocks, Lydes, Bells,
Wilsons, Allisons, Blamyres, Carlisles, &c., were the chief
names; Stanwix was also a great name between 1665 and
1724. In 1680 the guild numbered 51. In 1741 the
members of the guild honoured by handles to their names
are Cha⁸ Smithson gen, Thomas Stanwix Brig: Tho
Dobinson gen, Coll Gledhill, Thomas Fletcher esqʳ Ed
Pattinson Serg⁴; Rich. Hodgson Al (alderman) Rowland
Boustead Al, Edward Carlisle Al. John Snowden Al. Mʳ
Robert Eglesfield.

The plate consists of six pieces. (i) A small tumbler,
" Ex dono Geo Bell 1703." (ii) A posset cup, " The gift of
Col^ Thomas Stanwix." This has on it the butchers' arms,
viz., three bulls' heads couped, between two pole axes in
saltire—on a chief a boar's head between two garbs. (iii)
A tankard, on which, " The company of butchers in
Carlisle 1745." (iv) A cup, on which, " The gift of Mʳ Wᵐ
Nanson of London to the worshipful company of butchers
of the city of Carlisle 1791." On one side is the following
coat of arms :—Sable a chevron between three annulets
argent; crest, a bull's head. On the other:—Argent a tower
between two roses; on a chief gules a lion of England;
crest, the standard of Sᵗ George. This is a curious version
of the modern arms of the city of Carlisle. (v) A silver
salver, on which, " The gift of Col Samuel Gledhill
Citizen of Carlisle to the company of Butchᵐˢ Setemb 1710.
These are all fully described in the appendix to *Old
Church Plate in the Diocese of Carlisle*. There is a
legend of a seventh piece of plate having been stolen, but
the inventories of silver in the books do not bear
this out.

1. It is ordered and agreed that everie one of them shall be
faithful to other in all things lawfull and honest.

2. It is ordered and agreed upon by ye whole occupation that noe
outman shall occupie use or set up the trade of boutching
within this citty or ye liberties thereof untill such time as they
haue agreed with this occupation and that noe brothers son
nor apprentice shall sett up trade till they pay to ye occupacon
iii^s iiii^d *to be levied of their goods and chattels of ye party
offending rendring y^e* . . . .

3. If any outman not haueing agreed with this occupation shall
sett up trade or follow ye said calling in this citty or y^e
liberties thereof they shall pay to the occupation for everie
time they shalbe found offending therein 13^s 4^d to be taken
without fauor *to be levied &c.*

4. That whensoever any of ye occupation shall take an apprentice
he shall pay to ye said occupation 6^d and that noe man shall
take any apprentice within 6 years together upon paine of
6^s 8^d to be paid without fauor *to be levied as aforesaid.*

5. That none of ye occupation shall giue or take law one of
another without license of ye occupation first granted upon
paine of 6^s 8^d euerie default *to be levied as aforesaid.*

6. That none of this occupation shall make debate disorder or
brawling one with another upon paine of xiii^s iiii^d for euerie
offence to be *levied as af^{sd.}*

7. That if any of this fraternity shall know any mischief or false-
hood done or committed against any of his brethren of this
occupation by his or their apprentice or apprentices or by any
brother he shall show the same imediately without delcy in
secret to ye m^r or maisters of ye said apprentice or apprentices
upon paine of 6^s 8^d soe often as they shalbe proued to offend
in concealing ye same *to be levied as af^{sd.}*

---

* Taken from the oldest book. Throughout them words in italics are to be
understood as additions in another handwriting. Their date, as appears from
No. 16, is 1665.

8. That whensoever any brether of ye said occupation or any of their wines shall decease or depart this life they shall haue the whole light of ye occupation going before them to ye church and their children or apprentices at their departure shall have halfe light *to be levied as aforesaid.**

9. That noe brother of this occupation shall disclose or tell abroad any secret or privity which shall be spoken or done in and among ye occupation at any time upon paine of xiii^s iiii^d each offence it being proved *to be levied as aforesaid.*

10. That for ye better agreement and brotherly charitie amongst ye brethren of this occupation that none of them shall raile scold *give indecent languidge* or chide one with another upon paine ef xiii^s iiii^d for everie offence to be levied without fauor *to be levied as aforesaid.*

11. That none of this occupation shall at any time fellowe themselves with any outmen in buying or selling upon paine of iii^s $iiij^d$ for euerie offence *to be levied as aforesaid.*

12. That none of y^e occupation shall lend any axe gullie knife or other thing appertaining to their science to any out butcher upon paine of 6^d for euery offence *to be levied as aforesaid.*

13. That none of this occupation shall permit or suffer any outman to hang any flesh within his house or shop upon pain of iii^s iiii^d euerie offence *to be levied as aforesaid.*

14. That eurie one of ye occupation shall keepe their meetings at their quarter daies and at all other times upon lawfull sumons warneing giuen unto them by ye masters of ye occupation for the time being upon paine of iii iiii for euerie offence or default *to be levied as aforesaid.*

15. That none of this occupation shall buy any dead flesh of any person to ye intent to sell ye same again upon paine of xiii^s iiii^d for euerie offence.

---

* See a similar rule in the tailors' guild *ante* p. 147. The words in italics are rather meaningless in this case. Superseded by a later order of May, 1683.

16. That when any brother of this occupation is about y͏ᵉ buying of any beast and hath cheapened or bidden at the same none of this occupation shall outbide or go about to buy y͏ᵉ same on him enhanceing the price thereof without license of him that was first cheapner thereof or till he have of his own accord left y͏ᵉ same upon pain of curie offending herein 13ˢ 4ᵈ for curie offence *to be levied as aforesaid.*

All these orders and rules beforementioned were taken out of an antient parchment scrawl and transcribed by P. N.* for the benefit of this trade.

March 11. 1655.

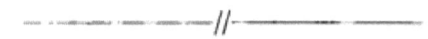

17. Allhallows quarter 2ᵈᵒ Novembris 1647. It is this quarter day ordered by y͏ᵉ occupation that if any brother thereof shall hane occasion of complaint against another the complaynant shall haue free liberty to propound his grievance and then y͏ᵉ party against whom y͏ᵉ complaint is made to alledge his lawfull defence moderately and without raileing or offensive words to be giuen by either party which being done ye͏ʸ without any further dispute shall not only submit themselves and y͏ᵉ differences to y͏ᵉ censor of y͏ᵉ rest of y͏ᵉ occupation then present but alsoe undergo what order or penalty shalbe set downe by them concerning y͏ᵉ difference then in question and soever shall transgress this order to be in amerciament xiiiˢ iiiiᵈ without any mitigation or abatement *to be levied as aforesaid and expeld y͏ʳ fraternity.*

18. Candlemas quarter 8ᵗʰ ffebruarie 1647. It is this day ordered and agreed upon by and with y͏ᵉ full assent and consent of y͏ᵉ whole occupation y͏ᵗ noe brother of this trade whatsoever shall hereafter forestall y͏ᵉ market in buying or under couller contracting with any person comeing to y͏ᵉ markett with any veales sheepe kidds lambs or any other kind of meate to sell belonging to this occupation untill such time as y͏ᵉ owner of

---

* Peter Norman. See an order of August 8, 1676, *postea,* p. 248.

such goods haue presented ye same themselves in open markett
upon paine of . . . euerie default without any . . or
abatement *to be leuied as aforesaid.*

Lammas quarter Aug 7 1655.

19. Ordered this quarterday with ye full assent and consent of this
occupation that ye sevrall apprentices shall carry and demeane
themselves decently towards ye maisters and brethren of this
company and whoever apprentice shall transgress this order his
maister or ye maisters of ye said apprentice shall for euerie
offence pay unto this occupation the sume of iii^s iiii^d *to be
leuied as aforesaid.*

July 11 1659.

20. It is this day ordered by generall consent or the major part of
this occupation that noe brother of this trade shall buy any
goods or sheep cowes oxen lambs kidds calves or any flesh
whatsoever from any boutcher whatsoever that is not a brother
of this fraternity *or from ye partner of ye any outer boutcher*
upon paine of 13^s 4^d for euerie ofense without any abatement
and that noe brother of this trade shall buy any goods directly
or indirectly of any outer boutcher nor x   x   his friends
upon ye paine of one lb if proued by one or more witnesses
to be leuied as afs^d

May 6 1662.

21. Ordered by generall consent that noe brother of this trade at
their meetings in ye guildhall on ye quarterday or otherwise
shall depart ye hall till they break up by consent without
license of ye trade then present or ye major part of them upon
of iii iiii for euerie such offense *to be leuied as aforesaid.*

22. Lammas quarter 1666 being ye 7th day of Augt Ordered this
quarter day with ye full assent and consent of this occupacon
y^t euery brother of this trade shall pay their severall prospective
amerciements and fines each year at or before Lammas quarter
to ye mr^s or undermaisters of this fraternity and whosoever
shall neglect to pay the same and to obey ye orders of these
trade shalbe debarred from takeing any apprentices nor his son
to have any benefit or to be brothered in to this guild till all
ye amerciements be paid as aboue said.

Lamas quarter Aug 4 1668.

23. Ordered this quarter day with yᵉ full assent and consent of this occupacon that euery brother of this trade that lines in the country shall pay to this occupacon forty shillings for euery apprentice he shall take before yᵉ apprentice be inrolled and that euery apprentice not being a brothers son shall pay viˢ viiiᵈ and euery brothers son iiiˢ iiijᵈ before he be admitted a brother of this society.

Lamas quarter Aug 2/70.

24. Ordered this quarterday that noe brothers son of this trade shall take an apprentice until himself be complete twenty-one years of age upon paine of forty shillings to be levied as above said.

Alhallow quarter Nov. 2 75.

25. Ordered this quarter day by generall consent that each brother of this trade shall repaire to the house wher the quarterday is kept (except the clark* at his glasse) and expend their 6ᵈ upon paine of euery person offending to be amerced 12ᵈ for euery default.

26. Ordered by yᵉ whole trade that yᵉ undermaisters doe demand what money any person owes to yᵉ trade by amerciements or otherwise and what person soever refuses to pay to arrest and prosecute them at law or for amerciements distresse and the trade to beare yᵉ charges and keep them indemnified.

Aug. 8 76.

Ordered this day by generall consent that Thomas Kidd be allowed to officiate as clerk to this trade and that Mʳ Peter Norman our clerk be excused from all amerciements at our guild in regard of his sickness and infirmitie.

May 6 1679.

27. Ordered this day by generall consent of the trade and occupation of butchers that Rich: Wilson nor any other brother of ffraternity shall fellow him or themselves with any outtmen or any that is not a brother of trade upon paine of   02 : 00 : 00 to be levied without abatement by the said trade.

---

* "At" must be meant for "have," i.e. the clerk to have his glass free.

May 8ᵗʰ 1683.

Ordered that every brother of this trade haueing due warneing shall attend the corps of every brother or brother's wife or child to the church and fro thence to the house or expend 4ᵈ upon paine of 6ᵈ for every ofence.*

28. November 3/97 Allhallows quarter then by the consent of the whole trade it is ordered that for the future noe butcher of this fraternity shall lessin† or say that any of the brotherhood sells or hath sold rotten or bad meat which may tend to the prejudice of any of this brotherhood upon paine iii iiij but such things shall be left to the clark of the market and the clerke of our ffraternity.

29. Ordered by the whole fraternity yᵗ if any of the said fraternity doe act any thing prejudicial or contrary to his oath or the orders of the fraternity nay yᵗ not only they but any of the fours or wardens yᵗ soe offends shall forfeit . . . benefit of the trade and be excluded the said fraternity.

May 7 1690.

Then was the voate put to the fraternity of butchers wheather after this quarter day any quarter days should be kept in one of the brothers houses or not and it is voted and caryed in the negative yᵗ there shall be none for yᵉ future.‡

July 28. 1690. No outman that follows the trade of a butcher shall upon any account whatsoever for yᵉ future take any apprentice unless yᵉ sᵈ maister dureing all the time live within yᵉ corpacon or suburbs & there apprentice soe taken shall live with his sd master & follow yᵉ sᵈ trade dureing all his 7 years.

August yᵉ 5º 1690. Same time it is then ordered that all brothers of the trade after their quarterly meetings in yᵉ guildhall shall

---

* This order supersedes No. 8, *ante* p. 245, which had become obsolete. This comes from another part of the book. There is another order on funerals in 1734.

† *Lessin*—to *lese* is to lie, see *Halliwell's Dictionary of Archaic Words*. Here *lessin* evidently means depreciate.

‡ See next rule but one for the repeal of this rule : and see several orders immediately following.

repaire to euery such house as is appointed for the quarter day and y^t their euery brother shall spend a twelvepence or else euery one for not so doing shall forfeit for ye benefit of the trade and to be levied by distress and otherwise of his goods an amercyment vi^s viij^{d.}

August 1696.　This Lamas qua^r it is agreed of and ordred by the whole fraternity of butchers that whereas their is seu^{ll} amercyments or fines due to the sd fraternity by seuerall of ye brotherhood wch they refuseing to pay to the und^r mast^{rs} who useth to collect the same for the use of the trade wee of the fraternity doe ord^r & deseire Mr Jos Read our clerk of the trade forthwith to commence sute in ye present und^r maisters name as he shall see cause & to pseeute the same & to agree and stay ye same & stay ye sd pcess if he sees cause for it and likewise wee of the fraternity with the whole consent of the same doe make this a standing ord^r for the future soe far as all moneys reced upon the account of any of these amercyments or fines afs^d all charges deducted the remaind^r then is to goe for the use of ye sd trade.

ffeb 7 99/1700.　Then the question being put for the quarter days to be at euery brothers house as formerly and put to the voat it is agreed of that the quarter dayes is to be kept at the brother's houses and to spend as formerly the houses only to find ayle pipes and tobacco and if any quarrell happen there where it appears that the man that begins the quarrell shall be amercyed for the benefit of the trade for every offence iii^s iiij^d and y^t all outmen is obliged to keep the said quarterday as aforesaid and to begin at the eldest & all y^t do not come shall be amercyed　x　x　viij^d

St Helens quarter 1705.
it is now agreed and ordered by the whole fraternity of butchers that every brother goe to Tho: Nauson this day being ye quarter day and there spend three shillings apece but after this day it is ordered that for the future every brother of this trade quarterly pay sixpence for the use of the trade to prosecute all such persons as doe damage to this trade of butchers and y^t in lieu of the money spent on the quarterdays at the brothers' houses and if any of the fraternity refuse to pay every quarter day his sixpence accordingly he y^t soe refuses is amereed one shilling and forthwith is to be distrained on for the same of the present undermasters.

Aug. 4th 1708. Whereas there is sev^{ll} amercymts due to this fraternity by sev^{ll} of the butcher trade it is this day in the guild chamb at this quarterly meeting that all such broth^r of the butchers as are soe indebted by amercymts be forthwith sued for the same and y^t Mr Jos. Read clerk to the s^d fraternity make preaction thereof till such amercymts be got upp.

Nov. 5 1708. Same time by the consent of the whole trade psent forty shillings delived to Geo Sowerby and Rob Gate 25^s of it to G Sowerby and xv^s to Gate is 40s and the remainder of that which paid out being iii^{li} is 2^{li} 16 8^d to W Rooke & iii^s & iiij^d paid unto the sheriff in expenses upon the writ the which as abovesd Jos Read Tho Crockbane and Thos Kidd rece^d of Mr Mansergh und^r sheriff being an egreemt for the inlargmt of Geo Sowerby Tho Blaylocke and Edw Gate butchers who was in custody at Roger Heydales* gaoler at suite of the fraternity of butchers for amercymt because they refused to pay the same.

ffeb 9 1708/9.
It is this day in the guild chamber agreed of and ordered y^t all bypast amercyments relating to any brother of this fraternity the same in all amounting to ye sume of eightie pound xii^s vi^d be remitted in consideracon of which these orders as underwritten is punctually to be observed and keept.†

first it is ordered and agreed of by the whole trade y^t from henceforth every brother of this fraternity is to pay sixpence every quarter day in there guild chamber for the use of the trade and y^t the money soe collected be deposited into the hands of the present undermasters and they to yield an account for the same to the trade once ayear or not as required this vi^d a quarter in lieu of ye xii^d formerly spent in the brothers houses.

---

* Debtors were imprisoned in the gaoler's private house, unless they could not pay his fees, then they went to the common gaol over the Scotch gate.

† This large amount of arrears must have arisen from a strike against the attendance on quarter days at brothers' houses. By rule 25 every brother was to attend and spend 6d. or forfeit 12d. In 1690 an order for the abolition of attendance was carried, but immediately repealed, and the amount to be spent raised to 1s. and the fine for absence to 6s. 8d. There was another order in Feb., 1699-1700, and again in 1705. Evidently there was great disunion over the quarterly drinkings.

Second that for the future ease of this trade and better payment of the same it is agreed of and ordered y^t whereas several brothers formerly pade iii^s iiij^d if absent at the quarter day y^t now for the time to come none shall pay at their quarterly meeting any more then one shilling a man if absent and amerced the same to be paid into the present undermaasters and they to yield an account once a year for it and all moneys relating to the fraternity when required.

Candlemas quar ffeb 7. 1710/11.　There was Mr Jemes Reed upon the resignation of his fath^r Mr Jos Read unanimously chossen and elected clarke to the fraternity of butchers with a true copie of Mr Reeds letter then to ye trade.

Carlisle febr'ry 7th 1710.

Gentlemen

　　　　　I have sent my son with the trades books it being that I have no minde to continueing yor clarke because my oth^r business concerns will not allow me to attend your qu'rt^r days. The und^r mast^rs account is right balanced and stated to this day being now a year & qurt^r since they came in : it is happiness to the fratternite I have left them out of everybodys debt but my owne and y^t not much considering y^t my purse was still open when the und^r mast^rs or any other wanted money.　Likewise y^t above eighty pounds amercyments have been very lately remitted to those of the trade few or none being taken of them for above this twenty years.*　my son desires to become a brother and its very like this may be a proper qut^r day he knows yor business of a clarke & I believe may be willing to serve you.

I am yo^rs
Jos Reed.

The amounts as appears by particulars due from the ffraternity to the above Jos Reed

14 „ 11 „ 1

Att ye quarterly meeting Aug ye 2nd 1727.　It is ye full consent and aprobation of this trade that ye 18 order inserted in this book be deligently observed for ye future on pain and penalty as is therein mentioned, viz 13^s 4^d for euery one offending.

---

* *Ante* p. 251.

Feb ye 5th 1728.   Its this day by ye whole consent of this company of butchers that for the futer euery of ye undermaisters or wardens of this fraternity shall be answerable for all such amerciements as shall happen to be in their time and they are hereby authorised to sue for them and the expenses attending thereby to be at the trades expence.

Allhallows quarter Nov ye 4. 1730.   Its this day agreed by ye majority of this trade that none of this fraternity shall buy any more goods of Thomas James ju^r upon ye forfeiture of 40^s as also that he shall continue a yearly man not any longer but atend his quarterly meeting at ye guild as other brothers does.

Allhallows quarter Nov ye 7th 1733. Its agreed on this day by ye full consent of this fraternity that if any brother of ye same shall kill or dress any manner of goods : for any person but what is for their own use and not to be exposed for sale shall be fined ye sume of 40^s for euery such fault soe committed.

Nov. 1734.   This day itt is ordered and agreed by the consent of this body that the whole body shall attend att the funerall of any brother or sister to attend them to ye church to be interred and likewise to return to ye house of ye deceased and spend there 6^d a peace upon the forfeiture of 12^d to be levied immediately.

Nov. 9 1737.
Whereas its made appear that frequent killing of goods doth hurt this fraternity it is ordered that noe brother of this trade shall present this markett with ane meat but what was killed against the markett day before upon ye paine of 6^s & 8^d for euerie such default.

In the guild of } Candlemas quar 4 ffebruary 1740.   Ordered by
butchers   } the consent of all the members of this fraternity who are here present this day that every brother of this fraternity shall for the time to come on the takeing of any apprentice to be instructed in the trade of a butcher pay to this guild the sum of ffive pounds.*   And it is in like manner ordered that no such apprentice shall be taken by any member of this ffraternity having another apprentice unless the former apprentice hath before that time served his sid master for the space of seven years.   And the better to enforce

---

* Raised to £10 in 1774, and to £20 at a later time.

this order no indenture of apprenticeship contrary to the tenor of the order shall be inrolled or allowed of in this guild nor shall any apprentice bound by such indenture at any time afterwards be admitted a brother of this fraternity.

In yͤ guild of ⎱ All Saints qͬ 3 Nov. 1742. The above order of butchers ⎰ the 4ͭʰ Feb. is hereby ratified & confirmed and also an order of this ffraternity dated 4ͭʰ Aug. 1668 & it is hereby declared and ordered that every brother of this guild living withͭ the liberties of this city shall on yͤ taking of every apprentice pay into the publick stock of this company as well the sume of five pounds mentᵈ in yͤ order of yͤ 4ͭʰ Feb. 1740 as yͤ sum of 40ˢ mentᵈ in the order of 4ͭʰ Aug. 1742.*

In the guild of ⎱ At a publick meeting of this company held at butchers ⎰ their comon guild or chamber this 30ͭʰ day of June 1742 it is ordered by the consent of the whole company then present that John Stordy the elder Thomas Sowerby John Pears and James Grayson be & from henceforth shall stand managers for this company to carry on certain prosecutions already commenced by the broͬˢ of this company agˢᵗ Joseph Dalton & John Slack for exercising the trade of butchers agst the form of yͤ statute in that case made and provided and that the said managers do carry on the prosecucon as they shall think proper and that they likewise carry on any other prosecutions against any other persons that haue exercised or shall exercise the trade of a butcher within the said city of Carlisle not being qualified by law so to do or not being entitled so to do by the custom of the said city or who shall in any other manner break in or incroach upon the antient libertys prescriptions rights and privileges of the sd company of butchers and for yͤ purposes afsᵈ It is ordered that yͤ sd managers or the survivor or survivors of them shall out of yͤ publick stock of yͤ sᵈ trade or of contributions raised for that purpose as they shall see most expedient pay off & discharge all such sum & sums of money as shall be due to Mͬ Tho Dobinson an attorney-at-law who has been employed in adviseing upon a state of the case of the said fraternity of butchers and in carrying on the prosecucon above mentᵈ and the said managers are hereby likewise directed & empowered to emply yͤ sᵈ Mͬ Dobinson in takeing further

---

* We do not find any order of 4th Aug. 1742 in the books. That of 4th Aug. 1668 is No. 23, *ante* p. 248. Clearly 1742 is a mistake for 1668.

advice upon this case and prosecuting such offenders as the s^d managers shall direct and the s^d managers are hereby empowered to apply the publick stock of the said trade towards the defraying of all such expences or if they shall think it more expedient shall by an equal poll rate or taxation to be made on every bro^r of the said company raise any such reasonable sum or sums of money as they shall have occasion for the purposes afs^d and such sum or sums of money as shall be so rated or assessed on each bro^r of ye sd company shall be paid to ye s^d managers or the survivors of them at such quarterly meeting of the said company as shall first happen after such rate or assesmt made and in case any deficiency shall happen by reason of the non payment of any of the sums so afsd assessed that then the sd managers shall in like manner make up such deficiency by a further equal assesmt by the poll rate as afsd and all such members of the fraternity as shall be rated & assessed by ye managers aforesd and shall neglect or refuse to pay ye sum or sums of money so assessed or rated upon them as afsd shall not be admitted bro^r of the said fraternity untill they shall have paid such sum or sums of money so rated & assessed upon them in maner foresaid.*

Aug. 6 1766.

It is this day ordered and agreed by ye whole fraternity this day present that for ye time to come every place man in his majesty's service is to observe his quarterly meetings or to pay sixpence for everic quarter day hes absent.†

Whereas the mayor &ct (*ante* p. 117).

Butcher guild

Thursday 17 Feb. 1785.

———————//———————

THE FRATERNITY OF BUTCHERS 1797,

RULES AND ORDERS TO BE OBSERVED.‡

THE BROTHER'S OATH.

You shall swear to be a true brother of the butchers, and shall at all times be obedient to the governors of this trade, and ready to

---

* The proceedings under this order are not recorded.

† These placemen seem to have been soldiers, of whom this guild had more than any other.

‡ These were ordered to be printed in 1801, and are here taken from a print of that date.

observe all orders and constitutions belonging to the same, and to the utmost of your power shall maintain and defend the same, and all the ancient rights and privileges belonging to the trade, being lawful and just. You shall duly and truly observe the quarterly meetings in the guild, and shall keep secret all private conferences, being lawful and just; and likewise all things belonging to the mystery of this occupation; and if any thing shall come to your knowledge that may tend to the prejudice or hurt of any member of this fraternity, that you shall timely acquaint them therewith, and to the best of your endeavours defend the same. All these things, and whatsoever else belongs to the duty of a brother of this trade, you shall faithfully perform and keep, to the utmost of your endeavours.

So help you God.

THE UNDERMASTER'S OATH.

You shall swear, well and truly to execute and perform the office of undermaster for the fraternity, for the year ensuing; you shall diligently and truly give notice and warning of the quarterly meetings held in your chamber, and all other meetings there, as by the clerk and ancients of the trade shall be appointed upon lawful and just occasion. You shall make a just and true account of all the amercements, fines, and such other money and goods as shall come to your hands, or shall be committed to your care or charge for the ensuing year, unto the whole company, at the end thereof.

So help you God.

THE CLERK'S OATH.

You shall swear that you shall well and truly execute the office of clerk to this company and fraternity of butchers, without favour or affection, malice or displeasure, to the best of your knowledge and skill.

So help you God.

THE WARDEN'S, OR ELDER'S OATH.

You shall swear you will well and truly execute the office as one of the elders or wardens of this trade or fraternity of butchers, and that you will use your interest to promote the benefit and advantage of the same, to the best of your knowledge and skill.

So help you God.

First Wednesday after Candlemas day, first Wednesday after the third of May, first Wednesday after Lammas day, and first Wednesday after All Saints.

Whereas various attempts have lately been made in this and other guilds, to obtain admission to their brotherhood, by persons having no claim or title whatever, we taking into our most serious consideration the violence of such proceedings; and for the better securing and preserving our rights and privileges as freemen of the city of Carlisle, do unanimously agree to the following resolution :

We repeal and declare null and void every rule, order, and institution, so far only as respects the notice given for meeting or assembling in the said guild, and in future order and direct that twenty-four hours shall be given to every brother, or left at his place of abode within the liberties of the city of Carlisle, or at the usual distance, before meeting or assembling in the said guild, all which meetings must be during the day.

Candlemas quarter, Feb. 4, 1801.

ORDERS AND RULES MADE BY THE OCCUPATION OF BUTCHERS BELONGING TO THE CITY OF CARLISLE, ARE AS FOLLOW :*

1. It is ordered and agreed, that every member shall be faithful to each other, in all things lawful and honest.

2. Ordered and agreed, that no person or persons shall reveal any secret or privacy that shall be spoken or done among the occupation. For every such offence he shall be fined 6s. 8d.

3. Ordered, that if any of the occupation shall at any time fellow himself with any out-man in buying or selling, he shall be fined 13s. 4d.

4. Ordered, that if any of the occupation shall lend any axe, gully, knife, or any things appertaining to their trade, to any out-butcher, he shall be fined 13s. 4d.

5. Ordered and agreed, that every one of the occupation shall keep their meetings on their quarter days; and at all other times, when occasion shall require, that they with great obedience come together upon lawful warning given them by the masters of the occupation for the time being, upon pain of 6d.

---

* These are all, down to No. 20, from the print of 1801.

S

6.   That when any brother of this occupation is in the act of buying any cow, oxen, sheep, lambs, kids, or any other flesh, and hath cheapened or bidden at the same, none of the occupation shall out-bid, or go about to buy the same over him, enhancing the price thereof, without the approbation of him who was the first cheapener thereof, or till he has, of his own accord, left the same.   Any person offending as above, shall be fined 13s. 4d.

7.   Ordered this quarter day, with the full assent and consent of this occupation, that the several apprentices of this trade shall carry and demean themselves decently towards their masters and brethren of this company ; and any apprentice transgressing this order, his master shall, for every offence, pay unto this occupation, the sum of 6s. 8d.

8.   It is this day ordered, by general consent, or the majority of this occupation, that no brother of this trade shall buy any goods, as sheep, cows, oxen, lambs, kids, calves, or any flesh whatsoever, from any butcher that is not a brother of this fraternity ; or from the partner of any outer-butcher, upon pain for the first offence 13s. 4d. for the second 2l. for the third 5l. without any abatement ; and that no brother of this trade shall buy any goods, directly or indirectly, of any outer-butcher, nor covereth by his friends, upon pain aforesaid, if proved by one or more witness.

9.   Ordered, by general consent, that no brother of this trade, at their meetings in the guild hall, on the quarter day, or otherwise, shall depart the hall till they break up by consent, without leave of the trade present, or the chief part of them, upon pain of 3s. 4d. for every such offence.

10.   Ordered, by the consent of the whole trade, that no butcher of this fraternity shall speak slightingly, or say that any of his brotherhood have selling, or hath sold any bad meat, which may tend to the prejudice of any of the brotherhood, upon pain of 13s. 4d. but that such things shall be left to the clerk of the market, and the clerk of this fraternity.

12.   Ordered, by the whole fraternity, that if any of the said body do act any thing prejudicial or contrary to his oath, in the orders of this fraternity, not only they, but any of the fours or wardens that so offend, shall forfeit for the benefit of the trade 13s. 4d.

13. Ordered, that any brother taking an apprentice for the time to come, pay to this guild 5l. And it is ordered, that no such apprentice shall be taken by any member having another apprentice unless the former apprentice hath before that time served his said master five years; and that no apprentice shall be allowed to buy any goods, such as cows, oxen, calves, sheep, lambs, or any other kind of goods belonging to their trade, until such apprentice has served his said master for two years, shall be fined 6s. 8d. for the second offence 13s. 4d. and to be paid before they are admitted a brother of that trade; and the better to enforce this order, no inden- ture of apprentice, contrary to the tenor of this order, shall be enrolled in this guild; nor shall any apprentice, bound by such indenture, at any time afterwards, be admitted a brother of this fraternity.

14. Ordered and agreed by this trade, that no brother, or brother's son, or apprentice, shall be allowed to kill any goods whatsoever, for any person that is not a brother of this trade, to sell in open market, or in hidlings.* If it be made appear against any one so offending, for the first offence 13s. 4d. for the second 2l. for the third 5l. if proven by one or more witnesses.

15. It is also agreed, by consent of this occupation, that no brother, or brother's son, or apprentice, shall buy any calves, or any other goods belonging to their trade, by weight. If any one so offends, to be fined 2l. for every offence.

16. Ordered and agreed, that no brother's son shall be allowed to follow the trade and occupation of a butcher, until he be full twenty-one years of age, without leave or licence of the said trade; and for such leave or licence, to pay forty shillings to the fraternity; upon refusing to take such leave and licence, he shall not be admitted a brother of this trade until the above sum be paid.

17. It is also agreed, that no brother, or brother's son, or apprentice, shall buy any calf, to return the caislip† in any state whatever, upon pain, for every such offence, 6s. 8d.

18. Ordered, by consent of the whole fraternity present, that each son of a brother of this fraternity, seeking to be admitted a

---

* *Hidlands* means secretly, see *Halliwell's Dictionary, Archaic, &c., Words. Hidlins* is anything hidden or put out of sight.—*Dickinson's Cumberland Glossary.*

† The *caislip* is the stomach, which is used in making cheese.

brother of the same, shall, before his admission, pay to the said fraternity the sum of 13s. 4d. And every other person in like manner seeking to be admitted a brother of the said fraternity, to pay the sum of 1l. 1s.

19. It is this quarter day ordered by the occupation, that if any brother hereof shall have occasion of complaint against another, the complainant shall have free liberty to state his grievance, and then the party against whom the complaint is made, to alledge his lawful defence moderately, and without railing or offensive words to be given by either party ; which being done, the parties without any farther dispute shall not only submit themselves to the rest of the occupation then present, but also undergo what order or penalty shall be awarded by them concerning the difference then in question ; and whosoever shall transgress this order, to be fined 13s. 4d. without any mitigation.

20. Ordered, this quarter day, with the full assent and consent of this occupation, that every brother of this trade shall pay their several amercements and fines to the master or under-master of this fraternity ; and whosoever shall neglect to pay the same, and to obey the orders of the said trade, shall be debarred from taking any apprentice, or his son to have any benefit, or be a brother of this guild, till all the amercements be paid.

The above rules and regulations to be in full force after the 1st of March, 1801.

————— // —————

Lammas quarter 7th August 1811.

Whereas the trade of a butcher has been much injured by persons following the same who have not served a regular apprenticeship of seven years and this guild hereof this day taking the same into consideration do appoint the following brothers to be a committee viz Richard Sowerby George Armstrong Joseph Norman Joseph Peascod and Robert Lamb and that such committee or any three of them shall have full power and authority to employ a proper person or persons to attend and see such following the trade of butcher kill and expose the meat to sale at the expence of the guild and the said committee or any three of them have like power and authority from this guild to prefer such bills of indictment on such persons as they think proper for following the trade & prosecute the same to con-viction out of the public money belonging to this guild.

St Helens quarter 5th May 1813.

Ordered by consent of the whole trade present that no brother of this fraternity shall be allowed to sitt down in this guild untill he pays all fines and arrears that stands against him. The undermasters shall have it in full power to turn them out upon all occasions untill they pay the whole sums that stands against them. That the undermasters may call upon any other brother present to assist them should there be any occasion. Any one refusing to aid and assist shall be fined five shillings each without any abatement whatever.

Feb. 7 1817.

It is ordered this quarter day by the general consent of the trade that several things have been stolen from the said company therefore they appoint a committee to take into consideration the best means of preventing thieves from stealing meat & also killing & slaughtering sheep out of fields & other goods belonging to any brother exercising the businesss.

Lammas quarter 7th May 1806.

It is this day ordered by general consent of a majority of the occupation that any brother taking an apprentice for the time to come pay to this guild twenty pounds.

St Helen quarter 7th May 1806.

Ordered this quarterday with the full consent of and approbation of this occupation that one guinea be paid out of the stock towards the funeral expenses of each brother belonging to this guild The above rule or order to be in force after this day : none to receive the above benefit but them that attended their quarterly meetings.

7 May 1817.

Ordered &ct that if any brother kill any kind of goods for any persons to be exposed for sale or even sold to persons after this quarter day will be liable to the fines of this guild without exemption whatever.

Lammas quarter day 1817.

Ordered &ct not to admit any person or brother of this guild off a quarter day [except] on 2 certain occasions during a contested election or if any person going abroad to leave the country and not likely to return : or if any brother knows any misdemeanour he is therefore to acquaint the trade withal.

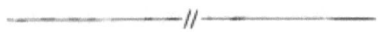

At the quarterly meeting of the guild or fraternity of butchers of the city of Carlisle held on Wednesday the 30th day of August, 1836.

It was proposed and seconded that the balance which shall remain in the hands of the clerk of the guild on the 8th day of February next and which will amount to the sum of six hundred pounds and upwards be then divided equally amongst all the members of the guild who shall be living on the 2nd day of Novr next or their representatves.

Resolved That the consideration of the above mentioned proposition be adjourned to the next quarterly meeting of the guild to be held on Wednesday the 2nd day of November next at 1 o'clock in the afternoon & that in the meantime notice of the above mentd proposition and also of the time appointed to take the same into consideration be given in all the Cumberland newspapers and in the Times the Morning Chronicle the Courier and Standard newspapers.

Resolved That the above mentioned notice be advertised once in the present month & once in the month of October.

At the quarterly meeting of the guild or fraternity of butchers of the city of Carlisle held on Wednesday 2nd day of November 1836.

The proposition made at last quarterly meeting of which public notice has since been given that the balance which shall remain in the hands of the clerk of the guild on the 8th day of February next be then divided equally amongst the members of the guild who are living on this day or their representatives having been again taken into consideration it was resolved that the said proposition be adopted and carried into execution.

Resolved That a list of the members of the guild be advertised in the Carlisle newspapers with a notice to all persons claiming to be members of the guild and omitted in that list to give in a claim as members of the guild before the first day of January next or that they will be excluded from the dividend.

That a statement be made out and submitted to the next quarterly meeting of the guild on the 8th day of February next of the balance of cash then in hand & of the sums due from members of the guild and that on and after that day each member of the guild on application to the clerk be paid his dividend after deducting all arrears due from him.

Resolved that Robert Brown Thomas Nanson (painter) & Robert Armstrong be a committee to carry this resolution into execution.

MISCELLANEOUS ENTRIES.

Candlemas qr 1656. It is this day ordered by genll consent that Rowland Darrance & Wm Wilson ju: now undermasters shall continue soe till Lamas qrtr Neither shall they be then discharged till they have leuied all ye amercimts & cleared their accompts.

Deliuered to the undermasters this quarterday wch they are to be accountable for 1 large couller of red & white sarsnet.*

1662. These psons following are amerced by genll consent for x x x & binding them to sessions & taking law one of another without acquanting ye trade therewith contrary to orders Thos Blaklock Rowland Darrance & James Blaklock therefore each of them amerced xs vid

Tho Blaklock & James Blaklock are by genll consent amerced for raileing & scolding in ye gild hall contrary to orders & therefore either of them amerced iiis iiijd

---

* They are also ordered to make a table frame and buffet, and to repair the chamber wall. Succeeding undermasters of this period receive "1 sarcent colour 1 staff for it & ribin 7 yards for staff each." In 1669, "ye arms of trade with lock and key of chamber door" are added.

1667. Geo Sowerby is fined for brawling words & thumping the table iii^s iiij^d *

1668. Candlemas. Ordered by generall consent that the vnder-masters provide 10/^s worth of good beere : cream cheese 2^s 6^d peice bread 2^s tobacco & pipes 2^s 6^d each and wine about 1^{li} bisket about 16^d & doe hereby engage to see ye undermasters pd what they lye out as afsd for this Alhallow Thursday next upon ye first quarter-day ensuing and whosever shall refuse to pay his pportion that then the vnderm^{rs} do distrain their goods for soe much.

1669. Rob Darrance was this trade amerced for saying Rob Small-wood was made a brother of this trade by means of the fflaggon pott being a gen^{ll} slander upon ye trade. Michael Barnfather was this amersed for calling John Robinson in presence of the trade "Rednosed Roger" 3^s 4^d

1670. James Sowerby was this day amced for scolding and abusive language and thumping agst ye clerks breast on Alhallows Thursday last & therefore amced according to order 3^s 4^d to be levied as afsd.†

Candlemas 1679. Rich Wilson amerced for saying that he did nott care for any of the trade nor for any of our forsworne oaths therefore we amerced him by consent the sum of 01^{li} 00^s 00^d remitted.

May 26 1679. Mr James Nicholson was then elected and sworn clarke of the fraternity of butchers & was also then sworne a brother of ye said trade.

November ye 4 1679. Information being made upon oath before this company or fraternity that John Pattinson a brother of this trade has joined himselfe in partnership in buying and selling goods with Thomas Tate als Mounsey of Stanwix an outman contrary to a former order of this guild the said John Pattinson is therefore amercyed xl^{s.}

Jo Ivison inform^{t:}

---

* Many similar entries occur : the words (very coarse words too) are frequently recorded. Fines for buying over brothers' heads, for fellowing with outmen, also occur.

† Thumping on the table (not on the clerk's breast) was a common offence at this period, as also was the abusing one Grayson. Who he was does not appear.

William Orsley is also amerced for trading as a partner with John Hill contrary to ye former order xl^s.

Tho Blaylock fil Robert
Wm Barnfather   } Inform^t.
Thomas James

Richard Wilson is amerced for railing and indecent words & giving the lye to George Sowerby jun^r contrary to former orders 3^s 4^d

3 ffeb 1679. Thomas Stanwix is amerced for slandering of Willm Barnfather & calling him " loose country rogue " in the presence of ye trade iii^s iiij^d pd 1^s & ye rest remitted.

Ordered y^t all the brethren of this occupãcon doe meet in their guild chamber on Shrove Tuesday next at ten of the clocke in ye forenoone to consult about the concerns of this trade and the masters to give particular notice hereof to all the country men brothers of this trade one day before and whosoever failes to appear (not haning a sufficient excuse) shall forfeit iii^s iiii^d. *

Persons amerced that went away ye last quarter day and went not to Robert Briggs house wher the quarter day was kept contrary to our order [Eleven, each fined 1/^s.]

July the 19th 1680. The names of those absent at ye meeting in the guild chamber† × × × Whereas the members of this trade or ffraternity have preferred two bills of indictment upon the stat of 5 Elizabeth ag^st Thomas Anderson of Stanwix & Richard Dufton of Itonfield for useing & exercising the trade of a butcher within the city of Carlisle contrary to the law. And whereas we suppose that ye said persons will make their defence at law by traversing the indictments or otherwise. Wee whose names are subscribed doe hereby order Thomas Sowerby and the undermasters to lay forth such sume & sumes of money in the managemt of these suits as Mr James Nicholson clerk shall direct and declare to be due.

---

* The record of the next quarter day does not show the reason of this special summons, but no doubt the two bills of indictment mentioned in the next order but one had their origin then.

† Nine, of which four are fined 6s. 8d., one *nil*, and the rest excused. The one fined *nil* is Mich. Barnfather, evidently a pauper, as he in other places appears in receipt of relief from the guild in company with sundry widows.

And we doe hereby promise that after all our public money is laid
forth & expended wee will severall pay to the psent undermasters
such further sumes or supplyes of money proporconally for & towards
yᵉ carrying on of the said suites or causes as shall at any time be
agreed by this fraternity or the maior part of those at any time
assembled in yᵉ chamber for that purpose to be due fitt & necessary
to be raised for the purpose aforesaid.   Witness oʳ hands the day
abovesaid.*

Feb. 1680.   Ordered that what brother of this trade shall hereafter
take any apprentice such apprentice shall dureing all the tearme of
his apprenticeship dwell with his master according to his indenture
unless this trade shall give leave to the contrary upon paine that noe
such apprentice shall be admitted a brother of this trade.

May 10ᵗʰ 1681.   Thomas Blacklock son of James is this day
amerced for giuing Tho Sturdy railing and abusefull words for
presenting him to the south leight† jury therefore we amerce him
iiⁱˢ iiijᵈ

Tho Blacklock son of James in the shambles & calling him rogue
therefore we amerce him iiiˢ iiijᵈ

May 9 1682.   Ordered that the undermasters by tenne peckes of
good malte against Assention day   3 pounds of biskett.

January 15 1682.   Ordered that a decent black funerall cloath be
bought by the vndermasters for the use of this fraternity   Ordered
also then that a new doore & a locke & key be provided for the
chamber doore & that the staires be also put into good repaire & the
vndermasters is to disburse moneyes for these things by the advise
& direcon of the clark & three or four more of this trade.

ffeb 5 1682.   Rob Smallwood is to lay downe unto the courtesy of
this trade for ameremᵗ for suffering outmen to hang meat upon the
crookes belonging to his house viⁱˢ viiijᵈ all remitted.

---

* 51 signatures : as all the absentees sign but Mich. Barnfather, the pauper,
the number of the guild, all told, was probably 52. Of the 51 signatures 33
are marksmen, and mark generally with the initial letter of their Christian or
surname : one or two use a combination of the two initials : others some arbitrary
sign. This litigation ended in 1682, when Thomas Anderson paid £5 and
expenses and submitted to the trade and was sworn a brother, as did some
half-dozen others, except Dufton, of whom we have no record.

   † Court leet jury.

August the sixth 1684 The day and yeare abovesd was ye fraternity of butchers in their guildhall and a motion was then made by ye senors of the trade for a new clark soe the question was put whether Mr Jas Nicholson should be continued clarke or yt Mr Jos Reed or Mr Kidd should be brought in It was carried in ye affirmative for Mr Joseph Reed the votes for him being twenty eight for Mr Jas Nicholson eight for Mr Kidd three.

Soe Mr Reed was sworn clarke as abovesaid by the wardens of the trade and admitted a brother of the same.*

Novem 4 1684. Then it is ordered by ye trade yt the said persons undr named doe meet upon Monday next in this guild between ye hours of 12 and one in ye afternoon to audit and state all ye accounts belonging to ye trade

Geo Sowerby	Thos Kidd
Robt Raskell	Thos Blacklocke
Tho Grayson	Tho Crockbaine
Tho Judson	Geo Sowerby senr
Rob Briggs	
Thos Sturdy	

Novemb 10th /84. Then meeting in ye guildhall by an order about stateing the accounts and adjourned to Jos Judsons and by a great part of ye trade spent their twelve shillings. Ordered Thomas Blaymire† to pay 12s by a generall consent.

1686. "1 mort cloth 2 pr cullers" handed over to new under-masters.

Aug 7 1689. Then according to an ordr antiently made by the fraternity of butchers that in caise any brother sued one another for money pticularly relateing to the trade that then they should pay 40s for ye use of ye trade soe yt it is now agreed unanimously by the trade to amerce Thos Blaylock accordingly 40s to be forthwith levyed.‡

---

* The reason for Mr. Nicholson's dismissal does not appear. For the end of Mr. Reed's term of office, see *ante* p. 252.

† Undermaster.

‡ The same year Tho. Grayson was fined 40s. for the like, but the trade gave him 14s. back in cash, he having, as shown by the next entry, paid the 40s. to the undermasters, who spent it in the Ascension-day ale.

Feb 5 1689/90. At this quarter it is ord^d by the whole consent of this ffraternity that whereas Thos Grayson had p^d 40^s upon ye account of amercit^s for surety of ye undermasters for ayle had for Ascension day without leave from the clarke & ye foures of the trade the s^d Tho Grayson submitting to ye trade it's ord^rd that the present undermasters pay him cash again fourteene shillings which is according^l p^d same time per Th^o Miller.

Lamas qua^r. The amount of what debt is due to ffeb 16 the fraternity of butchers as app^th

Thos Kidd debt 40^s	-	-	-	2 : 00 : 00
Thos James bulder debt 40^s		-	-	2 : 00 : 00
Geo Sowerby sen^r debt 20^s -		-	-	2 : 00 : 00
Thos Crockbaine debt 40^s -		-	-	2 : 00 : 00*

Allhallows qua^r 2 Novemb 92. Then upon the information of Edw Iveson on having bought 3 sheepe at Bleckall Thos Miller & Thos Stanwix butchers did goe to Rich. Sewell of Bleckall and told him not to trust the sd Edward whereupon the sd Edward did not get the sd sheepe and this being an aparent injury and not only contrary to fform^r order but . . . theerefore by consent of the whole trade amerc^d each of them xx^s.

Lamas qua^r August 4th 1703. Then did Mr Geo Bell of the city of Carlisle give to this ffarternity of butchers one piece of plate being a tumbler with his name &ct engraved upon it and wch was for admitting him a broth^r of this trade and for the remitting of his amercymts fmerly due to this trade for his being absent at the quart^r dayes.

1704. September 9. Then Christ Musgrave esq^r gave two guinneys to this trade wch was forthwith distributed amongst them and spent.

Sept 20 1704 It is agreed on by this fratternity of butchers y^t Tho Stanwix esq^r be made a brother of this trade therefore he is now admitted a broth^r of the same payd his fees and swore accordingly.

---

* These are loans on bond, with interest at rate of 1s. 2d. for 20s. yearly. The bonds are entered in the book, and against Sowerby is this note :—"1694 this by the whole consent of the trade is forgiven Geo Sowerby when in goale."

April 10 1705. Then did Thos Stanwix esq make a psent of a pece of plate to this fraternity it being a silv cupp.

St Helens quar^r 1705. Then did Mr Jos Reed upon the account of Sir James Montague & Coll Stanwix giue to this ffraternity xi^s to drink the queens health & their own.

Memo that in the guild hall Allhallow q^r it is agreed by the whole ffraternity that none shall buy any goods for one year aft^r this date of John Thompson Scotchman upon paine of vi^s & viii^d to the trade & iii^s iiij^d to the inform^t agst any one soe offending.*

ffeb 7 1709. That whereas there is an auntient ord in this book and made Allhallows qua^r 1647† that noe broth. of the ffraternity shall in the guild chamb^r on the qua^r days or any other day when the fraternity is met there about the trades business shall raile chide scold disturb or give any vndecent or unbecomeing language to one another butt shall not only pay xiii^s iiij^d to the und^{r}mast^r for the time being to be levyed of the offender forthwith for the use of the sd trade but be expeld the sd trade of butchers therefore this quarter day Geo. Sowerby is guiltie of the breach of the abouesd ord^r by very much disturbing the ffrattnity and hind'ring the busines of the qu$^rt^r$ day in y^e guild chamb soo is amercyed according to sd order xiii iiij.

Septr 28 1710. Then cam Lieut^t Collonell Samuell Gledhill and by y^e gen^l consent of this ffraternity was admitted a brother of the same accordingly and has taken his oath and payed his ffees.
On the day aboue being Sept 28 then did Coll. Gledhill giue to this trade one large silver bowl carv'd and one challice carvd.‡

St Helens qr May 2 1711. By a generall consent this day of the whole trade it is ordered and agreed that whereas Thomas Crockbane hauing not observ'd ye oath as a four or warden of this trade and contrary to the orders of the same hath abused & disturbd ye whole fraternity therefore the sd Thomas Crockbaine is turned

---

* Year not given, but between 1705 and 1708.

† This must be the order of Nov. 7, 1647, printed on p. 246, but the recital is a free paraphrase.

‡ Qu. Was the chalice silver ? It cannot be identified in subsequent lists. Is it the piece said to be stolen, *ante* p. 243 ?

ont from being a four of this trade and Thomas James senior elected in his room.

Sept 10 1719. Att a private meeting then Thos Fletcher esq is made a brother of this brotherhood taken his oath & given 40ˢ to the trade.

Allhallow qʳ Nov 5 1712. The same time came Mʳ Thomas Dobinson & by consent of this trade is made a brother of the same haveing taken the usuall oath & pd his fees accordingly being 6ˢ 8ᵈ

Candlemas qʳ ffeb 9 1714. Upon the petition of Thomas Blailock juʳ a prisoner in gaol it is agreed by this trade that yᵉ sum of six-pence per week be paid him by yᵉ undʳ mtʳˢ for ten weeks and the further sum of forty shillings when such sume will be sufficient to procure his discharge.

Lamas qʳ day 8 Aug 1716 Ordered this day that Thomas Dobinson of the city of Carlisle gent be requested to take upon him the office of clerke of this company & take the ppr and usuall oath of the sd office which the sd Tho Dobinson accepted of & was sworne according before the wardens of the sd company the day & year abouesd.

Candlemas quaʳ 8 ffeb 1720. Ordered that all amerciamts now un-paid be sued for and particularly Thomas Blaicklock & Richard Sowerby who were amerced 40ˢ each Wee whose names are here-unto subscribed doe promise to pay such contribution as shall be demanded of us towards sueing of Thomas Blaicklock senʳ & Richard Sowerby & others for the amerciamtˢ due to the company of butchers of Carlisle Witness our hand th 8ᵗʰ day of ffeb 1721.

49 names.

Lamas quartʳ 2ⁿᵈ Aug 1721. Ordered that John Wood & Willm Wood of Wigton & Thomas Staples of Brampton be indicted at the next generall quarter sessions for the county of Cumberland upon the statute of Eliz for exercising the trade of a butcher not haueing served an apprenticeship according to law ordered that att the next quarter day euery brother of this company doe pay unto the hands of the undermasters to carry on that prosecution 1/ˢ ordered that Mʳ Thoˢ Dobinson clerk of this company doe manage and carry on the said intended prosecution.

May ye 10 1727. Itt is agreed to by this company y^t they will remitte for ye future his attendance att ye quarterly meeting for repairing ye window in their guild chamber. Wittness my hand John Brown.

1727 Candlemas. John Clemetson amerced 10^e for bying over the head of Jo Nanson.

1727 June 12. Jo Nanson 3^s 4^d for throwing of y^e door out of its hinges & ile behaviour. He submitting was excused.

1729. Ralph Harley 10/ for buying a beast over Jo Nansons head.

1733 Nov. This day payed for y^e culler as appears $\wp$ receipt 2^{li} 11 . 0 and remains of y^e money collected for y^e same in my hand 8^s y^e whole sum collected being 2^{li} 19 . 0.

ffeb y^e 7 1770. This day William Lamb is amerced 40/s for buying a dead sheep and is amerced by y^e consent of y^e whole trade he acknowledged y^e fault y^e trade thought fit to return him back again £1 . 18 . 0.

1814. Cheque on Forster Bank   60
            4th Aug 1813
   —— — ——— Jan 1814   166
   ——————— Feb 20   20
       Money in hand   8 - 8 - 10
                  ——————
                   248   8   10

April 5 1816. The trade agreed to purchase that part of the guild which belonged to Charles King for £18 & they let the guild hall to Mr Tinlinson for a school at £8 - 10 per an.*

1822. Agreed this q^r day to give unto Rob Matthews the sum of 2^s 6 for getting a petition drawn by Mr Saul to be presented to the corporation to lower the shamble seats in the market.

---

* The guild hall contained other rooms than those belonging to the various guilds : the tenants of these held them, as the guilds did theirs, by *cullery tenure* of the corporation and could alienate them. For an account of this tenure see *Transactions Cumberland and Westmorland Archæological Society*, vol. vi, p. 308.

Chapter XIII.

EXTRACTS FROM THE COURT LEET ROLLS OF
THE CITY OF CARLISLE.*

Civitas ⎰ Turnus maioris sive curia leta ciuitatis Carlioli tenta
Carlioli ⎱ ibidem die veneris viz. vicesimo secundo die Aprilis anno
regni domine nostre Elizabethe dei gratia Anglie Francie et
Hibernie regine fidei defensoris &c 39 annoque domini 1597
coram Thoma Blenerhassett armigero tunc maiore ciuitatis
predicte Edwardo Monke et Willelmo Barwicke ballivis
eiusdem ciuitatis per sacramenta

Johannis Syde	Alexandri Knagge
Johannis Slater	Richardi Warwicke
Henrici Syde	Thome Grame
Johannis Calvert	Willelmi Wilson
Thome Barnes	Willelmi Hetheryngton
Thome Monke	Edwardi Barne

We find our selves great molested wth the poore that is strangers
therfore we crave your worshipe to be so good as to comand the
bedles to comand them forth of this cittye and that the bedles be
more strayth lock unto for doinge of ther dewtye for theye ar worthye
great punyshement for nott doinge of ther dewtye.

We crave your woorshipe to provid the cittycenes a sufficient
herd for this cittye and to allow him a sufficient stypent for doinge
and keapinge of the cittyes neatt and swine as your wo: and brethren
thinkith good for the cittye is greatly decayeth therby.†

* These extracts illustrate most excellently the transcripts from the
Dormont Book and the orders, &c., of the eight guilds, and are better for
that purpose than any number of footnotes.

† The herd would drive the citizens' cattle and swine to the Kingmoor,
and tend them there : he had a livery coat at the expense of the city.

We finde and present Charles Crockbaine Thomas Crockbaine George Crockbaine for forestallinge and regratinge of salmon sea trouts and all other kynde of fyshe contrarye the orders of this cittye therfore everye on of them in amearsyment v pounds except your worship cause this to be amended we are utterly undone.*

We find and present everye on of them that hath a bawne dogge unmusled after this daye to be in amearciment†   xii^d

We present Thomas Holme for that he doth kepe under him John Martin Scottsmane and Jane Pattinsone and Elyzabeth Pattinsone contrary the presentment at the last maior turne and therfore in amerciament   xx^s

Whereas we finde that John Prestmane servinge Mr John Morasby Mr Thomas Browne and Willm Willsone and in his said service did most deceitfully confederatte and compact wth one Rychard Dobsone and dyd cause him to take of the molter coarne nearly on pecqe to the use of the said John Preastmane and other sertaine mony to the valew of xxxvi^s yearly and therfore we crave that both Preastman and Dobsone be discharged for serving at any of ye mylls of this cittye and every man that shall retain them after this presentment to be in amercament v pounds and to be punyshed at your wo^r discretione to the example of others and further for a fyne we sett downe that he shall paye to the maior and baylyfes of this cittie ‡   xx^s

We crave your wo^r to be so good as to forese that both the waye at the new goytt§ and for amendinge of Eaden brige ende be spedely mended and that it be nott delayed and put of this somer but presently to forese it and that lykwyse Caldo brigg to be amended.

We crave your wo^r to inquyer for a bulle for the cittie is greatly damnyfied for lack of one.

We crave your wo^r to command the bellmane to mayke the conducts cleane and the walls for they are not well lock unto.

Good M^r maior whereas we finde in this cittye great defect for want of a sufficient mane to instruct the yonge childrene of this cittye therfor we crave your wo^r to be so good as to paie one for the

---

* *Ante* p. 83, rules 112, 117, and 118.

† *Ante* p. 70, rule 62. A bawne dog or bandog is a fierce watchdog of the mastiff species, crossed by a bulldog : see *Halliwell's Dictionary.*

‡ *Ante* p. 61, rule 27.

§ Goyte, or goat, a cut for water, a damcourse.

same purpose and to allow them sufficient wagies and to withdraw the wagies* both from the ushour of the hye schole and from Mongo Maysonne and to give itt to some that will instruct theme.

We crave your wor to comand the bedles to putt forth of this cittye Robert Bonehome and one Grace Towry.

In most humble maner dissiring yor worshipe to concider of me Archeles Dalton concerning the pavershipe of the citie that I may have your worshipes good will and fourthence in it for I think that I am as sufficient and fet for it as anie within this citie and so in it showing me that goodwill I am kept bound to pray for your worshepe

Your pour neighbour

To command   Archeles Dalton

We think good your wor shold consider well of this bill.

Charles Crokebaine, Thomas Crokebaine, George Crokebaine, Thomas Robson and Willm Mulcaster these fyve we fynd prevous offenders in forstalling and bying of salmon, hearings, and other fishe, wherefore we request yor worship wth the help of yor brethern, either to se these faults reformed, or else yf yt be not loked to, as we here present, we therefore do request you, that the statute provided against such offendors may be extended against them, as they well deserve, otherwayes yt ys in vaine upon or othes to present them when as you do not regarde yor owne in excueting of the same.

We present Robert Soulby for selling of unlawfull flesh wch was corny porke and therefore in ameriamt   iiis iiiid

We present and fynde John Payne, in Fishergaite and Thomas Steill to be unlawfull to remayne; and dwell wthin this cittie; and therefore we requier that they may be expulsed upon payne to him that letts them dwell wthin their house after Whitsondaye next xls

And further we order, and set downe, that all cottingers wch haith bene borne either in Scotland, or beyonde the blackeforde, to be avoyded, and expulsed upon payne to him that keaps him after Whitsontyde next †   xls

---

* The corporation paid one moiety of the salary of the usher of the high or grammar school, viz., £3 6s. 8d., which is ten marks. This appears from the chamberlains' accounts, but the amount is differently stated lower down.

† Ante p. 66, rule 46 and note, and p. 70, rule 63 and note.

We request yo[r] worship and the rest of yo[r] bretheren, that whereas John Robinson, and Edward Dalton, being beadells, and have no regard of their office, that yf they do not hereafter looke better to their office then they have heretofor done in keaping furthe vagabonds, and valient beggers, that they shalbe expulsed frome the sayd office, and their coits taken frome them, and others appointed to execute the same.

We present James Syde for keaping of his bawne dogge un-mossoled and therefore in amerciam[t]   xii[d]

We present Thomas Warwicke Rogersonne for hinging of sheip skynes in streat.

We present and fynde that yt is verie necessarie that the throughe gaite in Shapp vennell shalbe repayred and amended before Whit-sontyde next upon the citties chardge otherwise yf occasione serve yt wilbe verie hurtefull, and noysome to us all.

We request yo[r] worship and the rest of yo[r] bretheren that the xxvi[s] viii[d] wehe the usher of the heighe scolle had may be called backe, and retained to the use of the cittie untill such tyme as we shall thinke him worthy of the same, and likewise we request yo[r] worship to prefoure unto my lorde bushopp of Durhame a petitione for to request his lordshipp, that we may have a sufficient man appointed to teach o[r] children according to the ancient custome heretofore used.*

We request yo[r] worship that we maye have a sufficient man to be o[r] hird, and that his wadge may be amended at the sight and discreeone of yo[r] worship and the rest of yo[r] bretheren because the yeare is verie harde, and that he be had furth of hande for we have great neade of him for o[r] cattell.

We order and set downe that we may have a pecke, and a halfe pecke to remayne in the pillorye for measuring of corne both for the towne and countrie.

We present and fynde that John Moresbye laite maior [of this cittie of] Carliell about the xii[th] daye Marche last past 1596, did speake and reporte verie unhonest, undecent & unreverent, yea and verie slanderous words against yo[r] worship, yo[r] bretheren, and the

---

* *Ante* p. 273. The see of Carlisle was vacant from the death of bishop Meye, in February, 1597-8, to the consecration of bishop Robinson, in July, 1598. Probably the bishop of Durham was administering the see under a commission from the archbishop of York.

wholle corporacone of this citie of Carliell in saying that he conld buye a jurie in this cittie of Carliell for vi⁵ to go to the devell, and hell fire, and therefore we thinke him not worthie of that societye wch you do yet retaine him in, contrarie oᵉ order set downe at oᵉ last maiores turne.

We set downe and order that Archilles Dalton shalbe allowed to be the paver to this citie, and that he shall have the wages as others have had before, and we crave yoᵉ worship that he may be bounde to do all such like works as others have done before.

We request yoᵉ worship and the rest of the bretheren that the batlement of Caldobrig maye be amended bothe for the safegard of men and cattell.

We set downe that there shall be a sufficient learned man to teach and instruct the prties whome yoᵉ worshipe and yᵗ brethren thynketh most fettest and sufficient for the purpose that they may be fet for to come to the free scoole, and the xxvi⁵ 8ᵈ to be tayken from the ussher of the sayd free scoole, and gyven to him that so tayketh paines for teachinge of the sayd prties.

We set downe that as concerninge the cyties bull, yf a poore man had the bull in his keapinge he myght haue answered for hym, wch we thinke is a great deceaye to the cytie, wherefore we desyere yoᵉ worshipe and yoᵉ brethren to call of hym that had hym, and goot the cytyzens one as sone as may be.

We desyere yoᵉ worshipe and yoᵉ brethren to let us haue an able suffycient man for oᵉ hurd, and and as for his wayges and his cost we reffer that to yoᵉ worshipe dyscreation and yoᵉ brethren, and so lykwysse for oᵉ pavore.

Mᵉ maiore we request yoᵉ worshipe and yoᵉ brethren, whereas oᵉ neyghtbors hayth sustained great loosses by Cawdew bryge we therefore desyre yoᵉ worshipe that ye would consider of it and let the battlement be rayssed wherby neyghtbors may be kept harmles of their goodes.

Wheras yoᵉ worshipe hayth comanded us to serve God and oᵉ prence and you, and we oᵉ selves wyllinge to serve trewly to oᵉ consyens, so far as in us lyeth, we fynd oᵉ selvfes very sore abused and all other honest men that ar to be comanded by yoᵉ worshipe, in speaches uttered by John Morasbie wch ar thes followinge, that about the xii^th day of March last past 1596 or thereaboute the sayd John Morasbie should speake, that he could bye a jurye in Carlisle,

to say any thinge that he would require them to say, and to foreswere them selvfes, yea, not only to foreswere them selvfes, but also
to go hed longe into hell fyer, for vi⁸ yf thes may goe unpunished,
it is not for noe honest man nor none that is under yo͏ʳ worships
comandement to pass upon any jurye wherfore we desyere yo͏ʳ worshipe and your brethren to consyder of it, and as for his punisshment
we cannot set it downe, but we refere to yo͏ʳ worships discrecion and
yo͏ʳ brethren that all honest men, and all jurors, wch ar under you,
may be satisfyed by his punishment accordinge to his deservinge.

21ˢᵗ April 1619.*

Whereas it was ordered that everye free man and freholders and
inhabitants within this cyttie should be present and make theyr
appearances at everye courte leet within this cyttie for the service of
our souveraigne lord the kinge; therefore we fline and amereye such
person absenting him self contrary the paine   vi͏ᵈ

We amereye William Sympson for slandering Robert James to
be comon tayle teller to M͏ʳ Chancelor   vi͏ˢ viii͏ᵈ

We amereye Henrye Robinson for slandering M͏ʳ Blenerhassett,
and charging him with an untruth (being a justice of peace
      vi͏ˢ viii͏ᵈ

We amereye William Tomlinson being a florryner for assumyng
upon him to be a barbour and usinge the same to the hurte of some
of the same cyttie that doe exercise the trayd   iii͏ˢ iiii͏ᵈ

We order and sett downe, that the saide Tomlinson shall not use
the said ffacultye within the libertyes of this cyttie at any tyme
hereafter upon paine of amereyment   xx͏ˢ

We order and sett downe that the chamberlanes of this cyttie
shall build up and repaire the butts under the walles before the ffirst
daye of Maye next upon paine   xl͏ˢ

We request that M͏ʳ Maior and his breathren shall call for the
silver broad arrowes and the stock and the horse & nage bells† with
all expedytion to be imployed for manteyning of a horse race for the

---

* It is unnecessary to reprint the formal Latin heading of every court leet
roll, from which extracts are taken: it is sufficient to give the date.

† *Ante* p. 100, where the horse and nage bells are engraved. The silver
broad arrows do not exist, nor is any other race cup known but the bells: the
stock would be the race fund.

cytties use (upon the kinges moor) at such tyme yearely as theye shall thinke convenient, and to article that the same cup shall be brought in yearely as they shall thinke flittinge.

We order and sett downe that all that haue any swine wthin this cyttie shall eyther send them to the kinges more or kepe them close in theyr backside that they come not in open streat vpon paine of amercyment to everye one offending therein*   vi^d

And the hird to haue a penny in the month of the owners for his paines for every swine.

We request that Caldoe yeat be covered over for the avoyding of great dangers wch may befall his maties people and other inconveniences besides.

We order and sett downe that the bedles shall avoyd all beggers oute of this cyttie except ffre cytizens, or els to be avoyded them selves or to stand in the pillorye ffower market dayes every daye an hour at least.

We amercye Archiles Armestronge for keping his wief to play the milner, contrary the orders of this cyttie   iii^s 4^d

We amercye the wief of John Barwicke for keping of swine troughes in the hye streyt contrary the paine and therefore in amercyment according to the orders of this cyttie†   xii^d

We amercye John Martin for encroaching of the cyttie's inherytance according to the orders of this cyttie.

We amercye Thomas Hodge for slandering the merchants in saying that they bought harden cloath‡ in the merkett with a longe yeard and selling the same againe with a short yeard   iii^s iiii^d

25th October 1623.

We present Edward Durance of Castelgait for keeping of Thomas Pearson being a prentice & divers other at cards in mer.

vi^s 8^d

16th April 1624.

Wee present Thomas Blaymer of this town mere for that he abont xxvith of November last past did in open markett taxe Marmaduck Mangie then baylef of this citty to his great descreditt,

---

* *Ante* p. 65, rule 41.   † *Ante* p. 65, rule 41.

‡ *Harden* is coarse cloth.

and not only so, but disobayed the comandm[t] of the baylefs, and not only so, but afterwards did at the same tyme lye vilicant hands of his said bayleff, to the discouragement of honest men & them that hath and is to suply the said office of a bayleffe and therefore we order & inioyne him said Blaymer to come ether in open markett or open court & acknowledg his falt whither yt please the said bayleff will call him and when, as also wee amearcye him over & beside xx[s]

Wee present Willm Wilson butcher for buying a quick lambe wch M[r] Henry Bayns had or was about to buy yt, & the s[d] Wilson giving more for yt then the s[d] M[r] Bayns might have had yt for, this contempt done the xth Aprill 1624 in amar[t] iii[s] 4[d].[*]

Wee present Thomas Rashell of this towne for that thire was one barell of hearings apointed by John Callwell the first of his barell had to be sould for five hearings for a penye, now the fors[d] Rashell cam and bought the s[d] barell & sould y[t] for 4 hearings for a peny to the harm and damage & hurt of the markett and very ill example, & therfor in amercm[t], this contempt done about the 8th of Aprill 1624 vi[s] viii[d]

We present M[r] Thomas gent. laite maior of the cytie for noyt deliveringe the records of the cytie to M[r] Baynes nowe maior as he was formerly comandeyd to doe and contrary his oythe and orders of this cytie and therefore in amereyment accordinge the former paine x[li]

21st October 1625.

Whereas William Moresbye did make an escape, and departe out of the motehall after he was committed by M[r] Blennerhassett and his bailifes (therefore we doe amercye him) vi[s] viii[d]

And we order and sett downe that the saide William, shall repaire before M[r] Maior and his breathren in open courte and then and there submit himself to M[r] Blennerhassett and his bailifes and abide such censure as M[r] Maior and his breathren shall order and sett downe.

We present John Carliell (butchers John of Comersdell) for presenting unwholesome meate in the market and offering the same upon sale, and therefore we doe amercye him vi[s] viii[d]

---

* See *ante* p. 66, rule 44.

We request that the boke of orders belonging to this cittie, be duely and distinctlye read by the clerke at everye courte leet, that all free men may take notize thereof and thereby know what orders they are sworne unto for there are manie that do greatlie complaine that they never hard the boke of orders read, and therefore they know not wherunto they are sworne or otherwise that copies may be graunted to everye companie.

We present Robert Shipperd for not cutting downe so much of his apple tree as ys noysome to Henry Monke his barne, and therefore we amercy him   iii^s iiii^d

And we order and sett downe that he shall cutt awaye so much of the s^d apple tree as is noysome unto the s^d Henry before Candlemasse next upon paine of xx^s

We order that the clark for tyme present agaynst every lyte* correct his book of reeseants so as he shall call evere man by name befor the chardg be given upon payne for the clark his default xx^s

We present James Blaklocke younger glover for that he the third daye of October last 1625 did misreport and slaunder the wife of Alexander Addle smythe in calling her shepe stealer, and that she did recett Michaell Blaklocke sheats that were stollen : and therefore we doe amercye him for his slaunder   vi^s viii^d

We present William Salkeld milner of Herribye milne, and Thomas Rematye, for keping leading horses to forraine milnes and therfore we doe amercye eyther of them†   vi^s 8^d

We present Elioner the wife of Henry Tallentyer for baking bread usuallie upon the sabaoth daye before the sermon and therfore we doe amercy hyr   vi^s 8^d

We present Margaret the wife of Ambrose Carleton & Marye Barton for brewing (being foryners) and therefore we doe amercye eyther of them‡   vi^s 8^d

Wee present these under written as hocksteares and forstallers of this cittyes markett in byeing fruit butter and chease before markett bell ring contrary to cittys orders & therefore every of them in amercm^t §   vi^s viii^d

We doe amercye Isabell the wife of Thomas Nicholson for slaundering the wife of Thomas Shipperd in saying she did steale

* Court leet.   † Ante p. 61, rule 27.   ‡ Ante p. 69, rule 56.
§ Ante p. 84, rule 119. We omit to print the names.

shoes from her husband and burthned his children therewith to
excuse herself   iii⁵ i⁴

We amere the said Isabell for that she doth sett a swyne trough
in the street under the new motthall contrary to a former payne vi⁴

We amercie Robt Shepheard for his dunghill lying in the open
streate on the backside of the moothall contrarie the paine toties
quoties   vi⁴

We order and sett downe, that all such poore people, as have
eyther pension or allowance of this cittie shall content themselves
therewith, and not be clamorous or troublesome to strangers as
heretofore they have used to the great scandell of this cytie upon
paine that everye such clamorous begger shall forfytt theyr pension
and allowance.

We order and sett downe that if the bedles give way or sufferance
to such clamorous beggers to vex or troble strangers, that they for
theyr negligence shall lose theyr pensions and coats and with all
that they restraine forriners.

We order and sett downe that M^r maior and his officers shall
not suffer anie forriner, stranger, or other, to sell lint in faire tyme
within the motchall, and likewise to give charge to the sergeants to
kepe the hall safe from such people and if the sergeants be negligent
herein to be amerced   xx⁵

We order and sett downe, that woole, talloe, butter and cheise,
shall be weighed with the same weight at the motehall, that heretofore hath been accustomed ; and that lint should be weighed with
14^lb to the stone, and that both freemen and forriners shall waighe
with the same waight and whosoever shall use anie contrary waight
shall forfitt for everye default   vi⁵ viii⁴

Whereas forraine drovyers, butchers, and others doe kepe markett
and make marchandize for cattle on the kinge moore, before the said
goodes and chattles did present the markett by meanes whereof
much abuse hath been used, and manie stolen goodes sheltered,
therfore we order and sett downe that no such markett be kept hereafter. But whosoever shall buy any cattle before they present the
markett on Carlisle sands shall forfitt for everye default*   xx⁵

---

* Kingmoor is north of Carlisle Sands, and at an irregular fair held there,
it would be easy to sell stolen beasts and horses. On Carlisle Sands the
vendor of a horse had to enter it with the town clerk and produce some one as
surety that he was the owner. Several books of such entries are still in

We order and desire that Mr. maior and his officers for the tyme present and also for tyme to come shall cause all payns that is now made or hereafter shall be made to be openly proclaymed at Markett Cross of market day and also in parish churches presently after tyme of divyne service of the sabath day and that the clerke doe inrowle the said payns amongst other orders for the cittye.

20th April 1627.

Whereas the taylours of this cittie, in the faire tyme, doe worke some of them in the guild chamber; and an information hath been made unto us, that Andrew Foster did carrye into the saide chamber a fyrye coale, to take tobacco, in the faire tyme to the great danger of muche hurt that might happen therebye, therefore we order and sett downe, that not anie of the saide trade or anie other whatsoever shall worke in the sade guildhall, or in anye other guildhall for the avoyding of all danger upon paine of everye one offending to the contrarie.*   v^li

Whereas yt is informed that John Mathew of the citie of Carliell taylour that he from tyme to time, and at severall tymes, harbored recetted and intertayned common cut purses, detected persones and bad companye to the evill example of others and to the great hurte and anoyance of the kynges people therefore we doe amercye him the sade John Mathew for recetting of such bad persones   xx^s

And we order and sett downe that the sade John Mathew shall not hereafter harbour, recept, or entertaine anie such bad and detected persones upon pain of v^li and lose of the benefit of his trade within the cittie.

---

existence among the corporation muniments, styled "toll books for horses sold on Carlysle Sands," from which we extract the following :—

"John Armestrong of Cannebye, Scotchman, sold a blakgray filly 3 yeares to Leonard Ersdell of Cadbek, price liis vid pleg John Comson of the same. Edmond Greame of Mossbank hath sould a bay mere, fower yeare ould, two long white facies, cropt of the nere erce, to Anthony Richardson of the Maines, price lxs viiid pleg to John Holladay of Mossbank. James Harmestrong, Cattlowden, Scotsman sould a bay mere with a star, 6 yer ould, troting, to Tho Fisher of Walton Parish, price 30s pledge Tho Harmstrong of the same parish."

* The Guildhall or Redness Hall, ante p. 26 n, still survives ; it is a mass of inflammable timber, and dates from early in the 14th century. Wonder is it has escaped fire so long.

We doe amereye the clarke for not callinge by name everye inhabitant within this cittye att this court leat accordinge to a former order   xx^s

Wee present Scropp Snaden gentlm and Richard Slee and John Deithwick for ataching John Stodert in the night tyme in Michall Bayns house without licence of M^r mayor & therefore we doe amerce them for breech of the cittys libertyes   v^{li}

We present William Wilsome of Ratton rowe, for rescuing the wife of Randall Nicholson from the possession of Michaell Blakelocke late bailife, who did attach her for an execution, for the weh we doe amereye him   vi^s viii^d

We order and sett downe, that all such as have mastiffe dogges, shall kepe them allwayes musseled; upon paine of vi^d to everye one that kepeth ainie such, so often as the sade mastiffes shall be seane unmosseled.*

We present thes comon baikers, and brewsters, whose names are hereunder written, for grinding theyr corne at foraine milnes, severall tymes since the last leet.†

Whereas we are informed that the backsyde of Redness hall, both the ground walles and slates thereof are much ruinated and decayed therefore we request M^r maior, that his worpp, should cause his chamberlaines to repaire the said decayes with convenient expedition.‡

Whereas it hath bene formerlie ordered and sett down that all such poore people within this cittie as had eather pensions or allowanc of this cittie should content themselves therewith and not be troublesome and clamorous against strangers as usuallie they had bene to the great scandall and discreditt of this cittie upon paine that everie such clamorous begger should forfeit his pension and allowance and lykewise whereas it was ordered that the beadles should (not) give waie or sufferance to such clamorous beggers to vex or trouble strangers that they for their negligence should lose their pensions and coats &c we therefore order and sett downe all such pensions and citties benevolences as formerlie they had shalbe

---

* *Ante* p. 70, rule 62.

† We omit the names.

‡ The guild chambers in Redness hall, or the guild hall, were and still are held of the corporation by cullery tenure, and hence that body would repair the fabric.

deteyned and henceforth quite taken awaie from all such clamorous and troublesome beggers : and that neather pensions nor coats be given to the beadles that now be ; but that new bedles be appointed, such as wilbe carefull to doe their dewties, according to order and direction. And we desire that some of thes pensions be bestowed upon Archiles Bewlie, a poore distressed freeman, towards his maintenance.

17th October 1628.

We present for comon badgers forestallers of the markett, and buying greate quantities of corne and graine coming to the markett & converting the same into mault (making mault theire trade and occupation) to the annoyance of his mai^{ties} subjects.*

We request that the leaden spout that lies betwene the two houses of Readnes Hall be viewed and sufficiently repaired that water may have free passage without annoyance to the house or neighbours adjoyning thereto.

We order and sett downe that the aldermen of the cittie, bailiffes of the same, and ancient men of the best sorte shall attend and accompany M^r maj^{or} every Sonday to the sermon in their best attire upon paine of vi^d for every default unles they can make good excuse to the contrary.†

We request that the maj^{or} and bretheren may devise some convenient place neare unto the maj^{or} pue for placing the ancient baliffes and best sort of the cittie.‡

We order and sett downe that the baliffes of the cittie during the time of there office shall have and weare gownes, and likewise we order that all ancient baliffes and all such as are able to provide gownes shall provide and have them betwene this and Easter next upon paine

---

* *Ante* p. 83, rule 114. We omit the names.

† The sermon would be preached by the lecturer in St. Mary's church (the nave of the cathedral) : part of the lecturer's salary was provided by the corporation.—See *Transactions Cumberland and Westmorland Antiquarian and Archæological Society*, vol. vii, p. 312, &c.

‡ The mayor's pew or chapel was in St. Mary's church, in the nave of the cathedral, but was removed by the corporation in 1649 to St. Cuthbert's church.

We present the keepers of the pillorye, for taking more towle then theyr due*   iij^s iiij^d
And we order that if hereafter they doe use or offer the like iniurye that they shall lose theyre place.

We order and sett downe that if anye person digg or delphe for cley at a place called Caldoe Hill neare unto Botchardgate that all such persons so offending shall be amerced   v^li

We present these persons for keaping leading horses to the hinderance of the moulter graves of this cittie vizt: Robert Coocke and James Dunne for keaping a leading horse to Denton millne.†

Alexander Lowicke for a leading horse to Harrabye millne.

Robert Eales for a leading horse to Harrabye millne and Thomas Taylor for a horse to the Abbey millne.

We present theise persons following for digging and graving of flacks and turfes on the King moore they being forregners.

23rd October 1629.

We present thes persons following, for buying of beif and mutton of countrye butchers and selling the same againe in open market vizet James Syde and Lancellot Syde and therefore we doe amercye everye of them   vj^s 8^d

We amercye James Thompson and Agnes Rasshell for lying theyr dunghills against Saint Cuthbert churche yeard wall and therefore we doe amercy eyther of them   iij^s iiij^d

We present thes persones followinge, being kepers of comon ovens and bake houses for taking excessive dewes vizet George Wells (&c) and therefore doe amercye everye of them‡ vj^s viij^d

We order and sett downe that hereafter they take noe more towles for baking then heretofore hath bene accustomed and likewise that everye bakehouse kepe a paire of scailes and weights for weighing of bread as the statute doth allowe.§

---

* A plan of Carlisle in the British Museum, *tempore* Hen. viii, reproduced in Lysons, shews the pillory as a cage-like structure, in the market place, with a pillory proper on the top. The lower portion seems to have been used for keeping weights and scales, and the keepers of the pillory were the collectors of the city's market tolls.

† *Ante* p. 61, rule 27.

‡ *Ante* p. 70, rule 61.

§ *Ibid.*

We present Willm Stoddert the keper of the pillorye for taking of more then ordinarye towle   iij^s iiij^d

We present Robert Grame for taking suite against Thomas Sewell and his sonne at forreyne courts without licence of the magistrates of this cyttie and therefore we doe amereye him   iij^s iiij^d

We present John Bird sherifes clerke for serving of writs wthin the libertyes of this cyttie wthout acquainting the officers of the same cyttie therewith and therefore we doe amereye him according to the aintyent orders of this cyttye.*

23rd October 1633.

We order and sett downe that the tool of the horses be imployed yearely a part thereof towards the makinge of a free plate to be runn yearely upon the kings moore and the rest towards the benefitt of this citty.†

We request M^r maior that the three wates who now are allowed may continue and (be) commanded to play beginninge presently and soe continue untill Candlemas and to play both at Christmas and at all other times according to former custome except onely the Sabbaoth dayes and to have such allowance as formerly they have had.‡

We order and sett downe that the aldermen and brethren shall associate & accompany M^r maior att such times as he haith occasion and to sitt with him in place of judgm^t whereby he may have their counsell in doubtfull questions as formerly have been used according to ancient orders upon payne of iij^s iiij^d for every default.

Wee finde and amercy Thomas Baynes for entertayening and harbouring of apprentises mens children and servants and suffering them to play at cards and other unlawfull games in his house contrary to the statute and the orders of this citty and therefore we doe amercy him   xl^s

We present fine and amercy Andrew Foster for harbouring and entertayning honest mens children and apprentises att unlawfull

---

* *Ante* p. 11.

† *Ante* p. 100.

‡ The chamberlain's accounts show that the waits had coats and salaries from the corporation.

tymes and suffering them to tiple and drinke in his house and to waist their parents and masters goods and therefore we doe amercy him   xl^s

We amercye Xrofer Donnalt of Kirkbride for keeping an unlawfull measure for selling of salt to the cousanage & deceiveing of the kings people and therefore we doe amercy him   vi^s viii^d

We amercye Nicholas Hudson Robert Watson Willm Moresby & Andrewe Foster taylors for breaking their orders in taking apprentices before that their former apprentices had served five yeares and therefore we do amercye every of them*   xx^s

We amercy Jane the wife of Henry Clemetson for slandering Elizebeth the wife of Ralph Smith in sayinge she bought one goose at the crosse and stoole another and therefore we amercy her
iii^s 4^d

We order and sett downe that the well in Rickardgaite shalbe repayred with a mantle wall of a yeard height at the cost of the inhabitants next adioyninge who have the benefit of the said well betwixt this and the first day of December next and upon neglect of the said wall we doe order that the well shall be filled up.

We order and sett downe that the well in the markett place shalbe repaired and maid with a pump and stone trough as formerly it haith beene with all expedition for the common good of this citty and to be done att the charge of this citty.†

We order and sett downe that every maior and bailiffes shall from henceforth keepe 4 courts yearely vizt every qrter one for triall of debts and damages between party and party upon payne of x^{li} ‡

We order and sett downe that all butchers frequenting this markett shall bring the skinnes of their neate and sheepe fastened to some part thereof and that they shall not buy any kidds lambes or veales before the ringing of the markett bell upon payne of vi^s viii^d for every default.§

We order that donghills lyeing in Set Cuthberts vennell shalbe removed and carryed away once every weeke and the vennell to be

---

* *Ante* p. 148.

† This well is now closed and the exact site forgotten, but it was opposite the shop of Messrs. Thurnam & Sons ; it may have been the well, of Roman work, which St. Cuthbert was taken to see.

‡ *Ante* p. 73 n.

§ *Ante* p. 84, rule 123.   This was in the interest of the tanners.

maid cleane and swipt against the Sabbaoth day upon payne of iii^s iiii^d for every default.*

We order that Edward Murhouse shalbe the cittyes hird and and keepe the cattell upon the Kings moore as formerly haith beene used and to have such allowance as formerly haith beene given and we order that he shall sweepe and make cleane all the freemens chymneyes 4 tymes a yeare upon demand or att any time payinge to him for every dressing 1^d.

We order and sett downe that the lecturer of Set Maryes and Set Cuthberts shall have allowed unto him yearely the summe of six pounds thirteene shillings 4^d to be payed as followeth 3^{li} vi^s 8^d to be taken out of the maior his allowance for wine whosoever shall supply that place: and the other 3^{li} vi^s 8^d to be taken out of the cittyes milne rents and we order that the lecturer shall preach 4 sermons at Set Cuthberts yearely that is to say every quarter a sermon upon Sunday in the forenoone and likewise shall exercise and preach afternoon sermons upon the Sabbaoth as now is used.†

We order and sett downe that the booke of the orders and constitutions of this city shalbe scene and read openly in the common hall by the clarke at some freehold court yearly and every such trade or occupacon as shall desire a coppy thereof shall have the same granted unto them.

We present Thomas Stanwix gentl for keeping a leading horse att Harriby milne and for carricing of mault and graine out of this citty to grinde there to the annoyance of this cittyes milnes and therefore we do amercy him   xl^s

22nd October 1649.

We order that the three sergeants of this cittie shall carry their halberts upon their shoulders when they attend M^r maior and baliffes and likewise on the markett dayes and we entreat there may be three new halberts bought at the cittie's charge for the sergeants to serve them successively and we also order that the three sergeants

---

* St. Cuthbert's vennell was the access to the church of that name.

† *Ante* p. 284. See also *Transactions Cumberland and Westmorland Antiquarian and Archæological Society*, vol. vii, p. 312.

maces be made sufficient as is sett downe in the 7th article of the abstract of the citties charter.*

We amercy all such as after warneing given suffer their swine to goe unringed in the streets and church yeards everie of them who offend herein   vid toties quoties

We order that all the inhabitants in Set Cuthberts vennell shall make clean their forefronts every Saturday night and whosoever shall offend herein is to be amerised   xiid toties quoties

We order that the butchers shall present the markett with the hides and skins of all oxen kine and sheep web they shall bring to the same sub pena†   3s 4d toties quoties

We desire that all streets wthin this citty (wherein the decayes are) may be paved and amended and that Mr maior at his pleasure and at the charge of the citty would appoint such men as he shall thinke fitt to see the same finished.

We order that all the ringdikes in and about the liberties of this citty be repaired and kept winter and summer sub pena 3s 4d toties quoties.

We desire Mr maior that the conduits in and through the cittyes walles may be speadily clensed and what persons soever after the said clensing shall presume to lay any manure or dunghill neare the same to forfeit for every offence   vis viiid

We order that (according to an ancient order) the aldermen of this citty shall attend the maior upon every Lords day to the church in their gownes and likewise to attend the maior in the markett place at or before the sermon bell to the church sub pena vis 8d toties quoties and the common counsellmen to attend likewise sub pena 3s 4d toties quoties.

We order that the present baliffes of this cittie shall forthwith provide for either of them a decent gowne for the honor of this cittie sub pena   vli

We desire Mr maior that the sexton of the church shall ring six a clock bell called scholler bell every morneing at six a clock winter

---

* One of the halberts, purchased under this order, is still in existence. The three serjeants' maces were not made sufficient, but in 1650 three new ones were purchased for £12, and are now in use, while the older ones are in the Museum.

† Ante p. 84, rule 123, and ante p. 213.

and summer and alsoe nine a clock bell at night as heretofore haith bene accustomed and that he may have allowed him for his paynes and toward the charge of candlelight of the revenues of this cittie

40ˢ yearely

We desire that Willm Heslop piper may be permitted to goe his accustomed course playing evening and morning through the streetes and that he may have his livery formerly had with the charitable benevolence of those who   x   x   the course and love musick.

We order that the loning without the towne yet wthin the liberties called Porter loning may be wthin 20 dayes clensed by those neighboᵣˢ who adiogn upon it sub pena   viˢ viiiᵈ

We order that the dounghills wch lye against Sct Maryes church yeard walls may be spedily taken away and that noe dounghills be laid there hereafter sub pena   viˢ iiiiᵈ toties quoties

We order that all inhabitants wthin this citty doe not permitt their dounghills to lye in the streetes above 8 dayes and alsoe make their forefronts cleane sub pena*   viᵈ toties quoties

We present David Hodgshon for selling hardware in front of the shop of Willm Bushby on the markett dayes being noe freeman contrary to the order of this citty and therefore we amercy him
viˢ viiiᵈ toties quoties

We present George Taite als Mounsey for dressing of veale wch he presents to this markett wth sheepe sewett contrary to the statute and therefore we amercy him†   viˢ viiiᵈ

We desire that Mʳ maior aldermen and capital cittizens doe take into consideracon the great paines the bellman tooke in the sickness time and that he may have allowance out of the cittyes meanes; and that Mʳ maior be pleased that his wages may be augmented.

We likewise desire that the beadles and bellman may be remembered for their paines takeing in clenseing the conduits and dressing the streats.

We order that all the inhabitants betwixt Richardgaite and cittidale who have any gardens there shall clense the high wayes

---

* *Ante* p. 71, rule 66.   † *Ante* p. 83, rule 116.

betwixt their severall gardens and the walls wthin xx^{ty} dayes next followeing soe that there may be a free passage for cart and carriage, and upon default thereof we amercy them   3^s 4^d

We desire that the church yeard walls of both parishes may be speadily repayred and the gates maintained for the decency of the church and church yeard.

We desire that the mearestone now taken up betwixt Willm Robinson and Thomas Pearson may be sett downe and enquired who tooke up the same.

We desire that the pension for and concerning the child wch Willm Durrance now haith may be augmented for and towards the maintaince of clothes for the same.*

We desire M^r maior and the aldermen to take into consideracon the distressed condicon of two poore boyes freemens children to wit Hugh the sonne of Hugh Nanson and Thomas Willson the sonne of Thomas Willson late spurrier and that they may be putt to be apprentices or otherwise care taken for their future maintaince as alsoe the present as may be thought fitt.

The citty of } The court leet or the maiors turne of the citty of
  Carlile } Carlile holden there the eleventh day October in the
             yeare of our Lord 1651. Before Cuthbert Studholme
             esq^r maior of the citty afores^d Robert Colyer and George
             Marton bayliffes of the same.

We order y^t the inhabitants of St Cuthbert vennell shall make cleane their forefronts everie Saturday night and whosoever doth neglect we doe amercie 12^d for everie default.

Wee request y^t all ye streets in the cittie be paved and amended where the decayes are and y^t the constable of everie street or a sufficient man may oversee the same, till they be sufficiently repared at the charge of the cittie.

Wee order y^t the two bailiffes shall before the 24th of March next provide either of them a decent gowne upon paine of either of them   xx^s

---

* This would be a pauper child boarded out, as was the custom, with Durrance.

Wee desire y^t M^r maior will cause some one to view the citties milles and to see the houpes be made close, & the measures sealed in regard to abundance of complaints.

Wee order that a sufficient bull be kept in winter, and two in summer at the citties cost.

Wee order that all the ring dykes in both the friers* and all other ring dykes within the priviledge of this citty both within the walls and without be kept in sufficient repaire winter and summer. And whosoever shalbe found faultye in this order wee doe amercy everie of them   6^s 8^d

Wee desire y^t M^r maior and the aldermen will take bond of all such inhabitants who are not free that they may not be chargeable or burthensome to this citty.

Wee desire the maior aldermen & common counsell will continue the stipend unto Thomas Craghill usher of the grammer schoole wch hath beene alwaies heretofore paid qrterly by the cittie in regard both of his dilligence & abillity wch wilbe an encouragem^t to him for the continuance of his pains in the s^d place.

Wee present John Boweman being noe freeman of this city for keeping open shopp and selling merchant wares by retaile as well upon the week day as market day contrary to the priviledge of this citty not having compounded wth the companie of merchants and therefore doe amercy him   5^{li}

24th October 1655.

We present these parsons following for buying lincloth harne† and yarne before the markett bell ring Nicholas Barker (&c) we amearcy of them   iii^s iiii^d

We present Willyam Salkeld younger for suffering his beastes and swine lying without in the night time being offensive to Willyam Moorehouse and therefore we amearcy him   3 - 4^d

We present Mr Isaack Tully for not accompening M^r maior upon notice given by the Sariant contrary to an ancient order made, as may appeare therefore we amearcy him   iii^s iiii^d

---

* That is in the late precincts of both the grey and black friars.
† *Harne* is coarse cloth.

We order that the tenants under the moothall who hold theire shoppes of the citty shall make a sufficient wall betwixt shopp and shopp within twenty dayes after notice given upon paine of vi^s viii^d *

We order that the farmers of the wealock shall cause the markett place to be swept and made cleane every Satturday at night upon (pain) of xii^d every default.†

23rd October 1658.

We desire that the pavements of the severall streates of this cittie and liberties of the same where decayes are may be repaired at the citties cost namely Botchardgate without the gate Caldewgate betwixt the gates the causey without and the litle bridge over the dam Castlegate and Abbeygate and all other places within the liberties.

We order that all inhabitants of this cittie that buyes any corne in this markett shall grinde the same at the citties millnes upon pain of vi^s viii^d

We order that noe milner that farmes the citties milnes shall carry any corne to be ground to any out milne upon paine of vi^s viii^d every default.

We desire M^r maior that the markett bell may be rung winter and summer at twelve of the clock by the maior seriant.

We desire M^r maior that there may be a chimney erected and builded in Rickardgate heade a shorte table and a beddsteade for the use of poore prisoners being committed there.‡

We desire M^r maior that the sworne men both for flesh and fish that every markett they may take a strict view of both flesh and fish that it be good and wholesome for the sustenance of man that hereafter there be noe cause of complaint.

---

* The moothall was originally open on the ground floor : this space was let to tenants, who erected walls (as this presentment shows) and acquired fixity of tenure in their holdings, which the corporation has recently [1886] purchased at high prices.

† The "wealock" or weighhouse : the farmers of the "wealock" seem to have succeeded the farmers of the pillory as farmers of the market tolls.

‡ The city gaol was over Rickergate, or the Scotch gate.

15th October 1661.

We present Thomas Blacklock boutcher, for selling his beast skins [before ye beasts were kill'd] to John Tarne of Penrith & we amercie him   xiiis iiiid

We desire that ye well in ye market place be opened & a sufficient wall made about it, about a yeard in height with a close cover & a lock, wch we conceive may be usefull to ye inhabitants of the cyttie & also nessisarie in case of fire.*

We order that ye farmers of ye wealocke cause the market place to be swept & made cleane every Saturday at night, or before Munday at 12 o'clocke next ensueing, upon paine of every default   xiid

We order that noe inhabitant of this cyttie shall lay any maner against ye mainegard, but shall remove the same weekely & sweep & make cleane ye same upon paine of iiis iiiid every default.

We order that Robert Rigg shall remove his swine coat built against ye cytties wall within 40 dayes after notice given upon paine of   vis viiid

Whereas there hath been severall complaints made by Andrew Gaite for ye water wearing away his garth, or garden adjoyning Burrow mill, wch we conceive was occasioned by setting ye water that way in ye tyme of ye seidge for ye preservation of ye said mill, we desire Mr maior & counsell to take it into consideration & give him such satisfaction as shall be thought fitt.†

27th October 1662.

Whereas we are informed that Robt Sawer keepe a great dogg wch may be very hurtfull to children or servants and others, we desire Mr maior would send for ye sd Robt Sawer & cause him either to hang ye sd dog or keepe him musled for preventing of farther danger.

We desire that Mr maior would cause ye beadles to cleanse ye venell called St Mungo venall, and to open ye conduite, and cause the dung there laying to be carried away, it being hurtfull and noysome to ye scholars of ye high schole & other passingers and to be made cleane and carried away so often as there is occasion.

---

* *Ante* p. 287 n.   † A reference to the great siege of 1644-5.

24th October 1665.

Wee order that no fremens sonns servants or apprentices shall walke or goe abrode in the streets within this citty after tenn of the clocke in the night, except it be about ther fathers or masters business upon paine of punishm^t two howers in the stockes the next day after and further to be ordered by the maiors discretion.*

We order that if any persons within this citty doe entertayne any freemens sonns prentices or servants after x a clocke in the night, unlesse it be aboute ther fathers or masters business that every person offending herein shall be amerceyed for the contempt.

We order that if any person or persons hereafter cast any hott ashes in the common streete or laines or any other place else within the libertys of the citty the same shall forfett for every offence† 0ˢ 4ᵈ

Wee order that noe person or persons whatsoever shall winnow any corne in the open street or laines of this citty upon paine of every default‡   3ˢ 4ᵈ

We desire that M^r maior would please to take speadie course to cause ye pavements that are in decaye within the cyttie and liberties to be repaired as also that ye slates of ye gildhall be put in good repaire, and that two pecks be made and keept at ye pillearie for ye use of ye market.

23rd October 1666.

Wee present these persons followeing for not baiteing their bulls Tho : Blacklock and James Blacklocke, wee doe amarcy ether of them   iiiˢ iiiiᵈ

Wee present Robert Grame, Allixander Rittson, for lying two deed horses wthin the libbertyes of the citty, they being noysume, to the inhabytents of the same, and therefore we amersy each of them   11ˢ

Wee present Elizabeth Threlkeld and Issack hir sonn, for running a pitch forke into a sowe of Thomas Peats, therefore we do amercy them   iiiˢ iiiiᵈ

We order Anthony Atkinson glover to cut his thatch wch over reacheth ye wall of Cuth : Robinson soe y^t ye drope may fall upon ye pavement and not upon ye s^d wall, wthin twenty days after notice given upon paine of   iiiˢ iiiiᵈ

* *Ante* p. 69, rule 60.   † *Ante* p. 66, rule 67.   ‡ *Ante* p. 65, rule 40.

We order that if any person or persons doe sett any mastiffe doggs on fighting wch causeth great disorder in the streets, or such as doth manage them thereunto, be committed to the motehall for the space of twenty fower howers or otherwise to be punished as M^r maior shall think fitt.

20th October 1668.

Wee present Thomas Sowerby and Michell Craw for being abusive in the hall on the court leete day and departing thence before they had obtayned leave, therefore wee amercy eather of them   iii^s iiii^d

Wee order that noe butchurs within this citty shall kill, scald, or dress swine in the open streats of this citty upon payne of every default   iii^s iiii^d

26 October 1670.

Wee present John Nixon the bellman for not clensing the water-course the backside of St Cuthberts church yeard wall, contrary to aforesaide order therefore wee amersey him   vi^s viii^d

1673.

We present James Wiggon for killing of doggs & throweing their carcases over the walls being noysom of themselves, and to the danger of nighbours goodes goeing there therefore we doe amercy him   vi^s viii^d

We present John Waugh of Stanwix for cutting of whinns upon Kingsmoore therefore we doe amercy him   vi^s viii^d

We present Tho: Graham and Willm Coultard for lyeing their dunghills in the highway to castle feild therefore we doe amercy either of them   xx^s

We present Robert Durrance for overhearing the jury, & reveileing their secrets in the towne therefore we doe amercy him   xiii^s iiii^d and what further punishm^t M^r maior shall thinke fitt.

20th April 1682.

We present detor Tho: Smith deane of Carlile for his dunghill in the highwaye und^r ye wall of this citty, & we amercye him vi^s viii^d

We present Rowland Briggs of Atterby for graveing flax & pastering catle on the citty moore & we amercye him   xiii^s iiii^d

Wee present James Blacklock of Stanwix for occupying the trade of a butchur he haveing not served as an apprentis according to statute and therefore wee amercy him for every month foll : trade   xl^s

We humbly desire that a table of fees be written in Inglish & hung up in the inner hall.

We desire M^r maior to take into consideracon the great abuse of the Sabbath daye, by children playing in the streate wch if not suppress^d may bring judgm^t from God ag^t us.

21st October 1689.

We request y^t M^r maior would be pleased to take care about the observacon of the Lords day, and alsoe profaine swearers & drunkards.

We request that care be taken about the swine, as y^t they may be sent to ye Kings moore.

***

SCHEDULE OF THE COURT LEET ROLLS AMONG THE CITY MUNIMENTS.

22nd April	...	1597	27th October	...	1662
21st April	...	1619	24th October	...	1665
25th October	...	1698	23rd October	...	1666
16th April	...	1624	20th October	...	1668
13th May	...	1625	26th October	...	1670
21st October	...	1625			1673
20th April	...	1627	20th April	...	1682
17th October	...	1628	22nd October	...	1688
23rd October	...	1629	21st October	...	1689
23rd October	...	1633	25th October	...	1698
22nd October	...	1649	26th October	...	1703
11th October	...	1651	26th October	...	1730
24th October	...	1655	25th October	...	1734
23rd October	...	1656	20th October	...	1735
23rd October	...	1658			1735
15th October	...	1661			

Chapter XIV.

EXTRACTS FROM CERTAIN ROUGH MINUTES OF THE PROCEEDINGS OF THE COUNCIL OF THE CITY OF CARLISLE PRIOR TO ANY EXISTING ORDER BOOK.*

September 25 1666.

The city } It is ordered by the maior aldermen and comon council-
of Carlile } men of the city afores^d that noe inhabitant within the
liberties of the s^d city shall send or carry foorth or bring into this
city any corne or graine to or from Denton milne or to or from any
other outen milne upon paine of six shillings eight pence for every
default to be foorthwith levyed by the maior and bayliffes, and afterwards to be disposed of by the maior aldermen and council reparacion
of the farmers as they shall judge reasonable.

September 28 1666.

Whether the farmers of the tolls the last year shall have
abatem^t

To be abated			Not to be abated
50ˢ a year	40ˢ a year	5ˡⁱ	5 votes
7 votes	8 votes	2 votes	

What to be given to the chamberlaine

40ˢ	30ˢ	3ˡⁱ
17 votes	4 votes	3 votes

* Like the extracts from the court leet rolls, these illustrate the transcripts from the dormont book, &c. Some of them refer to matters which we cannot explain.

October 1 1666.

And. Wilson to be disfranchised.

He is to make submission in writing under his hand at or before the next court day.

Whereas Andrew Wilson of the city of Carlile did after he was comitted to the hall upon an execucon of his owne accorde depart thence without leave from Mr Thomlinson then maior John How and Thomas James then bayliffes or any of them It is this day ordered that for his offence done as afores^d he make submission in writing under his hand at or before the next court day.*

April 18 1667.

A plate   None
18 votes   —

The articles to be altered, and ye 1st plate to be rid for on Whitsun-Thursday.

June 17 1667.

Whether the maior and bayl^s shall be indempnifyed touching the arrest made upon Tho: Blackelocke.

Queries to putt to the recorder.

1. Whether bayle may be required of a responsible and resident freeman, the case being such that speciall bayle might be insisted upon at comon law.

2. Whether the bayle shall be demanded upon the arrest of the party, or in open court upon entering the plaint or declaracon.

March 4 1667.

What sume of money shall be given towards the maintenance of the m^r of Carlile free schoole during the pleasure of this corporacon if the dean and chapter provide a sufficient schoolm^r

18 voted 6^{li} 13^s 4^d †

September 25 1667.

Whether Jo: Bushby shall be committed if he refuse to submite for ye affront done to Mr Barwicke and Mr Thomlinson.

---

* *Ante* p. 77, rule 87. Mr. Wilson appears not to have been of "gentil demeanor."

† *Ante* p. 274.

He shall be comited soe long as M^r maior shall please—nemine contradicente.

Whether the difference betwixt ye citty and M^r Ed. James Mr Richard Monke and others, touching the 100^li and the last charges expended in suite concerning ye same, and consideracon for the same shall be referred to arbitracon.

To be referred.

21 voted.

October 14 1667.

Whether Mr James and others shall have the 10^li in dispute.

21 voted for £110.   6 voted for £120.

It was then voted that Mr James and others should have payed them the sume of 110^li.

October 18 1667.

Citty of } It is ordered by the maior ald^rm bayliffes and capitall
Carlile. } cittizens of ye s^d citty that George Barwicke and John Thomlinson gen two of ye aldrmen of the citty afores^d shall assigne and sett over unto Edward James and Richard Monke of the s^d citty merchants Edward Lowry and Francis Wood of ye same citty sadlers one bond or obligacon wherein Sir Wm Dalston kn^t and bar^t Sr George Dalston and Sr John Dalston kn^ts his two sonnes are bound to the s^d John Thomlinson then maior and the s^d George Barwicke in the sume of two hundred and ten pounds for paym^t of one hundred and five pounds as by ye s^d bond bear date 2nd of March 1666 more at large appeareth. And if the s^d bond shall not make up the sume of 110^li which this corporacon have promised to pay to them the s^d Edw: James &c upon the consideracon of p^rtended debt due to them from the s^d corporacon that then wee the s^d maior &c make up to them their extors adtors or asses what sume so ever shall be wanting.*

---

* It does not appear how the corporation became indebted to Messrs. James & Monke : probably they had advanced money for the corporation, which, after the siege of 1644-45, was in very low water pecuniarily. The bond for £105 with which the corporation paid those gentlemen probably represented money the corporation was made to advance in 1645 for maintenance of the royal garrison. See a paper by W. Nanson, on Carlisle 1644-45, *Transactions Cumberland and Westmorland Antiquarian and Archæological Society*, vol. vii, p. 48.

Jaury 21 1668.

Whether a pticular pson shal be imployed to manage ye cities bonds, Newcastle, and Apleby, and Duckets bill of . . .

19 voted.

Who shal be imployed.

M^r record^r* Mr Aglionby. 19 voted.—ye whole corporacon

August 3 1668.

Whereas an ord^r was ye 13 of July past made by this corporacon touching some grievances done to ye inhabitants of ye same by some of ye officers and sould^{rs} of the garrison of Carlisle as by ye s^d ord^r appeares we ye maior aldrmen bay^l and cap citz^{ns} of the s^d city haveing considered y^t ye effects of ye s^d ord^r may tend to prindice of ye said city, and y^t ye grievances therein complained of, may and will be redressed by Sr P. M. goun^r of ye s^d garrison. It is therefore this day ord^{r}ed that ye s^d ord^r shall at present be altogether null and void, and y^t Sr P. M. shall be acquainted with ye proposicon of ye corporacon touching ye s^d grievances and Mr Agl. shall also be acquainted therewith, and if redresse be not grted touching ye same grievances, y^t ye s^d ord^r do stand in full force wch ord^r being this day taken into further consideracon by us ye M^r ald^r &c we doe order y^t ye said ord^r shall be at prsent suspended and all further proceedings thereupon till a meeting of ye corporacon and a discouse be made with Sr P. M. concerning ye same and that M^r Jo. Agl : shall alsoe hane notice of ye said meeting that he may gine an acco^t how farr he has already proceeded upon ye former ord^r, and if Mr Aglionby doe appeare at next assizes at ye meeting of ye corporacon, that then he shall hane a copy of this ord^r, and a letter sent to him by the s^d corporacon.†

August 5 1668.

Whereas the sevrall persons whose names are hereund^r written did disburse for the use of ye corporacon the respective sumes of money likewise underwritten, for and towards the paym^t of the

---

* Mr. recorder was Thomas Denton, of Warnell, whose portrait is in the town hall, and who resigned in 1679 when John Aglionby, barrister at law, son of the distinguished royalist, succeeded him,

† What these grievances were does not appear. Sir P. M. is of course Sir Philip Musgrave. Some subsequent orders refer to these matters.

queenes joynture.* It is therefore ordered by the maior aldermen and capll cittizens now assembled in the guildhall of the s⁴ citty, that the s⁴ sevrall sumes of money shall be reimbursed to the said pties respectively upon the first day of Decembr next forth of yᵉ rents of yᵉ citties milnes then due and payable.

September 18 1668.

Whether yᵉ ordr of yᵉ 13 of July last past concerning some greinances done by yᵉ officers and souldly of this garrison shall be revoked or stand in force.

It shall be revoked.   To be respited till Monday next.
11 voted.   14 voted.

September 21 1668.

Whether the ordr of the 13 of July last shall be revoked, or it shall remaine in force, touching some difference between yᵉ garrison and yᵉ corporacon.

To be revoked.   It shall stand in force.
12 voted.   21 voted.

November 18 1668.

Whether yᵉ ordr of yᵉ 13 of July last and all ordrs touching yᵉ differences betwn yᵉ corpor & garn of Carlile shall be revoked.

Revoked.   28 voted.

Whether yᵉ order made yᵉ 1 of June 1668 whereby Mr Jo: Aglionby was authurized to prosecute and manage all yᵉ suites of yᵉ city &c. shall be revoked.

Revoked.   28 voted.   The s⁴ ordr is revoked.

December 30 1668.

Whereas J. A. ar. one of yᵉ aldrm of yᵉ s⁴ C. being appointed by Sr P. M. Bart govnor of Carlile to make his submission according to an ordr fro yᵉ kings maty and his most honrble councell did this day abovesᵈ make his submission and acknowledgmt accordingly in yᵉ prsence of yᵉ Mr aldr Bays and cap: citt: of yᵉ s⁴ city yᵉ deputy govnor of the gar of Carl and officers in these words foll—I. J. A. doe acknowledge &c.

---

* The fee farm rent of the city was included by the Crown in the marriage settlements made on queens Henrietta Maria and Catherine of Braganza.

Memorandu y^t ye day and y^r aboues^d Jo: A. esq^r one of ye aldrm of ye s^d city did publiqly in ye guildhall of ye city afod before ye M^r aldrmen B. and cap citizens of ye s^d city, and officers of ye garr of Carlile deliver in to be cancelled an ord^r formerly grted to him by ye corporation of Carlile afores^d wch ord^r was accordingly cancelled.

July 23 1669.

It being y^n referred to ye corporacon w^t money should be allowed to ye workmen, for building ye moothall, which they p^{r}tend is done, more y^n they were obliged to doe, by articles, and alsoe of fine pounds which was in ye courtesy of ye corporaco, it is this day aboves^d ord^{red} y^t 5^{li} shall be paid for ye extraorninary worke fourty shill for ye worke at ye door heads ten shill for ye finishinge and settinge ye office table and laying shelves there and 2^{li} 10^s of the fine ponds in o^r courtesy, wch 10^{li} is to be paid on St Matt. day next, and thereupo ye workmen to release ye corporaco of all demands whatsoever.

September 6 1669.

The din^r is not to exceed 4^{li} - 0
and ye wine   -   - 1 - 10^s

September 21 1669.

Whether there shall an abatem^t to Dr Tallantire of part of ye wealey rent* for last y^r and how much.

Abated

40^s	2 voted	
50^s	15 votes	Agreed y^t 50^s be abated to Dr Tallantire
45^s	1 vote	rest 2^{li} - 15^s - 0^d
20^s	1 ,,	

Whether Thos Bone shal be made free.
Respited till the eleccon day.

October 4 1669.

Whether any more than 4^{li} shall be allowed to Simon Taite for ye din^r on St Matt. day.

Allowed 2^{li} - 0^s 16 votes   Nil. 12 votes.

---

* Wealey, or weighhouse rent : the farmer of this collected the market tolls.

October 11 1669.

Ord^{r}ed that xx^s be abated to Mr Stanwix forth of the 25^{li} for ye shop, in respect of ye w^t of doores windowes and advanceing ye money before ye day, and bond to be delivered upo paym^t

December 3 1669.

An ord^r y^t ye quarter pensary due to ye poore of ye city to be p^d at St Thos day next, and noe more to be p^d by ye corporacon after ye form^r mann^r

December 10 1669.

Whereas ye sen'all psons whose names are und^r written haue this day disbursed and lent to this corporacon to supply ye necessary occasions thereof, ye severall sumes of money likewise und^r specifyed and to their respective names anexed, it it therefore ord^{r}ed by us ye maior ald^{rm} bayliffes and capll citizens of this city now assembled in ye guildhall of ye city afores^d y^t said sen'all sumes of mo: shal be reimbursed to ye s^d pties respectively their extors adtors and asses together with considaco for ye same upon ye 21 day of September next ensueing ye date hereof forth of the revenues of this city y^n due and payable and to ye pformance hereof we doe herby bind us and o^r successors.

September 16 1670.

Ordred y^t seven pounds be allowed for ye din^r on St Matthew day next besides w^t is to be disbursed for wine.

Ordred James Nicholson supply ye place of And^r this year and to haue xx^s for his paines.

September 21 1670.

Ordered y^t 15^{li} be abated to ye farmers of shire toll and Scotland toll for money by y^m lost at Dalston and other disbursements.

Also 5^s to be abated to Geo : Sowerby farm^r of King-Garth for disturbance in the work there.

March 18 1671.

Tho : Stanwix esq^r Mr Tho : Jackson and Mr Robt Wilson, ye 2 bayliffes, Mr Howe, Mr Hadocke, and Mr Lowry to view ye damb-head, and ye place where ye water overflowes upo wheat closes and to report it to the city.

May 18 1671.

Y^c expenses on 29 May next not to exceed 5^{li}

October 18 1671.

Whether a defence be made by ye city to Sr Wm Dalstons bill soe far as it concerns Mr Barwick . . . comission to be executed ye 25 instant onely.

A defence 14 votes.

Whether interrogaties to be drawn.

January 6 1672.

Whether Tho: Coulterd jun^r (who hath lately much priudiced ye city by a chargeable vexatious and causelesse suite) shall be disfranchised ye same being contrary to his oath, he being a freeman and sworne to maint ye cities franchises and customes &c—vide 1 art. of his oath.

Disfranchised 26 votes. Not—1 vote.

February 12 1672.

Ordered y^t 20 marks be laid out in repaire of ye weare at Priestbecke.

February 17 1672.

Ordered y^t a pson be sent to Yorke assizes to manage y^e businesse at suit of Vasey.*

July 18 1672.

1. The suite abo^t toll at Apleby to be defended.
2. The charters to be carryed to Yorke, y^e last and first.
3. Persons y^t can proue y^e usage abo^t takeing of toll to be inquired after, and apt persons for that purp$\cdots$s$\cdots$ to be provided to goe— not being freemen and to proue y^e manner and circumstances of y^e takeing.
4. Persons to be noiated to manage this tryall
5. Money to be provided for defraying y^e charge thereof, and what sume.

---

* The corporation had during the last half of this century much litigation concerning their tolls, particularly with Sir Francis Radcliffe, lord of the manor of Alston, and his tenants. After prolonged litigation, the corporation got a verdict at York. For an account of the litigation, see a paper by W. Nanson on the shire or county toll. *Transactions Cumbd. and Westd. Antiq. and Archæo. Society,* Vol. III, pp. 144 and 152. Many of the following orders show the corporation economising to meet the expenses of these suits.

September 13 1672.

Appointed to view ye weare und^r Caldewbriege and to direct ye amendm^t thereof, to prevent ye standing of ye castle mill

Tho: Stanwix ar	Mr Robt Jackson
Mr Baines	Roland Dickern
Mr Jackson	and Tho: Peat

September 23 1672.

That 7^{li} be allowed for ye diner on St Mathew day next, and y^t ye extraordinaryes be refered to M^r maior's discretion.

Things given in by ye now chamberlaines not hereafter to be allowed.

Barr moneye*—10^s—Beadles for emptying ye jackes. Pay and fire to ye co^{rt} leet jury. Makeing butts 13^s · 4^d Bedells for cutting dogberryes. Waiters on ye maior and bays 3^{li} 3^s Venison to ye messenger hereafter 10^s

January 9 1673.

Ord^{red} Mr Lowther haue his 4^{li} if it appeare to be unp^d and ye clerke to make search therein.

May 22 1673.

Mr Bird appointed solicitor for ye city.

w^{ht} salary allowed

to be allowed 6^{li} 13^s 4^d 17 votes

5^{li} 6 votes

Ordered 6^{li} 13^s 4^d to be p^d at St Mat day yrly

1 paym^t St Math day 74.

May 28 1673.

What terme ye milnes shall be lett for.

Whether singly and for 3 yeares or for one yeare or altogether for 3 yrs at ye old rent or for 1 yr.

The milnes to be lett singly for one yeare.

Ordered y^t ye milne damb bankes at Mr Aglionbyes close end shall be sufficiently repaired before Michaelmas next, and soe kept in repaire fro time to time by ye city or their farmers.

---

* An allowance to the sergeants for attending at the assizes, &c.

The 4 milnes for 4 months fro 1 June 73 lett to Mr Bushby for 30^{li} 5^s sureties Alexand^r Knagg Tho: Jackson.*

July 21 1673.

Whether an abatem^t shall be made of the record^{rs} salary considering he hath been very negligent in his place, and hath absented himselfe at seuall great court dayes and other times w^n ye affaires and concernes of ye corporacon required his attendance, and he had notice given.

An abatement to be made 20 votes.

Noe abate till he be discoursed with 2 votes.

Abated 5^{li} — neme contradic, except 2 voices onely.

September 22 1673.

Ord^r about Vasy to be entered, and Mr Bird to be consulted and ye thing to be done, and to be a publ concerne.

September 1 1673.

Whether the money recoued by Vasey be tendered in co^{rt} and a new tryall moved for,—and demand made of toll at Alston-moore in ord^r to a new action for toll there.

Wheth a din^r be provided on St Math day.

a dner 21 votes.

six pounds ordred for ye diner ordinaryes and extraordinarys.

September 19 1673.

Upon what condicons the milnes and the fishing to be lett and for what terme.

to be lett for 7 yeares ye farm^{rs} finding all repairs—being first putt in repaire ye farm^{rs} to leaue y^m soe: voted to be entered neme contradcte.

The tolls for ye ensueing yeare to be lett upo this condicon y^t ye farmers to be at ye hazard of all suites, and to be at all ye charge in collecting except only such suites as may happen betwn ye city, and such other psons as claime an exempcon, either by a more antient charter, or by prscripcon.

Also ordered y^t there be noe more free plates bestowed by ye city to be run for on ye king's moore or elswhere.

---

* *Ante* p. 61 n.

September 29 1673.

Whether seuall vacancies y^t now are, or hereafter shall happen be filled up out of ye counsell, and y^t the maior for ye time being reside in the city or loose his salary.

17 voted—nemine contradicente.   This order entered.

October 21 1673.

Whether the ord^r of ye 19th of Septem last touching the eleccon of aldermen within ye city of Carlile, shall stand, or be revoked.

to be revoked 15 votes   to stand in force 11 votes.

January 5 1674.

Whether Mr Wilson be restored to his place of alderman by vertue of ye writ of restitution.

Not to restore him, 6 votes.   To restore him to his pl, 3 votes.

Q.   Whether M^r maior and M^r recorder be desired to instruct Mr Bird (if not already concerned for Mr Wilson) to make a returne to ye writ.

They be desired to do it 6 votes.   Not to be imployed, 3 votes.

In case Mr Bird be imployed in ye businesse already—whether M^r maior and M^r recorder may not make choice of another fitt attorney to make ye returne and to haue an attorney und^r the corporacon scale and whether they are not to haue a sight of ye registers charters bookes pap^s and records or notes out of y^m for their directon in making ye s^d returne.

All these to be done, 7 votes.   Negative, 2 votes.

These to be entered in ye booke and an order inserted y^t ye maior and aldrmen haue ordered these things.

Anthony Stagg—in place of Cuth Robison dead—elected.

Robt Jackson jun^r—in ye pl of Steph Green gone out of ye country elected.

October 5 1674.

Armstrong 17 votes—chosen bedell.

Wallas   7   „

Dalton   14   „   —chosen bedell.

to haue allowed each of them yearely 1^{li} 13^s 4^d to be p^d quarterly, and pvided y^t if they doe not well demean themselves to be returned to ye old allowance or to be displaced.

The farmers of shire toll w^t abatem^t upo their losses sustained at Aldston moore* and for Jer. Davisons charges. 8^{li} 5^s 10^d—to be abated. Ordred ye 20^{li} to be p^d in by W. Nicholson to ye chamberlaine and ye s^d 8^{li} 5^s 10^d to be abated.

Ordered that M^r maior haue 10^{li} p^d him in p^t of the maior's salary for this yeare.

September 7 1675.

Ordrd y^t Mr Stanwix and Mr Haddock Ja: Nicholso and Ed: Lowry haue power to prepare witnesses and to ord^r ye managem^t of ye comission touching Sir Francis Radcliffe, and to send for such of ye corporaco, or others as they shall think fitt to advise and consult abo^t ye same and to imploy counsell to draw interrogator and further to advise therein and y^t ye chamb doe supply them with such sumes of money as they or any 3 of y^m shall und^r their hands declare is necessary to be disbursed therein and fro time to time to report their doings to ye corp and also to haue care of ye managem^t of ye businesse abo^t ye fishing, and to report ye same. Whether there be any entertainm^t on St Math day till ye suits of ye city abo^t tolls and the fishing be ended—or whether wine and w^t quantity &c.

A dinner 9 votes. A dinner but noe wine 1 vote. Wine only each pson one bottle 11 votes. Nothing at all 1 vote.

September 21 1676.

Whether 30^{li} 35^{li} or 40^{li} be p^d to Mr Duckett in full of his demands fro ye city, or w^t sume.

30^{li} 19 votes. 35^{li} 8 votes. 40^{li} 2 votes. 2^{li} 1 vote.

Notwithstanding ye form^r vote its agreed he haue 35^{li} and he to release the city genally. Entered.

October 30 1676.

Wh^t money be allowed Tho: Sowerby upon his petico. 3^{li} 13 votes. 4^{li} 3 votes. Nil 2 votes. 2^{li} 1 vote.

November 8 1676.

Waites 13 votes. Noe waites 8 votes.

Whether Todd be indemnifyed fro ye 9^{li} money taxed at Apleby. To be indemnifyed 18 votes.

---

* Owing to the litigation, *ante* p. 305 n.

08 : 07 : 04 ordered to be abated to ye farmers of ye shire-toll of their last years rent in respect of ye interruption of their collection of toll att A provided ye s^d farmers do give authority to such pson as this corporacon shall nominate to sue such as have not p^d their due toll att A and to retain y^e same w^n recoucred to y^e use of y^e corporacon also provided y^e s^d farmers doe give w^t assistance they may towards y^e recoucry of y^e s^d arrears of toll.

November 24 1676.

Mr^{dn} y^t 8^{li} 7^s 4^d was abated to y^e $farm^{rs}$ of y^e shire toll the last yeare for their losses sustained at Alston moore pvided &c.

Also 9^{li} 10^s allowed in Mr Haddock's hand for y^e costs ag^t Todd.

September 21 1677.

Ordered y^t y^e money be p^d to those y^t waited y^e last assizes on y^e maior and bayliffes and y^t fro henceforth y^e 3 $serg^{ts}$ not to haue any allowance for their attendance at y^e assizes and faires.

Ordered y^t nothing be demised by y^e name of Scotland-toll for y^e future save only y^e toll payable for great beasts or other beasts imported from Scotland or Ireland or other foreign countreys.

Ordered y^t Mr Hugh James of Rickerby haue xx^s allowed him for his paines about Sr Francis Radcliffes businesse.

Ordered y^t Mr James Nicholson and Mr Edw Lowry haue 4^{li} paid to y^m for their paines in goeing to Yorke and other places.

Ordred to y^e $farm^{rs}$ of y^e shire toll 4^{li} for their charges at Alston moore.

Ordred y^t Mr Joseph Reed $farm^r$ of y^e Scotland toll haue 50^s abated for his losses abo^t y^e differences about y^e two great tolls.

Whether Mr Jos. Reed shall be considred for y^e charges of y^e late suit ag^t him bro^t by Tho: Taylor: shall be considered.

Q. what allowance shall be given 19 votes. 17^{li} 19^s 17 votes. 11^{li} 1 vote. 18^{li} 1 vote.

March 25 1678.

What sum shall be allowed Wm How for his charges at suit. 40^s 17 votes.   Nil 1 vote.

Allowed 2^s quarterly to Margaret Dalton called little **Peggy** and to begin to pay at this quarter.

July 30 1678.

Whether ye rent of 3^{li} 6^s 8^d wch Mr Willm Wilson challenges fro ye corporacon as due to him in June last shall be paid for this yeare onely or not.

To be paid 20 votes. Not p^d 2 votes.

This order entered.

Whether or noe the said rent of 3^{li} 6^s 8^d shall be paid ye said Mr Willm Wilson for ye time to come.

Not to be paid 14 votes. To be p^d 8 votes.

Ordered.

December 9 1678.

Whereas it is found very conven^t and safe for ye city in these times of danger, y^t ye seuall inhabitants of this city who shall fro henceforth lodge any strangers, shall ye first night they shall lodge any such strangers giue in to ye cap^t of ye watch at ye maine guard at or before nine of ye clock at night ye names and surnames of euy such stranger or lodger, upo paine of 6^d for euy defalt to be levyed by ye bay^s of ye city for ye time being, and ye penalty to be disposed of by ye maior to ye poore within ye corporaco and this to continue in force till further ord^r

Whether or noe ye 3 . 6 . 8 paid to ye lecturer in the yeare 77 be continued to him for ye yeare 78.*

Not to be paid 15 votes. To be p^d 4 votes.

Ordred to be taken off.

January 28 1679.

Ordered y^t ye chist be opened and y^t Mr Aglionby haue ye pusal of certaine paps and evidences in a box.

Ordered y^t ye weare called ye goat be repaired, soe farr as ye corporaco are obliged to repaire, and y^t the lord Morpeth be moued to giue leaue to cutt downe a sand bed and willow bed on ye other side of ye water adjoining ye Swifts.†

Whether an abatem^t or noe abatem^t be made Mr Reed and to Mr Wm Nicholson and their ptners late farmers of ye cityes tolls.

Abatement 14 votes. Noe abatem^t 9 votes.

---

* *Ante* p. 284.

† Lord Morpeth was the lessee of the socage of Carlisle castle.

What sumes to be abated.

40^{li} to Mr Reed
20^{li} to Mr W. Nicholson } 8 votes

Ordered y^t 20^{li} be abated Mr Jos Reed and y^t 10^{li} be abated to Mr W. Nicholson.

Ordered that M^r maior and ye town clarke doe inspect ye accounts of Richd Wilson, alder Knagg and Edward Lowry touching their late suites and w^t they find justly due and expended, the same is hereby ordered to be p^d by ye chamblain.

Ordered y^t 40^{li} be taken forth of the chist.

February 27 1679.

Memorand that John Aglionby esq^r did then prsent to ye corporaco the kings ma^{ties} approbaco of his eleccon as record^r of this city, and was accordingly sworne and admitted record^r of the s^d city and tooke ye usuall oaths.

Ordered y^t 5^{li} be paid to Mr Richard Tubman ye county clarke as a gratuity for his charges and expenses in comeing fro his house to keep the seuall courts held here by ye present sher of Cumberland.

June 13 1679.

Ordered y^t Mr Wm Wilson haue paid to him ye sume of 3^{li} 5^s during his life yearly at midsumer, ye first paym^t to be on ye 24 of June 80—and y^t ye sume of 3^{li} 6^s 8^d a p^{r}tended rent due on ye 1 of June last for a watercourse be paid—and y^t an order under ye corpor seal be grated to Mr Wilso for ye paym^t of ye s^d 3^{li} 5^s— provided ye s^d Mr Wilson doe grant a release unde hand and seale to ye corporaco of all claimes and demands trespasses rents or pretences of rents for any watercourse to ye cities milnes and all other demands w^{t}soeu except ye s^d 3^{li} 5^s yearely.

September 4 1679.

Whether ye invitaco to St Math day din^r be left to M^r maiors discretio—or y^t he be limited to invite freemen onely.

To discretion 4 votes.   Limited to freemen 16 votes.

What sume to be allowed for ye diner and ale and beer— 6^{li} 13^s 4^d to be allowed.

Wine, tobacco and pipes to be p^d for besides.

Ordered y^t 20^s be p^d towards ye binding Jeremy Mason an apprentice after he is bound.

Whether ye salaries paid to ye master and usher of ye gramar schoole be stopped (after michas next) till further ord^r of ye corporaco.

Affirmatives 17.   Neg 2.

Whether M^r maior and such of ye corporaco as he shall nominate shall discourse with M^r dean about the businesse of ye schoole. Affirm. 7   Neg. 11.

October 25 1679.

Whether or noe the rioters on ye eleccon* day last shall be peeeded ags^t in ye crown office.

Affirmative 17 votes.   Negative 5 votes.

What persons to be concerned and peeeded ags^t

> Alexander Ritson
> Adam Robinson
> Richard Heath
> Thos Kidd
> Francis Atkinson
> Benjamin Sawer
> Tho Blakelocke jun
> George Wilson
> James Bell jun
> Tho Graham
> Robt Atkinson jun
> Tho : Thompson al^s Parker
> Timothy Haddocke

Whether these psons be peeeded ag^t
Affirm 17 votes.   Neg 3 votes

---

* The day of the election of mayor, viz, Monday after the feast of St. Michael the archangel, Sept. 29.   Timothy Haddock was the lessee of the corporation tolls, and as such had brought actions against many persons.   The anti-litigious party in the corporation seem to have got the upper hand, and hence all this riot and row.   Haddock was expelled the corporation and at once got a mandamus to be restored to his place as alderman.   The litigious party ultimately prevailed, and a fresh crop of toll suits commenced in 1684 and lasted for nineteen years, when the house of lords ordered a new trial.   The matter then slumbered until 1761, when litigation commenced which ended in 1774 in favour of the corporation, *ante* p. 305 n.

Mʳ Timothy Haddocke one of yᵉ aldermen of this city was then charged

To have been rude and disobedient to the prsent maior.

To have been guilty of yᵉ late riott on the eleccon day.

To have carryed on, and concerned in, and a promoter of vexations snites in the city agᵗ seuall persons—and that time be given to Mʳ Haddocke to answere yᵉ sᵈ accusacons till this day fortnight, and yᵗ copy of yᵉ ordʳ be given to Mʳ Haddocke.

November 8 1679.

In yᵉ guildhall there, the maior and court of aldermen assembled.

Question

Whether or noe this court (upon the information made agᵗ Mʳ Timothy Haddocke one of the aldermen of this city and entered upo record the 25ᵗʰ October last) haue recd such satisfaccon that the sᵈ Timothy Haddocke may be remoued fro his place of alderman of this city.

Remou.　Affirmat 6 votes.　Negat 2 votes.

November 20 1679.

Mʳ chancellor to haue paid 50ˢ quarterly for his stipend as lecturer, till farther order—accounting from Michaelmas last.*

December 12 1679.

Whether yᵉ charters and bookes and records of yᵉ city shall be produced and look'd into, to provide reasons, why yᵉ mandamˢ for restoring of Mʳ Haddocke is not obey'd.

Affirmd neme contradicente.

Who shall be appointed to attend this businesse, and to prepare yᵉ said reasons.

Mʳ Aglionby to draw and prepare yᵉ sᵈ reasons.

Mʳ maior and Ja. Nicholson to attend Mʳ Aglionby in searching yᵉ sᵈ charters and bookes &c and to haue power to keep yᵉ keyes and to open yᵉ chist and yᵗ Mʳ Aglionby haue 5ˡⁱ for his paines.

December 15 1679.

What sume shall be giuen to Thoˢ Denton esqʳ the prsent recordʳ as a gratuity upo resignacon of his place.

xxˡⁱ 21 votes neme contradicente.

---

* *Ante* p. 284.

Ordered y^t xx^{li} be paid to Mr Denton.

What sume shall be yearely p^d to Mr Aglionby as record^r of the city.

20^{li} 19 votes. 20 marks 2 votes.

to be paid at Chrismas yearely, the first paym^t to begin at Chrismas 1680.

January 17 1680.

Whether or noe ye chist be opened and xx^{li} taken forth and paid to Mr James Bird in part of his bill.

Affirmative 22 votes.

January 20 1680.

Whether or noe an abatem^t and what sume be made to ye late farm^{rs} of ye fishing called King-garth for ye yeare ended at Michaelmas last.

To be abated 3^{li} 10^s 14 votes. Nil 7 votes.

Mr Haddocke haueing this day desired a copy of ye order of his deprivaco and of such other orders contained in the Reg^r bookes, as doe relate to himself, it is ordered that ye towneclarke doe gine him a copy of ye s^d ord^r of deprivaco, and of all other ord^{rs} in this reg^r particularly relating to himselfe, wch he shall by writing under his hand specially nominate and request fro ye s^d towneclarke.

Mr Haddocke desires copies of two cancelled ord^{rs} relating to Thomas Coulterd, and ye ord^{rs} of his disfranchisem^t and restitucon, and the ord^r of Mr Haddock's deprivacon.[*]

May 8 1680.

Whether or noe there shall be any further pcedings in ye crown office ag^t Tho Kidd and others menconed in ye peticon annexed upo ye riott comitted upo ye last eleccon day of ye maior &c or y^t ye same shall be withdrawne.

Noe further prosecucon 13 votes. To be psecuted 10 votes.

June 9 1680.

Whether or noe the ord^r of the 25th of Octob last, for the psecucon of certaine psons in the crowne office for a riott comitted on ye eleccon day last, be revived and confirmed and ye persons therein named prosecuted, and ye order of ye 8 of May last revoked,

---

[*] *Ante* p. 305.

or that they be freed from further prosecucon and the s⁴ ord⁴ of yᵉ 8 of May confirmed.

To be prosecuted and yᵉ first ord⁴ to stand 13 votes.   Not to be prosecuted 9 votes.

September 10 1680.

Whether or noe Tho Mason (a capitall citizen) shall be remoued from yᵉ place (haueing been scuall yeares absent) and neglected to doe yᵉ service &c.

To be remoued 7 votes.

Whether or noe yᵉ place of Tho Coulterd, and John Nicholson two capital citizens (being old and infirme and not capable to doe any service for yᵉ corporaco and haue desired to be freed fro any further service be remoued fro those places.

Remoued 7 votes.

March 6 1681.

Whether anything shall be abated to Mr. Timothy Haddocke forth of yᵉ arreare of 67ˡⁱ or to Tho: Taylor—Roland Hegeale another of the farmers now in arreare.

Noe abatem⁴ 16 votes.   Abatem⁴ 2 votes.

Whether or noe six hundred acres of yᵉ kings moore shall be lett to farme, to be taken upp at such places as the farmer shall thinke fitt.

To be farmed ut supra—15 votes.   Neg—1 vote.

March 8 1681.

Ordered y⁴ 3ˡⁱ be giuen in cock plates.

Three hundred acres that is to say 15 score acres to be lett only.

Whether for 3 lives or 21 yeares.

3 lives—14 votes.   21 yeares—7 votes.

6ˡⁱ — for what rent this is to be lett.*

July 4 1681.

By yoʳ maᵗⁱᵉˢ late gracious declaracon† to secure and maintain &c.

x   x   x   x   x   x   x   x   x

---

* These minutes record the commencement of very disastrous transactions for the citizens of Carlisle, *ante* pp. 118 n. and 142 n.

† "A declaration of the reasons for dissolving the last two Parliaments," which "raised over England a humour of making addresses to the king, as it were in answer to it." Burnet's *History of His Own Time*, Vol. I, p. 500. See also Rapin, &c. In the first of these two parliaments Carlisle was repre-

and that all the benefitts of it are so fully secured to us by y^{or} ma^{ties} late gracious declaracon to secure and maintain &c.

Whether or noe the addresse or draught p^{r}sented by M^r maior as it is amended shall be perfected and sent up to ye kings ma^{ty}

Whether or noe this addresse be sent to Sr Chro Musgraue solely to be presented to ye king or to Sr Philip Howard and Sr Chro: Musgraue.

To whom this addresse shall be deliuered to be presented to ye king.   To Sr Chro: 18.   To S^r Ph: H: and Sr Chro: M. 12.

Whether to be sent by pticular messenger or by ye post.   By pticular messenger 12.   By y^e post 17.

October 3 1681.

Ordered y^t applicacon be made to y^e dean and chap^r to remoue y^e prsent schoolmaster and y^t a new one be provided.

Whether this applicacon be made.   Affirm 27.   Neg 5.

Ordered y^t y^e schoolm^r be remoued, and y^t xx^{li} $\wp$ ann be paid to a new schoolm^r, pvided y^e dean and chapter doe provide a fitt and able person to supply y^e s^d place, and that such master be not made a petticanon.

Ordred y^t y^e succeeding maior 3 aldermen and 3 of y^e councill to inspect y^e last yeares accounts and to report y^e same to the corporacon and y^t they also be appointed to approve of ye security to be giuen by ye farm^{rs}

viz Mr Warwick	Ja. Nicholson
Mr Tallentire	Mr W. Nicholson
Mr Lowry	Mr Jefferson

September 21 1681.

Ord^{red} by the court of maior and aldermen y^t ye case relating to M^r record^r, whether his place of alderm be void or not, be stated, and referred to some eminent counsell to giue his opinion And Jo : Agl : esq^{re} now record^r hath prmised y^t howsoever such counsell shall declare his opinion as to the vacancy or not vacancy of ye place of alderman neverthelesse he is to resigne his said place of alderman at or before Lady day next.

---

sented by Sir Christopher Musgrave and Sir Philip Howard, but in the second the tory Sir P. Howard was replaced by the whig Lord Morpeth, *ante* p. 17. *Cumberland and Westmorland M.P.s*, p. 40.

December 8 1681.

Whether or noe the stipend of twenty pounds ordered on St Mathew day be . . . . to the grammar schoole, be withdrawn.

To be revoked and ye xx^{li} withdrawn 18.   Negat. 8.

December 19 1681.

Whether or noe Thomas Kidd shall be deprived of his place of a capitall citizen of this city.   Deprived 3.   Neg 4.

December 20 1681.

Whether or noe the vote passed yesterday in relaco to Thomas Kidds deprivaco, shall stand in force or that ye said vote shall be revoked and made void.

Revoked 4 votes.   To stand 3 votes.

Whether or noe Thomas Kidd shall be deprived and removed fro his place of a capitall citizen of Carlile.

Deprived 4.   Neg. 3.

March 10 1683.

Ordered y^t an ord^r be made to call upp all such debts and sumes of money as are due to ye city by Mr Joseph Read or any other pson.

Ordered y^t Mr James Bird be imployed to make returne to ye two writs of mandam^s brought by Mr Joseph Read and Lancelott Jefferson, and y^t M^r record^r may haue ye inspeco of such charters and records as he shall think necessary for the better instructing of Mr Bird therein.

Ordered y^t direcons be given to ye farmers of Kinggarth fishing to repaire ye garth as formerly, and y^t ye corporaco will consider ye same w^n finished, and y^t applicaco be made to ye Duke of Norfolk or his officers about ye gote there.

Ordered y^t Priestbeck weare be repaired with w^t convenient speed may be—at or before Michaelmas next.

Ordered y^t ye Goose green be lett to farme to Mrs Ann Baines for her life, at ye old rent of 6^d yearely.

Ordered y^t 8^{li} worth of plates to be fought for by cocks be bought, whereof 4^{li} to be given by ye city to be fought for on ye last weeke of Aprill.

Ordered y^t M^r Jo How now maior hane allowance to build his house at ye new sun one foot or thereabouts further into ye street then it now stands.

Ordered y^t ye 4 keyes of ye chist be in ye hands of ye maior for ye time being and Sr Geo Fletcher baron^t one of ye senior aldermen, and Mr W. Nicholso and Mr Jenkin Pow 2 cap. citizens.

Edward Blakelocke of Carlisle glou elected a capitall citizen neme contradicente.

April 9 1683.

Then ordered that all persons as well forreiners as freemen may have full power to bid at and take to farme any of the citys revennues gineing good security for the rent of the same and that any person tho: noe freeman proferring more money then a freeman shall be accepted before him.

July 14 1683.

Whether the addresse to his ma^{ty} shall be sent by ye post, or by a pticular messenger.[*]

By a pticular messenger 24 votes.   By ye post 3 votes.

What messenger—Mr Reed nem^{ne} contradicente.

Octobe 31 1683.

Ordered y^t the weare beyond Caldew bridge be repaired.

November 10 1683.

It is ordered by ye court of maior and aldermen now assembled &c. that a copy of ye articles ag^t Mr Reed be delivered to him, and he required to answere to them on Thursday next, the 15th instant.

Ordered also y^t Mr Reed doe pduce the vouchers to his acconnt to the towneclerke ag^t Thursday next.

May 22 1684.

The toll for all forrain goods imported at Whitehaven Workington and the adjacent creeks, and ye tolls of all goods exported there, and the toll for all goods going out of ye county at Drumelrayes, and ye toll of all leed oare goeing out of ye county at Alston Moore be lett for 5 yeares to Mr Haddocke und^r ye yrly rent of 1^{li} to be pd at St Mathew day yearely, except and alwayes reserved forth of this

---

[*] Address of congratulation to the king on his escape from the Rye House plot.

lease all toll due for horses and cattell imported or exported at any place w^tsoever. Mr Haddock to be at ye charge of collecting these and to indemnify ye corporaco fro all manner* of charges.

August 5 1684.

Whether or noe it not ye duty and interest of this corporaco to surrender their charter to the kings ma^{ty}.

It is the duty and interest of ye corp soe to doe 28 votes. Nem^{ne} contradicente.

Ordered y^t the charter of this city be surrendered to ye s^d kings ma^{ty} by an instrum^t under o^r comon scale, and M^r maior, ye aldermen, and como councell, or soe many of them as can conveniently meet doe during ye time of this next assizes wait upo Sr Geo Jefferyes l^d cheife justice of England one of ye judges of this circuit, and that his lo^rpp be requested to receive ye s^d charter, and ye insstrum^t of resignaco, and p^rsent ye same to ye king.

Whether or noe ye charter and scale be taken forth of ye chist, and secured till such time as ye instrum^t of surrend^r be ready for ye seale, and y^t ye same be affixed then delivered to ye l^d cheife justice.

Ordered also that ye charter and also ye comon scal of this corporacon be put into ye hands of the maior for ye due execution of ye s^d surrender and that ye comon seal be thereunto by him affixed.†

September 15 1684.

Ordered the day and yeare abovesaid that there be two peices of plate provided to be runn for on Tuesday and Wednesday the 23 and 24th of this p^rsent the first plate to be of the value of 10^{li} ye other of 5^{li}.

Ordered that the councell meet the 22^d of September and there doe the businesse ussually done on St Mathew day and that a dinner be provided by M^r maior for which the councell to allow 6^{li} 13^s 4^d beside extraordinarys.

---

* The Corporation having won in the litigation commenced in 1672, a fresh litigation commenced, in which the point was whether lead ore was liable to pay toll, and whether goods and merchandise coming to the county by sea were liable. See *ante* p. 305, and *Transactions Cumbd. and Westd. Antiq. and Archæ. Society*, vol. iii, 144, 152.

† For an account of the surrender of the charter, see *ante* p. 17 and 18.

That upon the request of Wm Bushby he have leave to build on the place where the pillory now stands and that he place the flagg posts and conveniencys in the place backwards next Tho: Birds shopp without any anoyance to the streets.

September 22 1684.

Ordered ye milnes be viewed and forthwith repaired.

Ordered y^t M^r record^r be desired to represent to ye duke of Norfolke ye case of ye goat at King-Garth.

Ordered y^t 6^{ll} 11^s 8^d be allowed to Mr Timothy Haddocke for charges expended by him at Whitehaven.

Mr John How jun^r chosen capitall.

Tho l^d bpp* chosen freeman.

Henry Fletcher esq^r

Mr Basill Fielding.

Robert Blakelocke.

October 4 1684.

Whether Mr Story to be made freeman.

Affirm 16.   Neg 14.

December 26 1684.

Ordered y^t on Tuesday next a dinn^r be provided at the recepts of y^e new charter.

Y^t the 8 companies wth their colours stand in their ord^r as called in the call booke, and a guinea to be given to each to drink y^e kings health.

A guinea to y^e guards—y^e like to y^e gun$^{rs.}$

Ringers at St Maries 10^s at St Cuthberts 2^s 6$^d.$

Y^e countrey men to be directed to goe to Mr Hen Pattinson and to haue in drink xx^s and to increase or lessen y^e rate according to y^e number.†

---

* Thomas Smith, bishop 1684 to 1702. He was a local man and probably a member of the guild of tanners, to whom he gave a tankard.   *Ante* p. 165. For Basil Fielding see *ante* p. 20.

† For the new charter, see *ante* p. 13 and *ante* p. 186.

May 18 1685.

Ordered y^t Mathew Armstrang haue paid him yearely only viz 5^s ⅌ q^rter.

Michael Barnfather to have ye like.

This is for their salaries as bedells.

May 14 1686.

This day Mathew Caipe merchant was sworne freeman of this city.

The plates to be sent for, and ye races to be run, on Tuesday and Thursday, in ye first weeke in June.

October 3 1687.

Whether or noe the maiors salary of 40^li be advanced to 100^li ⅌ ann upo consideraco of his taking upo him ye defraying of ye charge of all treats, and publicke entertainments and gratuities to poore, travellers, and other casualties, excepting treating ye king, or some of ye royall family.

Affirmed—28 votes.   Nem^e contradicente.

Ordered also y^t ye s^d 100^li be paid at lady day and St Mathew day—yearly.

Ordered y^t 5^li apeice be p^d yearly to ye 2 bayliffes at Lady day and St Mathew day, and they are to receive all amciamts &c.

April 27 1688.

Then ord^red in full councill that the charter of this city be taken out of the chest and carryed to Mr Gilpin deputy recorder of this city to peruse in reference to ye managem^t of the city affaires.

Then ord^red that such bookes as are necessary for ye corporacon be forth with provided.

May 14 1688.

Then ordered that there be 2 plates provided at the charge of the corporacon one of the price of 9^li and the other at 6^li to be run for on Kingmoor on Thursday and Friday in Whitsuntide weeke.

GENERAL INDEX.

INDEX OF PERSONS.

www.ingramcontent.com/pod-product-compliance
Lightning Source LLC
Chambersburg PA
CBHW051118120726
47905CB00005B/1327